THE CHILDREN'S HOUR

Stories of Today

A BOOK TO GROW ON

Consultant Editor for
Stories of Today

MABEL L. ROBINSON
Author, Associate Professor
Columbia University

CONSULTANT EDITORS FOR THE CHILDREN'S HOUR

CAROL RYRIE BRINK
Author
Newbery Prize Winner

JULIA CARSON
Author and Biographer

IRVING CRUMP
Editor and Author

HELEN DEAN FISH
Editor and Author

WILHELMINA HARPER
Anthologist, Librarian
Redwood City, California

WILLIAM HEYLIGER
Author,
Editor of Literature for Youth
The Westminster Press

SIDDIE JOE JOHNSON
Children's Librarian
Dallas Public Library

CORNELIA MEIGS
Author and Teacher
Newbery Prize Winner

NORMA RATHBUN
Chief of Children's Work
Milwaukee Public Library

MABEL L. ROBINSON
Author, Associate Professor
Columbia University

MARGARET JONES WILLIAMS
Director of Elementary Education
Cornell College, Iowa

MARJORIE BARROWS, *Editor*

Stories of Today

MATHILDA SCHIRMER
Associate Editor

DOROTHY SHORT
Art Editor

THE CHILDREN'S HOUR

PRINTED IN THE UNITED STATES OF AMERICA

Acknowledgments

The editor and publishers wish to thank the following publishers, agents, authors, and artists for permission to use and reprint stories, poems, and illustrations included in this book:

ARTISTS AND WRITERS GUILD, INC., for "Punch Has an Adventure" from *The Barkingtons* by Robin Palmer, published by Harper and Brothers, New York, and copyright by Artists and Writers Guild, Inc., with illustrations by Flavia Gág.

DODD, MEAD & COMPANY, INC., for "Waino and Ivar Meet Honk the Moose" from *Honk the Moose* by Phil Stong, copyright, 1935, by Phil Stong, with illustrations by Kurt Wiese.

DOUBLEDAY & COMPANY, INC., for "Mr. Dooley Disgraces His Family" from *Marty Lou* by Mary Dickerson Donahey, copyright, 1925, by Doubleday and Company, Inc.; and "The Old Coach Road" from *Taxis and Toadstools* by Rachael Field, copyright, 1926, by Doubleday and Company, Inc.

HARCOURT, BRACE & COMPANY, INC., for "The Middle Bear" from *The Middle Moffat* by Eleanor Estes, copyright, 1942, by Harcourt, Brace & Company, Inc.

HOUGHTON MIFFLIN COMPANY for "An Island Christmas" from *Douglas of Porcupine* by Louise Andrews Kent.

LONGMANS, GREEN AND CO. for "Story Hour" from *Susan's Year* by Siddie Joe Johnson, copyright, 1948, by Siddie Joe Johnson.

JULIAN MESSNER, INC., for "The Cream-colored Pony" from *Gypsy Luck* by Chesley Kahmann, copyright, October 26, 1937, by Mabel Chesley Kahmann.

WILLIAM MORROW AND COMPANY, INC., for "Ellen's Secret" from *Ellen Tebbits* by Beverly Cleary, with illustrations by Louis Darling, copyright, 1951, by Beverly Cleary; and "Gallons of Guppies" from *Henry Huggins* by Beverly Cleary, with illustrations by Louis Darling, copyright, 1950, by William Morrow and Company, Inc.

L. C. PAGE & COMPANY, INC., for "Christmas Eve at Reginald's," "The Rule of Three," and "The Street of Memories" from *Beacon Hill Children* by Elizabeth Rhodes Jackson.

RANDOM HOUSE, INC., for "False Summer" from *Bright Island* by Mabel Louise Robinson, copyright, 1937, by Random House, Inc.

RINEHART & COMPANY, INC., for "Clarinda, 1869" from *The Four-Story Mistake* by Elizabeth Enright, copyright, 1942, by Elizabeth Enright Gillham; and "Randy at the Art Gallery" from *The Saturdays* by Elizabeth Enright, copyright, 1941, by Elizabeth Enright Gillham.

CHARLES SCRIBNERS' SONS for "Rusty—Movie Star" from *The Smiths and Rusty* by Alice Dalgliesh, copyright, 1936, by Charles Scribners' Sons.

RALPH FLETCHER SEYMOUR for "The Christmas Path" by Anne Higginson Spicer.

STORY PARADE, INC., for "The Penny Walk" by Anne Molloy, copyright, 1948, by Story Parade, Inc.; and "Smoky" by Marion Holland, copyright, 1946, by Story Parade, Inc.

'TEENS (The American Baptist Publication Society, The Judson Press) for "Frisbie Cures the Doctor" by Charles Coombs.

THE VIKING PRESS, INC., for "A Winterbound Adventure" from *Winterbound* by Margery Bianco, copyright, 1936, by Margery Bianco.

EDITH MASON ARMSTRONG for "The Mason Children on the Roof" first published in *Child Life Magazine*.

JANET NORRIS BANGS for "Snowfall."

MARGERY WILLIAMS BIANCO'S estate for "Dolly Joins the Circus."

NANCY CLINTON for "Guppies Are Best."

MARJORIE FISCHER for "Rococo Skates" first published in *Story Parade*.

HELEN TRAIN HILLES for "All Mutt," "Handsome Is," and "Living Christmas."

MARGARET LEIGHTON for "Independence Day for Davy," first published in *Child Life Magazine*.

ADELAIDE LOVE for "Circus Drums" and "The Best Ride of All," first published in *Child Life Magazine*.

CORNELIA MEIGS for "The Sandpipers," first published in *Child Life Magazine*.

CONSTANCE SAVERY for "Spindleberries and Pam."

MARGUERITE DAVIS for illustrations for Elizabeth Rhodes Jackson's "Rule of Three" and "Christmas Eve at Reginald's."

GENEVIEVE FOSTER for illustrations for Chesley Kahmann's "The Gang's All There."

FLORENCE AND MARGARET HOOPES for illustrations for Constance Savery's "Spindleberries and Pam" and Margery Williams Bianco's "Dolly Joins the Circus."

KEITH WARD for illustrations for Helen Train Hilles' "All Mutt," "Living Christmas," and "Handsome Is."

Contents

Elizabeth Rhodes Jackson

STREET OF MEMORIES

ILLUSTRATED BY *Matilda Breuer*

THE Prince and Princess used to belong to Mr. Brackett. He lives on the street floor, and we live on the next floor, and old Mrs. Lavendar lives on the top floor.

There are three of us. Jack is my older brother, and Beany is my younger brother. I'm Dee, and I'm eleven. Somebody said to Beany once, "There are three of you Corey children, aren't there—two boys and a girl?" and Beany said, "No, there are four of us—Jack and Dee and me and Reginald."

Reginald is our dog. He has brown eyes, and his hair is black and white. The rest of us have blue eyes and light hair.

We first got acquainted with Mrs. Lavendar by accident. The accident happened to Beany, and this is the way it came about.

We live on one of the oldest streets in Boston, on the river side of Beacon Hill. The old brick houses have alleys at the back or through their cellars, and we play tag in them. The

1

alleys all run into each other and make a sort of maze. You run up an alley and climb over a couple of fences and down another alley and through a gate, and there you are, in another street.

We were all playing, one day after school, and Beany went to climb a fence and fell, right on his face. Beany would, you know. He's always the one of us who has the falls. He bruised his forehead and skinned his nose. He was very brave about it and didn't cry, although the tears were in his eyes.

We took him home, Jack and I, walking one on each side and holding his arms. He could walk perfectly well, of course, but he seemed so wounded and so brave that we held him up; and we got him home all right.

But when we took him upstairs to our hall, the door was locked, and Mother was out. Beany had been brave so long that he couldn't wait any longer, and while I was fumbling in the regular place for the key, he burst out into a long, sad wail. Then a lady on the floor above, who was a stranger to us, leaned over the banister and said, "Bring him up to me."

Her apartment was very lovely, with beautiful old furniture and soft, thick rugs on the floor and huge silver candlesticks on the mantel. But there was no fire in the fireplace, though the day was cold, and she had a shawl around her shoulders, a beautiful white silk shawl with an embroidered border.

She took Beany on her lap, and he was glad to be there, and he let her wash the dirt off his face very gently with warm water. Then she held him in her arms, and Jack and I sat on the rug, and she told us about her son, when he was a little boy, and about a dog he once had. It was a very interesting story.

That was the way we got acquainted with Mrs. Lavendar by accident. The way we came to find the Prince and the Princess was through Mrs. Lavendar.

Mother calls the street we live on the Street of Memories for two reasons. One reason is that memories of the past are still living there. Two blocks from our house, in the big park called Boston Common, is the spot where the British soldiers embarked, the night that Paul Revere got ahead of them on his

2

famous ride. Two blocks the other way, Oliver Wendell Holmes used to live. He was a doctor who wrote poetry. He loved children, and he knew every boy and girl who lived near him on Beacon Hill.

And Miss Louisa M. Alcott, who wrote *Little Women*, has walked on our street many and many a time. She's such a special sort of person to children that her memory would hallow any street. I love to walk up the hill to see the little brick house where she and her sister lived—Jo and Amy—in their struggling days. And on the way home I pass the stately mansion where she lived when she was successful and famous.

The other reason Mother calls it the Street of Memories is because of the little shops all up and down the street that sell old, quaint, antique things. Some of the shop windows are very artistic, with nothing but two colonial chairs and a desk, or perhaps one pink rose in a pewter porringer with a camel's-hair shawl background. But we like best the ones that have the windows crowded so full that you can't see everything at once and keep discovering new and interesting things.

Mr. Brackett's is like that, on the street floor of our house.

3

His show window is just jammed with things. There are three ship models, and some colored bottles with heads of Washington and Hancock on the glass, and a battered old lantern, and a glass paperweight with colors in it, and andirons, and silhouettes in tiny frames, and an inlaid snuff box, and a pair of china dogs, and a luster tea set, and hanging up are old engravings and faded samplers.

We were all three looking into Mr. Brackett's window one day, when Mrs. Lavendar came out and saw us there. We knew her very well by this time.

"Mrs. Lavendar, do you see this ship's model," said Jack.

"It looks like all sorts of adventures," she said, and then she saw something else and caught her breath a little.

"How long have *those* been here?" she said. "I haven't seen them before."

She was pointing to a pair of china figures about a foot and a half high, a lady and gentleman in elaborate, old-fashioned dress. The lady had wide skirts and high powdered hair and flowers on her breast, and the gentleman had a ruffled shirt and knee breeches and buckled shoes. Though the ruffles and the flowers and the buckles were small, they were just perfect and very delicate, and the faces were exquisitely beautiful.

"I'm sure those are mine," said Mrs. Lavendar, very low. Then she walked into Mr. Brackett's shop.

"She's going in to buy them!" we said, but presently she came out without them and almost walked past us without speaking, and then she remembered us and smiled and went on.

We told Mother about it. "Why do you think she didn't buy them?" asked Jack.

"Probably Mr. Brackett's price was too high," said Mother.

"Oh, but Mrs. Lavendar's rich, Mother," said Beany. "You ought to see her apartment."

"I'm afraid she isn't, Beany," said Mother. "Mrs. Lavendar's husband is dead, and her son gave his life in the war. Though she used to have a great deal of money, now that she's old, she has very little. She goes out almost every day to help a dressmaker with sewing."

4

"I wonder if that's why she doesn't have a fire in the fireplace," I said.

We often went up to see her, and her apartment was usually cold. Of course, the house is supposed to be heated from the cellar, but we always have two log fires going in winter, to help out.

Our house is one of the old ones on the Street of Memories. They were once beautiful residences, but some of them, like ours, have been made over into apartments, with shops on the first floor. So the plumbing and heating are old-fashioned, and we have a great deal of trouble with them.

Ladies who come to see Mother always say, "What wonderful carved woodwork!" and "How I envy you your quaint fireplaces, dear." But it isn't so pleasant when the water pipes freeze.

A week later we had cold weather, and cold weather in Boston is *very* cold. I don't believe even the North Pole is much colder than the Street of Memories in winter! When we came home from school, we were glad to get to the fire in the living room, and we all told Mother how cold it was outdoors.

"I was going to suggest that you go up to see Mrs. Lavendar," she said, "but perhaps it's so cold that you ought to take a fire with you. I'll ask her."

I followed her up the stairs and heard her saying, "Mrs. Lavendar, would it bother you if the children made a little call?"

"I'd love to have them," said Mrs. Lavendar. "Only, I'm afraid the room is rather cold. I can't seem to get enough heat."

"It's a very poor heating system, isn't it?" said Mother. "We've had to have a hearth fire today. Jack will bring up some wood, if you don't mind the litter. He knows how to build a fine fire."

We were soon on the way up, Jack with a basket of logs and Beany carrying the paper bag of kindling and I with the hearth brush.

Beany, poor child, tripped over the rug and dropped the bag. It split open, but Mrs. Lavendar was very nice about it, and I

5

swept up the debris, and it was all right.

Jack made a glorious fire, and we were very cozy. Knowing Mother as I do, I suspect she planned the whole thing just to get Mrs. Lavendar warm.

While we were all sitting there as happy as could be, Beany suddenly spoke up. Beany too frequently says things he shouldn't—I suppose because he's such a child—and what do you think he said this time?

"Mrs. Lavendar, how did your china figures come to be in Mr. Brackett's antique shop?"

We tried to hush him, but Mrs. Lavendar answered him.

"I sold all the furnishings of my house some years ago, Beany, except what I have here, and the china Prince and Princess went with the rest."

"Are they a Prince and Princess?" I asked.

"That was the name my boy had for them, Dee. He was very fond of them when he was little." And somehow, from the way she said it, I knew that she missed the china figures.

Then Beany piped up again. "Why did you have to sell your furniture, Mrs. Lavendar, when you have so much money?"

We couldn't hush him at all, but Mrs. Lavendar understood, and she only smiled and said, "I haven't much money, dear. I had some, but it was stolen from me. So I had to sell the furniture to get money to live on."

"How was it stolen?" said Beany, all interest.

"It isn't a very pleasant story," said Mrs. Lavendar, "but I'll tell it to you. When the war came, it stopped my income. All my money was in a business that couldn't go on until the war was over."

Beany nodded, though he didn't understand. Jack and I partly did.

"My son's salary was enough for us both till he went to war. Then we sold our house. We planned to invest the money so that I'd have enough to live on till he came back."

"I see," said Beany, trying to be polite.

"One afternoon, my son came in with the money from the sale. He wouldn't take a check, because sometimes checks can't

6

be changed into money. He went to the bank himself with the man who bought the house, and the man drew the money in bills and gave it to him—forty thousand dollars."

"Whee! That was a lot of money, wasn't it!" said Beany.

Mrs. Lavendar smiled at him. "There wasn't time to take the money to our bank for deposit that day. Banks, you know, close early in the afternoon. So my son brought the money home to me, and it was stolen that same day."

"Who stole it?" we said together.

"I never knew," said Mrs. Lavendar. "I can't imagine who would. Not the servants. They'd been with me for years. Someone must have come in, but I don't know how. It's always been a mystery."

"Where was it?" we asked.

"In the Governor Winthrop desk," said old Mrs. Lavendar. "That very desk there against the wall. My son said, 'I'll put it in here, Mother.' I saw him with his hand on the open leaf of the desk. I said, 'Yes, that's a perfectly safe place.' But I didn't lock it. I went to the train to see my son off. I was so confused and troubled in mind—it was so hard to part with him. So I forgot to lock the desk! And when I went to get the money, next day, to take it to the bank, it wasn't there."

"This very desk!" said Beany, touching it.

"Oh," said Jack, "there must be a secret drawer or a cubbyhole back of one of the pigeonholes."

"There always is, in storybooks," I interrupted.

"Just think," Jack went on. "There's forty thousand dollars hidden somewhere inside that desk!"

"Then Mrs. Lavendar will be rich again," said Beany, happily.

"If we can only find it," I added.

But Mrs. Lavendar shook her head. "I've known this desk all my life, dear," she said. "It was my great-grandfather's. I know every nook and corner of it. It has no secrets."

"May we try?" Jack asked. "May we look through it?"

"Of course you may," replied Mrs. Lavendar. "I'll take out all the papers, and you may open all the drawers."

Jack felt in each cubbyhole in turn.

"What are you feeling around for?" Beany wanted to know.

"For a sliding panel," said Jack. "There might be a little secret cubbyhole at the back."

He felt and pressed and pushed in all the pigeonholes.

"Well, I guess not," he said. "But let's take out the drawers."

"Yes," I said. "The money might have slipped back of the drawer and got stuck there."

So we took out each drawer in turn and felt inside.

"It's no use," Jack said at last. "We've tried everything."

"Oh dear," said Beany. "I was so sure we'd find it!"

I noticed that the beautiful silver candlesticks were not on the mantel, and Mrs. Lavendar was wearing a little black sweater instead of the embroidered shawl. I was afraid Beany would notice and ask if she had had to sell them, too, but he was so interested in the desk that we got away without his asking any more questions.

For several days Jack and Beany and I talked together about the money, and tried to guess how it had been stolen, and made up stories about finding it again for Mrs. Lavendar. Then we forgot all about it for a while, for Christmas began to come.

We were busy as could be, writing our Christmas wants and our Christmas lists, and making things, and counting our savings to buy presents, and going shopping at the Five-and-Ten,

8

and painting Christmas cards, and doing all the things that belong to Christmas.

Each one of us painted a card for Mrs. Lavendar, of course, and it was while we were doing this, one snowy day, that I happened to think of something.

"Oh dear, I wish we could buy the Prince and Princess and give them to Mrs. Lavendar for Christmas," I remarked.

"That's just like you, Dee," said Jack. "One of those brilliant ideas that there's no way of carrying out."

I knew he didn't mean that to be as unpleasant as it sounded. It was just that he wanted so much to do it, and felt sure that we couldn't.

"Let's ask Mr. Brackett how much they are, anyway," said Beany. "Maybe we could buy them. I'll ask him."

Beany's always so hopeful. Jack and I knew it was useless, because we'd already spent so much of our money for Christmas. But Beany went down to ask Mr. Brackett and came back soon to tell us.

"Seven dollars and fifty cents!"

He said it just as cheerfully as if we had seven dollars and fifty cents right there, but of course Jack and I had very little hope.

We got our banks out and counted what we had left. Jack had two fifty-centses and a quarter and four dimes. That made a dollar and sixty-five cents.

I had four quarters and three dimes and two nickels and two pennies, and that's a dollar and forty-two cents altogether.

Beany had eight nickels and three pennies and a Chinese coin that Mother got in change from the laundry, by mistake. The Chinese coin didn't count, so he had forty-three cents. We added it all up, and it was three dollars and fifty cents, and that wasn't nearly enough.

But we did manage to get the money and buy the Prince and Princess after all, and this is the story of how we did it.

We were playing tag in the back alleys a few days later, and by mistake we tipped over an ash barrel. When we went to pick it up and put back the junk we had spilled, we found that it

9

was a most unusual collection. There were old bundles of letters tied with faded ribbon and photographs and some good kodak films.

Someone had just moved out of the house, and there was no one around but a cleaning woman. We went into the backyard and showed her the films through the window and asked if we could have them. She said yes, we could have anything we found in the backyard.

Then Beany spied a double row of store milk bottles at the back gate, and he had a happy thought.

"Look," he said, "we could get five cents apiece for those milk bottles, and then maybe we could buy the Prince and Princess for Mrs. Lavendar."

We asked the cleaning woman if it would be all right to take the bottles. She said, "Land sakes, yes! I can't lug all those back to the store."

There were thirty-one of them, and we had to make four trips. That gave us a dollar and fifty-five cents. So we had five dollars and five cents, altogether.

"Perhaps we could beat Mr. Brackett down," said Jack. "People always do bargain for antiques, you know."

So we took the one dollar bill and the four dollars and five cents in change and showed them to Mr. Brackett. We told him that was all the money we had or hoped to have, and we asked if he would sell us the pair of china figures.

"You expect me to sell them for five dollars and five cents?" said Mr. Brackett, indignantly. "Why, I could have sold them ten times over for that price. Seven-fifty is my figure, and not one cent less than five-fifty."

"We haven't got five-fifty," said Jack.

"Five-fifty," Mr. Brackett said again. So we went out to talk it over.

"We almost have it," said Jack. "Only forty-five cents more to get. Let's all think hard."

"I know," I said. "Mrs. Fuller offered me twenty-five cents once for bringing back Nimrod. I'll go and get it now."

Mrs. Fuller is a lady who lives several blocks away. We

hadn't known her till one day when I met her looking into every alley and calling, "Kitty, kitty, kitty."

"Little girl," she said, "have you seen a large, dirty, white cat with a black spot on his back and a black tail?"

I knew the cat she meant. "Only," I said, "he isn't white now. He's almost maltese."

"I know what you mean," she said. "He was white when he left home, but I'm sure he could pass for maltese now."

So I told her I'd find him and bring him home if I could.

A day or two later, when we were playing hide-and-seek, I saw him hiding behind a barrel, and I coaxed him out and took him to her house. He was battle-scarred and very wild, but after he had lapped up a saucer of milk, he started washing his face and began to feel more at home.

Mrs. Fuller told me the story of his life. "He was a street cat till he was a year old," she said. "Then we began to feed him whenever he came around. Little by little, he's grown to feel that our house is run solely to give him a home and meals when he cares to turn up here. In winter, he condescends to spend the season with us; but as soon as spring comes, he has a longing for the great open spaces, and he deserts us for the back alleys. Then he forgets that we exist. He doesn't even come home when he's hungry, and I lie awake nights wondering

11

when he had his last full meal. He knows we're talking about him. See his self-conscious expression. Nimmie, you old villain, where have you been? In somebody's ash barrel?"

"What's his name?" I asked.

"Nimrod," she said. "He's named after Nimrod, the mighty hunter in the Book of Genesis, in the Bible. Our Nimrod is the best mouser that ever was born. That's why I cherish you, you ingrate," she said to him, "not because of affection for you."

Nimrod rubbed his head on her shoe and put up his paw just like a little dog. Mrs. Fuller picked him up and hugged him, all dirty as he was, and then she tried to give me a quarter. Of course I wouldn't take it. I said I was glad I could be the means of restoring Nimrod to his home.

But now that I thought it over, it seemed to me it would be right to take that quarter and use it towards our fund, so I went over to call on Mrs. Fuller. She was at home, the maid said, and I was received by Mrs. Fuller in a room where Nimrod reposed on a blue cushion. He was white and sleek and sleepy and looked as if he had never seen an ash barrel in all his life.

"He's our winter cat now," said Mrs. Fuller. "He leads a double life. I am very glad to see you, dear."

I didn't tell her about Mrs. Lavendar and the Prince and Princess, as Beany might have. I only said, "I need some money for a Christmas gift, and I thought perhaps you'd be willing to have me change my mind about the quarter."

"Yes, indeed," she said. "I don't have to lie awake at night for Nimrod now, but I often wake and feel I did wrong not to insist on your taking that quarter. I'm so glad you came."

She got up and found her pocketbook. "Indeed," she said. "Nimrod's so precious to me that I think it's worth fifty cents to me to have him back." And she offered me a half-dollar.

Of course, I couldn't take that. I said, "No, thank you, Mrs. Fuller, I couldn't take fifty cents; but I do need just forty-five cents to get this gift, and if you feel Nimrod is worth that, I'd be glad to take it."

So Mrs. Fuller fished around in her pocketbook and found the change, and I went, after she had asked me to come again.

12

There was a great shout of joy from the boys when I got back with the forty-five cents. We went right in to Mr. Brackett's and bought the Prince and Princess.

They were a little bit dusty, and Jack thought we ought to put them into the bathtub and wash them. But Mother thought not, because we might chip them or wash off the color. She said that Mrs. Lavendar would know best how to clean them.

Then we started to wrap them in Christmas paper, but Mrs. Lavendar might break them in opening them. Besides, it would be more fun to have them burst on her startled vision when she opened the door.

Jack wanted to be the one to carry the Prince, and I wanted to carry the Princess, and Beany felt very bad about it.

"It's just because I'm the youngest," he said. "I always get the worst of it. I have to take turns with you filling the wood basket and going to the store, but no one ever takes turns with me being the youngest. And Mrs. Lavendar was my friend first."

So we told him he could be the one to say, "Merry Christmas, Mrs. Lavendar, we've brought you a present." So it was settled that way.

Christmas Eve is very beautiful on Beacon Hill. All the houses are lighted with many candles in every window. The curtains are drawn back so that everyone can see inside the homes. The houses are all very beautiful to see, because most of them were built in early days and have winding mahogany staircases and lovely paneled walls; and many of them have beautiful tapestries and paintings.

A great crowd comes from all over Boston, so that you can hardly move through the streets, but everyone is quiet and reverent. It is almost like having church outdoors, especially after the carols begin.

The Christmas carols are sung by musical groups that come from different parts of the city. They sing in front of the houses, especially around a tiny park called Louisburg Square, which is halfway up Beacon Hill.

The people inside the houses listen to the carols. Sometimes the people in the street sing right along with the carolers.

13

Mother always takes us out for a little while before bedtime, after we have lighted dozens of candles in our own windows.

This Christmas Eve we asked Mrs. Lavendar to go out with us, but she thought she would get too tired. So when we came back, we thought we'd sing some carols to her. We sang, *Silent Night, Holy Night* and *The First Noel*, and stood outside, looking up at the candles in her windows. Mrs. Lavendar liked it very much.

It's such an exciting feeling to wake on Christmas morning and see the stockings all humpy and a candy cane sticking out of the top! But this Christmas morning when I opened my eyes, I had a special feeling that something very joyous was going to happen, and then I remembered that we were going to take the Prince and Princess up to Mrs. Lavendar.

Right after breakfast we went upstairs, Jack carrying the Prince and I carrying the Princess, just as we had planned.

Halfway upstairs I caught a glimpse of Beany's face. He had a scratch across his chin where the grocer's cat had scratched him when he tried to pet her, and he had such a sad look that I was sorry for him.

"It must be hard to be the youngest all the time," I thought.

Besides, Mrs. Lavendar *was* his friend first. So I said, "Here, Beany, you take her," and I put the Princess carefully into his hands.

"Oh!" said Beany.

We got to the top of the stairs, and Jack looked around and saw how it was, and he said, "Oh, well," and he put the Prince into my hands. So after all, it was Jack who lifted the brass knocker and said, "Merry Christmas, Mrs. Lavendar, we've brought you a present," when she opened the door.

When she saw the Prince and Princess, she said, "Oh, you dear children!" very softly.

Then she said, "Their home is on the desk, dears, one on each side of the picture."

What she meant was a photograph of her son in a silver frame. I walked across the room and put the Prince on the desk very carefully, and Beany came after me, carrying the Princess.

But when Beany stepped on the corner of the rug near the door, it slipped under his foot and down he came—crash!—on the floor. Beany *would!*

Mrs. Lavendar stooped to pick up the pieces, and it was like her to think of Beany's embarrassment instead of her loss.

"I'm sure we can mend the Princess," she was saying. "I have some china cement—" and then she gasped and picked up something from under the pieces and held it out for us to see.

It was a roll of bills that had been inside the hollow Princess!

"The money wasn't stolen!" she said slowly. "It was there all the time."

She sat down with the bills in her lap, and I could see her hands trembling. We children couldn't say a word. All those bills!

"I begin to understand," she said. "My son was standing by the desk. I never thought of the Princess—but of course he would put it there. He always did put things there. From the time he was quite small, he used to stow all sorts of treasures through that hole in the base. He thought of course I saw him put it there, and no one else would know."

15

We had a great rejoicing after that. Jack went out into the hall and shouted for Mother so loudly that she came running up all breathless.

The first thing she did after she heard the news was to make a cup of tea for Mrs. Lavendar, who was looking very pale. Then we passed some of our Christmas candy, and Beany nearly choked on a chocolate with a nut in it.

Since then, Mrs. Lavendar hasn't gone out to do sewing any more. The silver candlesticks are back on the mantel, and she wears the white silk shawl and has a fire, too, on cold days. And she has mended the Princess with china cement so you can't see the cracks at all, unless you get up very close.

THE CHRISTMAS PATH

Anne Higginson Spicer

Far though we wander
Among the world of men,
Once a year a little path
Leads us home again,
Leads us through a starry night,
To holly on a door,
To stockings by the chimney
And toys on the floor . . .
Every home's a sacred place
A star may shine above,
If it hold a memory
Of child-and-mother love.
The world's way's a wide way
And leads me far a-roam,
But the little path to Christmas
Can always bring us home.

Beverly Cleary

GALLONS OF GUPPIES

ILLUSTRATED BY *Louis Darling*

Every afternoon after school Ribsy waited
for Henry under a fir tree in the corner of the schoolyard. Four
days a week they ran home the shortest way, past the park, up
the hill, and through the vacant lot.

On Fridays, however, they walked home the long way round
past the Rose City Drugstore, the Supermarket, the Ideal
Barber Shop, and the Lucky Dog Pet Shop. At the pet store
they stopped while Henry bought two pounds of horse meat
from Mr. Pennycuff.

Henry liked to go to the pet store. The windows were full
of puppies and kittens and, just before Easter, rabbits and baby
chicks and ducks. Inside there was usually a parrot or monkey
and once there had been a deodorized skunk. Henry thought
it would be fun to have a skunk following him around, but
when he found it cost forty dollars he gave up the idea.

17

But best of all Henry liked the fish. One side of the store was covered with rows of little tanks. Each aquarium contained green plants that grew under water, snails, and a different kind of tropical fish. Henry always stopped to look into each tank. He liked the dollar-sized black-and-silver-striped angelfish and the inch-long orange moonfish with their velvety fins and tails. He thought the tiny catfish were fun to watch, because they stayed on the bottom of the tanks, rolled their eyes, and used their whisker-like barbels to feel around in the sand for food. Mr. Pennycuff explained that the fish came from all over the world, but most of them came from jungle rivers where the water was warm. That was why they were called tropical fish.

One Friday when Henry went to the pet store he saw a sign that read:

SPECIAL OFFER

1 pair of guppies
fish bowl
1 snail
aquatic plant
package of fish food

ALL FOR 79¢

"Jeepers!" said Henry. "All that for seventy-nine cents!" He looked at the fish in the bowls. Each bowl held one plain silvery-gray fish almost two inches long and one smaller fish with all the colors of the rainbow. "That really is a bargain!"

"It certainly is," agreed Mr. Pennycuff. "Shall I wrap up a pair for you?"

Henry felt around in his pocket. The silver dollar his grandfather had given him was still there. He watched the little rainbow fish chase the silvery fish and decided he had to have a pair of guppies. After all, it was his very own money he was spending. He would keep them on the dresser in his room. They would just stay in his room and swim quietly around in their bowl. He didn't see how his mother could object to two quiet little fish that didn't bark or track in mud or anything.

18

"I'll take a pair," Henry told Mr. Pennycuff, and watched him fasten waxed paper around the top of the bowl with a rubber band and put it into a bag.

"Now be sure to put the bowl near a heater in cold weather so the fish won't get chilled and catch ick."

"Ick?" said Henry.

"Yes, ick. It's short for *ichthyophthirius*. When the fish get chilled, they catch ick and are covered with tiny white spots."

"Gosh," said Henry. Maybe there was more to keeping guppies than he thought.

"Oh, don't worry," said Mr. Pennycuff. "They can stand water down to sixty degrees. If it were that cold in the house, you'd have the heat on."

That sounded easy. "How often do I change the water?" asked Henry.

"You shouldn't have to change the water. The snails help keep it clean. Just give the fish a tiny pinch of food once a day. It's only when the fish don't eat all their food or when you have too many fish in a bowl that the water gets dirty." Mr. Pennycuff gave Henry his change.

"I didn't know that," said Henry. "I'm glad you told me. Here, Ribsy." He handed Ribsy his package of horse meat. The dog took it in his mouth, and they left the pet store. "You'll have to carry your meat all the way home today. And don't you stop and try to eat it before we get home, either. It has to last you a few days."

Ribsy wagged his tail and trotted on ahead of Henry with his meat. Henry tried to walk without jiggling the package. He didn't want to slosh the guppies any more than he had to. When Ribsy was half a block ahead of Henry, he dropped his package and looked back at Henry. Then he began to tear the paper off the meat.

"Hey! Cut that out!" yelled Henry. He started to run, but the water in his fish bowl sloshed and he had to stop.

Just to be safe Ribsy picked up his meat, trotted farther down the sidewalk, and finished tearing off the paper.

"Stop that! You—you—you old dog!" Again Henry tried to

19

run. This time he held the bowl straight out in front of him, but the water still sloshed.

Ribsy gobbled part of the meat and then trotted ahead with the rest of it in his mouth. Just as Henry was almost close enough to reach for the meat, Ribsy put on a burst of speed.

"Ribsy! You come here!" The dog ignored Henry. "I'll get you for this!" Henry was really angry now. He set his package of guppies on the sidewalk and ran after his dog. This time Henry caught up with him.

Henry grabbed one end of the meat and pulled. Ribsy, growling deep in his throat, hung onto the other end and pulled. The dog had a better grip on the meat because he could sink his teeth into it. Henry found that raw meat was cold and slippery.

"You let go that meat!"

Ribsy growled more fiercely. He sounded as if he meant it. The harder Henry pulled, the louder Ribsy growled.

Henry was sure Ribsy wouldn't really bite him, but just the same he knew it was not a good idea to annoy any animal when it was eating. Anyway, he couldn't stand there all afternoon playing tug-of-war with a piece of horse meat. His guppies might get cold.

"All right, you old dog! Go ahead and eat it and see if I care. You'll just have to eat canned dog food the rest of the week." He went back to his guppies while Ribsy wolfed the rest of the meat, licked his chops, and then, with his stomach bulging, followed slowly at Henry's heels the rest of the way home.

When they reached Henry's house on Klickitat Street, Henry opened the door and yelled, "Hey, Mom! Come and see what I bought with the silver dollar Grandpa gave me."

"I'm afraid to look," answered his mother from the kitchen. "What is it this time?"

"Fish."

"Fish?" Mrs. Huggins sounded surprised. "Did you want me to cook it for dinner?"

Henry carried his package into the kitchen. "No, Mom, you don't understand. Not dead fish. Live fish swimming around in a bowl of water. They're called guppies."

"Guppies?"

"Yes. Just two little fish. I'll keep them on my dresser and they won't be any trouble at all. They were on sale at the pet shop. They were a bargain. See, Mom?" Henry gently lifted the fish bowl out of the bag.

Mrs. Huggins put down the potato she was peeling. "Why, Henry, what pretty little fish!"

"I thought you'd like them." Henry was pleased.

His mother bent closer to the fish bowl. "But, Henry, what are those little dark things in the water?"

"What little dark things?" Henry looked closer.

"Why, they're baby fish," Mrs. Huggins exclaimed. "There must be fifteen or twenty."

"Baby guppies!" Henry was delighted. "Look, Mom, did you ever see such teeny-weeny little fish? Golly, they're so little just about all you can see are their eyes and their tails."

Mrs. Huggins sighed. "Henry, I'm afraid they won't be teeny-weeny little fish very long. They'll grow and then what are you going to do with them?"

"I don't know. I'll ask Dad." Henry was worried. "Maybe he knows about baby guppies."

21

But when Mr. Huggins came home from work, Henry was disappointed to learn that he knew nothing about little guppies. "Why don't you get a book about guppies from the library?" he suggested.

Mrs. Huggins said there would be time before dinner, so Henry found his library card and he and Ribsy ran all the way to the library.

"Hello, Henry," said the lady in the boys' and girls' room at the library. "Have you come for another book about gienats and orges?"

This was a joke between the librarian and Henry. When Henry had first started reading fairy tales by himself he returned a book and asked for another about gienats and orges. He felt a little silly about it now, although he secretly thought gienats and orges sounded better than giants and ogres.

"No, I want a book about guppies," Henry answered. "I have some baby guppies and I don't know how to take care of them."

The librarian found a book on hobbies with a chapter on fish, but it did not tell much about guppies. "Just a minute, Henry," she said. "Maybe there is something in the adult room." She returned with a thick book about tropical fish. It was full of colored pictures. "I'm sure this will help you," she said, "but I'm afraid it's too hard for you to read. I'll let you take it out on your card if you think your mother and father will help you with it."

"Sure, my dad will help me."

The librarian stamped the book on his card and Henry, proud to have a grown-up book stamped on his library card, ran home with it.

After dinner Mr. Huggins sat down to read the fish book while Henry went to his room to watch his guppies. This time he counted thirty-eight babies. After a while his father came in with the book in his hand. "This is a mighty interesting book, Henry, but you're going to need some more fish bowls. According to this book you can't keep so many fish in one bowl."

"But, Dad, where will I get more bowls?"

"Maybe we can find something in the basement."

So Henry and his father rummaged through the basement until they found a gallon jar Mrs. Huggins used for making dill pickles.

"This should do," said Mr. Huggins. They carried it upstairs and washed it. Mr. Huggins filled it with hot water and carried it into Henry's room. "Now when the water cools we can move some of the little guppies. They can't live in cold water right out of the faucet. They need water that has stood or hot water that has cooled. While it's cooling, we can make a net." He found a piece of wire and bent it into a circle. Mrs. Huggins took an old stocking and sewed it to the wire to make a little fish net.

Henry and his father took turns catching the tiny fish with the net and moving them into the pickle jar. Henry was surprised that such small fish could swim so fast.

The next day and every day after that Henry looked at his guppies the first thing in the morning. When he came home from school he looked at his guppies before he went into the kitchen for something to eat. His fish grew and grew. As the weeks passed the big guppies had more little guppies. The little guppies grew up to be big guppies and had little guppies of their own. Henry had hundreds of guppies. He couldn't find any more pickle jars so he started using his mother's quart fruit jars. He couldn't keep many fish in a quart of water.

Henry had jars on his dresser. He had them on the table by his bed. He put jars on the floor all around the edge of his room. When he had one row of jars all the way around the floor, he started another row.

"Goodness, Henry," his mother said, "pretty soon you won't be able to walk in here."

"If you keep all your guppies," said his father, "by the end of the year you'll have over a million fish in your bedroom!"

"Golly!" said Henry. "A million fish in my bedroom!" Wouldn't that be something to tell the kids at school!

Henry was glad when summer vacation started. It took him so long to feed his fish that he no longer had time to play with the other children on Klickitat Street. He spent all his allowance on fish food, snails, and plants for his jars. He slept with his windows shut if he thought the night were going to be cold. He wasn't going to have his fish getting ick if he could help it.

All day long the boys and girls in the neighborhood rang the doorbell and asked to see Henry's fish.

Finally his mother said, "Henry, this can't go on. You must get rid of some of those fish. You'll have to give them to your friends."

Henry liked each fish so much he couldn't decide which one he liked best. They were all so lively, swimming around in their fruit jars. Henry didn't see how he could part with any of them, but now that he was on the third row of jars around his room, he decided to try. He started asking his friends in the neighborhood if they would like to have some fish.

Scooter didn't think he had time to take care of fish. He delivered the *Shopping News* two days a week.

Mary Jane said her mother wouldn't let her have any fish. Mary Jane's mother was very particular.

Robert said he would rather come over and look at Henry's fish than take care of guppies of his own.

Finally Beezus said she would take one fish. Beezus' real name was Beatrice, but her little sister Ramona called her Beezus and now everyone else did too. Beezus and Ramona already had a cat, three white rats, and a turtle, so one fish wouldn't make much difference. It took Henry a long time to decide which guppy to give her.

Then one morning Mrs. Huggins came home from the Supermarket with three lugs of apricots in the back seat of the car. When Henry helped her carry them into the house, she said, "Henry, run down to the basement and bring up about twenty quart jars. These apricots are so ripe I want to start canning them right away."

Henry went down to the basement. He did not come back with twenty quart jars. He came back with four. "These are all I could find, Mom," he said.

"Oh, dear, and one of them has a crack." Mrs. Huggins looked at the three lugs of apricots. Then she looked at Henry.

"Henry," she said, and he knew from the way she said it she meant whatever she was going to say, "go to your room and bring me seventeen quart jars. And don't bring me any jars with guppies in them, either."

"Yes, Mom," said Henry in a meek voice. He went into his room and looked at the jars of guppies. He guessed he did have too many fish. But they were such nice fish! He got down on his hands and knees to look at his pets.

"Henry!" his mother called. "I am starting to pit the apricots. You'll have to hurry!"

"O.K." Henry took his net and started catching the smallest guppies. The only thing he could do was to move them in with the other fish. He hated to do it, because the fish book said they shouldn't be crowded. When the guppies were moved, he carried the jars into the kitchen and poured the water down the sink.

"I'm sorry, Henry," his mother said, "but after all, I did tell

25

you some time ago that you couldn't go on putting guppies in fruit jars."

"I know, Mom. I guess I'll have to think of something else." It took Henry the rest of the morning to feed his fish. He had to put the tiniest pinch of the finest fish food into each jar. He could hear Robert and Beezus playing cowboy in the vacant lot. Ribsy trotted into his room, watched him a few minutes, and then went outdoors. Henry began to wish he were outdoors, too, but he couldn't let his little fish go hungry.

Late that afternoon Mrs. Huggins drove downtown to pick up Henry's father after work. When they returned, Henry saw his father carrying more lugs of apricots into the kitchen. He had a feeling he knew what was coming next.

It came.

"Henry," his mother said, "I am afraid I'll have to ask you for some more fruit jars."

Henry sighed. "I guess I'll have to double them up some more." He started to go to his room and then turned back. "Say, Mom, are you going to can anything besides apricots this year?"

"Yes, tomatoes and pears. And I thought we might go out to Mount Hood and pick huckleberries. You like huckleberry pie during the winter, don't you?"

Henry certainly did like huckleberry pie. He liked it any time of year. He went to his room and moved more of his guppies. Tomatoes, pears, and huckleberries. He could see that his mother would need all her fruit jars before the summer was over. That would leave him his original bowl and the gallon pickle jar.

"Hey, Mom," he yelled. "Are you going to make dill pickles, too?"

"Yes, Henry."

There went the pickle jar. By the end of the summer Henry would have to move the hundreds of fish he had now, and goodness knows how many more, back into the bowl. There would be so many fish there wouldn't be room for any water.

That settled it. Henry decided he would have to get rid of all his guppies. He hated to do it, but if he kept even two he

26

would soon be right back where he was now. It would be nice to have time to play outdoors again. Henry made up his mind to take every one of his fish back to the Lucky Dog Pet Shop. Maybe Mr. Pennycuff could have another sale.

Henry was chasing a guppy with the net when his father came into the room. He told his father what he planned to do. "I sure hate to do it," he mourned, "but I can't keep a million guppies in my bedroom." He looked sorrowfully at his fish.

"I know, Henry. I hate to see the fish go, too, but they're getting out of hand. I'll tell you what to do. Catch all the guppies and put them into the pickle jar. It won't hurt them to be crowded for a little while. Right after supper I'll run you down to the pet shop in the car."

Henry sadly packed up his fish, and after supper he and his father and Ribsy got into the car and drove to the pet shop. Ribsy liked to ride in the car.

"I brought you a lot of guppies," Henry said to Mr. Penny-cuff. "I hope you can use them."

"Use them!" exclaimed Mr. Pennycuff. "I certainly can. I haven't had a guppy in this store since the sale. Let's see them."

While Henry unwrapped his pickle jar, his father looked at the tanks of tropical fish along the wall.

"I should say you do have a lot of guppies," said Mr. Penny-cuff. "Nice healthy ones, too. You must have taken good care of them." He held the jar up to the light and looked at it closely. It seethed with gray guppies, rainbow guppies, and baby guppies of all sizes, swimming round and round. "Hmmmm. Let's see. We-e-ell." Mr. Pennycuff continued to stare at the fish.

Henry couldn't understand why he was muttering to himself that way. He had given Mr. Pennycuff the guppies and now he wished he would return the pickle jar so he could go.

"Well, now," said Mr. Pennycuff, "I guess these fish are worth about seven dollars. I can't give it to you in money, but you can pick out seven dollars' worth of anything in the store you want."

Seven dollars! Henry was astounded. Seven dollars' worth

of anything in the pet shop! He was rich! He had been so busy thinking about getting rid of the guppies that it had not occurred to him they might be worth something to Mr. Pennycuff.

"Hey, Dad! Did you hear that? Seven dollars!" Henry shouted.

"I certainly did. You'd better start looking around."

"Take anything you want, sonny. Dog collars, kittens, bird seed. Anything."

Henry tried to decide what he would like. Ribsy had a collar and leash and a dish, so he didn't need anything. He looked at the kittens. The sign read, "Kittens. One dollar each." They were cute, but Henry decided he didn't want seven dollars' worth of kittens. Ribsy would chase them.

"You don't have any skunks on sale for seven dollars?" he asked hopefully.

"No, I haven't had any skunks for a long time."

"I'm glad to hear that," said Mr. Huggins.

Henry looked at the tropical fish. Then he looked all around the store and came back to the tropical fish again. He stopped to watch a little catfish busily digging in the sand. Suddenly Henry knew that the only thing in the store he really wanted was more fish.

"Could I keep a catfish in my fish bowl?" he asked Mr. Pennycuff.

"No, sonny, they have to be kept in warm water. They need an electric heater and a thermostat in the water to keep the water the right temperature." He held up two long glass tubes. One looked as if it were filled with sand and the other with wires. "See, this is what I mean. They fit into the corners of an aquarium like this and keep the water warm all the time." He fitted them into the corner of a little tank on a table.

"How much does that cost?"

"The tank is three dollars and the heater and thermostat come to four. That makes seven dollars."

Henry was disappointed. "I wouldn't have any money left for a catfish, and the only thing I really want is more fish."

"You know, Henry, I hoped you'd say that," answered his

father. "I hated to see those guppies go as much as you did. If you buy the tank and heater and thermostat, I'll buy the fish."

"Gee, Dad, that's swell! Let's get a little catfish!" Then Henry thought of something. "Do catfish have as many babies as guppies?" he asked Mr. Pennycuff.

"Oh my, no. Catfish rarely have babies when they're kept in tanks. They mostly have them when they live outdoors in ponds and rivers."

"Swell!" said Henry. "That's the kind of fish we want. Won't Mom be surprised!"

GUPPIES ARE BEST

Nancy Clinton

I like snakes and snails and mice—
I think they all are awfully nice.
And I like ants who crawl around
And work in ant hills on the ground,
And fireflies who like to flit
At night with all their headlights lit,
And shiny little worms who squirm
To show it's fun to be a worm,
But way ahead of all the rest
Guppies are best!

Marjorie Fischer

ROCOCO SKATES

ILLUSTRATED BY *Seymour Fleishman*

T WENTY pairs of shoes clattered up the marble steps inside the Metropolitan Museum. The class was having Art today, and Miss Ryan had taken them to see the pictures. Miss Ryan walked beside the line, looking forward and back along the double row of children.

Mary Ann was at the very end of the line, even behind Frances, the girl she was supposed to be walking with, who was her best friend in a way. Miss Ryan looked back at Mary Ann and her glasses caught the light, so that for a second you couldn't see Miss Ryan's eyes.

"We can't have any loitering, Mary Ann," said Miss Ryan. "Close up the line."

Mary Ann stepped up and then fell back again. This would be a good place to roller skate, she thought; the floors were hard wood, and today most of the galleries were empty. You could go shooting down the galleries and around corners yelling like anything. You could stop yourself with statues so big and heavy they couldn't fall. You'd go swinging around the statue with the force of your rush, just holding lightly with one hand to the statue, and then you'd take off again, rolling, shooting, yelling. If you had skates, you could. Mary Ann didn't have any skates. Skates were what she had particularly wanted for a long time, for it seemed as if everyone she knew had skates. Sometimes when she was in the park—if she had skates—she wouldn't just shoot along, she'd swing, she'd glide, almost like dancing, and then she could play tag with Frances and the other kids who had skates. Maybe next Christmas—but Christmas was a long way off, and so was her birthday.

The twenty pairs of shoes clattered along the galleries. Here and there Miss Ryan would hold up her hand, the shoes stood still, and Miss Ryan told them about this picture or that, her glasses sometimes reflecting the pictures very small and curved, as if her glasses were mirrors.

Miss Ryan stopped before a medium-sized picture of a table with a bottle of wine, a loaf of bread, a knife, and a basket of fruit. It wasn't bad, Mary Ann thought, leaning. Then she stood straight. Right at one side of the picture was another picture on an easel. It was a medium-sized picture of a table with a bottle of wine, a loaf of bread, a knife, and a basket of fruit. It was, in fact, a copy of the picture on the wall and so exactly like it that, except for the frame around it, nobody could have told one from the other.

"How is that, Miss Ryan?" asked Mary Ann.

"Artists get permission from the Museum to come in and copy," said Miss Ryan. "This is a very famous picture, so naturally artists copy it."

"I'd never," said Mary Ann. "I'd rather do my own, even if it was bad."

Mary Ann loitered behind the class, standing before the easel and looking from one picture to the other. Maybe the paint was still wet on the copy, she thought. It would be easy enough to find out, but of course she shouldn't do that. Her right hand reached out all by itself, and her forefinger pressed against the picture on the easel. Oh, heavens! It *was* wet. She felt the paint slide a little under her finger.

Mary Ann hurriedly caught up with Frances and stepped along beside her.

"I saw you," whispered Frances. "You're just lucky Miss Ryan didn't see. Did it leave a mark?"

31

Mary Ann didn't answer. She walked along beside Frances, not leaning at all and breathing rather fast.

Miss Ryan walked on, with twenty pairs of shoes clopping behind her. They walked and stopped, walked and stopped. The pictures were like windows, Mary Ann thought, and through them you saw how people used to look. Then they went through rooms full of furniture, and you could see how people used to sit and write and sew and sleep. There was one enormous bed with a canopy over it, and the canopy of rose silk was held up with carved, golden Cupids leaping through the air and holding carved wreaths of flowers.

"This is Rococo furniture," said Miss Ryan.

Rococo, Mary Ann thought to herself. It might be the name of something to play, or a pigeon cooing, or something you shouted as you slid along on roller skates.

"Rococo," Mary Ann said out loud, and Frances looked at her and repeated it after her.

"Rococo," said Frances.

"Rococo," said Mary Ann, trying it out as a pigeon.

Mary Ann and Frances began to laugh. They hit against each other as they walked. "Rococo!" they said, and swayed away. They walked and looked, walked and looked. Mary Ann began to lean again. She was *tired*.

"All right, children," Miss Ryan said at last, "that's enough for today. You may turn right around as you are and we'll find our way out."

The class turned, and Mary Ann and Frances were at the

head of the line. They walked along, past the furniture—
"Rococo!" said Mary Ann and Frances, swaying against each
other. They walked past pictures and pictures. Now they were
in the room where the picture on the easel had been.

"Look," said Frances, "the copy's gone."

Mary Ann was next to the wall. She leaned along as she
walked, and when she came to the medium-sized picture of the
table with the bottle of wine, the loaf of bread, the knife, and
the basket of fruit, she gave such a loud cry that everyone
stopped.

"Look!" cried Mary Ann. "It's the other one. The real one's
been stolen!"

"How can you tell?" said Frances.

"Quick!" cried Mary Ann. "We've got to tell someone important."

Miss Ryan came between Mary Ann and Frances.

"What is the meaning of all this noise?" she said.

"The picture!" said Mary Ann. "The real picture's been stolen.
This is the one that was on the easel."

"Nonsense," said Miss Ryan.

"Honestly!" cried Mary Ann. "We must tell the head of the
Museum right away."

"Come along, now," said Miss Ryan. "I never heard such
nonsense in my life."

By this time one or two people in other galleries had heard
the racket and were standing about trying to find out what had
happened. A guard in a blue uniform strolled in and told everyone to keep quiet—this was the Museum, in case they'd forgotten.

Miss Ryan was getting ready to march them straight out;
Mary Ann saw that. Miss Ryan would never believe her, and in
the meantime the picture would be gone.

"I must tell someone," cried Mary Ann. She spun about,
before everyone, not knowing where to go. She began to run,
back along the way she had come, because the class and Miss
Ryan and the other people and the guard were on the other
side. She ran past pictures and pictures, dodging people or

33

bumping against them, and everyone turned to look, and then—there came the clatter of nineteen pairs of shoes, running along the galleries after her.

Mary Ann came to the furniture room, and there were two guards coming toward her, one from each doorway, and she ran around two chairs and a desk, and there were the guards still coming toward her, and the nineteen pairs of shoes clopping along faster and faster. She sprang over the rope around the Rococo bed, and the guards came nearer. They reached out their hands for her, and she leaped on to the bed and stood on it. How hard the mattress was, like a board! She ran a little one way on the bed, under the canopy, and as both guards ran to get her, she doubled about, leaped from the bed, sprang over the rope, and made off again, with everyone clopping after her.

She ran out into a marble hall, and at her left she saw a door marked—marked—why, it was marked Office of the Director.

The DIRECTOR. She turned about and swung open the heavy door and dashed inside, just as everyone caught up with her.

"A picture's been stolen," gasped Mary Ann to the people in the office. "I know it's been stolen. You just come along with me and I'll show you. No one believes me, Miss Ryan or not even Frances, but I'll show you. Only, hurry!"

While she was talking, a nice old man had come out of an inner office, and Miss Ryan and four guards had come through the outer door.

"Let's just go along and have a look to make sure," said the nice old man. "It's pretty hard to steal a picture here, but just to make sure."

Back they went, all of them, first the nice old man and Mary Ann, then Frances and Miss Ryan, and then the class, and the other people, and the guards. When they got to the picture, the nice old man put on a pair of glasses with a black ribbon attached to them, and he looked at the picture very carefully. After quite a while he turned to Mary Ann.

"This is a very good copy," said the nice old man, "but it is a copy. The real picture has been stolen. I am going back to my office now. Won't you wait for me outside?"

While they waited for the nice old man, Miss Ryan told Mary Ann that she quite understood how it was, that Mary Ann

S. Fleishman

35

had really *had* to run. When the nice old man came out, he had a great book bound in blue leather in his arms.

"This is for you, Mary Ann," he said. "It has colored pictures of most of the pictures in the Museum. It even has the stolen picture. If it had not been for you, the theft might not have been noticed until the picture had been taken out of the country. You have done a very remarkable thing; almost anyone would have been fooled by that copy."

"I guess I couldn't be fooled," said Mary Ann.

"Here's the book then, Mary Ann," said the nice old man.

Mary Ann took the great book bound in blue leather and said thank you, politely. The nice old man watched her.

"Maybe there was something you specially wanted, Mary Ann," he said, "besides the book."

"She wants roller skates," Frances burst out.

"Roller skates it is," said the nice old man, and he called a nice young man from his office.

In a few minutes Mary Ann and Frances were going down the steps outside the Museum with the nice young man. The rest of the class and Miss Ryan stood and watched Mary Ann and Frances climb into an automobile and waved to them.

"How did you know about that copy, Mary Ann?" asked the nice young man as they drove along.

"I pushed the copy with my finger and it left a mark," said Mary Ann. "Right in the middle of the basket."

"Oh, so that was how," said Frances. "But I wouldn't tell on you."

"Neither would I," said the nice young man. "What do you say, Mary Ann and Frances, skates first or sodas first?"

"Sodas," said Frances.

"Skates," said Mary Ann, "she's got skates. Anyway, I marked the picture."

"Oh, all right," said Frances.

"I thought we could make up a new game," said Mary Ann. "Rococo Skates."

"What!" said the nice young man.

"Something like tag on skates," said Mary Ann.

36

Cornelia Meigs

THE SANDPIPERS

ILLUSTRATED BY *Janice Holland*

THE TWINS, Susan and Lawrence, were very fond of birthdays, not on account of the presents and the cake with candles, but because they liked having one day out of the whole year that really belonged to them.

"A winter birthday is very nice," said Susan, "with skating and sliding and popping chestnuts in the fire in the evening. But a summer birthday—"

"A summer birthday, after we go down to the shore," Larry interrupted, "would be as much fun as a winter one."

"And we are two people, even if we are twins; we have a right to more than one birthday between us."

They decided, therefore, to choose for their summer birthday the fifteenth of August—a date that satisfied both of them.

So it happened that, before the sun had quite got up to show the world that the fifteenth of August was to be a bright, cloudless day, two sturdy figures came out of the brown cottage, slipped through the gap in the wall and crossed the field on their way to the beach. They made their way down the wet, shining path, for they had got permission to begin the day with a picnic on the beach.

The sandpipers were having their breakfast, too. Their slim little black legs all moved alike; their quick bills all dipped together as they followed a wave as it slid back down the sand, followed it out and out, seeking along its shallow, curling edge for the delicious morsels that they alone can find. Then, when the wave came in again, back they all came running, keeping just ahead of the curving line of water that reached for their toes and could not quite touch them.

Sue and Larry sat very still and watched the birds after they had finished their own sandwiches and milk. One sandpiper out

37

of all the flock seemed tamer than the rest and several times came very close, seeming to regard them with great curiosity. It did not run just as the others did, but minced and sidled as it moved along.

"It just walks like—" began Larry.

"Like that lady who came to see Mother yesterday," Susan said. "Let's call her Mrs. Jackson, after Mother's visitor."

Beyond the big boulder upon which they had spread their breakfast, they heard a strange knocking noise.

Close against the rock, something was floating and bobbing, something that had been carried in by the tide and now seemed to be in two minds whether to stay where it was or to float away to sea again. At first they thought it was a boat; but when they climbed down to look closer, they saw that it was a tub, a very big tub with heavy oak staves and solid hoops. The crew of some ship had accidentally dropped it overboard, perhaps.

"It is so big that if we get in, I do believe it would carry us," declared Larry.

"And if it sank we would only get a little wet in the shallow water," Susan added. So, without more ado, they scrambled in.

The tub turned slowly round once or twice and then went sailing off, riding the sun-touched waves as gaily as the yacht that they had just seen go out of the harbor. It seemed as though their new boat had been looking just for two children who were having a birthday picnic on the beach and who now were to have a birthday sail. They passed the broken rocks that fringed the shore, they drifted by the tiny island with its tufts of green grass and at last were moving straight across the harbor toward the open sea. The water became rougher, and the tub began to pitch.

"Isn't it—isn't it time we went home?" Susan asked suddenly.

"I wonder how we make the tub go the other way," Larry answered.

They had never thought of that! Larry took off his sweater and spread it between them for a sail. That changed their course a little but did not stop their moving out to sea.

"We may go ashore on the outer island," said Larry. "See,

38

Larry took off his sweater and spread it between them for a sail.

we are drifting toward it now. Oh, Susan, don't cry."

"I won't," Susan answered, gulping bravely. They were both beginning to be frightened; but they knew it was better not to say so. In vain they spread their knitted sail to its widest limit; in vain they hung longingly over the side of the tub and watched the shore of the second island slide past. Their heavy craft bobbed on the waves and carried them steadily onward.

"Put down the sail, Susan," cried Larry of a sudden. "If we go now the way we went before, we will touch that rock over there. Tilt the tub to this side; that will help too."

Unwillingly their clumsy ship changed its course, turned, lurched and sidled, and at last bumped against the flat, weed-grown rock. They scrambled out.

"Now," said Larry, "we're safe, but we will have to stay here for a little while until somebody comes for us."

But the time passed, long minutes to the impatient pair, and then a long hour. The tide had turned and was coming in. The water covered the still pools where the snails and the crabs lived, came over the weeds and ledges, and crept higher and higher. They moved once and then again, to keep their feet out of the lapping ripples.

"Larry," cried Susan all at once, "will the water cover the rock to the very top? Will it, Larry? Perhaps we ought to get into the tub again."

"I don't know," he faltered, and at the quiver in his voice Susan buried her face on his knee with a wail.

"Oh, why did we come?" she sobbed, and Larry could only pat her shoulder, since he had not voice enough to answer.

"Sue," he whispered, after a minute, "look there, and keep very quiet."

A cheerful sound—"pweet, pweet"—came from the farthest ledge of rock. There stood a little gray sandpiper, with its head cocked on one side, staring at them with round, bright eyes. It moved a step or two toward them and stopped again.

"It's Mrs. Jackson," whispered Sue, so very low that not even the shy bird could be frightened.

Mrs. Jackson it was indeed, with the same plump body, neatly fitting wings and quick, black feet. She hesitated and sidled nearer, then hesitated again. Finally with a satisfied chirp that seemed to say that she had made up her mind that her visitors were friendly, she flew to the highest corner of the rock and settled down over the crevice in the stone.

"She has a nest!" cried Larry.

"Hush," warned Susan, "if we creep up very quietly, perhaps she won't fly away."

Very cautiously they climbed nearer and nearer, while Mrs. Jackson, although she cocked her eye and fluttered her wings nervously now and then, did not stir from the small gray nest that was built so carefully against the gray rock. She seemed not to mind even when the twins sat down, one on each side of her, but chirped contentedly to herself or perhaps to the round little sandpiper babies still hidden in the eggs.

The tide rose, the tub knocked against its moorings and seemed preparing to sail away again. Should they go with it? Was there more danger here than there? Susan's eyes were brimming with tears again when Larry smiled in sudden delight.

"Don't you see," he whispered, "that if Mrs. Jackson built her nest here, it must be safe from the tide?"

"Good, dear Mrs. Jackson!" exclaimed Susan. "She—" But she broke off suddenly. "Larry, listen! What do you suppose it is?"

A tiny cheeping noise seemed to come from close by, but not from Mrs. Jackson. She sprang up, as excited as were the twins, and perched on the edge of the nest. Instead of three eggs, there were now only two, and one small ball of gray fuzz. "Chip—chip!" came the sound again, and right before their eyes a second egg hatched and then the third, turning into faintly moving masses of down with wide, yellow mouths.

"Oh!" exclaimed Susan, and "Oh," it seemed Mrs. Jackson cried also, as she flew away on the instant to fetch her new family something to eat.

The twins hung over the nest, watching, so eagerly, the clumsy movements of the little birds that they did not hear a new sound behind them.

"Well, would you look at this!" exclaimed an unexpected

voice, and a white-clad sailor came climbing up the rock. The yacht that they had seen sailing out of the harbor had put in toward the island and was riding the waves a hundred yards away. Her boat lay moored where the tub had landed.

"We thought we saw two heads above the ledge," said the sailor, "and that it was no place for children. How in the world did you get here? You're pretty far out, you know."

Larry stood up to point out their vessel; but by this time it had floated away to sea and then disappeared, either sunk or drifted out of sight.

"We came in a tub," he told the man. "We would like very much to go home now, please."

The sailor took them into his boat and rowed them ashore. Sue, sitting in the stern, told him all about what had happened to them as they were celebrating their summer birthday.

"And we are going to keep away from tubs for all of our birthdays, always," she said.

Larry, listening in the bow, slowly nodded his head, as he looked at their new friend.

"If it hadn't been for Mrs. Jackson and you," he began, but did not finish. He watched the water as they came nearer and nearer to the shore, wondering whether something might happen, even yet, to keep them from getting safely home. There were ten waves between them and the edge of the sand, then five, then three, now only two and now the last one carried them up the beach—safe! He could see their basket standing on the rock just where they had left it, with two inquisitive sandpipers, cousins of Mrs. Jackson's, examining it. They had been gone some hours, but, since everyone thought they were still having their picnic breakfast on the shore, no one had come to look for them.

They thanked the sailor and watched him as he rowed away. It was pleasant to know that their adventure had brought them a new friend. The tide had played its old, old trick on them, but now they were safe on land again. One last, sparkling wave came snatching at their feet and seemed to laugh as it ran after them, while they, laughing too, ran up the beach.

Margaret Leighton

INDEPENDENCE DAY
FOR DAVY

ILLUSTRATED BY *Janet Smalley*

IT ALL began right after school closed, when Davy found the lucky stone.

A whole year had passed since the Hills first moved into the Old House. After a glorious summer of freedom among the acres of fields, grove, and meadows, Bob, Nancy, David, and Barbara started to school in the red brick building that stood at the crossroads. Back and forth through the changing seasons the feet of the four children wore a little path down the hill, through the orchard, across the brook on the stepping stones, to the roadway at last. And there they were soon joined by other children going in the same direction—friendly children, easy to know and easier to like.

Nancy Hill loved every step of the way that crossed their own land. In the early fall they had to stoop when they went through the orchard, so low did the weight of the red apples and bronze pears bend the boughs of the trees. Beside their path the long, yellow grass grew cloudy with purple asters. Then the first frosts came, catching the leaves of the little maple trees in the hollows and kindling them to scarlet. With the coming of midwinter something happened that was rare in the mild Virginia climate—a snowfall so deep that their hill became the gathering place for the neighborhood sleds and skis!

Then earliest spring brought foamy clusters of wild cherry blossoms—delicate as a fairy's frozen breath, thought Nancy— and flat drifts of dogwood, flowering in the shadows of the grove. The tall hemlock trees in front of the house were tipped with tender green, and at last the honeysuckle was blooming again, perfuming the air in honor of summer, here once more.

Davy had found the stone when, assisted by Nancy, he was building a dam across the brook in the tulip grove just where the wild grapevines dangled down to make such fine swings. It *was* an odd-looking stone. Its color was different from any of the others there; it was smooth and egg-shaped and dark, and all round it, as neatly as if painted, ran a white ring.

Old Caesar, the colored caretaker and gardener, pushing a wheelbarrow load of dead sticks that he had gathered for kindling wood, came past just as Davy was examining it.

"What you got dar?" he asked, pausing.

"Just a stone, but it's sort of a funny one."

Old Caesar took the stone and turned it over in his hands. "No, suh! Dis ain' jus' a stone!" He shook his head solemnly. "Dis yere one ob dem lucky stones. See dat white ring?" He handed it back, his old face wrinkling into a grin. "You keep it always by you. You'll soon fin' out it bring you good luck. Yes—suh!"

"What sort of luck?" David looked at the stone with new respect.

"Any kin' ob luck you need." The old man paused, looking down at David sharply, then nodded again. "Wid dat stone in his pocket, a boy hadn't ought to be skeered ob nothin' ever again, nohow," he said.

"Do you mean, like getting my head under water when I swim, or crossing the pasture where Mr. Forrest's bull stays, or setting off fireworks next week on the Fourth?" David's eyes shone.

"Dat's right. Ob course dat stone don't gib you no leave to get sassy wid no fireworks or no bulls!" Caesar shook his head severely. "But it sure look to me like a right powerful luckpiece. Yes—suh!" He picked up the handles of his wheelbarrow and moved on, and they heard him say "Yes—suh!" again, as he disappeared among the trees.

David wiped the stone carefully on the end of his shirt-tail which, as usual, was hanging out. Then he put the stone into his pocket and went on with his building. Davy had great plans

43

for this dam. He had made a little water wheel, one that really worked and could turn a shaft. If he could make the dam force the water strongly enough past his wheel, there was no limit to what he might do with it! So intent was he that he really didn't think much more about the stone, and Nancy forgot it almost immediately, too.

A short procession, consisting of Barbara, her fat white duck named Billy Miller Hill, and Nicky, the family dog, came to call Nancy and David back for lunch. As they left their work and reached the lawn in front of the house Nancy was surprised to see how dark the air had grown. Great black clouds were rolling across the sky, pushed by a rapidly rising wind. A mutter of thunder sounded and, just as they won the shelter of the porch, big drops thudded on the tin roof.

Before they were even seated at the table the rain had begun in earnest. It came with such force, driven by a gale of wind, that doors and shutters began banging all over the house. The four children, their mother, and Maysabelle, the cook, hurried to make everything fast against the storm. Swiftly the flashes of lightning came, followed each time more and more closely by thunder.

"That one struck near by!" said Bob, trying to peer through a streaming windowpane.

David came clattering down the front stairs from his room where he had been shutting and locking his windows, but instead of rejoining the others in the dining room he ran straight out of the front door.

"I'm going to get my water wheel before it's flooded out!" he called back over his shoulder.

"He oughtn't to go down among those tall trees in a storm like this!" said Mother, looking worried.

Bob and Nancy both started after David to call him back, but they had barely reached the front door when a flash of lightning and a clap of thunder came at exactly the same instant and with such force that it almost stunned them both. And then, from the direction of the tulip grove, came another sound, a tremendous, rending crash that seemed to stop Nancy's

44

heart. David had already disappeared among the trees—he was nowhere to be seen!

Bob and Nancy stared at each other. The same thought must have come to them both at once, and to Mother, too. Without a word all three ran out of the door, across the soaking grass, through the rain that beat so fiercely against their faces, toward the grove. There was a queer smell in the air, Nancy noticed, a sort of chemical smell. Her ears rang. And then, out of the wood came Davy, running as hard as he could with his head down, clutching his water wheel against himself as if it were a football.

"Davy!" cried Mother, hurrying him into the house. "Oh, Davy!"

"That tree almost fell on me!" David's red cheeks had lost their color. "I heard the lightning crashing round in the tops of the trees, so I just grabbed up my wheel and ran. And then the tree fell, right across the dam!"

Now that it was over, Nancy's knees began to shake so hard that she had to sit down. She couldn't think of anything to say, but just patted David's wet shoulder. From across the table little Barbara stared at him, too, her spoon halted halfway to her mouth.

Even Bob, looking at his small brother, couldn't seem to find words. "What a lucky guy," he said at last.

45

Suddenly David's eyes grew round and solemn. He put his hand into his pocket and pulled out the stone he had found in the brook that morning. "I reckon Caesar was right, and that this *is* a lucky stone!" He fingered it reverently. "I'm going to keep it with me, always, just like he said!"

But in the beginning, no one really understood just how much faith David had in the magic powers of his lucky stone. The first that Nancy noticed was when David's bedtime came that evening. Now, although Davy was nearly nine, he still had a great dislike of the dark. He *said* it was a dislike, but the rest of the family suspected that fear played a large part in the feeling. He had even been known to go to bed an hour before his own time just to have Barbara's company up the long, dark stairs where so many of the boards creaked strangely, and where the shadows cast from the light in the hall below crept up along the wall behind one.

But tonight, although the rain had made the summer dusk as dark as that of winter, Davy took his lucky stone out of his pocket, gave it a brisk polish, and marched up the long stairs without a single protest.

And then, the next morning, Nancy saw David riding his new bicycle down the lane, and for the first time he was riding it "nohanded," a feat which he had long lacked the nerve to try.

46

"Look, Nance! See what I'm doing," he shouted as he sailed past her. "My lucky stone has sure begun to work!"

When, that afternoon, Davy plunged into the swimming pool that had been built where the brook widened in the meadow, and, without hesitating, swam with his head under the water all the way to the other side, even Bob noticed. David clambered up on the bank, panting, and Bob saw then that he was holding his lucky stone tightly in his fist. His trunks had no pocket big enough to hold it.

Feeling his responsibility as the oldest, Bob lost no time in trying to explain to David how foolish it was to believe in such a thing as a magic stone. But with no success.

"Caesar says it's a lucky stone and Caesar knows more than you!" said David indignantly. "Besides, I know it for myself. Didn't it keep that tree from falling on me? If it can ward off lightning, it can do *anything!*"

"Isn't it all right for Davy to *believe* in it?" asked Nancy anxiously of Bob, when David was out of hearing. Nancy herself was never too sure just which was magic and which was science. They were both equally wonderful and confusing to her. "At least he isn't scared of the dark any more, and this swimming is a good thing, too."

"That part's all right, maybe," agreed Bob, "but it wouldn't be good for him to begin *depending* on any old stone. You know that!"

The rapid approach of the Fourth of July now filled everyone's mind. The Hills had combined with other families in the neighborhood to plan a great occasion. There was to be a field day for all the children—and grownups, too—with sports and contests and games, followed by swimming. Then, in the evening, there would be a picnic supper to which everyone was invited. Last of all, for the grand climax, a great display of fireworks would be set off in the field in front of the house, where everyone could see!

Slowly the days passed. As the Fourth drew nearer, from all over the countryside came the sound of explosions and poppings and reports, set off by children who were too impatient to wait

47

for the holiday to come. But not the Hills! They had made a solemn agreement among themselves to save *everything* in the big heavy carton for the great day itself.

On the morning of the third, Mother and Maysabelle went early in the car to market in the village to get in all the supplies that would be needed for the picnic.

Bob and Nancy had a big job before them, too. They carried a hatchet, a hammer, a long measuring tape, a ball of twine, and an armful of stakes down into the far end of the field in front of the house. They were to mark off the course for the foot races and to arrange the places where all the different contests were to be held. Prizes would be given for each event. Nancy herself had wrapped the packages in red and blue paper and sealed them with big white stars.

As they worked, Nancy could see Barbara and David practicing cart wheels on the soft grass in front of the house. Plump little Barbara was especially good at them. She seemed to turn over and over without effort, as lightly as a dandelion puff.

Maybe Barbara would win one of the prizes! Nancy hoped so.

From the highway came a few intermittent bangs and pops. A group of boys were walking along, setting off firecrackers as they went. Stopping to hold the end of the tape measure against a stake, Nancy spied a four-leaf clover deep in the grass. While Bob pulled the tape across the field to measure the distance for the races, Nancy shut her eyes to think of a good wish.

And then, while her eyes were still shut, she heard a strange noise, a sort of swooshing sound, and a squeal from Barbara. Looking up, Nancy saw a skyrocket soar over the hemlock trees from the road beyond, strike the square tower on the corner of the roof with a resounding thud, and bounce back to land, still sputtering fire, on the very edge of the gable!

The boys disappeared down the road as fast as they could go. From the far end of the field Bob gave a shout, and then, to her horror, Nancy saw that where the rocket had lodged a thin curl of smoke had begun to rise, dark against the brightness of the sky! With every passing instant it seemed to grow thicker and blacker!

48

Bob began to run toward the house. Then David, who had stood rooted, suddenly darted through the front door. Before Nancy and Bob had reached the edge of the lawn they saw him climbing out of an attic window to the ridgepole of the roof.

Bob stopped in his tracks. "Get back in there, Dave!" he roared.

But David continued to climb out, pulling a long-handled broom behind him. "The roof's on fire! The rocket's caught among some pine needles that are stuck to the shingles there!" he shouted back.

"Never mind—you get back in there before you break your neck," shouted Bob.

David merely grinned and waved his hand. Then, carrying the broom before him like a tightrope walker's pole, he started out along the peak of the roof.

Nancy was unable either to move or to speak! She could only stand there and stare up at David's yellow head outlined against the blue sky so high above them. Now he had reached the very point of the gable where the rocket had stuck. With one easy sweep of the broom he knocked the whole mass over the edge.

It fell slowly, streaming bright sparks as it came, to land, charred and smoking, on the grass almost in front of the three watchers. Then Nancy noticed that Barbara, dancing up and down at her side, was shouting something up to David.

"Be *very, very* careful, Davy!" she called. "Because you don't have your lucky stone up there with you. It fell out of your pocket when you were turning cart wheels. See—I found it!" She held it up.

Over Barbara's curly head Nancy's eyes met a sudden answering fear in Bob's. Both their glances flew back to the figure of David, looking so small up there on the high peak of the roof. He was staring down at Barbara, at the stone in her hand. His mouth fell open, and, before their eyes, his face seemed to turn white. Nancy heard Bob give a sharp gasp, and she pressed her own hands over her mouth to hold back the scream. Was Davy going to fall?

Then Bob stepped forward. "O.K., Dave!" he shouted. He spoke slowly, so that there would be no chance of David missing what he said. "It was you, not the stone, that put out the fire! Just you. Now turn 'round and trot back the way you came!"

For all his confident words, Bob's voice sounded cracked and shrill. The long moment of suspense was almost more than Nancy could bear. Then she let her breath out again, for she saw David close his mouth firmly and lift his head. Slowly he turned round. Then, balancing with the broom again, he ran lightly back across the roof to the open attic window and climbed in!

Halfway up the attic stairs Bob and Nancy met David coming down, still carrying the broom. Before any of them could speak Barbara came toiling up behind them, much out of breath.

"Here's your lucky stone, Davy," she said, holding it up.

David took it from her, but he didn't put it into his pocket.

"I reckon this belongs in my mineral collection," he said. "It's a pretty stone, anyway."

Bob slapped Davy on the shoulder so hard that he nearly knocked him down the stairs. "That's right, old timer! You don't need it any more." Then he grinned. "Your Independence Day came a day early, didn't it, Dave?"

51

Robin Palmer

PUNCH HAS AN ADVENTURE

ILLUSTRATED BY *Flavia Gág*

THIS is Patsy's day at the dentist's," Mrs. Barkington announced one morning, "so I am going downtown with her after school. You boys can have a good time taking care of Punch."

Jim groaned, but Roddy was never at a loss for words when he found himself in a difficult situation.

"I'm sure Punch should go to the dentist, too," he said. "He acts as if he's getting another tooth."

It was a good enough idea, but Mrs. Barkington didn't hear it. She had a dreamy expression on her face. Roddy knew there was no use talking to her when she looked like that. So did Jim.

"She isn't listening," he said. "Come on. We'll be late for school."

They started down the street, feeling very gloomy indeed.

"It's one of those days," Roddy remarked, "when everything goes wrong. You wait and see."

"Oh, Punch isn't that bad," said Patsy. "The trick is never to let him get out of your sight."

"We know that," answered Roddy coldly. "It means we can't do a single thing all afternoon but sit and look at that baby. Leave him alone for just one minute and he finds an ink bottle or a box of eggs or something that makes a mess. It's all very well for *you* to talk, Patsy—you don't have to stay with him."

"Would you rather go to the dentist?" asked his sister.

Jim laughed. "We would not," he said.

"Well, no, I suppose not," Roddy admitted. "It's an unlucky day for all three of us."

That afternoon he and Jim stood at the window and watched their mother and Patsy go down the street. On the floor beside them Punch was cheerfully pulling the books out of the bookcase.

"What shall we do with him?" asked Jim.

Roddy drummed on the windowpane with his fingers. "We could take turns watching him, of course," he replied. "One of us could read while the other one watched."

"Who wants to read?" said Jim.

Roddy started to say, "I do," but instead, he stopped and listened. Then he threw open the window. "What's that?" he asked.

A long way off Jim could hear the sound of bells ringing and whistles blowing. It grew louder and louder. Clang, clang, CLANG!

"A FIRE!" cried Jim. "Here comes the hook and ladder."

Roddy leaned out of the window. "It must be near here," he said. "Let's follow the engines."

"What about Punch?"

"Why, we'll take him along. He may never have another chance to see a fire. Come on, Punch."

As he spoke, Roddy grasped one of Punch's arms, and Jim took the other. Off they went, out the door and down the street. More engines passed them as they ran, and they could see smoke a few blocks away. They would have gone faster if it hadn't been for Punch. He lifted his feet from the ground and let his brothers carry him by the arms.

"Use your legs," said Jim. "What do you think we are, anyway?"

Punch chuckled and kept his feet up.

"Of all the stupid tricks," panted Roddy. "They ought to keep babies in cages until they get big enough to have sense."

"If only mother didn't feed him such a lot," Jim replied. "He weighs too much. I bet he weighs as much as a four-year-old. Put your feet on the ground, Punch, or I'll drop you."

Punch chuckled again.

"He knows you won't," grunted Roddy.

They went on, hurrying as much as they could with such a burden, until they came to the block where the fire was. It

53

was crowded with people. Firemen had tied ropes across the street to hold them back.

"If we could just wiggle through the crowd," said Roddy, "we might be able to see something."

But you can't wiggle through a crowd when there are three of you together. Roddy let go of Punch's arm.

"Jim can hold him," he thought, "while I find a good place to stand."

At almost the same instant Jim had the same idea.

"If I were on the other side of this man," he said to himself, "I could see something. Roddy will hang on to Punch." So he let go of his brother, too.

Of course Punch could see even less than Jim and Roddy; he was so small. In front of his nose was the wide blackness of a woman's coat. He couldn't see to the top of it and he couldn't see to the side of it. He looked down at the pavement. It was dirty, but that didn't bother Punch. He realized that his only chance to go forward was to get on his hands and knees, so down he got.

Punch was used to crawling, even in tight places. In and out he went, around one pair of feet after another, until he was in the very front row. Then he went under the rope.

The fire was a most exciting one and all the people were looking up at it, so nobody noticed Punch. He paused for a minute, wondering what to do next. In the basement window of the house he saw a small kitten. Punch was very fond of cats. He crawled at top speed right into the building where the fire was.

The older boys didn't get through the crowd so easily. Jim wriggled and squeezed with all his might, but he only managed to wedge himself between a tall man and a very fat woman. He couldn't see the fire any better than before, and he felt as if all the air were being pressed out of him. It was a tight, uncomfortable feeling.

"No use staying here," he thought. "I'll pull myself out and find Roddy."

Pulling out was harder than it sounds. In fact it was just as

54

much of a squeeze as pushing in. But Jim did it. He backed away from the crowd and took a deep breath. Then he saw Roddy running toward him.

"Where's Punch?" cried Roddy.

Jim had forgotten all about Punch.

"I don't know," he answered. "I thought you had him."

"But I left him with you," gasped Roddy. "Where on earth do you suppose he is? We'll never find him in this crowd."

"It has only been a minute or two," Jim said. "He can't have gone far. Let's call him."

They walked up and down shouting. "Punch! Punch! Come here."

But Punch didn't come.

A man in the crowd turned to look at the boys. "Have you lost your dog?" he asked.

"No," answered Roddy. "It's our little brother. He's only a baby. Have you seen him?"

"No, I haven't," replied the man, "but I'll try to help you."

He spoke to other persons in the crowd. "There is a baby boy lost," he said. "Does anyone see him?"

One after another they began to look, but the answer was always the same: "No, he isn't here. He isn't here."

"Where can he have gone?" asked Jim. "We *must* find him soon. He'll be so frightened."

"Let the boys go forward," the man suggested. "Make way for them to get through."

Some of the people stepped back and others moved aside, so Jim and Roddy managed to get right up to the rope. They could have had a perfect view of the fire, but they were thinking too much about Punch to notice that. And Punch was nowhere to be seen.

"Oh, dear," cried Jim. "If only I had held on to him! What shall we do? What shall we do, Roddy?"

"He must be here," answered his brother. And then a horrible thought occurred to him. "Unless someone picked him up," he said. "You know he is kind of cute— Oh, LOOK!"

Jim gave a shout. One of the firemen was coming out of the

55

burning apartment house. He had Punch in his arms, and Punch was hugging a little cat.

The boys dodged under the rope and started to run across the street to him. But before they had gone three steps, heavy hands were laid on their collars and a gruff voice asked: "Where do you think you're going?"

They looked around at the blue coat and brass buttons of a big policeman.

"Don't you know what that rope is for?" he said sternly.

"Yes," answered Roddy, "but the fireman has our baby brother. He just brought him out of the fire. Please let us go to him, sir."

The policeman had his back toward Punch or he might have been more sympathetic. As it was, he said: "That's a likely story! Everyone was out of that building twenty minutes ago."

"Everyone else may have been," cried Roddy. "But not Punch! Really it's true. Mother had to take Patsy downtown to the dentist, so she left us to look after him."

"You're quick with your tongue, aren't you?" asked the policeman.

At that moment Punch saw his brothers and waved to them.

"Look at that," Roddy said. "Look at that if you don't believe us."

The policeman turned around. "For goodness sake!" he exclaimed. Then he took the boys across the street.

Punch smiled sweetly at them. "Kitty," he said. "Got kitty."

"He stopped to save the little cat," explained the fireman. "Isn't he a fine boy? I wish he were mine."

"He's ours," said Roddy, and there was a note of pride in his voice. Suddenly Punch seemed quite worth claiming.

"Their mother is at the dentist's," the policeman remarked. "It will be a shock to her to come home and find the house like this."

Jim and Roddy exchanged glances.

"I guess I'd better take the three of them around to the station-house," the policeman went on, and he sighed because he hated to miss the fire.

Then Roddy began to think quickly.

"Mother expects us to be at our grandmother's house," he said. "It isn't far from here. Don't you think we should go there and wait for her?"

The policeman scratched his head.

"You see," continued Roddy, "it would be a *real* shock to her to hear that we were at the police station." He was quite sure this was true.

"I believe you're right," answered the policeman. "I do believe you're right."

He took Punch from the fireman and handed him over to his brothers. "Run along now," he told them. "It isn't safe for you to stay here."

The boys held Punch firmly by the shoulders, and took one look at the fire before they started to make their way through the crowd. Then they found, much to their surprise, that Punch had become a hero.

"Look at that baby," someone said, "he went right into the fire to save his kitten. What a brave child!"

"You have a fine little brother," a stout old lady told them. "You must be very proud of him."

Another person tried to pat Punch on the head, but his brothers gripped his arms and hurried along home.

"Whew!" cried Roddy, when they were out of the crowd. "That was a narrow escape. We might have landed in jail."

Jim nodded. "I was scared for a minute," he said.

Roddy looked down at Punch. "What are we going to do with the kitten?" he asked.

"Take it home, of course," Jim replied. "It's just a little tramp cat, all thin and hungry, I'm sure it doesn't belong to anybody. We'll have to feed it a lot."

And later, when they told their mother what had happened, she agreed with Jim.

"Poor little kitten," she cried. "He might have been burned up. I'll get some milk for him."

Anne Molloy

THE PENNY WALK

ILLUSTRATED BY *Janet Smalley*

THE day-before-Christmas wind blew a-
cross the bare, brown ground. It rocked the sign above the
store window by which Rose and her friend, Nancy, stood. It
swung the boughs of the great Christmas tree in the park across
the street and rattled its bright red and green and blue light
bulbs. It whipped wind tears from Rose's eyes.

"Let's try one more store," she said to Nancy. "Maybe it will
have a present I could buy Dan with my penny. Let's try once
more."

"Let's," said Nancy.

They went into the red store next door. They walked up and
down its aisles. They looked at presents, hundreds of them. But
there wasn't one for a penny that they could see.

"Maybe the lady over there will tell us if they have any
presents for a penny," said Rose. "Let's ask her."

"Let's," said Nancy.

Rose stood up on tiptoe, her penny in her hand. She leaned over the counter in front of the lady and said in a loud voice, "Any presents for a penny, lady?"

The lady banged open the cash register drawer.

"This is a five-and-ten cent store, little girl," was all she said. She scooped dimes and nickels from the drawer, then snapped it and her mouth shut.

"Oh," said Rose. She sank back on her heels and turned to Nancy. "No presents for a penny," she said.

Together they walked through the swinging door into the wind. This time the tears it whipped from Rose's eyes weren't wind tears.

"There's nothing I can buy for Dan with my penny. There's a blotter I made in school for my father, there's the calendar I made for my mother. Why don't schools let you make presents for brothers?"

"Because there isn't time, with all we have to learn about," said Nancy.

And Rose agreed. There wasn't time.

"But what good is my penny if it won't buy anything for Dan?" she asked. Then she smiled and answered her own question. "It's good for a penny walk anyhow. Remember, we took one last summer. You toss a penny up and if it lands on your hand topside up you take the first street to your right. And if it lands bottomside up you take the street to the left. You do that every time you come to a crossing. The penny decides for you which way to turn. Let's take one now. You can't tell what we may see or find."

"Let's," said Nancy.

Rose let Nancy have first throw.

Nancy tossed the penny into the air and caught it in her two cupped palms. "The head is on top," she said, studying the penny. "That means we turn right first."

They walked past several more stores on the main street and then turned down the first street leading from it to the right.

The penny had made a good choice for them. Once they left

60

the stores behind they saw only fine houses on both sides of the street. Now that darkness was almost here, the great houses were lighting up. Never had Rose and Nancy seen such bright Christmas trees as they saw in the front windows of every house; never had they seen such gay lights as were strung around front doors and porches. They said "Oh" or "Ah" in front of almost everyone.

"I'll push Dan over here in his stroller tomorrow," said Rose. "Seeing all this will be almost as good as a present."

At last another street cut across this one of fine houses.

"My turn to find out whether we go right or left," said Rose. Up she tossed the penny and caught it on the back of her hand.

"Tails this time; we turn left," she said. "I hope we'll be as lucky this time."

For a while it didn't look as if they were. The farther they walked, the smaller the houses became. Some had no bright red or green lights at all. And the wind blew strongly behind them now as if it wanted to hurry them off the street.

Worst of all, a black dog suddenly rushed out at them from an open gateway. He stood in front of them and raised his head in bark after bark. Nancy and Rose stood still. They were too afraid even to turn around and go away.

After a long while the dog was so near they could see his white teeth shining in the lamplight. After a longer time, the front door of the house through whose gate the dog had come opened. A woman leaned out.

"Prince, stop that barking," she called. "Don't be afraid, little girls, he won't hurt a fly."

But Prince kept on barking until the woman came out and down the path. Prince stopped his barking now and ran in wiggly circles.

"Come in the house a minute," said the woman. "I'll show you something to make you stop looking scared. Don't mind Prince."

She caught Prince's collar and marched him into the house. Rose and Nancy marched behind, straight through the door and into the warm, spicy kitchen.

61

"Look here," said the woman, and held out a tray. On it were rows of molasses cookie Santa Clauses. They had white frosting beards and red frosting caps, and eyes and buttons of currants.

"Oh," said Rose and Nancy together.

"Take one, each of you," said the woman.

"Thank you," they said. They each took one and marched outdoors.

"I'm going to save my cookie for Dan," said Rose. "It will be almost as good as a boughten present."

"I'm going to eat mine," said Nancy, "but you may have the legs." She snapped the cookie Santa Claus' crisp neck with her teeth.

By the time they had eaten the cookie they came to another street. Nancy took her turn at tossing up the penny. It fell head up into the cup of her palm. They turned right, into the new street.

Here the houses were far apart. The wind blew between them more strongly than ever. Rose's hand holding the cookie for Dan ached with the cold.

"The penny didn't pick us a very good street to walk on this time," said Rose.

But she was wrong, for this street later turned out to be the best of them all.

As they passed a big white house they saw the wind tugging at a wreath on a lighted front door. It flapped the ends of the wreath's big bow. Then, with a howl, it tore the wreath from its fastenings and rolled it over and over like a hoop, down the path and away up the street.

Rose and Nancy chased the rolling wreath. Every time they caught up with it, every time they had their hands stretched out to reach it, a gust of wind hurried it away from them.

"Oh, dear, we'll never get it," said Nancy.

At last, under a street light, the wreath slowed down. Rose fell on it to make sure of stopping it. She did stop the wreath from rolling on, but at the same time she broke in two the Santa Claus cookie. Oh, dear, now she had nothing for Dan at all!

62

She and Nancy sadly ate the cookie as they carried the wreath back to its owner's house. Here Rose rang the doorbell.

An old lady not much taller than Rose and Nancy opened the door.

"Thank you for returning my wreath," she said, "but come in, do. Your noses are as blue as your eyes with the cold. It's colder than Greenland today, to be sure."

Rose and Nancy went inside, and the old lady closed the door behind them. Then she pointed to a suitcase and a bag on the floor near a table.

"Why should I be complaining of the cold when I'm going off to the sunny South? Yes, in half an hour the taxi man's coming to take me to the train to Florida and I'll spend the winter there with my boy, basking in the sunshine."

A trilling bird song interrupted the old lady.

"If it weren't for that Pip, the dear, I'd be a happy woman. But would you believe it, there's nobody, high or low, wants to take the poor creature. Here I'm leaving in half an hour, and not a soul have I found to take him, not even as a favor to an old friend. Afraid they might be put to trouble by a little bird. But come, my dears, come see this Pip of mine and see what a beautiful bird he is."

63

Rose and Nancy went with the old lady to her dining room, and there in the window hung a golden cage. It jounced and jiggled, for inside the golden bars was a green-gold bird. In the most saucy manner it twittered and twirped, swooped and sung, bobbed and blinked at them.

"There he sits, the poor creature, showing off and throwing seeds on my clean floor as if he didn't have a care in the world. Pip, my bird, how could anybody not want you? If it weren't for the long days you'd have to spend on the train, and the nights, too, I'd take you South with me," said the old lady to the bird.

If the time hadn't been so short and if the bird hadn't been so beautiful, and if she hadn't needed a Christmas present for Dan so badly, Rose never would have had the courage to say what she did.

"What about me? Could I have Pip?" she asked the old woman. She sounded bolder than she felt.

The old lady turned from the bird to Rose.

"And why not? You look like a good, reliable girl. Why not? I'll phone the taxi man to take you and the birdcage and the bag of bird feed home before he takes me to the station. Where do you live, child?"

Rose told her the name and her street and number. The old lady called the taxi man at once. While they waited for him to come Rose told how she and Nancy happened to be so far from home. She was so happy at having a golden bird for Dan's present she would have talked bravely to even the gruffest stranger.

"It was really the penny that brought us here, wasn't it, Nancy?" she asked.

"Yes, the penny found us the street, and the wind found us the house," said Nancy.

"Lucky penny, lucky wind," said Rose.

"And a lucky time of year is Christmastime," said the old lady as she wrapped the bird's cage for the cold trip ahead.

The taxi man's horn at the door answered a gay, "Yes, yes."

64

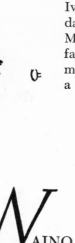

IVAR and Waino had been hunting all day in the mountains above Birora, Minnesota. When they entered Ivar's father's livery stable to get warm, they met a most unexpected visitor. It was a moose!

Phil Stong

WAINO AND IVAR
MEET HONK THE MOOSE

ILLUSTRATED BY *Kurt Wiese*

WAINO was in the corner between Papa's desk and the wall. Ivar knew, really, that the air gun wouldn't kill a moose. He picked up a pitchfork and went bravely to the door.

The doorknob twisted again. "You get away from there," Ivar shouted. "Go on back in the woods where you belong."

There was a pause. "What's the matter in there? Why's the door locked?"

"Papa!" Ivar said, and threw back the bolt.

Ivar's father was not fat but he was about as big as two men. His face was all pink and white and his eyes were as good-humored as Ivar's. He smiled at the two boys, now.

"What's the matter?" he asked again. "You look like you yust seen a ghost." Because he had spoken only Finnish and Swedish as a boy, it was still hard for him to say "J." He said "Y" instead. Ivar, who was an American boy, said "J" but he never noticed that his father said "Y." He always heard him speak that way.

"A moose," Ivar said.

"A moose," Waino added.

"What!" Then Ivar's father laughed, and the floor shook a little. "You yust seen a moose, what? Well, he wouldn't chase you here."

"Out in the stable," Ivar told him.

Ivar's father laughed a good deal, and everything shook. "A

65

moose in the stable. I think you've got a bat in the belfry, Ivar.
I guess a horse got loose. You go up and see if your mother has
any errands—I'll take care of the moose."

"It's a moose, Papa—honestly!"

"You should see things straight, Ivar," his father said. "A
Suomi should see things straight. It is a horse, and because you
were afraid you say it is a moose. Come on, we'll see this moose,
now. A Suomi should not be afraid, either—"

He opened the door and stepped out into the aisle. "We
will see."

An instant afterward he scooped the two boys up in his strong
hands and almost threw them back into the office. He followed
them and locked the door. "It's a moose," he said.

Ivar's father thought for a moment and then the same stub-
born bravery that had made Ivar go out against the moose made
his father rise and go to the door. "You lock the door after me
and stay here. We'll see about this. If I call, you go out the
window and run for the policeman."

He opened the door and went out, but Ivar disobeyed. He
was not going to let his father talk to a moose unless he was
there to help. He walked out quietly behind his father, so, of
course, Waino went too.

The moose had eaten so much hay that he was growing sleepy.
He still nibbled at the hay, which he could just reach as it hung
over from the loft, but he didn't want it very much. Only, since
the hay was there, he might as well eat it while he had the
chance.

"Wonderful!" said Ivar's father. "How could anything eat so
much? You please shoo now," he added to the moose.

Honk rolled one eye toward him and went on eating. This
made Ivar's father angry. "Hay costs twenty dollars a ton. You
have already eaten a ton.. How do you pay?" In fact, the moose
had stuffed himself with hay, after the long, hungry days in the
woods, until he looked like a balloon that had been blown up
only at the front end. The other end was still skinny.

"It's honestly—"

"Yes, I know," Ivar's father interrupted him. "It's a moose.

66

How he got here, I don't know."

"The winter is bad—maybe he was cold."

Ivar's father smiled at Waino, at the same time keeping an eye on the moose. "Not cold—mooses don't care if it is cold. But I guess he was hungry. He must have come here in the afternoon when nobody was looking."

"What are you going to do with him, Mr. Ketonen?" Waino asked eagerly. For a young boy he always showed a very practical mind.

"What am I going to do with him?" Ivar's father said, a little bit crossly. "What does one do with a moose? I am going to do what one always does with mooses."

"What's that?" Ivar asked curiously.

"I am going to shoo him out of my barn. What will the horses think?"

"What *will* they, Papa?"

"They will think I don't keep a good livery stable. Mooses!"

At this moment Honk's legs collapsed. He felt very good, but tired. He rolled one eye at the people and then he sank on his side and rolled himself once or twice. After that, with a contented sigh, he went to sleep.

This made Ivar's father angry again. "You get out of here. You can't sleep here." He prodded the moose in the side. Honk did not even open his eyes.

Ivar began to feel a little sorry for the moose. He could see how sleepy the animal was and he thought of mornings when

67

he had had to get up to go to school in spite of the fact that he was having a splendid time sleeping.

"I wish I was mean enough to stick him with a pitchfork," Ivar's father said unhappily. "Listen, you!" he said fiercely to the moose. "If you don't go away I'll get the policeman; and do you know what he'll do to you? He'll shoot you."

The moose did not open his eyes even then. He said "HAAAWNK" very softly and sleepily.

"All right," said Mr. Ketonen firmly. "Ivar, you go for the policeman."

"Aw, Papa—!"

"Aw, Mr. Ketonen—!" said Waino.

"Can I run a livery barn with a moose in it? He'll eat me out of house and home. He'll get in the way. Besides, mooses are dangerous."

"That one isn't, Papa. Look at him."

"How do we know what he'll be like when he wakes up? You go get the policeman, Ivar."

"All right."

Ivar and Waino left the stable. Night had fallen—it was almost suppertime—and the bright corner lights of the little mining town twinkled and glittered on the snowy streets. They found Mr. Ryan, the policeman, in the mayor's office, over the fire station. His belt with its two enormous revolvers was hung from a nail on the wall. He was reading the evening paper.

He merely glanced over his paper at Ivar and Waino.

"Well," he said severely, "I knew when I saw you start out with that gun you'd get into trouble. What've you done? Killed a moose hunting out of season—or maybe several mooses?"

The boys knew that this was a joke, but they were too breathless to laugh.

"Papa wants you to come put a moose out of his stable."

Mr. Ryan liked to joke. He stared at them for a moment and then he frowned.

"Playing jokes on an officer of the law, uh? I'll just take you back to the jail and let you pick your rooms right now. And remember," he said slowly, "what we have here for supper is bread and water—and that's what we have for breakfast and for dinner."

"No, Mr. Ryan, please, it isn't a joke. Papa wants you to come put a moose out his livery stable."

"No, Mr. Ryan, please, it isn't a joke—" Waino said.

Mr. Ryan grinned and reached for his belt. For a minute he'd thought the boys were trying to make him believe a real moose was in the stable and then he remembered that "moose" was Minnesota slang for a big man.

It was pretty late for tramps up on the Iron Range and, anyway, Ivar Ketonen (young Ivar was named for his father) was about as big a "moose" himself as anyone would want to see. He wasn't the kind that would ask for help or need it, usually.

At the same time, if Ketonen needed help he might need it pretty badly. Mr. Ryan started at a swift walk that made the boys trot. Mr. Ryan was a small Irishman but he was very strong and braver than he was strong.

"What's this moose doing?" he asked Ivar.

"He's asleep, Mr. Ryan."

Mr. Ryan laughed. "We'll give him a better place to sleep up here in the jail. Did he make any trouble?"

"No, he just ate a lot of—"

"Oh, broke into the house, uh? Well, that's bad." Mr. Ryan grew serious. "He oughtn't to have done that. We'd have fed him and let him go tomorrow. Now, I guess, we'll have to keep him. That's bad—breaking into places."

"Yes, sir," Ivar said anxiously.

"He steal anything?"

"No, sir. Just a lot of—"

"Nothing but food, poor fellow. Well, we'll see what we can do for him. He must have been mighty hungry. Didn't know enough to come around to me. I'd have fed him and given him a bed. He might be all right after all." Mr. Ryan hated to arrest people—he hated to see them get into trouble. But he wasn't afraid to arrest *anybody* if he thought he deserved to be in trouble.

Waino said timidly, "He's a kind of a sad moose, Mr. Ryan."

Mr. Ryan sighed. "Poor fellow. Hungry and just saw a door open. It's been a hard winter. We'll see what we can do."

They had come to the door of the livery stable. Mr. Ryan believed the boys when they said the "moose" was sad, but he didn't know how much they knew about tramps. He hooked his thumb over the edge of his belt close to one of the revolvers and opened the door quickly.

"Ivar?" Mr. Ryan called to Ivar's father.

"Frank?"

"Everything all right?"

"Everything is not all right. What are you going to do about this moose? What's he doing here?"

Mr. Ryan walked quickly and boldly down the aisle. The boys heard him gasp. "It's a moose!"

"I said it was a moose," Ivar told him. He added, rather anxiously, "What are you going to do with him, Mr. Ryan?"

Waino said, "What are you going to do with him, Mr. Ryan?"

Mr. Ryan did not know what to do. He was too soft-hearted to shoot a sleeping moose, so he phoned the mayor, Mr. Nels Olavsson, who in turn phoned the members of the city council, Mr. Lunn, Mr. Town Clerk Hulburd, and Mr. Councilman Hoaglund.

.   .   .   .   .

An hour later they were all sitting around a table in Ivar's father's office looking very puzzled.

"You can't shoot him—a sad moose like that," Mr. Olavsson was saying for the hundredth time.

"No—the poor fellow, he's starving!" Mr. Lunn said.

"You mean he *was* starving," Ivar's father corrected, thinking of his hay.

"I'll tell you," Mayor Olavsson said finally. "The town will pay for the hay, and Frank can stay here tonight with his revolver. If the moose makes any fuss, then he must shoot him. But if he just goes away, everything will be all right."

They agreed on that. Sometime in the night Honk went quietly away.

70

"You get away from here," Ivar shouted. "Go on back in the woods."

Charles Coombs

FRISBIE CURES THE DOCTOR

ILLUSTRATED BY *Hascy Tarbox*

LEM BURGIN is usually as cheerful as a cat in a salmon cannery. But on that particular morning, when he came to the back door in answer to my call, I could see trouble written all over his freckled face.

"Lem," I said, "it can't be *that* bad."

"It—it's Frisbie," he said solemnly.

"You mean he has disappeared? Run away?" I'm afraid I wasn't very careful at hiding the hope in my voice.

"Frisbie is ill," Lem explained.

"And I suppose you walked the floor all night with a sick skunk," I scoffed.

"It might be serious, Ned," he said. "Come on in and have a look at him."

"You've got him in the house?"

"Why not?"

"Thanks, but I think I'll stay out here where a guy has a fifty-fifty chance of making a clean break, should Frisbie become incensed at something."

"Have it your way," Lem said. "But someday you'll learn to appreciate Frisbie."

"Don't hold your breath. On second thought, it's a good idea, when you're around Frisbie."

Lem went back into the house, letting my gay humor pass unheeded. Quickly he came back carrying an apple box. I eased cautiously to windward, as Lem set the box on the lawn.

"Come on, Ned," Lem said impatiently. "He's not going to bite you!"

"Look, pal, I've never been worried about Frisbie biting me."

I moved in closer, then. I wasn't really as afraid of Frisbie as I let on. After all, we had been through quite a few ad-

71

ventures together, Lem, Frisbie, and I. And, as yet, neither Lem nor I had had to bury any clothes. Still, I never wanted to be caught off guard.

Well, Frisbie did look somewhat peaked, at that. He turned his shoe-button eyes up toward us. His teeth were making a sort of clicking sound. I'll admit I was somewhat moved by the poor little fellow's sad appearance.

"Skunk fever," I said professionally.

"No, I think he has a sticker in his ear," Lem corrected. "Notice how he holds his head over to one side. See the swelling? Look close, Ned."

Well, maybe I was moved, but not that close.

"We've got to take him to a doctor," Lem said.

"A doctor! Lem, you're the guy to take to a doctor, if you think anyone would let you within a block of his office with Frisbie."

"There's Doctor Boland down on Cypress Street. He's a veterinary."

"Cats and dogs," I reminded him.

"A good veterinary should know about all animals."

"Even skunks?"

"Skunks are animals. Come on. That sticker or whatever it is may be working its way toward Frisbie's brain!"

"Skunks don't need brains," I said, but I fell in beside him, as he started toward town. "You know, Lem, Doc Boland has the reputation of being very high priced, even for treating far less complicated animals."

But Lem's sense of economy was blinded by his love for Frisbie. He didn't answer.

We arrived at the white stucco building which housed Doc Boland's dog-and-cat hospital. The barking of dogs and the meowing of cats filtered through the partition that separated the waiting room from the rest of the building. We waited and made sufficient noise to attract anyone's attention who might be in the back room. Still, no one showed up.

"Bolands live in a house in the rear," I said. Maybe the doctor's eating lunch. Let's go see."

72

We found him back there, all right. He was an elderly man, not given much to smiling. He had a fringe of white hair that formed a windbreak around a patch of arid scalp. He peered out at us over his bifocals.

"What's on your minds, boys?" he said. "If you had gone into the office, I'd have known you were here."

"We did go inside," I said.

"You did? Then that buzzer must be out of order again." He pointed to the wire that ran back from the hospital and disappeared into a small square box under the porch eaves. "Well, anyway—here, Myra," he spoke to the cute little three- or four-year-old girl who had been sitting on his lap, "you'd better get down now so I can see what these boys want. My granddaughter," he explained proudly.

"She's sure a cute trick," I said, cootcheecooing her under the chin, then watching her run pell-mell around the house. Always good business to get in solid with the kids, I thought. Might help Lem when the bills were written.

"I—I have a sick animal here, Doctor Boland." Lem suddenly came to life.

"Well, you've come to the right place. Must be a small one. Let's have a look in that box, and—whoa! Hey, what kind of a joke—get that thing out of here!"

Well, I think Lem could have stood anything but to have a man whose profession is animals take such a sudden offense at Frisbie. The look of disillusionment that cast a cloud over Lem's face was pretty awful to behold. As for me, I was never one to defend Frisbie. In fact, Frisbie had never needed help. But this was different, somehow.

"Lem's skunk is friendly and tame, Doctor Boland," I said quickly, quite astounded at the sound of my own words. "And he's ill. Even a sick skunk deserves some sort of care."

"Not by me." Doctor Boland stood adamant with his back to the wall. "Take him to the dog pound or the city incinerator, or——"

That was dangerous talk for anybody, with Lem around. And the very fact that he didn't challenge Doctor Boland's

73

thoughtless remark convinced me of just how concerned Lem was over Frisbie's health.

"I—I'll pay you whatever you ask," Lem said in a sort of choking voice.

Well, a tasty carrot like that dangling before his nose was more than even Doctor Boland could seem to ignore. He began to breathe somewhat more easily, and I could almost hear the adding machine in his mind making mental calculations.

"All right, if you guarantee that he's harmless. What seems to be the trouble?"

"I think he has a sticker or something in his ear," Lem explained.

Doctor Boland moved slowly closer, but kept his hands well to himself. "Sort of looks like it, at that. All right, bring him into the hospital. We'll give him some ether and see what we can find."

"Ether?"

"Of course. I wouldn't touch him without putting him to sleep first. We do it most of the time with any animal."

Lem seemed to accept it philosophically. He even held Frisbie, while Doctor Boland applied the ether-saturated cloth over Frisbie's tiny black nose. First the sweat broke out on

74

Lem's forehead, then he got pale. For a minute I thought he was going to faint.

"There it is," Doctor Boland said, laying down a long pair of tweezers, which were grasped around a long foxtail-like sticker. "Quite a bit of infection in there, but this penicillin will straighten it up in a hurry. You'd better get your friend a drink of water," he said to me. "You'll find a water cooler down the hallway. Don't get near those dog cages. There are two or three mean ones."

Well, he didn't have to tell me twice. As I went down the middle of the corridor, a couple of big mutts lunged at the wire as though nothing would make them happier than to tear me limb from limb.

Lem was gulping the water when the phone rang. Doctor Boland soon returned. "I have to go pick up a dog down on Elm Street," he said. "You might as well ride over with me. That animal will be some time coming out of the ether. The fresh air will do you good. Especially you, young fellow," he indicated Lem, who was still rubbery in the legs. Lem seemed unwilling to leave Frisbie.

"Come on, Lem," I prompted. "He'll be okay."

Doctor Boland changed the cardboard clock in the door window to *Back in 10 Minutes*, and we were soon headed for Elm Street to pick up a fancy mutt that needed a bath.

Having had some difficulty in locating the little Pekingese which had hidden in a closet at the very mention of a bath, it was somewhat after ten minutes when we returned to the dog-and-cat hospital. On the way back, Doctor Boland had hinted of various and sundry charges for anesthesia (imagine having to gas a skunk!), penicillin, professional services rendered, to say nothing of what he called extraordinary expenses. I could see that he was planning to clear up whatever mortgages might be hanging over his head. It was going to be a sad time for Lem, on a fifty-cents a week allowance.

We went on in the door. And the minute we stepped inside, I had one of those unexplainable feelings that something was wrong. There seemed to be more noise coming from the

75

animals beyond the office partition. The inner door was ajar.

And suddenly from beyond it came the unmistakable crying of a child. The sound froze us momentarily in our tracks. I say "us," but I think it was Doctor Boland's sudden stiffening, as he dropped the Pekingese to the floor.

"Myra!" he gasped. And I remembered that Myra was his granddaughter. I also knew intuitively that Myra was not allowed in the dog-and-cat hospital.

Ordinarily, it might not have been such a startling situation. But the throaty growling of a dog sifted through the many sounds. That growling did not come from the area of the heavy wire kennels. One of the dogs was out.

And, from the sound, it was one of the mean ones.

Lem went through the door, with me right at his heels and Doctor Boland crowding close behind.

What we saw was enough to make anyone turn and run. Right in the doorway that led to the kennels stood a large, wild-eyed dog. His teeth were bared. He lunged, then jumped back; he lowered his head and swayed this way and that.

"Grampa! Grampa!" The little girl was crowded back into a corner of the small operating room opposite the doorway to the kennels.

On the floor between her and the doorway which framed the drooling dog stood a small black-and-white furry object. His tiny teeth clicked angrily, as he held the large animal at bay.

"Frisbie!" Lem said, but he didn't move to pick up his pet. Frisbie seemed to have things well under control.

Doctor Boland hurried the girl out into the waiting room and closed the door. "Give me that chair," he said, and I could tell that he was having trouble with his voice. The realization of what that dog might have done to his granddaughter was enough to make us all lose our voices.

I slid the chair over to him, and he moved in toward the dog, relieving Frisbie of his vigil.

The dog wasn't mad; he was just mean. But Doctor Boland knew how to handle him.

76

Then he came back and sat down heavily. The sweat was pouring off his forehead. "We—we've told her a hundred times not to come back here," he explained.

"Kids will be kids," I said.

"There should be padlocks on those kennel doors," Lem said.

"There will be," Doctor Boland said. "There will be!"

Well, there was no sense in anyone bawling out anyone. It was one of those things that could have been very, very serious —had it not been for a certain little fellow who wasn't afraid to stand up to anything or anyone.

"It's well that—Frisbie came out of the ether in time," Doctor Boland said. "Son, if that animal ever needs any attention of any kind, bring him to me."

"He could probably use an occasional bath," I put in helpfully, and the doctor never batted an eye.

Funny thing, too, Lem never did receive a bill from Doctor Boland. And he can't figure out why every once in a while there's a case of dog-and-cat food left on his doorstep.

"But, Ned," he says, "I didn't order any dog-and-cat food."

"Frisbie likes it, doesn't he?"

"Likes it? And how!"

"Then stop worrying." I say, "Frisbie ordered it, and he paid for it in full."

Constance Savery

SPINDLEBERRIES AND PAM

ILLUSTRATED BY *Florence and Margaret Hoopes*

P AM did not like Uncle Anthony. The other little girls were much shocked at her distressing lack of taste, for they thought that there was nobody in the world like Uncle Anthony. They sometimes vied with one another in saying how much they loved him.

Ursula said, "I love Uncle Anthony mountains high."

Grace said, "And I love Uncle a hundred golden pounds."

Fat little Elaine said, "I love Uncle Anthony as deep as the sea."

But Pam just shrugged her shoulders and said, "I don't love Uncle Anthony at all!"

When Pam said that, she would meet with disapproving looks from Ursula, Grace, and Elaine.

"But Uncle Anthony is so very nice!" said Ursula. "Think what lovely games he plays with us."

"I don't like him!" said Pam decidedly.

"But he asks us to tea in his rooms!" said Grace.

"I don't like him," said Pam.

"But he gives us presents and tells us stories!" said Elaine.

"I don't like him," said Pam.

And in spite of all they could say, she refused to change her mind.

Ursula, Grace, Pam, and Elaine lived in the quadrangle of a college in an old university town in England. Their father was the dean of the college; his house stood in a corner of the quad, with six steps running up to the front door. Uncle Anthony had two rooms on the other side of the quad, and people called him an undergraduate. There were more young men in the college

78

than the little girls could count, but none of them equaled Uncle Anthony in any respect whatever. Uncle Anthony was the most wonderful person who had ever lived. He had seven silver cups; he belonged to all the teams and clubs and societies; he rowed for his college; he had his cricket Blue; he was going to get a First.

But still Pam didn't like Uncle Anthony.

There was a reason for her dislike, a reason so old and worn that everyone had forgotten it, except Pam herself. This was the reason: Pam's baby brother had been christened Terence Anthony instead of Gregory George. Pam had chosen the names Gregory George herself because she thought them the most beautiful names in the world, and she was bitterly disappointed when Mother said that baby must be called Terence after Father and Anthony after Uncle Anthony.

"But need he be christened Anthony?" she said. "Couldn't he be called Terence Gregory George?"

But Mother answered, "I think not, dear."

Then Pam said, "Couldn't he be christened Terence Anthony Gregory George?"

"Oh, Pamela, no!" said Mother.

And no coaxing would make Mother change her mind. A little later Pam unfortunately overheard Mother telling Uncle Anthony about the names that baby's third sister had chosen for him. Uncle Anthony put his head back and roared with laughter.

79

"Terence Anthony Gregory George!" he said. "Poor little beggar—what a bunch of labels!"

Pam had never forgiven Uncle Anthony for that. She would not call Baby Tony by his family title; she preferred to speak of him as Terence at any time when she could not avoid using his name. When he and she were alone together, she called him Gregory George because she felt that Gregory George was the name that really belonged to him. And she could not stop disliking Uncle Anthony, although Tony had grown into a fat creature of two and she herself was old enough to do lessons with a governess.

Uncle Anthony knew that Pam disliked him. The knowledge did not make him any less kind to her, but he was most careful to refrain from teasing her because he knew that nothing is more annoying than to be teased by an enemy. So he was polite to Pam and comforted himself by teasing fat little Elaine twice as much as was fair and just. Elaine did not mind in the least; she grew fatter than ever under the treatment.

It was Uncle Anthony who planned the expedition to the wood where the spindle trees grew. Pam heard all about it when she came into the schoolroom after the morning walk. Mademoiselle had taken Ursula, Grace, and Elaine down to the river to watch the college eights at practice; but Pam had chosen to go into the town with Nurse and Gregory George. She had thus missed an important piece of news.

When they told her about the promised treat, her heart became almost too full for words. They were to have a half-holiday that afternoon; they were to drive with Mademoiselle to the wood; they were to have tea at a cottage; they were to pick spindleberries. Pam's eyes were widely opened, but she did not see the schoolroom table and chairs and her three sisters —all she saw was an endless wood of spindle trees laden with fruits of red and orange in four-lobed beauty.

For Pam loved spindleberries. Uncle Anthony brought home armfuls every year from the distant woods where they grew, and Pam would creep alone into the drawing-room to gaze at their dark rose color and orange seeds. Sometimes Mother would give her some branches to put in the schoolroom, and then Pam would be happy for days. She would never allow the vase to be emptied until all the berries were withered, and even then she would save the seeds to make yellow and green dyes for her dolls' clothes. The dyes never lasted, but each year she tried them again in the hope of greater success. Every autumn she had hoped to find spindleberries herself and had hoped in vain. Now she felt that happiness was at hand.

"And Uncle Anthony is coming to drive us, and that is the best news of all," said Grace.

"Uncle Anthony!" said Pam, a black scowl settling down on her face. "He will spoil everything. I don't want Uncle Anthony."

"Now don't be naughty, Pam," said Grace very severely.

And Pam whirled around in a tempest of wrath.

"I don't want him. He makes silly jokes which I don't want to hear. He is always laughing, and I hate it. I wish he would stay at home. I don't like Uncle Anthony!"

"O Pam, what a wicked girl you are!" cried Ursula.

"Uncle Anthony is a pig!" said Pam.

There was a dreadful silence.

"That is the wickedest thing you have ever said about him," said Ursula. "We cannot allow you to be so wicked, Pam. We must tell Father."

Pam's rosy face went pale and her boldness departed. "Oh, please don't," she faltered.

But Ursula and Grace were trembling with indignation.

"I am afraid we must," said Ursula. "It is such a dreadful thing that you said that Father must know how naughty you have been. We shall write the words on a piece of paper; for they are too wicked to be spoken aloud. We wouldn't say them for anything."

"But Father won't let me go to the spindleberry picnic!" sobbed Pam, quite broken down.

"That cannot be helped," said Grace and Ursula.

Then they took a piece of paper and wrote on it in large letters:

"Pam says Uncle Anthony is a pig."

This done, they marched downstairs to the Dean's study, followed by a weeping Pam and a frightened fat Elaine. The Dean was known to be very particular about their manners, and Pam's unruly tongue had more than once brought her into trouble. At the thought of Father's stern rebuke, her chubby knees shook under her. And then there was that wonderful picnic! As certainly as night follows day there would be no spindleberry picnic for Pam, and she felt that to stay at home would kill her.

When they came into the study, the Dean was standing by a bookcase, stooping over a book in a way that meant he must not be disturbed. Uncle Anthony was sitting on a corner of the desk, a newspaper in his hand.

"What's up?" he whispered, as they trooped in.

"It is too shocking to tell you," said Grace. But she showed him the paper, because it was likely that he would hear the story sooner or later.

Pam felt very much ashamed when she peeped under her eyelashes to see what he thought of her. But she was angry, too. If it were not for Uncle Anthony, she would not have been standing here in disgrace between two jailors, waiting for sentence from the Dean. It was too much to bear.

"Why not put in some commas?" Uncle Anthony asked, without showing any surprise at sight of the five wicked words.

"Does it need commas?" said Grace, much surprised.

"Two would improve it," said Uncle Anthony. "One after 'Pam' and one after 'Anthony.'"

Grace added them, although she secretly thought that they were unnecessary. Uncle Anthony looked carefully away from Pam's shaggy head.

"What do you children want?" asked the Dean, coming up to the desk.

"Father," said Grace, "something very wicked has been said in this house, and we thought you ought to know. We have written it down on a piece of paper."

Then she gave the paper to the Dean, and went away with Ursula and fat little Elaine. Pam thought that Uncle Anthony ought to have gone away with them, but he stayed where he was.

The Dean unfolded the paper and read out in his severest voice:

"'Pam, says Uncle Anthony, is a pig.'"

Then he put on his glasses and said, "A disgracefully impolite remark! I am much displeased. What have you to say for yourself, Anthony?"

Pam gave a start of surprise and bewilderment. How odd her words had sounded, and what a curious mistake Father had made! But of course horrid Uncle Anthony would hasten to explain.

Uncle Anthony put down his newspaper and stood up.

"Nothing, sir," he said.

It was not the way in which he usually spoke to his brother; it was the way in which the other undergraduates spoke to their Dean. Pam thought that Father answered like a Dean, not like a brother.

"Nothing?" he said. "Certainly, there can be no excuse for such vulgar rudeness."

Then Uncle Anthony received the stern lecture that properly belonged to Pam. It was so severe that Pam held the edge of the desk in alarm. How shocked and indignant Father was! How harshly he spoke! Mother's entrance made him stop in the middle of a stinging sentence.

"You may go," he said to Pam. "I do not think that your uncle will speak of you so rudely again."

Pam walked over to the door with her eyes on the ground and her head in a whirl. She stumped upstairs to the schoolroom and looked at the others in sulky triumph.

"I am going to the spindleberry picnic after all, you horrid things! There!" she said.

It was not long before the whole story came out. Great was the horror of the three little girls, who could hardly believe their ears.

"Uncle Anthony did it on purpose!" said Grace. "It was the kindest thing I've ever heard of. I should think, Pam, that you must feel very sorry for having been so nasty to him. He must have known that those commas would make the sentence read differently. But why didn't you tell Father the truth?"

"I didn't want to," replied Pam angrily. "Uncle Anthony

could easily have told. He was an old silly not to tell. You are all cruel to me. And I hate Uncle Anthony."

Then she climbed into the red armchair with the shiny back and the red buttons, pressed her nose in a hard way against the nearest button, and refused to look at the others. It was plain that Pam was in what Nurse called "a taking." Grace and Ursula did not try to reason with her. They took fat little Elaine into a corner and talked to her about the nobleness of Uncle Anthony.

And Pam bumped her nose against the red buttons and said to herself, "It was only a scolding, and a scolding doesn't count. If it had been me, it would have been losing the spindleberry picnic as well. And if he hadn't been a pig, I wouldn't have called him one. He deserved to be scolded, he did."

Luncheon was a silent meal. They always talked French at lunchtime on Tuesdays, but they did not know any words likely to prove useful in a quarrel. So they had to sit mute, feeling very uncomfortable.

Mother and Tony came out under the archway to see the party set off for the picnic. Mother did not say anything about the pig-affair; but even if she had wanted to speak, she could not have gained a reply from Pam, who sat hunched in a ball at the back of the car.

Father's chauffeur began to make preparations for the start. Grace asked, "Mother, where is Uncle Anthony?"

"Uncle Anthony isn't coming this afternoon," answered Mother. "He asked me to allow Morgan to drive you instead."

The car drove away, carrying three disappointed little girls and a fourth who felt uneasy in her mind. No one spoke a word all the way; and as soon as they reached the wood, Pam took to her heels and ran away from the others.

The woods were beautiful in their autumn red and gold. Pam filled her arms with glowing spindleberries and tried to pretend that she was perfectly happy. But in spite of this pretense she took great care to avoid Grace, Ursula, and Elaine.

At last she ran into them by mistake, and they closed around her.

"Do you know why Uncle Anthony didn't come this after-

85

noon?" said Grace. "Ursula and I have guessed, and we think that Mother did not like to tell us. It is a most horrible reason, and it is all your fault that he has been gated, Pam."

"I don't know what 'gated' means," said Pam in an exasperating voice, kicking at the pebbles in the path.

"Oh yes, you do," said Grace. Her own knowledge was small and doubtful, but she made the most of it. "Being gated is not being allowed out of college. It is what Father does to the undergrads when they are wicked. We believe that he has done it for the first time to Uncle Anthony. That's what has happened. He has gated Uncle Anthony for the wicked word you said. And it is an enormous disgrace for the Dean's brother. Everyone in college will know, and everyone in the university, too. I hope you will be ashamed forevermore because of what you have done."

Then Ursula and Grace were surprised, for Pam charged between them so suddenly that she nearly knocked them down. All her spindleberries flew right and left as she dashed like a little mad thing down the path and over the fence and out into the road beyond. In awe and astonishment they watched her scuttling along the road like a rabbit till her blue coat and black tam vanished in a distant blur. And they went to tell Mademoiselle.

Pam covered the ground at a rate that amazed even herself. She tried not to think as she tore along; but thoughts could not be kept back, unpleasant though they were. She could not run all the way; and as soon as she was tired enough to be obliged to walk slowly, the thoughts crowded upon her faster and faster. It was a very sorrowful Pam who at last crept into the quad and up the six steps of the corner house. She went into the study without knocking, so anxious was she to make her confession as quickly as she might.

"Why, Pam!" said Uncle Anthony.

Father was nowhere to be seen. Pam never knew quite how it came to pass that the next minute she was telling Uncle Anthony about everything, her face so closely pressed against his tweed coat that it was wonderful he contrived to hear any words at all.

"So you ran all the way back to save your hateful uncle from disgrace, Pam?" said Uncle Anthony, very gently. "That was kind of you, dear."

"You're not a hateful uncle; it is me that is hateful," sobbed Pam. "Are you truly disgraced forever, like they said?"

"Well, not this time," said Uncle Anthony, with a twinkle. "You see, Pam, the Dean didn't gate me—that was just a little mistake on the part of Ursula and Grace. I didn't come with you this afternoon because I thought you would be happier alone—see? But I didn't stay in college—I have been playing hockey."

"I see," said Pam, and she put her arms round Uncle Anthony and hugged him hard.

When the Dean came in, he showed no surprise at the unusual sight of Pam on her uncle's knee. Over her head Uncle Anthony grinned at his brother in the friendliest way; and Pam fancied that there was something like a smile on her father's face.

It was not hard to tell Father the truth when one could keep fast hold of Uncle Anthony's hand all the time; and for some reason known only to himself Father did not say one reproving word. Afterwards Pam wondered why Father seemed to know her story almost before she told it, and why he and Uncle Anthony were so very much amused at some private joke which they did not explain to her. However, at the time she was too happy and too penitent to ask herself any questions. It was bliss enough to be forgiven and to have tea with Mother and Father and Uncle Anthony in the firelight.

When the others came home, they found Pam playing with Tony in the nursery. Her face was pink and her eyelids were red, and she was calling him Tony as if she had done it all her life.

"Here are your spindleberries," said Grace coldly. "We brought them back for you in spite of your being so wicked."

"Thank you," said Pam. She took the rosy bundle into her arms and marched off with it. A little later Ursula saw her running across the quad, the spindleberries in her hands. She went up to Uncle Anthony's scout, who was standing at the entrance to his master's staircase. And leaning out of the window, they were surprised to hear her say clearly, "Will you please put these in Mr. Lennox's rooms?"

The scout took the flowers, and Pam came back to the corner house and went on with her game.

And the others never knew that a piece of paper went with the berries, all tightly folded over lest the scout should read the words on it. The paper said:

"To Uncle Anthony with very best love from his sorry Pam."

Soon after the Smiths moved from New York to their home in the suburbs, Rusty, a small cocker spaniel, showed up on their doorstep one morning and remained as their dog. Every day Susan and Greg discovered some new trick he could do, and one of these led to this unusual adventure.

Alice Dalgliesh

RUSTY—MOVIE STAR

ILLUSTRATED BY *Esther Friend*

ONE of Rusty's tricks was to wait for the word of command before he crossed a street. Susan and Greg soon found out that when they came to a crossing Rusty would sit firmly down on the edge of the sidewalk. Then he would look up at them with a question in his eyes. The first time this happened the children wondered what to say to him.

"It's all right, Rusty," said Greg.

Rusty sat perfectly still.

"Come on, Rusty!"

Rusty did not move.

"Go, Rusty!"

At that Rusty got up and crossed the street with the children. "Go" was the one word that could make him move from the sidewalk.

When Father heard about it he said, "That dog must have grown up in a city. Most city dogs have to learn to wait at crossings."

One day Susan had a slight cold and could not go to school.

89

In the afternoon she and Rusty walked over to the school to meet Greg. When Greg came out Susan and Rusty joined him.

"Look," said Susan. "They are taking movies of some of the children."

"I know," answered Greg. "The pictures are for a Safety First campaign. The children show how to cross a street safely."

The Smiths and Rusty stood on the sidewalk and watched the movie men at work. A group of children stood waiting for a signal. When the signal was given they looked to right and to left of them, then crossed the street. The camera clicked busily.

"I wish they had asked us to be in one of the pictures," said Susan. "Why didn't they?"

"The sixth grade was asked," explained Greg. "They didn't ask the younger children."

The movie men were packing up their camera and getting ready to leave. Greg and Susan had to cross the street, and as usual Rusty sat on the sidewalk and waited for the command.

"Look at that!" said one of the men. "The dog is trained to wait at crossings. We ought to get a shot of him with the children."

Greg and Susan wondered if they were hearing rightly. The man who had spoken came up to them.

"Say, kids," he said, "would you mind doing that stunt with the dog for us?"

Would they *mind?* Greg and Susan were almost speechless. At last Greg managed to say, "Sure, we'll do it."

The children and the dog went back to the other side of the street because the cameramen wanted the school in the background of the picture. Greg began to feel cold and funny inside. Suppose Rusty did not do it right? He had never made a mistake, but this time he might. They walked along the sidewalk, Rusty tugging eagerly at the leash. Click, click, click went the camera. They came to the edge of the sidewalk, and Rusty sat down. He looked up at Greg.

"Go, Rusty!" said Greg.

They crossed the street. The camera clicked, then stopped.

90

"Fine!" said one of the men. "That will make a swell picture."

"Where will it be shown?" asked Greg.

"It's part of the newsreel for next week. You could see it at Radio City Music Hall," answered the man.

"Oh, Greg!" said Susan. "Radio City! Do you suppose Father and Mother will take us?"

"We'll ask them."

Father and Mother were much interested to hear about the safety film.

"I'll find out what the main picture is," said Father. "If it's right for you to see we can all go to it."

When Father came home that night the children rushed to him. "Did you find out about the picture, Father? Did you? May we go?"

"I did find out," said Father. "It's a Shirley Temple picture, and I think it's one you would enjoy."

"Goody! When do we go?"

"I think you'll have to wait until Saturday so that I can go too," said Father. "Mother can drive the car in, and I'll meet you at Radio City."

Saturday seemed a long way off.

"Suppose it rains," said Susan.

"Oh, a little rain won't make any difference," said Mother. "We'll go rain or shine."

The days went by slowly. At last Saturday came. It took only forty-five minutes to drive from Greendale to Radio City, but to Greg and Susan the drive seemed much longer than that. The road went by so slowly, first the Parkway, then the Park, then Riverside Drive. At last they were on Fifth Avenue and the tall white towers of Radio City came nearer and nearer. The parking place was crowded, and it took Mother a long time to park the car. It seemed years before they were really out on the street again and walking over to the Music Hall.

"Susan," said Mother, "can't you *walk?*" It was true that Susan was not walking, she was skipping.

"I don't mind if you skip," Mother went on, "but if you get too excited you know what may happen."

"I'll be sick! I'll be sick! I'll be sick!" sang Susan happily.

"Yes," said Greg. "Then when they show our picture you'll be lying down in one of those fancy dressing rooms and you won't see it." At that Susan stopped skipping and walked sedately beside Mother. Father met them at the corner of the street.

The Music Hall glittered with lights. Shirley Temple's name sparkled at them from above the entrance.

The children were a little startled. It had almost seemed as if the lights should say:

GREG, SUSAN AND RUSTY in SAFETY FIRST

"Do you suppose our picture is on now?" asked Greg.

"I'm sure I don't know," answered Father. "And for mercy's sake remember that your picture is only a very small part of a newsreel and will take only a few minutes."

"We know," nodded Susan.

"I'm not so sure," said Father. "To hear you talk about it you'd think it was the whole show!"

The Smiths had bought their tickets now and were going in the entrance.

"It always makes me think of a fairy palace," whispered Susan to Greg. Greg pretended not to hear, for Susan's fancies were two years too young for him.

"Let's go upstairs," he said. "I like to sit up there and see the lights in the ceiling change color."

Going up in the elevator Susan turned a funny pale green. Greg looked at her anxiously. Suppose they had to stop now and take her downstairs! He did not feel safe until they were actually in their seats. The stage show was on.

"Gosh!" said Greg. "That means we have to see a whole lot of dancing and Shirley Temple before our picture comes on."

"Greg!" whispered Mother. "Stop talking, stop worrying, and enjoy yourself."

Greg did stop worrying and began to enjoy himself very much indeed. The show was a good one. Shirley Temple's picture was fun, and there was a Mickey Mouse cartoon.

Then the announcement of the newsreel flashed on the screen. Greg pinched Susan, who gave a shrill squeal. The lady in front turned and looked at them severely.

"Children!" said Mother.

"He pinched me!"

93

"Be quiet, Susan," hissed Greg. "Our picture's coming any minute."

The newsreel was rather dull. There seemed to be a great deal of it and a great many pictures that did not mean anything to the children. At last——

SAFETY FIRST!

As the words came on the screen Greg and Susan sat on the edge of their chairs. They pinched each other joyfully. They rocked back and forth. They kicked the seats in front of them. The lady in front turned and glared again.

"Greg! Susan!" said Father in his fiercest whisper. "If you can't behave I'm going to take you out."

That sobered the children a little. The safety picture was on the screen now. There were many children crossing the street. Yes, there was the sidewalk in front of the Greendale school! Two children came walking along. The boy was holding the end of a leash and tugging at the leash was a cocker spaniel.

"It's us!" said Susan right out loud.

"Go!" said the boy in the picture. "Go, Rusty!" The children and the dog crossed the street, and the picture faded out.

"Come, children," said Father. "We're going home."

"Can't we stay and see it over again?" asked Susan.

"I should say not! But if it is shown in Greendale you may go and sit as long as you wish."

They went downstairs and out into the street. Greg and Susan were still more or less in a daze and neither of them spoke until they reached the parking place.

"Think of Rusty being in the movies," said Greg as they got into the car. "I wish he could have seen himself."

"All we needed in the theater was Rusty," said Father raising his eyebrows. "I have never seen two children wriggle so much."

"That's just because we were extra excited," explained Susan. "Next time we'll sit as still as mice."

SUSAN and her aunt Ann are living in
the home of queer old Mrs. Patrick,
who won't let anyone see some historic letters belonging to her. Ann, a
writer, needs to consult them. In this
very interesting part of the book
Susan sees one of them.

Siddie Joe Johnson

STORY HOUR

ILLUSTRATED BY *Matilda Breuer*

MISS West had suggested Story Hour at the
Public Library early in the fall. It was one
of the best things Dalport had to offer its
young fry, she said. Miss Jeffries, the Children's Librarian, told
the stories on Wednesday afternoons at the Main Library downtown. Mary Kate and Donald had discovered the Story Hour
with Susan. There they had met children from all the other
schools of Dalport. Small Mexican boys and girls were there,
talking in two languages as easily as Susan talked in one. Susan
liked their musical voices, the different rhythms their Spanish
speech made, the velvet throatiness of their laughter. There
was one girl, especially, whom Susan liked. Her name was
Carmelita Chapa, and she seemed to get the same pleasure
from Miss Jeffries' stories that Susan did.

Mary Kate admired the dresses of the little girls from Miss
Holiday's exclusive girls' school. As for Donald, he struck up a
warm friendship and rivalry with some big boys who lived
down close to the Viaduct. They went barefoot even in really
cold weather, but they liked the same kind of stories Donald
liked, and they bragged that they could play better football in
their school than he did at Berry.

Story Hour was certainly one way to know Dalport, at least
the young part of it. It was almost like the counter at the five-

and-ten cent store. Different languages were spoken, different kinds of clothes were worn, different sections of town represented—north, east, south, west. Children came to know each other who would never have become acquainted otherwise.

Miss Jeffries was glad to see them—every one of them—always. She knew exactly what books would please the big boys Donald found so fascinating. They knew she knew, too, and talked to her the way they talked to each other. Susan wondered sometimes if Miss Jeffries, from the boys' telling her about it, couldn't probably play as good football as any of them.

Sometimes Miss Jeffries talked Spanish with the Mexican children. She introduced Susan to biography and books about history. Susan was thrilled. That was the kind of writing Ann did. Maybe she would grow up to do the same. She and Mary Kate always checked out one poetry book to read aloud to each other. Of course, they had their lighter moments, too. Mary Kate was reading stories about teen-age girls now. And Susan could even like an almost poor book if it was about a dog. Not that Miss Jeffries would ever let a really poor book walk in her library door!

One afternoon in early winter, they sat watching Miss Jeffries light the Story Hour candles. Susan forgot—just as she imagined Miss Jeffries forgot at such moments—that this was an old, rather run-down library, that they needed a new Story Hour room badly, that, on afternoons like this, logs should have been set alight in the fireplace they did not have. The place became, for the time being, a place of enchantment.

The story was a special one today—the first real winter Wednesday they had had. Miss Jeffries was telling Hans Christian Andersen's "Snow Queen." Gerda and Kay came to life in the candle-lit room. The chickens of the Snow Queen fluttered and flew. The little robber maiden brought a cluck of approval from the boy sitting next to Mary Kate.

Just as Gerda was nearing the Snow Queen's palace, Susan glanced at Carmelita, who sat beside her. Susan and Mary Kate always saved a seat for Carmelita near them. Carmelita's eyes were open, but she looked almost as though she were asleep.

Her lips moved as Miss Jeffries said the Hans Christian Andersen words. Susan was sure Carmelita could tell a good story her own self.

Finally, Miss Jeffries brought Gerda and Kay back home. "And it was summer again." The story was over.

Miss Jeffries always selected some child to blow out the candles. Today, it was the tousle-headed boy in blue jeans who sat at the back of the room with Donald. He stumbled up to the front and blew at the candles like a boy in a dream. Susan remembered her own birthday candles and her wish. Would it ever really come true? All of it? The boy slouched back to Donald again, still in a dream. Miss Jeffries was not content with her children discovering the world about them—the sometimes very strange world of each other. She gave them another world, as well, a world in which Snow Queen and children like Gerda and Kay were just ordinary beings. A magic world.

But, when Story Hour was over, Miss Jeffries sometimes had to bring them back from that magic world.

"It is your turn now," she said today. "I have told you stories for a long time. Now it is your turn to tell them to me. We are going to have a Storytelling Tournament right here in this room. Any boy or girl in Dalport who wishes to enter may. You may make up your own story, if you like. Or take one from a book. You might even retell one that you have heard me or some other storyteller tell. But be ready by next Wednesday to tell your stories, and we'll draw numbers to see who goes first. We'll have the stories every afternoon for a whole week—from next Wednesday to the Wednesday after that.

Susan and Donald and Mary Kate went home intent on the stories they were going to tell. Mary Kate decided that she would use a picture-book story because it would be short and easy to learn.

"With lots of repeating in it," Mary Kate said.

Donald wanted an adventure story—a mystery, or one about ghosts, probably. Susan didn't know. She would like to write her own, but she couldn't think of a plot.

After she had told Donald and Mary Kate good-bye—she

97

wouldn't even have time to play with Doodle before dinner—
she went slowly up the front steps of the apartment.

Ann did not meet her at the front door, but Mrs. Patrick did.
For a minute, Susan was a little frightened.

"Your aunt's over at that magazine place. Your friend, Mr.
Barcus or whatever his name is, called half an hour ago. Said
she had to read proof or something. You can eat dinner with
me." She sounded a little grudging, as though it were a favor
she didn't quite want to grant.

"Thank you, but—" Susan knew it was a favor she didn't
want to receive. She had eaten one meal with Mrs. Patrick,
and that had been sort of fun. But to go to Mrs. Patrick's apartment at a regular mealtime! She didn't think she'd be able to
swallow. Or say a word. And what was Mrs. Patrick doing in
their apartment, with Ann gone?

"You come on, young lady." Mrs. Patrick always seemed
capable of reading her mind. "Your aunt said for me to come
in here and watch for you, if I wanted you to eat with me. So
come on."

Susan followed her. If Ann and Mrs. Patrick had planned it,
there was no use arguing, though Susan could fix a good enough
dinner for herself.

Susan was surprised when she saw the table Mrs. Patrick had
set for them. Flowers were on the table, a pretty cloth, and
what Susan guessed must be "company" china and silver. There
were even candles to be lighted.

"Thought I'd show you I could keep house, too," Mrs. Patrick
said. For once, Susan saw what she thought was a twinkle in
Mrs. Patrick's sharp eyes.

The meal was very good: fried chicken drumsticks—you
could select your own pieces of cut-up chicken at the market
up on Berry—mashed potatoes and gravy, spinach with hard-
boiled egg on top.

"Children always like drumsticks," Mrs. Patrick explained.
"And spinach is good for you."

As the candlelight flickered, Susan found herself talking a
great deal. She told Mrs. Patrick about the storytelling

tournament and her own lack of a proper story to tell.

"I know the very thing!" Mrs. Patrick left the table abruptly. They had finished their pieces of apple pie, anyway. Susan wished she could make an apple pie—one just like Mrs. Patrick's.

But what was Mrs. Patrick doing? She was fumbling in her desk drawer, pulling out a pile of old letters. Oh, glory! Were they the letters from Sophronia Compton? How Susan wished for Ann. Why, if Ann could get her hands on those letters, she'd be in such a seventh heaven, she'd be willing for them to have half a dozen houses of their own—even if they had to "keep" every one of them—and for Susan to have a kennel full of puppies in the backyard of each one.

"Have a letter here from a friend," Mrs. Patrick said. "Written a long time ago. Most people know what's in the letter—been enough curiosity about it and feature stories written on it. All a lot of trumped-up foolishness, I say! More mistakes in every one of those features than you can count on your fingers. But in this letter she tells me all about it—just how she felt that day General Sam Houston was wounded, and what he said to her and all. She tells all about how she nursed him back to feeling good, too. And how she happened to meet up with this Colonel of his—the one she afterwards married."

It was the Sophronia Compton material, all right. If only she could get it in her hands! But she'd memorize every word and tell Ann. Wouldn't Ann be surprised! And now, Susan was almost as interested in the letters for their own sake as Ann could have been.

"Now, what you can do," Mrs. Patrick said, "is to make your own story out of this, tell it in your own way. And there won't be another story even to come near it."

Susan closed her eyes and opened them again. Yes, it really was Mrs. Patrick sitting there. She couldn't believe it, not really. Mrs. Patrick had acted like a normal human being all evening. That was almost more of a miracle than the letters. It was another discovery.

So Susan helped Mrs. Patrick with the dishes and thought about making her story around the central figure of historic old Sophronia. Then Ann knocked on the door, and it was time to go home.

Susan told Ann, of course, about the letters. Ann shook her head.

"I'll just have to do without them, I guess. She hates writers. Feature writers have sort of messed up the Sophronia legend. But even the part you remember is worth something, Susie. Only—I'll have to have the letter itself to quote from, or my work will be worth little more than the worst of the feature stories that have just been based on other feature stories—and on what the writer could imagine. I'll have to quote date and place." Ann was silent for a moment, then she said, "I've asked her about the letters."

Susan was surprised. She had not known that Ann had ever mentioned the letters to Mrs. Patrick. That was the worst about being a little girl. Grownups so seldom took you into their confidence.

"But—" Ann laughed. "There's no use asking. Remember what she told you—that she'd never let me see them at all, if I asked for them. Luckily, I've only asked *about* them."

Even so, Susan and Ann felt pretty good about Susan's having seen the letters. It seemed a little better than nothing.

100

The story Susan worked up around the one letter Mrs. Patrick had read to her really was "better than nothing." Susan did not have a chance to tell her story the next Wednesday, but Donald did. And Donald was voted the best storyteller of the afternoon. As Miss Jeffries said, still laughing over Donald's story, when she read the judges' decision, Donald's story might not have been the most finished product in the world, but it certainly had lots of life in it. As in everything else, Donald went at story-telling with vim and vigor. He was, as Mary Kate expressed it, a good hard storyteller.

Mary Kate did not win the next afternoon, though her story was neatly and charmingly done. Carmelita told hers that same Thursday, and there couldn't have been any doubt in anybody's mind—even Mary Kate's—as to which of all the ten stories told was best for the day. Carmelita's eyes, when she told her story, were just as they had been when she listened to Miss Jeffries telling one—wide open, but asleep. Carmelita was gone from the world of the Story Hour room to the world of her story. She, like Susan, was discovering. The story that she told was a legend of old Mexico, a legend of her people. Susan loved it.

And then, on Monday afternoon, before the run-off on Wednesday, Susan told her story. She did not win first place all by herself, but she did tie for it with Donald's tousle-headed friend from the Viaduct district. The boy, strangely enough, told one of Hans Christian Andersen's stories, just as Miss Jeffries loved to do. He told it with unexpected delicacy and grace, so that all of them were surprised, seeing both the boy and their beloved Nightingale with new eyes.

On Wednesday, for the run-off, Miss Jeffries lighted the Story Hour candles again. All of the winners from the individual days would tell their stories over once more. And the judges were well-known newspaper and radio people and one speech teacher from the University. Susan knew, too, what the prizes were—prizes given by one of the Dalport bookstores. First prize was Audubon's *Birds of America*; second prize, a new and lovely edition of Hans Christian Andersen; and third prize, a copy of Kenneth Grahame's *Wind in the Willows*.

Susan had seen Carmelita looking at the prizes. Turning the pages of *Birds of America*, she had murmured, *"Qué hermosa! How beautiful!"* She had called her younger brother and sister up to look at it, too. Susan was going to tell her own story as well as she could, but she hoped Carmelita would win.

The boy from the Viaduct drew the first number today. He told his story again, even more delicately than he had before. Susan, who was reading a biography of that "ugly duckling," Hans Christian Andersen, himself, wondered if the boy were not a great deal like the famous writer of fairy tales. After the boy, came Susan's turn. She saw Miss Jeffries nodding with approval. Miss Jeffries had been very interested in Susan's writing her own story about a real character.

Donald was not quite so good as he had been on the first day. His mind was on football. He didn't scare the audience quite so much, and his exuberance seemed to be straining at the leash—straining to get out on a football field.

Last of all was Carmelita. Again that look in her eyes, again that liquid little-girl voice casting a spell. Susan glanced at the two younger Chapa children. Their eyes, as they listened to their sister, were exactly like Carmelita's, shut to the outside world, but opened wide on a world of fantasy and legend.

The judges conferred. And then Miss Jeffries announced the decisions. First prize to Carmelita. The younger brother and sister went up with her to receive the *Birds of America*. It took all three of them to carry it, for they were all three in such a daze they didn't seem to have much strength.

Second prize to the boy that Susan now called "The Ugly Duckling." He deserved a book of Hans Christian Andersen, Susan thought.

Susan squirmed a little as Miss Jeffries conferred again with the judges before announcing the third prize. She didn't think she had won it—she owned a copy of *Wind in the Willows*, anyway—but Donald's and Mary Kate's eyes were signalling her loyally. And it might put Mrs. Patrick in an especially good humor if she had something to show for the gift of the material from the letters.

"And now I want to give a prize of my own," Miss Jefferies said.

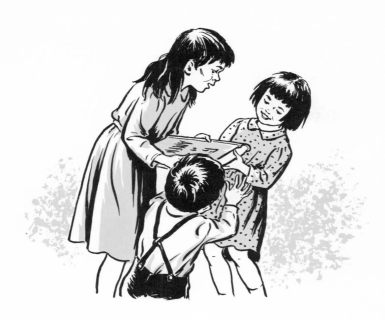

Third prize, Miss Jeffries said, holding up the lovely *Wind in the Willows*, went to Marjorie Brown, one of the daintily dressed little girls from Miss Holiday's school. Susan could hear Donald's "Oh, shucks!" quite clearly. He had not been expecting it for himself, either. He had not told his story like a boy expecting it. Storytelling, after the first fine flurry of it was over, was not exactly in Donald's line. If he could have sung a song now! Or played a piece on the piano—or caught a pass—

But there Miss Jeffries was again, another book in her hands.

"And now I want to give a prize of my own," Miss Jeffries said, "a new dog book that has just been published. It goes to a storyteller who arranged her own story from original materials about a real person and a real event. I like that use of history—of things that happen all around us—of stories that our elders, people we know, tell us about the past of our own state. Susan Brent, this is for you."

Susan was glad that hers was a special sort of prize. Now she would have something to take home to Mrs. Patrick. And to Ann. A dog book, at that!

Marion Holland

SMOKY

ILLUSTRATED BY *Gladys Peck*
AND *Eleanor Osborne Eadie*

THE whole family was getting ready to leave for the cottage in New Hampshire where they spent their summers. "Then that's the way we'll do it," said Father to Mother. "You take the plane to Boston tomorrow morning and catch the afternoon train to the lake. That will give you time to get the cottage opened and everything ready while I drive up in the car with the children and the heavy luggage."

"But, Father," argued Andy, "why can't I go on the plane, too, with Mother? Gee, I've never been in a plane in my whole life. Why can't I go on the plane, too?"

"Because you can just as well go in the car. It costs too much to send you in the plane just for the fun of it. And one more thing—I will *not* drive all the way to New Hampshire again with that awful cat in the car."

"But, Father," wailed Anne, who was sitting on the floor cuddling the big Persian cat, "we've got to take Smoky! Why can't he go in the car with us?"

"Maybe you've forgotten what happened last year, but I haven't," said Father grimly. "We stopped for gas in Baltimore, and Smoky got out and climbed on the filling station roof. It took forty minutes to find a ladder and get him down again. And in Philadelphia, he jumped out the window and ran down the middle of the street in all that traffic—and it took two policemen and the whole family an hour to round him up again. Not to mention the way he yowled all the way and dug that big hole in the upholstery—"

"Yes, I remember," said Anne hastily. "But he's a whole year older, now, and he'll behave better. Won't you, Smoky?"

104

Smoky opened one green eye and shut it again. Sharp curved claws crept out from an enormous paw and hooked quietly into the best rug.

"Scat!" shouted Father. "Get off that rug! I wouldn't mind that cat being such a complete nuisance," he went on in a reasonable tone of voice, "if he were the slightest use in the world. But what good is he? Won't eat this, won't eat that. Sleeps in the best chair. Won't catch mice—why, there are mice in the pantry right now, dying peacefully of old age—"

Smoky elevated his superb plume of a tail and stalked majestically from the room. "Oh, Father," cried Anne. "Now you've hurt his feelings again!"

"All right, all right, he can go. But not with me. That's final."

"Maybe we could ship him by freight," suggested Mother mildly. "Of course, it would take several days—"

"Smoky would hate that. Couldn't he go on the plane with you?" asked Anne.

"I don't know whether planes take cats as passengers," said Mother doubtfully.

"Call up and see," urged Andy.

They called up. Yes, the plane would take a cat, but not as a passenger. He would have to be crated and weighed in, and travel with the rest of Mother's luggage. "Say—why couldn't I go as luggage, too?" shouted Andy. "I wouldn't cost anything extra. Just crate me and stick a sign on, saying, 'Savage dog, do not disturb—'"

"You," said Father, "can march down in the basement, right now, and fix up a crate for Smoky. A good strong one."

Anne and Andy found a box in the basement and bored a few holes in it for air and fixed a lid with hinges and a latch. "The lucky dog—cat, I mean," grumbled Andy as he drove the last nail. "Getting to ride in a plane—and I don't suppose he'll even have sense enough to enjoy it."

"Look, what about Smoky if there should be an accident or something?" asked Anne anxiously. "You know how it always is in the movies, people jumping out of planes with parachutes. Are there cat parachutes?"

"Say, that's an idea. Have we still got that big hunk of parachute stuff that Uncle Jim brought back from the Pacific?"

By dinnertime the cat parachute was finished. The large, circular piece of nylon was attached by strings to a fancy leather harness that Smoky had once gotten for Christmas but never cared much about. Andy wanted to test it on the cat, but Smoky took one good look at the contraption, dug four sets of claws into Andy's arm, and departed rapidly over the back fence. So they found a piece of oak in the woodpile that weighed about as much as Smoky. They fastened the harness around this and dropped it out of the attic window. At first it fell like a stone, then the chute billowed out and the piece of wood descended sedately, swaying gently from side to side.

"Let's not bother Mother and Father about this," said Andy thoughtfully. "I'll leave it in the crate for tonight, and we'll put it on him in the morning before we start."

Next morning, while their parents were loading the car for the trip, they found a small can of sardines looking forlorn and forgotten on the pantry shelves. They lured Smoky into the basement with this and quickly buckled on the harness while he was happily eating ninety-eight cents' worth of imported Norwegian sardines in olive oil. The parachute, folded neatly, fitted into the bottom of the box, and they bundled the cat in on it. Andy slammed and latched the lid and waited for the explosion. But Smoky was full of sardines, and besides, he had been out all night. He curled up and went to sleep.

He woke up, though, when the crate was put in the car. You could tell that by the noise. "That cat," said Father.

At the airport, there were quite a number of people standing around where the luggage was being weighed in, and they were all interested when Smoky's crate was set on the scales. It suddenly rose up in the air an inch or two, all by itself, and came down again with a crash that jiggled the weights on the bar. The noise was really something to hear—not exactly a howl, and not exactly a growl, but something about midway between the two. And it wasn't the noise, so much as it was the vibration. The whole scales quivered.

106

"My land," exclaimed an elderly lady, peering over her glasses. "There ought to be a law!"

Smoky's crate was loaded aboard with Mother's suitcase, and Mother got on with the other passengers. Andy, waving as the big plane taxied down the runway, could not help feeling that an airplane ride was wasted on a crated cat and a lady who, even if she was his mother, couldn't tell a P-39 from a C-54.

"When do the passengers put on their parachutes?" asked Anne, watching the plane grow smaller and smaller.

"Parachutes?" said Father. "Why, they don't bother with parachutes in these big passenger planes. They're as safe as trains. Safer, maybe."

"Oh," said Anne. "All that work and we needn't have bothered. Poor Smoky."

"What about Smoky?" asked Father, starting the car.

Anne and Andy looked at each other, feeling foolish. "Nothing," they said.

"That's fine," said Father. "I would be just as glad to hear nothing about that cat for the rest of this trip. When I think about the way he ate the biggest fish I caught all last summer— It wasn't so much that I grudged him the fish, but he might at least have waited until I had taken a picture of it."

They found plenty to talk about without mentioning Smoky again. Late on the second day, the car turned into the dirt road leading to the cottage, and Andy leaned out the window, yelling, "I see the lake!"

"I see the pier!" shouted Anne.

"I see Mother!" shouted Andy. "Hi, Mother! How was the plane ride?"

"Did Smoky just hate it?" asked Anne, jumping from the car.

"The plane ride was fine," answered Mother. "But—oh dear, I hardly know how to tell you. Such a day as I had yesterday. The man at the airport office in Boston kept talking about whether it was our liability or the company's, and there was a reporter who kept asking questions and *asking* questions—why, he seemed to think the whole thing was funny! And that terrible old lady kept saying, 'I'm going to write to my congressman.' It's a wonder I didn't miss my train!"

"What *is* this all about?" demanded Father.

"Smoky," said Mother.

"Yes, where *is* Smoky?" asked Anne, looking around.

"Gone," said Mother.

"Gone where?" asked Andy.

"Oh, dear. Well, sit down and I'll get it over with. You see, just before we came in at Philadelphia—we stopped at Philadelphia and New York on the way—anyway, somebody opened the door to the little place up front where the hand luggage goes—and everything happened all at once. Smoky must have gotten out of his crate somehow. Andy, are you sure you had it fastened properly? Anyway, he just shot between the man's legs and came flying down the aisle. Such confusion! Everybody dodging and yelling, but Smoky doubled back into the luggage place, and the man had him cornered against the far door, and then—oh dear—"

"And then—what?" demanded Anne breathlessly.

"And then—that door opened, the co-pilot it must have been. And Smoky simply sailed past him, right up to where the pilots sit, and shot out that little side window and disappeared into a cloud—"

"Oh no!" cried Anne. "You don't mean Smoky jumped out the window, and he's—"

"Well, yes, dear. You know how Smoky is—was, I should say." Anne burst into tears. "And the strangest thing about it," went on Mother, "was that he must have gotten tangled up in someone's scarf, because he was dragging this long white thing

109

behind him. Only it was bigger than a scarf, really, more like a nightgown. Though I can't imagine where he would have gotten hold of a nightgown, and nobody complained about missing one—"

"But that was his parachute!" cried Andy excitedly. "Did it open all right?"

"His *what?*" exclaimed Father and Mother.

"Parachute. We made him one. He had it on in the crate."

"If you wrapped something around Smoky, no wonder he clawed his way out of the crate," said Father severely. "He probably thrashed around and got so tangled up in it he could hardly move."

"Well, I wouldn't say that," said Mother thoughtfully. "He was moving, all right. I don't think I ever saw anything move any faster."

"But don't you see?" cried Andy. "Stop crying, Anne. If it opened all right, he probably made a perfect fourpoint landing somewhere. All we have to do is find out where the plane was when he jumped, and go back and get him. We can start right now."

"We can *not,*" said Father, in a very final sort of voice. "Just make up your mind that Smoky is gone. Parachute, indeed. It's too bad, of course, but that cat has just jumped out of one window too many."

"Oh, poor Smoky," wailed Anne. "And we can't even have a funeral."

"When we get home again, we'll see about getting you another cat. One that will eat table scraps and be glad to get them. One that will catch mice," said Father.

At about this time, a farmer named Paxon in Pennsylvania was saying to his son, "Bill, I want you to keep your eyes open around the chicken-house. Something is after those baby chicks. There were four missing today, and I found tracks in the mud near the water pan."

"Tracks? Gee, what kind of tracks?"

"Well, that's the funny thing about it. Big tracks. Bobcat, I'd

110

say, but I never heard of any bobcats around here."

"Bobcat? Golly!" Bill raced down to the chicken-house. There were the tracks, all right, and they certainly looked enormous. When he returned to the house, he had something in his hand. "Look, Dad, what I found stuck on a nail by the chicken-house door. Like a piece off a handkerchief, or something. Maybe it was a tramp that took the chicks."

His father scrutinized the piece of cloth and shook his head. "A tramp would go for frying chickens—or old hens. But I never heard of a bobcat carrying a silk pocket handkerchief. Ask your mother if this could have been torn off something of hers."

Mrs. Paxon ran her fingers over the scrap. "Why, this is real fine material. I haven't got anything like this, and if I had, I wouldn't be wearing it around the chicken-house."

"Say!" cried Bill. "We got a fine first-class mystery to solve!"

"Fine or not," grumbled his father, "if any more chicks turn up missing, I'm going to solve it with a shotgun."

The next day there were more chicks gone, and fresh tracks. "It's a bobcat, all right," said Mr. Paxon, loading his shotgun. But that afternoon, Bill dashed in from the pasture with another and much larger piece of cloth. "Found it caught in that mess of blackberry bushes," he explained. "Looks like your bobcat is a mighty fancy feller." His father scratched his head. But his mother took the piece of material, exclaiming, "Why, that will make a real nice handkerchief. I'll just square it off and put a little hem on it. Find me a bigger piece, son, and I'll have a new Sunday dress."

The next morning there were more chicks missing, and that night something tipped over a can of pig scraps on the back porch. It rolled down the steps with a clatter that woke Mr. Paxon. He jumped to the window and stared out across the moonlit farmyard. "Well, I'll be dad-blamed," he muttered in a shaken voice.

"What is it?" The bobcat?" asked his wife sleepily.

"Blamed if I know," he replied. "But I'd be willing to go into court and swear it's got a white tail over a yard long!"

The next morning Bill hurried through his morning chores.

111

He intended to take his dog and go bobcat hunting. He dumped wood into the box by the kitchen stove and piled old newspapers beside it. A headline over a little item at the bottom of a column caught his eye. "Cat Leaps From Plane" he read. While he was reading the short story under the headline, a plane zoomed overhead, already losing altitude for its stop at Philadelphia. Day in and day out, as regular as clockwork, the big passenger planes swept over the farm; even the chickens hardly bothered to look at them any more. Bill ran to the door and watched the plane out of sight. Then he reread the piece in the paper. He looked at the date on it, then tore it out and put it in his pocket.

"Why not?" he argued with himself. Anyway, he could find out, maybe—quietly, without getting laughed at. "Think I'll go bobcat hunting, Dad," he announced. "What'll you give me if I catch it for you?"

"If it is a bobcat," replied his father cautiously, "there might be a bounty on it. But go easy—better take the dog with you."

Bill did not answer. The dog was the last thing he wanted to take along, now. He made a quiet visit to the pantry and set off, with a large hunk of cold fried fish in his pocket.

It was a strange bobcat hunt. Bill walked back and forth across the pasture, calling in a soft, coaxing voice, "Here kitty, kitty, kitty. Come puss, puss." He thought he heard a rustle under the tangle of blackberry bushes where he had found the second piece of mysterious cloth. Of course, it might be rabbits. Or the wind. But he sat down close to the bushes and laid the piece of fish on the ground beside him. He kept very quiet, except to go on calling gently, "Kitty—kitty—kitty—"

The stealthy rustle in the bushes commenced again. Soon Bill could make out two glowing eyes. Inch by inch, an enormous cat worked his way out. A couple of times Bill thought he was stuck on something, but he pulled himself free. As soon as he could reach the fish, he began eating hungrily. Bill reached out and touched him. He growled, but went right on eating.

"Poor puss, nice kitty," said Bill, stroking the long fur. It was all matted with mud and burrs. "Why, kitty," he exclaimed.

112

"You're all tangled up in something." With his pocket knife he cut the cat free. Then he held up the tangle of dirty strings and shredded cloth and whistled. "So that's where the stuff came from. Cat, did you *parachute* out of that plane?"

"Prrraow," said the cat, licking the last of the fish flavor off its chops.

Bill's hands parted the fur over the harness. "Smoky," he read on the little metal plate. "Well, come along, Smoky." The big cat allowed himself to be picked up and carried. "Mother! Dad!" shouted Bill, running back to the house. "Come and see your chicken thief! And you're wrong about bobcats, Dad—they *do* carry silk pocket handkerchiefs!"

"Oh, the poor thing," cried his mother. "I wonder if he's hungry."

"Hungry!" retorted her husband. "*Hungry?* With all those chickens in him? Not to mention whatever he got out of the pig bucket!"

"But where did he come from?" asked Mrs. Paxon. "Why, he's a beauty!"

Bill showed them the clipping, and what was left of the parachute. "It doesn't say anything about a parachute," he admitted, "but look, it says, 'Valuable Persian cat, property of—' Gosh, there wouldn't be *two* of them!"

P.E.

His mother said, "It gives the address. Why don't you write to the people? Maybe there's a reward."

"That's right," laughed Bill. "A bounty on bobcats! Shall I write, Dad?"

"Never mind the bounty," said his father. "But somebody ought to pay for all those chickens. Go ahead and write."

When the letter arrived in New Hampshire, Andy shouted, "I told you so!" and Anne was so happy that she burst into tears all over again.

"I suppose it really is Smoky," said Mother cautiously.

"I'm afraid so," said Father. "The letter describes the harness and everything. But what are we going to do about it?"

There was quite a long pause, and Mother said gently, "I'm afraid the only thing to do is to drive down, and thank the people, and bring Smoky back."

"That cat," said Father, but in a defeated tone of voice.

The day Smoky arrived home, Anne and Andy washed and brushed and fed and petted him within an inch of his life. "That cat," said Father to Mother as they were going to bed. "But apparently he had to forage for himself while he was gone. He must have learned to catch mice. That's something."

In the dark living room of the cottage, Smoky stalked over to the largest chair. He sharpened his claws on it for a while, then he leaped lightly onto the seat. He kneaded a hollow place in the cushion, turning around and around, and settled down with a rhythmical purring. After a while, a very small mouse crept in from the kitchen. It paused in the middle of the floor. Smoky opened one green eye and looked at it. Then he closed the eye and settled down more comfortably into the curve of his fluffy tail.

Smoky was home again.

Chesley Kahmann

THE GANG'S ALL THERE

ILLUSTRATED BY *Genevieve Foster*

JACK CRAMER scuffed through the new snow. At the corner street lamp he stopped, as Scotty Hanson had told him to do, and pulled a piece of paper from his pocket —the paper Scotty had put into his hands only a minute ago with the instructions, "Read it at the corner."

The street lamp now shed a blurry light over the white paper, and the fast-falling snow began to wet it, but Jack had no trouble, reading the tall, black-crayoned words:

YOU ARE HEREBY ASKED TO BECOME A MEMBER OF XDY AND SUMMONED TO APPEAR AT THE NORTHEAST EDGE OF WILLOW WOODS AT FIVE O'CLOCK TOMORROW MORNING!

"Gee!" said Jack. "Scotty Hanson's gang, inviting me to join!"

He had lived in Hawkton only three weeks. It was almost unbelievable that this gang had really chosen him. He turned around to see if Scotty had followed. No one in sight, he started home.

He remembered taking Scotty up to his room, and Scotty's looking at the life-saving medal and the riflery medal and the scroll saying he had passed his canoe test at Camp Waumahok, which he had attended for the past two summers. He remembered Scotty's saying, "Gee, you sure did a lot of things in that camp!" Ever since, Scotty had been asking hundreds of questions. It was undoubtedly Scotty who had interested XDY in him.

Jack turned in at his driveway, waded through drifts to the house. On the porch he stamped his feet and shook himself in general to shed what snow he could. Then he entered the house. A jerk at the collar unsnapped his black leather jacket. Another jerk and his mackinaw cap was off and on the coat rack. Then he was in the living room, facing his father who was reading his paper.

"Gee, Dad, this sure is a swell town! Scotty Hanson's gang's asked me to join!" he began.

"Gang?" asked Mr. Cramer. He fluttered his paper. "Who's in it?"

"Oh, Scotty Hanson, and Dick Foster, and—"

"Henry Parker belong?" Mr. Cramer asked.

"Gee, Dad, he's not the kind a gang would ask!" Jack said.

"I don't see anything wrong with Henry," Mr. Cramer said. "Well, is John Drake in then?"

Jack shook his head. Quickly, however, he said, "If there's an initiation fee, I'll earn it easy enough shoveling snow. Gee, you ought to see how deep the snow is, already!" He rushed to the window. "Boy! By morning we ought to have eight feet!"

Mr. Cramer seemed uninterested in the depth of snow just then.

"What does this gang do?" he asked seriously.

"They—" But for his life, Jack couldn't think of anything except that on Saturdays the boys went places—and how was a person who wasn't a member to know where? After all, a gang had to have *some* secrets!

Mrs. Cramer came into the room. Jack told her the news, impressing upon her how unusual it was that he, a new boy in town, should have been so honored by XDY. Mrs. Cramer frowned.

"Those boys," she said, "were going through Mr. Melrose's pasture and broke the fence—and his cattle got out. Mrs. Garner told me so!"

"The fence was rotten!" Jack cried. He'd heard the whole story. "The cattle would have gotten out anyhow. Old Melrose just blamed the gang—"

116

Mr. Cramer raised his eyebrows.

"Besides," Jack continued, "Mrs. Garner's got it in for XDY because her son Frank wasn't asked to join!"

"Well, come to dinner, anyhow," said Mrs. Cramer.

After dinner Jack went upstairs and set his alarm for four o'clock.

"I'll know the password before long!" he thought, as he undressed. He glanced up at the fluttering *Camp Waumahok* banner stretched across one wall and the medals on the board beneath, grateful that Scotty had seen and liked them.

There was a knock at the door. At Jack's, "Come in!" Mr. Cramer entered, twirling the chain that hung from the knife pocket to the watch pocket across his stomach. He cleared his throat, then said, "Son, you're new in town," and twirled his chain some more. "I'd go slow. Not join a crowd unless I was sure—"

"I am sure!" insisted Jack. "Gee, Dad, they're swell fellows!"

"No doubt," said Mr. Cramer. "But what would you get 'for your money'?"

"Everything!" Jack said. "All the privileges of the gang—"

"Which are—"

"Well," said Jack. "You can't know all the privileges until you're *in!*"

"I don't approve of gangs," said Mr. Cramer. "They lead to mischief. People talk about this one. Now I don't mean you to be unfriendly to anyone. But don't join without looking it over longer."

"Dad!" cried Jack. "That's not fair!"

But that was all there was to it. Mr. Cramer walked out of the room and downstairs.

In bed, Jack lay thinking. Not be unfriendly to anyone. But not join! What would the gang think? But he'd meet the boys at five and tell them—have it over as fast as he could.

He fell asleep at last but through the night kept waking. One o'clock—ten past two—eighteen after three—then five minutes of four. He shut off the alarm before it had had a chance to ring. He looked out of the window. The snow was deep.

117

He was about to start dressing when he saw a light flashing about in the upper windows of the garage which stood perhaps a hundred and fifty feet back of the house.

"Burglars!" Jack thought. But he knew there wasn't anything in the whole garage a burglar would want. The Cramers didn't have a car. Downstairs there was only junk—crates and old automobile licenses which a former tenant must have left behind. Upstairs there was nothing.

Suddenly the upper windows were dark. Light appeared downstairs. Then the front door opened. Four boys filed out.

"Some of the gang!" Jack gasped. Scotty—Dick—the other two he couldn't make out. What were they doing there?

At five o'clock Jack was at Willow Woods waiting for the gang to appear. How would he begin his explanation? How—

But flashlights were already dashing out from behind the trees. Soon Jack was the center of a circle. With no other greeting, someone cried, "Eighty-seven—ninety-four—blindfold!" Bill Cole, with cloth in hand, approached Jack.

"Wait!" Jack said, stepping back. "Wait!"

"Scared of a blindfold!" Two boys grabbed his arms.

"Listen, I say!" Jack shouted. He wriggled away from his captors. "I've got to tell you now— I *can't join!*"

"Not join!"

"Why'd you come then?"

118

"You can't make fools of us!"

"Say it again, yellow! All we were going to do was blindfold you and lead you to our meeting place!"

So they thought he was a coward, did they? Not joining because of the blindfold!

"It's not that!" Jack cried. "It's—"

But louder voices drowned his words. Then Scotty edged up to him, saying, "You sure did let me down. What do you mean, you can't join? You let me think—"

"Forget him, Scotty!" Dick called out. "We're lucky to find him out! What'd we tell you—"

"I'd like to belong," Jack said. "But I can't—right now—"

"All right, if that's the way you feel about it," Scotty said. "Seems to me you could give a reason, though."

XDY moved away from Jack, went into a huddle. Jack turned, scuffed through the snow towards home, feeling more alone than he had ever felt before.

Home again, he walked around the house. The sight of the garage reminded him of Scotty and Dick and the two others who had made that early morning visit there. What had they wanted? He found himself entering the garage, a few minutes later. He passed the crates and license plates, climbed the stairs.

"Gee, they'll all have it in for me, now!" he kept thinking.

Upstairs the windows were small, but enough light crawled through to show a vacant room except for a box over in a corner. Suddenly something jumped out of that box, came scooting across the floor.

"Foxy!" gasped Jack, recognizing Scotty Hanson's fawn cocker spaniel.

Foxy wagged her short tail wildly and seemed glad to see him. From the box came squeals and squeaks.

"Gee! Puppies!" Jack said, following Foxy back to the box. "Nine of them!" Two black and white ones, three fawns, two dark browns, and two blacks.

But from below came sounds. Feet on the stairs. Voices. As the door opened, Bill said, "It was such a swell place, too!"

A moment later Jack faced XDY.

119

"Well, what're *you* doing here?" asked Dick Foster.

"It's my garage," said Jack. "I was looking around."

"We've come for 'em," said Bill, nodding toward the puppies. He didn't look friendly any more. "Now you've decided not to belong, we've come for 'em!"

Foxy licked her babies contentedly, seeming to know no one would hurt them.

"Where're you going to take them?" asked Jack.

"I don't know," answered Scotty distantly. "But somewhere!"

With little questioning, however, the story came out. The boys, thinking Jack would be a member of XDY, had supposed the garage would be available to the gang's possessions. They had moved the dogs there that morning. Scotty's mother had said she wouldn't have a thing to do with this new litter. Foxy had had pups before. They had run all over the house. Like ants, she had said; you couldn't get rid of them. So this time she had said that Scotty could even give Foxy away if he couldn't dispose of the puppies.

"Gee!" said Jack. It seemed a shame to keep moving them. "Why don't you leave them here? They aren't bothering anybody."

Everybody looked surprised.

"You—you *mean* it?" Scotty asked.

"Sure!" said Jack. "It's a swell place for them. They'd be warm enough, with some blankets—"

Silence. Glances among the boys.

"Well, maybe it *would* be better'n moving them again!" Dick finally said. "It's a job in all this snow. We could bring food here—" He looked at Scotty, as if for support.

"It's—it's not our usual way of doing things," Scotty said seriously. "We don't let outsiders know our business. But—well, this is a big exception."

"But you've got to promise not to tell anyone!" Dick said.

"Sure!" said Jack. That was easy enough. Was there any harm offering a home to a bunch of dogs? He hadn't joined the gang, had he?

The boys started to leave. Scotty and Jack were the last.

"You see," said Scotty, at the door, "we've been meeting in this garage almost a year—while the house was vacant. I wouldn't tell you, except we're not going to meet here any more, now your family's moved into the house and—and you're not joining the gang!" He paused, then asked, "Say, what've you got against us?"

"Nothing!" said Jack, scuffing the snow. "You ought to know that."

"It's your father then!" At Jack's silence, Scotty added, "I guess the gang won't be so hard on you if its—*him!* Gosh! You can't help—"

"If you're quiet enough about it," Jack said, "I guess you could keep on meeting in the garage. It doesn't interfere with—anybody!"

The boys gone, Jack found the snow shovel and cleared away the tracks around the garage. Then he worked on the sidewalks, clear around to the front door so it wouldn't look suspicious. As he shoveled, he wished his father knew about the dogs—how the gang of which he had disapproved was a humane gang, protecting homeless dogs. But his father couldn't know.

Later Jack sat at breakfast with his family. If his father had known about his going out so early that morning, at least he had the decency not to mention it. Jack tried to be natural and take part in the family conversation, but suddenly he found it hard to talk or swallow food. A horrible thought had flashed through him. Had the gang asked him to join just because they wanted to meet in the garage? Because they needed a place for the puppies?

Breakfast over and his father gone to work, Jack hurried upstairs, snatched the dark blue blanket from his closet, and went out to the garage. He found Foxy still mothering her puppies. He draped the blanket around three sides of the box. *Camp Waumahok*, in large letters, came at the top. But the puppies still shivered. They had probably been used to heat, at Scotty's.

Heat! In his very attic was an electric heater which Grandma Cramer used when she came to visit. But nobody was using it now. He hurried to the house. Soon the heater was in the garage, connected to the light socket.

"You won't freeze *now!*" he said, patting Foxy's head.

Every day he visited the dogs, sometimes meeting Scotty there, or one or two others, but never the gang as a whole. He brought Foxy dog biscuits, purchased with part of his allowance, and milk and left-over meat until the day a black-crayoned sign appeared over Foxy's box:

Dog getting too much food at wrong hours. No feeding except by owner.—S.G.

In the corner stood a fifty-pound sack of brown meal—to be mixed with water, the directions said.

Two weeks later Scotty and Jack met in the garage.

"The gang," said Scotty, seriously, "had some plans, but we're —sort of changing them. We thought maybe we could do some things you did in your camp. We got the idea, seeing the blanket every time we came up here." He nodded toward the *Camp Waumahok* blanket.

"Sure! You could!" said Jack.

122

"What we need," said Scotty confidentially, "is equipment, and that takes money. So we thought maybe we could all start earning a little, and—buy a boat, maybe, or whatever we needed."

"It's a slick idea!" said Jack.

"But we thought it'd be foolish to go on with it unless we knew—you'd—show us how to do things—" Then, quickly, "That's the only reason I'm telling you the plan. The gang generally doesn't do things like that—tell outsiders. This'd be an exception."

"There're canoe tests—and life-saving— Gee! Millions of things!" Jack cried. His father would approve of that.

From then on he spent his evenings thinking back over the activities of Camp Waumahok, to be ready for XDY.

One day Mr. Cramer said, "I saw Scotty Hanson shovelling snow at Mr. Green's—and Dick working in the drugstore Saturday. I guess the gang's split up."

Jack said nothing. XDY was keeping its business to itself, as usual.

Then came the day when Mr. Cramer opened the electric bill.

"Sixty-nine dollars and fifty cents!" he gasped.

"It must mean six dollars and fifty cents," Mrs. Cramer said. But Jack felt very cold.

"Gee! It's the heater!" he said. "I—I've been using a heater—in the garage. Got some dogs out there. It was cold—"

He told about Foxy's having pups and Mrs. Hanson refusing to keep them and how he himself, of his own free will, without any suggestion on Scotty's part, had offered the garage, knowing Foxy wasn't a barking dog and wouldn't bother anybody.

"Well, son," said Mr. Cramer, "you may go out and turn off the heater and see that the dogs go back to your good friend, Scotty. We'll deduct eight dollars for the house bill—*and you can start earning the rest: Sixty-one fifty.*"

"Gee!" said Jack.

At six o'clock that evening not only Scotty, but every member of XDY appeared. Solemnly they divided the pups, then filed out into the snow, saying good-bye to Jack at the back door.

Jack went into the living room, an uncomfortable place with a lot of thoughts going on, and no one speaking. In the long silence, Mr. Cramer scanned his paper. Then, like a fire alarm, the doorbell rang. Jack answered. On the porch stood XDY.

The boys, each with a dog under his coat, walked into the

living room. They formed a half circle around Mr. Cramer who seemed rather dazed at the sight of the boys and the dogs' heads sticking out of the coats.

"Our gang invited Jack to join," Scotty said, "but Jack wouldn't. But now he's in trouble we'd—like to treat him the way we would if he was a member. We've earned a little money around town, for some things we needed—"

"Like a boat—to have tests the way Jack did at camp," said Bill.

"But we've had a meeting and decided to work toward the electric bill first—and equipment later. We've got fifteen dollars saved up, already—and we'd like to give it to you toward the bill—"

"And the rest as soon as we make it," Scotty added.

"Gee!" said Jack. "You don't need to do that. I'll earn it, somehow! Gee!" If he had been a girl, he might have cried.

But Scotty shook his head. Looking straight at Mr. Cramer, he said, "I hope you won't say anything about it to anybody. XDY doesn't generally tell its affairs to outsiders."

"No," promised Mr. Cramer. "No, I won't say anything. Thanks for coming."

Then the boys were gone. And so was Mr. Cramer, for he went straight out to the kitchen to talk to Mrs. Cramer.

Two days later Jack opened an envelope which had arrived in the mail. Scrawled in tall, black-crayoned letters were the words:

YOU ARE HEREBY SUMMONED TO APPEAR BEFORE XDY AT FIVE O'CLOCK SATURDAY MORNING AT THE NORTHEAST CORNER OF WILLOW WOODS.

Then, in parenthesis, in the lower left-hand corner:

YOUR DAD SAYS IT'S O.K.

Helen Train Hilles

ALL MUTT

ILLUSTRATED BY *Keith Ward*

ONY woke up with a gulping feeling that something was going to happen. He lay flat on his back in bed, his heart almost thumping straight through him to the mattress. It was a little like the breathless feeling you got just before Christmas—except that at Christmas you were sure something *nice* was going to happen.

Today was the day of the Pet Show.

Tony kept his eyes tightly closed. Then slowly he stretched out one freckled arm in the candy-striped pajama sleeve, till it hung over the edge of the bed. He heard a little thump and then a faint sniff. Then he felt warm breath on his knuckles, and a wet, cold nose. He waited. In a moment he felt a rough, sandpapery tongue covering his fingers with short, timid licks.

Tony sighed, and some of the hard lump went out of his throat. Then, forgetting, he moved his hand. There was a gentle yelp, and something heavy scuttled under the bed.

"Doggone it!" sighed Tony. "Now I've gone and scared him and he was getting *so* good!"

He rolled out of his bed and crawled under it.

126

"Come, Handsome, nice doggie," he coaxed, a little breathlessly, because of his cramped position. Nothing happened. Tony came out from under the bed, sat down in a resigned sort of way on the floor, and waited patiently.

By degrees Handsome inched himself forward until the heavy head that Father said reminded him of a bulldog stuck out from under the box spring. Next came two forepaws, one on either side of the head. The paws didn't look as though they belonged to Handsome at all. They had a sort of delicate, curly, French-poodley look that went oddly with his heavy head and ferocious jaw.

Tony coaxed him farther out. Even he couldn't help being surprised all over again at the black and white fox-terrier thinness of Handsome's middle. A laugh started inside of Tony. But he was very careful not to let it come out, because he didn't want to hurt Handsome's feelings, particularly today.

Handsome was all the way out from under the bed now, his long feathery tail brushing the floor like a mop. Mother said she was sure there was some setter in him.

"How could I have entered him in the Pet Show?" thought Tony in despair.

Of course it was all Tom Green's fault. Tom Green had started all the teasing that Tony had to stand, and Tom Green had given Handsome the name that made Tony hurt inside every time he heard it.

Tony'd never thought of entering Handsome till he'd met Tom whistling along the street only two days ago.

"Hi!" said Tom loudly. "I got some raw meat here for my alligator." Tony set his jaw.

"Hi!" he said. Tom Green needn't be so cocky about his old alligator. He knew it was the only alligator in town. So he'd be bound to win with the alligator entry in the Pet Show.

"Too bad," said Tom with a smirk, starting to walk on, "*you* haven't got anything to enter."

Tony's mouth opened of its own accord and, before he had time to shut it, he heard his voice saying: "I'm going to show H-Handsome." (The name had stuck.)

"W-What!" Tom's jaw dropped, and he looked so funny that Tony got over the unexpected feeling that his own words had given him. Tony gulped.

"Sure," he made himself say airily, and walked on. Tom recovered himself enough to yell at Tony.

"Ya!" he jeered. "I'd like to know where that will get you! Handsome isn't handsome—he isn't even *anything!*" The words cut into Tony's back. He quickened his steps. As he rounded the corner he heard Tom's last words.

"He doesn't even wag his tail!"

Once around the corner a dreadful weight sank on Tony. What had made him say that to Tom? He didn't want to show Handsome! And Tom was right. Handsome wasn't handsome— he wasn't anything, *yet!*

You couldn't explain to Tom Green or anyone else how you felt about Handsome. When you found a pathetic looking dog on your lawn, and you were the only person he'd ever let come near, you just *had* to take him in. And because he was so scared of everybody, and ran with his tail between his legs at the slightest sound, it made you feel even sorrier for him. Some-body must have been horrid to him—probably somebody like Tom Green.

Tony had worked gently and patiently with Handsome, and the dog really had improved. He wasn't very much scared with Tony alone, now—only if Tony forgot and raised his hand or dropped something. Yesterday Handsome's tail had given a thump on the floor that might almost be called a wag. But with other people, Handsome hadn't improved much.

And in an hour or two now Tony and Handsome would be at the Pet Show.

Tony looked down at Handsome. The dog's head was on his knee, and he was looking up at Tony with big bulldog eyes. Tony felt his own eyes water a little.

"If *they* could only see you now—just your head, I mean, without the rest of you!" he whispered huskily. "You look almost h-handsome!"

Tony got to his feet resolutely and started dressing. Dressing didn't usually take Tony very long, but this morning he brushed his tow head even in the back, and put on a bright tie and tied it very carefully.

Ready! Tony opened the door and called to Handsome, still hopeful that someday Handsome would follow. He didn't. Tony's patience cracked.

"Oh, all right, *stay* there!" he yelled. "*I* don't care if you want to be so dumb!" Then he ran back. "I'm sorry, I didn't mean to hurt your feelings," he whispered. But Tony's bluff slipped over him again as he walked into the hall. He whistled as he slid down the bannisters and bounced into the dining room. Father and Mother and Jane were having breakfast. There was a ring of puffed rice around Jane's place.

"Hello, Son," called Father, in a hearty, hollow voice that didn't fool anybody, least of all Tony.

"We've got wheat cakes, dear," said Mother in a sweet, anxious voice.

"Hello," said Tony. He poured himself a glass of milk.

"It's a beautiful day—" began Mother.

"For the Pet Show!" burst out Jane, emerging suddenly from her mug, a white milk mustache glistening on her upper lip.

Mother and Father looked at each other, then started talking very quickly, both at once.

"Jane thought she'd show the baby mouse," said Mother, "the one that got caught on the flypaper and we washed off."

"In a saucepan, so's he can't crawl up the sides," said Jane, her face anxious under the thick black bang that covered her forehead.

"Not a bad idea," said Tony.

"Of course there will be ever so many dog entries," said Father, much too casually. "That's the biggest class and no one can expect to win with so much competition."

"Better be going," said Tony, gruffly. He knew Father was being kind, and he could not bear to have anyone be kind to him just now. He rose from the table.

"We'll get ready," said Mother.

"You all going?" asked Tony.

"Certainly," exclaimed Father. "Promised Mr. Green we'd come and see him judge."

When Tony reached his room, he opened his top bureau drawer and took out something carefully wrapped in tissue paper. It had taken all his allowance for weeks, and it exactly matched the color of his tie.

He looked down at Handsome.

"If you don't like this—well, you're just crazy," he said firmly. He leaned down and gently fastened the shiny green patent leather collar round Handsome's neck and snapped the matching leash to it.

Handsome sniffed, but didn't scratch at it.

Suddenly the window shade flapped. Handsome tried to scuttle under the bed, but Tony had the leash tight in his hand. Handsome almost, but not quite, pulled Tony over. Tony set his teeth.

"You've just *got* to come now," he said desperately.

Without looking back Tony pulled Handsome along with all his strength. By the time he reached the stairs Tony's nose was beaded with perspiration, between the freckles. Handsome, he thought, weighed a ton.

Down the stairs they went, Handsome sitting, his fox-terrier body, ending in his setter tail, landing with a thump at each step.

It was easier to pull Handsome along the slippery floor at the bottom of the steps to where Father and Mother and Jane were waiting.

"My mouse is in here!" said Jane, holding out her saucepan, covered by a clean dish towel. Father and Mother looked at Handsome and his new leash.

"Why!" exclaimed Father in his hollow, this morning's voice. "Doesn't he look—look unusual!"

The whole family were on the pleasant, wide street now. The street was usually quiet, but this morning it was alive with children, parents, and animals, and strange yelps and noises were in the air. All the action on the street was surging in one direction, towards the Bakers' large field.

130

The noise was too much for Handsome. He shivered, turned, and tried desperately to claw his way back into the house.

"You can't!" Tony whispered between gritted teeth. He turned and scooped up the heavy dog in his arms. It was a much warmer day than he had realized.

Tony struggled along for a few steps without Father and Mother noticing him, because Father and Mother were calling greetings to friends and trying to restrain Jane, who was jumping up and down, sing-songing, "I've got a teeny mouse! I've got a teeny mouse!" Then Father saw, and flashed a quick look at Mother.

"Here, I'll take him," he offered.

"No—you—won't," panted Tony. He could stand it if he just looked straight ahead and didn't listen to the cheery sounds and squeals around him. Handsome weighed a lot, but he looked quite well as he lay there, confidently, his big head hanging

131

over Tony's right arm, which was beginning to go to sleep. He could see the field now—only a few more steps.

Walking ahead of him was the broad back of Mr. Green, the judge. Next was Tom, carrying a cigar box with holes punched in the lid. For a fleeting moment Tony envied him. How light that tiny alligator in a cigar box must be!

The Bakers' field was already trampled all around the temporary platform that Mr. Baker had laid down specially for the show. For quite a circle around it parents, children, and pets were surging in confusion. Pets were straining at leashes, held in arms, lugged in boxes, and through the din you could hear the Cullens' parrot squawking, "Go home! Go home!"

Tony sat down on the grass a little way off from the platform. Handsome was still trembling, but there were so many people that no one noticed. Tony saw that some of the other pets were frightened, too. He felt a little better, and he could rest his arms.

There was a hush of human voices as Mr. Green got on the platform and clapped his hands. The animal voices, of course, went right on. Mr. Green cleared his throat.

"The first class," he announced, "seems to be birds. Will all the entries please step to the platform?"

The crowd murmured with interest as a long line of assorted children filtered through the mob to the platform, birdcages held on high, then stood giggling before Mr. Green, who looked a little uncertain as to what he was supposed to do.

"Put all those——all those things down on the floor," he directed, looking at the frame of birdcages which encircled him.

All the birdcages were set down—small wooden traveling ones, gold-colored wire canary ones, the Travises' green-painted one that had a stand that made it loom high above the others, even though there was only a rather forlorn pair of lovebirds in it; and the Cullens' parrot protesting loudly over being placed on the drafty floor of the platform.

The twittering of the disturbed birds started the other animals off. Dogs strained at their leashes and there were loud yelps and low snuffling noises.

132

"Hold your pets tight!" directed Judge Green through cupped hands.

Tony was watching everything with interest. No one had noticed either him or Handsome, and the dog was resting quietly on his knee, making only a few whuffly, soothing noises in his throat, because he had a touch of asthma.

Luck was with Mr. Green. It might have been hard to judge the birds—but a hush descended on the whole audience, even stilling the animals, when pale little Joe Malloy got down on his knees and, opening the door of his shabby little wooden cage, whistled softly to his bird. There was a gentle, fluttery little noise that even Tony could hear and a flash of something tiny and primrose colored; then Joe stood up, holding out his arm. A little yellow canary was perched on the boy's scrawny wrist, not at all scared. Amid the friendly roar of the audience you could hear a tiny clear trill.

No one was sorry when Joe got the first blue ribbon of the day.

Next came the alligator class. Tom Green was the only entry. Mr. Green must have known it, thought Tony, but he slipped his spectacles up on his forehead and boomed,—

"Any other entries?"

There was a polite silence while Tom waited confidently for his prize. And when he got his ribbon there was just enough applause so Mr. Green's feelings wouldn't be hurt.

Mr. Green disposed of all the rabbits next. And then a tiny little girl got a ribbon for a chipmunk she had rescued from a cat.

Then Mr. Green called the mouse class. Tony stiffened. Jane's class. He hadn't realized how many mice there were in town. Almost as many children filed up to the platform as in the bird class! There was a very fine-looking cage held above the heads of the Maloney twins. Tony's heart sank as Jane stumbled through the crowd carefully holding her saucepan at arm's length. All the others were *white* mice! Mr. Green adjusted his spectacles and looked over the squealing mice carefully. Then he looked at Jane.

133

"Let's see yours, Jane."

"Mine's just a *regular* mouse," said Jane. Everyone laughed. She put down the saucepan. Suddenly Tony saw Ned Reynolds' cat. It flashed toward the saucepan. "Look out!" he shrieked. "Oh, Janey, look out!" Jane whirled, bewildered. Then quick as a flash she sat down on her saucepan. Ned Reynolds came forward sheepishly and collected his cat. There were yells from the crowd:

"Good work, Janey!" "You take good care of your mouse!"

Mr. Green selected the finest white mouse and awarded it the ribbon. Then he turned to Jane.

"You win the field-mouse ribbon," he announced kindly. Jane looked pleased but perplexed.

"He isn't a *field* mouse," she protested. "He's a *flypaper* mouse!" The audience looked at one another. Mr. Green's face grew quite red, but Tony could tell it was a pleasant red.

"What do you mean, Janey?" the Judge asked.

" 'Cause Mother and I found him on a flypaper and washed him off!" piped Jane. Mr. Green cleared his throat.

"We'll change the award!" he said impressively. "Miss Jane Fiske gets a ribbon for the most original way of acquiring a mouse."

Tony beamed. He felt almost as though he'd gotten a prize.

"Anything else to clear up before we start on the dogs?" asked Mr. Green. The old weight hurled itself down on Tony's chest. He'd almost forgotten the dog class. He gulped. There was no reply to Mr. Green's question. Mr. Green took a drink of water.

"All right, bring up the dogs, and we'll get this thing over," he said genially.

There was a scramble as the dog owners made their way to the platform. Tony, heart thumping so loudly he was afraid Handsome might feel it, waited till almost everyone was at the platform. The less rustling around there was, the less scaring to Handsome. Handsome didn't need to be pulled. With a terrified look around him, Handsome stuck close to Tony's legs, almost tripping him. And with a final heave Tony got Handsome up on the platform, where he sat, on the very edge, pushed against Tony. Mr. Green was looking at a small, brown, Pomeranian-seeming dog, who was yapping at him.

"Take him over there—" he began; then he caught sight of Handsome, and Tony, unhappily, could feel his eyes freeze to him. "Upon my word!" exclaimed Mr. Green. "What's that?" Tony could feel the flush that seeped up from his collar to his forehead. "That's—that's my dog," he said defiantly.

Mr. Green turned his attention to the others. The big airedale-looking dog of the Maloneys was straining to get at the Booths' Pomeranian-like one, an old backyard enemy. The platform was crowded with assorted pets, all dogs, if not all unmistakable varieties of dog. Mr. Green was frankly bewildered. But he knew so many dogs from outside contacts that it wasn't so hard after all. He walked around the platform, looking intently at each. And every few minutes his eyes returned, as if fascinated, to Handsome. Tony was getting more and more uncomfortable.

"A most—most amazing dog," he heard Mr. Green murmur.

Tony flushed again. Was he making fun of Handsome?

"You can get down, and you, and you," said Mr. Green, and three dogs, held by their leashes in disappointed childish hands, climbed down off the platform.

Each time Mr. Green sent another dog down, the platform grew less crowded, and the dogs left on it were plainly visible. Tony grew unhappier. Why put it off? Why couldn't he tell Handsome and Tony to get down and get it over with?

One more dog out. Another—another—only five dogs left! It got more and more strained. It was like a bewildering game of "going to Jerusalem," one chair going at a time, leaving so few.

Four dogs left! Tony twisted Handsome's green patent-leather leash around his knuckles so tightly that his knuckles grew white. What was happening, Tony asked himself.

The yappy Pomeranian was left, a pretty little dog with a horrid disposition; Bob Barrows' sort of poodle, the trick dog of the community; a teeny pup—and Handsome.

There was a breathless pause; then the teeny puppy was sent down. Three dogs left!

135

Then Mr. Green walked around the platform, pausing to look intently at each of the three dogs left. He stopped at the poodle.

"Put him through his tricks!" he said to the poodle's master. The boy made him roll over, play dead dog, and shake hands.

Mr. Green nodded. Then he looked at Handsome, with that same perplexed, strange look in his eye.

Mr. Green walked to the edge of the platform.

"Folks!" he said. "This is the biggest class and the most difficult to judge. However, I feel sure you will agree with my decision when I award the first prize to the Booths' Pomeranian. He has by far the best points, technically, of any dog here!"

The applause was loud, and Tony nodded. Mr. Green had done right. But why, why had he kept the rest on the platform? Mr. Green raised his hand.

"But we are giving other ribbons in this, the biggest class," he said. "The next goes to this near-poodle, the most intelligent and best trained dog in the show!"

This time the applause was deafening. It roared in Tony's ears. The dreadful feeling that something was going to happen came over him again. He didn't breathe as Mr. Green raised his hand for the last time.

"The next prize," he said, "goes to Tony Fiske's dog, Handsome—for having more different kinds of dog in him than any other dog at the show!"

The wave of noise was deafening. Loud clapping filled the field, clapping for Handsome! Tony felt weak. He looked at Mr. Green with eyes that suddenly felt wet. He tried to speak when Mr. Green handed him the ribbon, but no words would go up his throat. He got down on his knees to pin the ribbon on Handsome, burying his face against Handsome's big head.

Then suddenly he straightened up and stared.

Handsome was wagging his tail!

Edith Mason Armstrong

THE MASON CHILDREN
ON THE ROOF

ILLUSTRATED BY *Janet Smalley*

THE big house on the shore of the little lake was full of visitors, and the Mason children were wild with delight. Half a dozen cousins with their fathers and mothers had come up from the city early Saturday morning.

"Come on!" said Ros. "Everybody choose sides for a mock battle on the kitchen roof!"

There were thirteen Mason children—ten boys and three girls. They had the best times in the world, for there were so many of them that there was always something going on. They were very happy in their home in the city, but they were always happiest when June came and it was time to go to their summer home. It was on the shores of a quiet little lake in the country, where their father had bought a rambling old country house and ten acres of woods and fields and hills and valleys. The house had been added to from time to time, so that there were a number of different roof levels, including the low roofs over the porches; and playing on them was one of the children's favorite pastimes.

137

The three girls circled around Eleanor, the one girl cousin among the visitors, and dumping her suitcase on the hall settee, followed their brothers who had disappeared on a run round the corner of the house.

"Hurry!" panted Edie, as they took hold of hands, "or the boys will get all the cucumbers!"

"Dear me!" said Eleanor. "What are we going to do?"

"Just you wait and see!" returned Ethel, the oldest of the four girls, and as they arrived at the kitchen porch she began immediately to strip wild cucumbers from the vines which covered the roof and lattice enclosure. The others did likewise and the boys, who had already amassed a pile of the soft, wild fruit, which was to serve as ammunition, began choosing sides.

Hunny and Ros were captains and flipped up a coin to see which would hold the kitchen roof first. Ros won, and in an instant he and his men were scrambling up by means of the latticework and taking their positions on the low porch roof.

"Hi, Hunny! Get us off of here, if you can!" he shouted, and with various cries of defiance from both sides, the mock battle began.

Maurice winged his cousin Elmer on the ear with one of the soft, squashy missiles, and another one caught Norman on the chin. The defenders on the roof, ducking wildly for cover, tried to return the fire.

"We've got them on the run, we've got them on the run!" shouted Hunny. "On, on, my braves!"

Ros and his supporters did not stop to answer Hunny's challenge with poetry, for it was known to be Hunny's habit to break into quotation in moments of excitement, but they responded with a concerted attack which succeeded in repulsing the brave enemy's attempt to take the roof by storm. The two leaders, breathing hard and choking with laughter, engaged in a hand-to-hand struggle, Ros endeavoring to keep Hunny from making the last step from the lattice to the roof, while they poured into each other's faces a rain of soft cucumbers.

"More ammunition!" shouted the intrepid leader of the attacking party, while his followers raged below him, ready to

138

follow if he should gain the roof. Edie stood next to him at the
foot of the ladder with a hat full of cucumbers.

"Gimme yours!" ordered Hunny, reaching down. But Edie
hesitated. Hunny had taken her doll that morning and hid it
in a tree. She was tired of his teasing.

"Get some cucumbers for yourself!"

Hunny only took time to give her one astonished look, for he
had quite forgotten the incident of that morning, then he
ducked his head and with a wild shout of encouragement to his
side jumped over on to the roof. His followers swarmed after
him, and there was a brief interchange of shot which forced the
defenders of the roof to leap for safety to the hillside below.

The battle soon developed into a sort of "follow your leader"
race, and before long the last boy was down on the ground,
tearing over the lawn to find something new to do. The girls
did not try to follow them, but instead climbed over the roofs
of the rambling house until they reached the highest one of all.
There they seated themselves comfortably astride the ridgepole
and began cracking hazelnuts spread out there to dry.

"Isn't it glorious up here?" sighed Eleanor. "You can see
way down the lake!"

And indeed their lofty perch did command a wonderful view of the valley, with the little lake sleeping in the hot sunshine, the great trees on the island just across from the house showing as in a mirror.

Edie cracked a specially large nut and offered it to her cousin.

"I'm so sorry I didn't let Hunny have my cucumbers."

"Never mind," consoled Ethel. "You can do something to make up."

"I suppose so!" agreed Edie, rising carefully, for a party on the roof, though one the Mason children were very fond of, required a nice sense of balance.

"Now, see what you've done!" said Margy, for in spite of Edie's caution, she had knocked some of Margy's cracked nut-meats down the side of the roof.

"Never mind!" said Edie. "I'll get them for you!" The roof was high, but the nuts had stopped halfway down the shingles, so the little girl did not hesitate to scramble after them.

But she forgot to reckon on the fact that she had not worn her rubber-soled tennis shoes that day; and as she tried to climb back with the nuts in her hands, she slipped and slid down several feet nearer the roof's edge than she meant to go. It frightened her. All in a moment the roof seemed miles high. She glanced toward the lake far below and laid her head down on the shingles.

"I guess I'm going to fall," she announced unsteadily, as the others, not sure if she were in danger or not, peered at her from the ridgepole.

Lemonade was being served on the front veranda to the visiting aunts and uncles, when a little girl with big black eyes and ashy lips came running at full speed. It was Margy.

"Oh, Daddy! Come quick!" she gasped. "Edie's falling off the roof!"

At this astounding information, the lemonade drinkers, as soon as they could realize what the child was saying, were thrown into a panic.

"What roof? Where?" they cried, rising suddenly and spilling thimbles, magazines, and ashtrays upon the floor.

But a quiet boy who was sitting on the steps below his elders, absorbed in a volume of Carlyle's *French Revolution*, grasped the situation at once. It was Hunny, and jumping to his feet, he seized his sister's hand and made for the easiest place to scale the roof, the grown people following as fast as they could.

In all her life Edie had never heard a more welcome sound than her brother's voice as he saw her plight.

"Keep cool," he said in even, cheerful tones. "Hang on just a minute longer and I'll have you safe up again!"

Ever since Margy had gone for help, Edie had been nerving herself against the fear of falling. She did not let herself look down but gazed up piteously at Ethel and Eleanor, who continually urged her not to let go and assured her that help would surely come.

Yet, in spite of herself, she began to slide slowly nearer and nearer the edge of the roof, until now she crouched only a foot away from it. Digging her fingers into the warm shingles, she hardly dared to breathe for fear she would feel her body move an inch or so downwards. But at the sound of Hunny's voice, strength came back to her. She dug her leather toes more confidently into the crack of the shingles and with pleading eyes looked up at him as he stood above her.

The situation was tense—Hunny saw that. It would have been too much of a risk to go down to the little girl. He could manage it himself, but he could not pull her weight up the steep incline without help from above, and Ethel and Eleanor were unable to give it. But Hunny had a plan. Stripping off his leather belt, he buckled it tightly around one foot; then grasping the ridge-pole with both hands, he lowered the length of his body down the roof.

"Catch the belt, Edie, and pull yourself up to my foot. Then climb the rest of the way on me!" he ordered.

Edie was past thinking for herself, but could obey when Hunny spoke. If he said she could do it, she knew she could.

"Take hold; don't be afraid!" came the steady voice of command.

A strange thing happened. Edie knew she was in danger; she saw that the other girls had their hands over their faces to shut out the sight below; yet suddenly all fear left her, and the only thought that came to her was her regret that she had refused to give Hunny the hatful of cucumbers when he had asked her for it. Well, if she did as he told her now and climbed up where the others were, she could tell him she was sorry! She must do it!

Raising her hands quickly, as he told her, she balanced a second, then caught the strap. The touch of it gave her confidence and hanging on with all her might, she hunched her way along until she came to her brother's foot. The rest was easy. The feel of his sturdy body, attached as it was to brave hands which clutched the ridge with whitened knuckles, brought back all her powers. Climbing carefully but nimbly over him, she was soon sitting astride the roof with Ethel's and Eleanor's arms around her. She heaved a deep sigh of relief.

"Come on," said Hunny, as though nothing unusual had happened. "They are waiting for you."

Looking down Edie saw that the whole family, as well as the guests, were gathered on the lawn below, watching the rescue in a silence they did not break until rescuer and rescued were standing safely on the ground once more.

After supper that evening, the family were sitting on the front porch talking about the little girl's narrow escape. Over a neighboring hill the planet Venus rose, luminous and bright; on the lawn the children were chasing fireflies.

"To think she might have fallen if it hadn't been for Huntington!" said Mrs. Mason to a group of sympathizing aunts; and from the corner of the veranda near by, where the glowing ends of cigars made sparks in the darkness, came Mr. Mason's voice.

"Yes, quick-witted lad—my boy Hunny!" he said.

Edie, who was sitting on the steps, wiggling her feet in the grass, heard every word. Tears came to her eyes at the thought of her courageous brother. She had been wanting to thank him all the afternoon but it was so hard to find a chance. If she didn't hurry it would be time to go to bed. She looked around hastily. Yes, there was Hunny, down at the shore. She could just see his dim figure, bending over a fishline he had set for the night. Not even hearing the voice of the governess calling from the hall, "Children! Children! It's time to come in now!" she raced down the sloping lawn to the pier.

"Hunny," she said breathlessly, "is that you?"

"Yes," her brother answered without astonishment, "it's me."

They stood, silent a moment in the starlight; then Edie said softly, "I'm sorry I didn't give you my cucumbers, Hunny."

And the boy understood. His sister was trying to thank him for rescuing her that afternoon.

"That's all right, Edie," he said, and to the little girl's infinite joy and peace he put his arm around her shoulders and walked with her up to the big lighted house.

143

Eleanor Estes

THE MIDDLE BEAR

ILLUSTRATED BY *Ruth van Tellingen*

WHEN a play was given at the Town Hall, Sylvie was usually the only one of the four Moffats who was in it. However, once in a while the others were in a play. For instance, Rufus had been the smallest of the seven dwarfs. And once Janey had been a butterfly. She had not been an altogether successful butterfly, though, for she had tripped on the sole of her stocking, turning a somersault all across the stage. And whereas Joey was rarely in a play, he was often in charge of switching the lights on and off.

Jane liked the plays at the Town Hall. In fact she liked them better than the moving pictures. In the moving pictures Jane always found it difficult to tell the good man from the bad man. Especially if they both wore black mustaches. Of course the pianist usually played ominous music just before the bad man came on the scene, and that helped. Even so, Jane preferred the plays at the Town Hall. There she had no trouble at all telling the good from the bad.

Now there was to be a play at the Town Hall, *The Three Bears*, and all four of the Moffats were going to be in it. Miss Chichester, the dancing-school teacher, was putting it on. But the money for the tickets was not going into her pocket or into the Moffats' pocket, even though they were all in the play. The money was to help pay for the new parish-house. The old one had burned down last May, and now a new one was being built. *The Three Bears* was to help raise the money to finish it. A benefit performance, it was called.

In this benefit performance, Sylvie was to play the part of Goldilocks. Joey was to be the big bear, Rufus the little bear, and Janey the middle bear. Jane had not asked to be the middle

144

bear. It just naturally came out that way. The middle Moffat was going to be the middle bear.

As a rule Joey did not enjoy the idea of acting in a play any more than he liked going to dancing school. However, he felt this play would be different. He felt it would be like having a disguise on, to be inside of a bear costume. And Jane felt the same way. She thought the people in the audience would not recognize her as the butterfly who turned a somersault across the stage, because she would be comfortably hidden inside her brown bear costume. As for Rufus, he hoped that Sylvie, the Goldilocks of this game, would not sit down too hard on that nice little chair of his and really break it to bits. It was such a good chair, and he wished he had it at home.

Mama was making all the costumes, even the bear heads. A big one for Joey, a little one for Rufus, and a middle-sized one for Jane. Of course she wasn't making them out of bear fur; she was using brown outing flannel.

Now Jane was trying on her middle-bear costume. She stepped into the body of the costume, and then Mama put the head on her.

"Make the holes for the eyes big enough," Jane begged. "So I'll see where I'm going and won't turn somersaults."

"Well," said Mama, "if I cut the eyes any larger you will look like a deep-sea diver instead of a bear."

"Oh, well . . ." said Jane hastily. "A bear's got to look like a bear. Never mind making them any bigger, then."

Besides being in the play, each of the Moffats also had ten tickets to sell. And since Rufus really was too little to go from house to house and street to street selling tickets, the other three Moffats had even more to dispose of. Forty tickets!

At first Jane wondered if a girl should sell tickets to a play she was going to be in. Was that being conceited? Well, since the money was for the new parish-house and not for the Moffats, she finally decided it was all right to sell the tickets. Besides, she thought, who would recognize her as the girl who sold tickets once she was inside her bear costume?

Sylvie sold most of her tickets like lightning to the ladies in

145

the choir. But Joey's and Janey's tickets became grimier and grimier, they had such trouble disposing of them. Nancy Stokes said she would help even though she went to a different parish-house. She and Joey and Jane went quietly and politely up on people's verandas and rang the bell.

"Buy a ticket for the benefit of the new parish-house?" was all they meant to say. But very often no one at all answered the bell.

"They can't all be away," said Nancy. "Do you think they hide behind the curtains when they see us coming?"

"Oh, no," said Jane. "You see it'd be different if the money was for us. But it isn't. It's a benefit. Why should they hide?"

One lady said she was very sorry but she was making mince-meat. "See?" she said, holding up her hands. They were all covered with mincemeat. So she could not buy a ticket. Not possibly, and she closed the door in their faces.

"She could wash her hands," said Nancy angrily. The children called this lady "mincemeat," ever after. Of course she never knew it.

146

Yes, the tickets were very hard to sell. But little by little the pile did dwindle. If only everybody were like Mrs. Stokes, they would go very fast. She bought four tickets! Jane was embarrassed.

"Tell your mother she doesn't have to buy all those tickets just 'cause all of us are in the play," she instructed Nancy.

But all the Stokeses insisted they really wanted to go. And even if none of the Moffats were in it, they would still want to go, for the play would help to build a new parish-house. What nice people! thought Jane. Here they were, a family who went to the white church, buying tickets to help build a parish-house for Janey's church. She hoped she would be a good middle bear, so they would be proud they knew her.

At last it was the night of the play. The four Moffats knew their lines perfectly. This was not surprising, considering they all lived in the same house and could practice their lines any time they wanted to. And, besides this, they had had two rehearsals, one in regular clothes and one in their bear costumes.

When Jane reached the Town Hall, she was surprised to find there were many features on the program besides *The Three Bears*. The Gillespie twins were going to give a piano duet. *By the Brook*, it was called. A boy was going to play the violin. Someone else was going to toe dance. And Miss Beale was going to sing a song. A big program. And the Moffats, all of them except Mama, were going to watch this whole performance from behind the scenes. They could not sit in the audience with the regular people with their bear costumes on, for that would give the whole show away.

Jane fastened her eye to a hole in the curtain. Mama had not yet come. Of course Mama would have to sit out front there with the regular people, even though she had made the costumes. The only people who had arrived so far were Clara Pringle and Brud. They were sitting in the front row and Jane wondered how they had gotten in because the front door that all the regular people were supposed to use wasn't even open yet.

When Jane wasn't peering through a hole in the curtain,

Joey or Rufus was. Each one hoped he would be the first to see Mama when she came in. Or now and then they tried to squeeze through the opening at the side of the asbestos curtain. But the gnarled little janitor shook his head at them. So they stayed inside.

Sylvie was busy putting make-up on herself and on the dancers' faces. Jane watched them enviously. The only trouble with wearing a bear costume, she thought, was that she couldn't have her face painted. Well, she quickly consoled herself, she certainly would not have stage fright inside her bear head. Whereas she might if there were just paint on her face. "Somebody has been sitting in my chair," she rehearsed her lines. She stepped into her bear costume. But before putting on her head, she helped Rufus into his bear uniform. He didn't call it a costume. A uniform. A bear uniform. Jane set his head on his shoulders, found his two eyes for him so he could see out, and the little bear was ready.

Joey had no difficulty stepping into his costume and even in finding his own two eyes. Now the big bear and the little bear were ready. Jane looked around for her head, to put it on. Where was it?

"Where's my head?" she asked. "My bear head."

Nobody paid any attention to her. Miss Chichester was running back and forth and all around, giving an order here and an order there. Once as she rushed by, causing a great breeze, Jane yelled to make herself heard, "How can we act *The Three Bears* unless I find my middle bear head?"

"Not just now, I'm too busy," was all Miss Chichester said.

Everybody was too busy to help Jane find her head. Sylvie was helping the toe dancer dress. Joey was busy running around doing this and doing that for Miss Chichester. And the little old janitor was busy tightening ropes and making sure the lights were working. Rufus could not be torn from a hole in the curtain. He was looking for Mama.

Jane sighed. Everybody's busy, she thought. She rummaged around in a big box of costumes. Maybe her bear head had been stuck in it. She found a dragon head and tried it on. How would

148

that be? She looked in the mirror. The effect was interesting. But, no, she could not wear this, for a bear cannot be a dragon.

Goodness, thought Jane. The curtain will go up, and the middle bear won't be a whole bear. This was worse than tripping over her stocking the time she was a butterfly. Maybe Joey and Rufus somehow or another had two heads on. They didn't, though, just their own. Phew, it was warm inside these bear costumes. Jane stood beside Rufus and looked through another small hole in the curtain. Oh! The big door was open! People were beginning to arrive. And what kind of a bear would she be without a head? Maybe she wouldn't be allowed to be a bear at all. But there certainly could not be three bears without a middle one.

"Don't worry," said Rufus, not moving an inch from his spot. "Lend you mine for half the play . . ."

"Thanks," said Jane. "But we all have to have our heads on all through the whole thing."

The Stokeses were coming in! Jane felt worried. The only person who might be able to fix a new bear head for her in a hurry was Mama. Oh, if she had only made a couple of spare heads.

But Mama wasn't coming yet. Jane resolved to go and meet her. She put on her tam and her chinchilla coat over her bear costume. Then she ran down the three narrow steps into the Hall. She crouched low in her coat in order not to give away the fact that she was clad in a bear costume. Nobody on this side of the curtain was supposed to know what people on her side of the curtain had on until the curtain rolled up. Surprise. That's what was important in a play.

Mr. Buckle was coming in now, walking towards the front row. Jane stooped low, with her knees bent beneath her. In front her coat nearly reached the ground. From the way she looked from the front, few would guess that she was the middle bear. Of course her feet showed. They were encased in the brown costume. But she might be a brownie or even a squirrel.

"Hello, Mr. Buckle," said Jane. "I'm in a hurry . . ."

"Where are you going, middle Moffat?" he asked. "Aren't you the prima donna?"

"No. Just the middle bear."

"Well, that's fine. The middle Moffat is the middle bear."

"Yes. Or I was until I lost my head."

"Oh, my," said Mr. Buckle. "This then is not your head?" he asked, pointing to her tam.

"Yes, but not my bear head. I don't mean bare head. Bear head! B-e-a-r. That kind of head."

"Mystifying. Very mystifying," said Mr. Buckle, settling himself slowly in a seat in the front row.

"You'll see later," said Jane, running down the aisle.

She ran all the way home. But the house was dark. Mama had already left. And she must have gone around the other way or Jane would have passed her. Jane raced back to the Town Hall. There! Now! The lights were dim. The entertainment had begun. Jane tried to open the side door. Chief Mulligan was guarding this entrance. He did not want to let her in at first. He thought she was just a person. But when she showed him her costume, he opened the door just wide enough for her. The bear costume was as good as a password.

The toe dancer was doing the split. Jane tiptoed up the three steps and went backstage, wondering what would happen now. The show always goes on. There was some comfort in that thought. Somehow, someone would fix her head. Or possibly while she was gone her middle bear head had been found. She hoped she would not have to act with her head bare.

Miss Chichester snatched her.

"Oh, there you are, Jane! Hop into your costume, dear."

"I'm in it," said Jane. "But I can't find my middle bear head."

"Heavens!" said Miss Chichester, grasping her own head. "What else will go wrong?"

Jane looked at her in surprise. What else *had* gone wrong? Had others lost worse than their heads?

"Where's the janitor?" Miss Chichester asked. "Maybe he let his grandchildren borrow it."

Jane knew he hadn't, but she couldn't tell Miss Chichester for she had already flown off. And then Janey had an idea.

"I know what," she said to Joey. "Pin me together." And she pulled the neck part of her costume up over her head. Joey pinned it with two safety pins, and he cut two holes for her eyes. This costume was not comfortable now. Pulling it up and pinning it this way lifted Jane's arms so she had trouble making them hang down the way she thought a bear's should. However, at any rate, she now had a bear head of sorts.

151

"Do I look like a bear?" she asked Rufus.

"You look like a brown ghost," Rufus replied.

"Don't you worry," said Sylvie, coming up. "You look like a very nice little animal."

"But I'm supposed to be a bear, not a nice little animal," said Jane.

"Well," said Sylvie, "people will know you are supposed to be a bear because Rufus and Joey both have their bear heads on."

So Jane resigned herself to not being a perfect bear. She tried to comfort herself with the thought that she would still be in disguise. She hoped her acting would be so good it would counterbalance her bad head. "Somebody has been eating my porridge," she practiced.

Miss Chichester appeared. "The janitor said 'No,' " she said. She thoughtfully surveyed Jane a moment. "Hm-m-m, a make-shift," she observed. "Well, it's better than nothing," she agreed with Jane. But she decided to switch the order of the program around in order to give everybody one last chance to find the middle bear's real head. She sent Miss Beale out onto the stage. Everybody hoped that while Miss Beale was singing *In an Old-fashioned Garden*, the head would appear. But it didn't.

"Keep a little in the background," said Miss Chichester to Jane. "Perhaps people will not notice."

"If I can only see where the background is," thought Jane. For she found it even harder to keep her eyes close to the holes cut in her costume than it had been to the real ones in her regular bear head.

Now the heavy curtain rolled up. It didn't stick halfway up as it sometimes did, and Sylvie, Goldilocks, in a blue pinafore and socks, ran out onto the stage midst loud applause. The play had begun! Sylvie had a great deal of acting to do all by herself before the three bears came home. But she wasn't scared. She was used to being on the stage alone.

Jane's heart pounded as she and Joey and Rufus waited for their cue to come home. If only she didn't trip and turn a somersault, for she really could not see very well. Somehow

152

she managed to see out of only one eye at a time. These eye holes must have been cut crooked. One hole kept getting hooked on her nose.

"Now!" Miss Chichester whispered. "Cue! Out with you three bears."

Joe, Jane, and Rufus, the three bears, lumbered out onto the stage. They were never supposed to just walk, always lumber and lope.

The applause was tremendous. It startled the three bears. The Town Hall was packed. Somebody must have sold a lot of tickets.

"There's Mama," said Rufus. He said it out loud.

He wasn't supposed to say anything out loud except about his porridge, his chair, and his bed. But anyway he said, "There's Mama." Jane could not see Mama. Lumbering out onto the stage had dislocated her costume so that now she could not see at all. Fortunately the footlights shone through the brown flannel of her costume so she could keep away from the edge of the stage and not fall off.

The Moffats all knew their lines so well they did not forget them once. The only trouble was they did not have much chance to say them because the applause was so great every time they opened their mouths. At last, however, they reached the act about the three beds. An extra platform had been set up on the stage to look like the upstairs of a three bears' house. The three bears lumbered slowly up the steps.

Suddenly shouts arose all over the Hall:

"Her head! Her head! The middle bear's head!"

"Sh-sh-sh," said others. "See what's going to happen."

As Jane could not see very well she had no idea what these shouts referred to. She had the same head on now that she had had on all during this play so far. Why then all these shouts? Or had she really stayed in the background the way Miss Chichester had asked her to, and the audience had only just discovered about the makeshift?

"Oh," whispered Joey to Jane. "I see it. It's your real bear head, and it's on the top of my bedpost."

153

"O-o-o-h!" said Jane. "Get it down."

"How can I?" said Joe. "With all these people watching me?"

"Try and get it when you punch your bed," urged Jane.

Joey was examining his big bear's bed now. "Hm-m-m," he said fiercely. "Somebody has been lying on my bed. . . ." But he couldn't reach the middle bear's head. He did try. But he couldn't quite reach it, and there was more laughter from the audience.

Jane pulled her costume about until she could see through the eyehole. Ah, there was her head! On the post of the big bear's bed. No wonder people were laughing. What a place for the middle bear's head. Here she was, without it. And there it was, without her. Jane resolved to get it. Somehow or other she would rescue her head before this play was completely over. Now was her chance. It was her turn to talk about her bed. Instead, Jane said,—

"Somebody has been trying on my head, and there it is!"

Jane hopped up on Joey's bed. She grabbed her middle bear head.

"Yes," she repeated. "Somebody has been trying on my head," but as she added, "and here it is!" the safety pins that held her makeshift head together popped open. The audience burst into roars of laughter as Janey's own real head emerged. Only for a second though. For she clapped her middle bear head right on as fast as she could and hopped off the bed. Goodness, she thought, I showed my real face, and I didn't have any paint on it.

Unfortunately Jane still could not see, for she had stuck her bear head on backwards. But the audience loved it. They clapped and they stamped. Bravo! Bravo! Bravo, middle bear! Big boys at the back of the hall put their fingers in their mouths and whistled. And it was a long, long time before Jane could say,—

Somebody has been sleeping in my bed," and the play could go on. At last Rufus discovered Goldilocks in his little bed, and she leaped out of the window. That was the end of the play, and the curtain rolled down.

When the bowing began, Miss Chichester tried to send Jane in backwards, thinking the back of her was the front of her. Fortunately, Rufus held Jane by one paw, and Joey held the other. So she didn't get lost. And the three bears lumbered dizzily on and off many times, sometimes with Sylvie, and sometimes alone. And somebody yelled for "The mysterious middle bear!" It must have been the oldest inhabitant.

Miss Chichester turned Jane's head around for this bow, and at last Jane really did look like a perfect middle bear. Furthermore, she could see out. There was Mama, laughing so hard the tears were rolling down her cheeks. And there was Nancy Stokes with all the Stokeses, and Olga was there. And there was Mr. Buckle beaming up at the stage. Jane bowed and lumbered off the stage. She felt good now. Acting was fun, she thought, especially if you could be disguised in a bear uniform. And this time she had not turned a somersault across the stage as she had the time she was a butterfly. True, she had lost her head. But she had found it. And the show had gone on, the way people always say shows do.

Moreover, the Moffats had nice warm bear pajamas to sleep in for the rest of the winter. Of course they didn't go to bed with the bear heads on. But the rest of the costumes were nice and warm.

Elizabeth Rhodes Jackson

RULE OF THREE

ILLUSTRATED BY *Marguerite Davis*

ONE Fourth of July, we three children and Reginald were left all alone on the island. Of course, Mother wouldn't have deserted us on a holiday except for something very important. It was right after breakfast, and firecrackers were popping all around the lake, when between pops we heard someone shouting and yoo-hooing on the shore.

We looked across, and there was Mr. Bassett, who lives on a farm and brings us vegetables and eggs. So Jack rowed across, and Mr. Bassett had a telegram for Mother.

"Stationmaster said it came last night," he said, "but there wasn't nobody comin' this way, so he kept it till I drove by. But I never thought you'd hear me, with all the cannonadin'."

Jack knew the telegram must be from Daddy, because Daddy hadn't come the night before, when we were expecting him. Mother read it to us: *Aunt Charlotte in Boston tomorrow only. Hopes to see you.*

That meant, of course, that Mother would have to go to Boston.

Aunt Charlotte is our great-aunt, and she's very old. She thinks children should be seen and not heard, and when we are noisy, she says, "Mercy me!"

So we weren't at all happy to think of giving up our Fourth of July on the island to spend the day at a hotel in town trying to be quiet. We told Mother that we'd much rather stay at the lake, and we said we'd be very trustworthy.

"But *Fourth of July!*" said Mother, looking worried. "It's such a dangerous day."

"We'll keep out of danger," Jack promised.

"We won't leave the island," said Beany.

"We can paint our painting books," I suggested.

"We-ll," said Mother reluctantly, and she began to get ready, all the time telling us what not to do while she was gone.

"And when Daddy and I come home," she said, "we'll all have fun doing the firecrackers together." And so Mother went to Boston.

We didn't do anything, of course, that Mother had told us not to. We very carefully didn't do any of the things she said not to do while she was away. We didn't throw stones for Reginald to chase, and we didn't go out in the boat, and we didn't set off a single firecracker. We very carefully didn't set off any firecrackers, because she told us that three times, and it was the last thing that she called to us from the boat.

But she didn't once say, "Don't climb the pine trees."

We sat on the piazza and painted our books and listened to the "pop-pop-pop, bang, boom," all around the lake.

About halfway through the morning, when we were getting tired of painting, Albert rowed across the lake to visit us and brought three packs of firecrackers.

"I thought maybe you didn't have any. I didn't hear any noise over here," he said. "I brought a pack for each of you."

We thanked him very much and showed him our box of fireworks inside the camp and explained that we couldn't set them off till Mother and Daddy came home.

Albert understood and said, "All right. I'll keep these for myself."

He sat on the piazza with us and set them off, one cracker at a time, so they lasted a long while.

"We've got a big flag out, over at our house," he said proudly.

"We have a flag, too," said Beany. "Daddy'll put it up when he comes."

"Let's put it up now," Albert suggested.

So we brought it out and worked for a while trying to set up the pole in the ground. But it would lean sideways!

"I'll tell you where the flag would look best," said Albert. "At the very top of one of the tall pines."

"That's a keen idea," said Jack. "Let's do it."

We looked around for a good pine tree. The trouble with pine trees is that they keep on growing at the tips of the branches, but the lower limbs die and break off. So the big pines all around our camp, about a hundred years old, I guess, grow up straight and tall, higher than a house, before the branches begin, and there's nothing to pull yourself up by.

"I know," said Beany. "Let's climb up to the top of that easy maple that has a branch bending down. Then we can reach the lowest branches of the pine tree and swing across."

He pulled himself up to the low branch of the maple and began to climb.

"You'd better be careful," said Albert. "You're too little to climb that high."

"I'm not!" Beany was indignant. "I always remember the rule of three."

"What you mean, the rule of three?" asked Albert.

"Daddy told it to us," explained Beany. "You have four things to hold on by when you climb a tree—two hands and two feet. And you must always keep three of them holding on, and only reach with one at a time, in case a branch should break."

"That isn't the way monkeys do it," argued Albert. "I've seen them at Franklin Park, and they can swing by one hand."

"They can even swing by a tail," Beany retorted, looking

158

down on Albert from the maple tree. "But we're not monkeys."

Jack was still on the ground. "This other pine tree is taller," he said. "The flag would look better there. And we can reach it, if we get up on the roof and then climb up that oak and then crawl across on that long branch up high there. Only, I can't climb and carry the flag, too."

"I'll carry the flag," I said. "I can reach it up to you and then climb up where you are."

"You can't climb a tree," said Albert. "Girls can't climb trees."

"Of course she can," said Jack. "Dee can climb any tree you ever saw."

He went in for some cord and then got up on the roof by way of the piazza railing, and I reached the flag up to him, and then he gave me a hand, and I got up beside him. Then he climbed the oak tree a little way and waited there till I handed him the flag and climbed up to him. Then I took the flag again, and he went up a little farther, and so we kept going till we were as high as the lowest branch of the big pine. It spread right across to our oak, and we got a foothold on it while we were still holding to the branches of our tree.

After that, it was easy, going up the pine. It was like climbing a ladder, and we took turns climbing and holding the flag. Only, we had to be very careful about dead branches, and Jack said to me, "Don't forget the rule of three."

"Hey, look at me," shouted Beany, from his own tree. "See how high I am!" But I couldn't see him because the pine needles were so thick around me.

Then suddenly, instead of pine needles there was clear sunlight with blue sky overhead, and we had reached the top and were swaying there in the wind!

All around below us were layers of green branches, and beyond, far below, the blue lake and boats like toys and roofs of toy cottages on the shores. Then there was a circle of woods and, beyond that, farms and woodland like a checkerboard, and cutting through them a long white ribbon that was Route One, with little dots moving on it for cars.

Jack pulled the cord out of his pocket. I held the flagpole

steady while he tied it to the very top of the tree, and the flag floated out in the breeze.

Then we came down. Jack went first, because it wasn't so easy as going up, and he could tell me where to find footholds at the hard places.

When we got to the ground, we stood off to see our flag. It looked very beautiful floating out straight against the wide blue sky, and I thought of America, *"beautiful for spacious skies."*

Albert raised his hand in salute and began, *"I pledge allegiance to the flag,"* and Jack and I joined in. We all three stood up very straight and said it all through.

Then Albert said suddenly, "Why, it's raining. I felt a drop on my hand."

We looked up. It wasn't rain. It was tears. Beany was 'way up there, far above us. He had climbed up to his own tall pine by way of the easy maple. He had reached up to a branch too far above his head and had pulled himself up till he was doubled up over it with no foothold, and he was balanced there, seesawing on his stomach.

"Beany must have forgotten the rule of three," said Albert.

"Hold tight!" Jack called. "Don't let go!"

Beany never answered. But some more shiny drops came glittering down.

"Don't let go, Beany!" Jack called again. "I'm coming!"

He went up the maple as fast as he could climb.

"If Beany should let go, we'd have to put the flag at half mast!" said Albert, gloomily.

I couldn't see how Jack was going to get Beany down. I didn't see how Beany could stretch down to get a foothold, unless Jack lifted him off the branch; and Jack couldn't let go of the tree to lift him without losing his own balance.

I stood looking up till my neck ached, watching Jack as he went up, up, that tall pine. Once I heard a branch crack, and he swung his feet quickly over to another branch, and then the broken limb came crashing down. And then he was there, with his hands on the big branch below Beany.

160

I watched him pull himself up till he was kneeling on the branch, holding by his hands to a stump of a limb next to it, so that his back was level like a floor under Beany's feet.

I couldn't hear what he said, they were so far above us. But I saw Beany, still doubled up over the higher branch, fumbling with one foot till he found Jack's back. Then Beany stepped on Jack's bent-over back and straightened himself till he could get his hands on the upper branch and so let his feet down to the lower one.

Jack steadied Beany's feet for him on the lower branch, and when Beany had found his foothold, Jack swung down to the next branch. So they both came safely down again to the maple, Jack coming first, each time finding the easy way for Beany's feet, and then down the maple to the ground.

I just hugged Beany when they got down, and I would have hugged Jack, but I knew he wouldn't like it with Albert there.

Just then we heard our car tooting on the mainland, and we all ran down to the wharf. Mother and Daddy were on the other side, waving to us. They got into the boat that Mother had left on the shore, and Daddy started to row.

Mother leaned forward and said something to him, and he stopped rowing and looked around. Then he and Mother both gazed up at the flag, floating above all the tall pines, the highest thing in sight except the clouds. Then Daddy began to row quite fast, and soon they were at the wharf with all of us crowding around and Reginald barking great shouts of welcome.

Mother explained that Great-aunt Charlotte had had so many people she wanted to see in one day, that Mother had stayed for only a little chat. Then she and Daddy had hurried home so that we could set off our fireworks.

We all came up the walk together, and Mother stopped short. "Why, what's this?" she said in surprise. She was looking at the litter of burnt red paper all over the grass.

"Oh, those were Albert's firecrackers," said Jack.

"He brought them to give to us," I explained.

"But we didn't fire off a single one," said Beany, "because you said not to."

162

"I set them all off myself," explained Albert.

"I see," said Mother.

"How did the flag get up there?" Daddy asked.

"Jack tied it there," said Albert.

"But it was Albert's idea," Jack added, wanting to be generous.

"You mean Jack climbed that tall pine all by himself?" said Mother.

"Oh, no," said Jack quickly. "Dee came up, too, and helped me."

"Mercy me!" said Mother. She sounded like Aunt Charlotte.

"I climbed a tree, too," broke in Beany proudly. "I climbed that one, see? 'Way up to where those two big branches are. But I couldn't get down again, and Jack climbed up so I could stand on his back."

"It was very brave of Jack," I told Mother, "because if Beany had upset his balance, they'd both have fallen."

"There's to be no more climbing pine trees around here," said Daddy in a very firm voice.

"Oh, but Daddy, we'll have to take the flag down," said Jack. "The colors have to be lowered at sunset."

"We can consider that later," said Mother. "How about lunch?"

After lunch we set off the firecrakers. Daddy helped and Mother watched. We had a lot of fun, but before we had quite finished, there was a thunderstorm. So we all went inside the camp and tossed the firecrackers out through the door as we lighted them.

The wind blew terrifically, and in the midst of the thunder and lightning, there was a great crash on the roof. We all thought that a tree had fallen, and we ran out to look. It was our flagpole, blown down by the wind, and there was our flag draped over the chimney, flapping furiously.

So we didn't have to climb the tree to lower the colors after all, and we never have climbed the pines again. We do go up in the maple trees and the oak trees, though.

But sometimes when I'm going to sleep and the wind is blowing, I think for a moment that I'm swaying again at the top of the big pine, with the lake far below. And it seems to me that I can reach up my hand and touch the sky.

Helen Train Hilles

LIVING CHRISTMAS

ILLUSTRATED BY *Keith Ward*

"L ET'S have some sort of binge at Christmas," said Ricky, sticking another marshmallow lazily on the end of the long toasting fork. He really didn't want another marshmallow, but there were so few left it seemed a shame to waste them.

"Like what?" said Jock, suddenly emerging from behind one of the books he'd found in the attic and was rereading. The Sherwood family—Ricky and Jock with their sisters, Twig and little Bumps, and Father and their stepmother Phil, of course —were sitting by the fireplace in the living room of their house in Maine. The room looked exciting and unfamiliar. Snow frosted the edges of the windowpanes. The fire shone in queer lights on the bare floor and on the pieces of furniture that were still done up in white sheets, for the house was only half open for the Christmas holidays.

"Oh, like—like—" Ricky stood up and turned his back on the fire. "Like—a party, with a whole lot of kids—and gobs of Christmasy food, and presents, and slews of contests at different things—"

"We could have a sliding-down-the-hill-on-trays contest!" Jock was on his feet, too, now.

"And a barn dance—" from Twig.

164

"And bobbing for apples!" put in Bumps, who'd come awake. Her eyes shone sleepily. She was hooted down.

"That's Halloween!" said Ricky scathingly.

"We'll each choose our own contests," said Twig, who was feeling peaceful.

"And we'll decorate the whole barn with lights and Japanese lanterns," went on Ricky, as though it were all decided. "And there are millions of kids we can ask. Herb (he was the electrician's son and a great crony of the Sherwoods) and Mazie at the post office, and Tom's nephew, and—"

"And Molasses—you know, who comes on the ice-truck with his father," added Bumps.

"Oh, it'll be swell! A—a community Christmas!" said Jock. Father looked at their shining faces and flashed a quick look at Phil.

"Hold on!" he said. "Who's going to pay for all of this—and do all the work?" He looked pleasant but firm.

"Why I—but you—" began Ricky, a little shamefaced. *He* certainly couldn't do it, because he only had a dollar and thirty-nine cents left from his whole allowance and Christmas presents still unbought. The others all took a deep breath. They'd never thought of that.

"You thought we'd do it," continued Father. "Well, we've already done quite a lot for you. Most of you wanted to leave New York and come up here on your vacation." Here Twig gave him a guilty look. "So we opened the house and lugged you up here—no mean job—and I think we're entitled to a little rest. There's only Tom and his wife to help—and they're busy with their own house and the animals. Besides, it'll be expensive—"

"Not so very," said Ricky slowly. "Just prizes and decorations and food and—" he stopped. It *did* sound a lot when you counted it all up.

"Look here," went on Father. "We don't mean we don't think it's a good idea. We do. We just don't want you to think it's easy as pie—no pun intended—or that it doesn't cost anything. If you *really* want to do it, go ahead. If you'll take on

165

the job and do the work yourselves and give the prizes, Phil and I will provide all supplies, as a joint Christmas present to all of you!"

There was a dead silence. The children realized it was a fair proposition. It was a swell idea, but it *was* a lot of work, and how about going without any other Christmas present? Bumps was the first to speak.

"Molasses would have such a good time. He loves to eat," she said.

"I vote we do!" said Twig suddenly. She'd been the one that had been disagreeable about wanting to stay in the city and go to parties, and she had a guilty conscience.

"And we'll all be sick to death of just us by Christmas," said Jock.

Ricky struggled with himself. It was his own idea, but he had a two-page typewritten list of the things he wanted for Christmas. He looked a little glum. Then:

"Come on!" he said. "Let's go to bed. We've got a heck of a lot of things to do and only a week to do them in!"

The next day fled by, and the only thing that got done was the planning. Tom, the coachman, gave messages to the guests when he went for the mail, and they had twenty-two acceptances by the time he came home, and they kept thinking of more children they wanted to ask.

"It'll be a mob scene!" wailed Twig, whose first attempt at pie had failed dismally that morning.

Everyone went around with a pad, writing down things to be added to Father and Phil's supply list, which was already a small volume.

They were only going to have turkey and mashed turnips and cranberry sauce and candied sweet potatoes and stuffing and rolls and nuts and raisins and three kinds of pies and chocolate cake, which they decided was the very least you could eat. But Twig was a wiser girl when she wrote down the list of all the ingredients they would need just to make these few things!

Then they had to get paper plates and napkins and arrange

166

long tables (made out of clotheshorses and boards). And they almost forgot to put the marshmallows to be toasted and corn to be popped on the Family's list!

Then there was decorating the barn, and filling bags with hard candy—and on top of all that Ricky who always did things wholeheartedly, decided they ought to do something for the Family! It was his idea to decorate Phil's best beloved big pine tree that stood behind the barn and have a living Christmas tree. Even with the help of Herb, who was a wizard at lighting, providing everything wholesale, it took all the money the children had and left them penniless.

"Listen!" said Twig, coming in wearily one afternoon from the kitchen. She'd already burned herself twice, but luckily Dr. Wetherill, who'd taken out Bumps's appendix and was a great friend of the Family, had come to spend Christmas. So the burned places were covered with neat bandages and yellow grease and were the envy of the others. "We've still got to arrange our contests and decide about prizes. I choose the dancing contest—and I'll give a five-dollar bill!"

"For heaven's sakes!" said Ricky, annoyed with her for setting such a high standard, "you must have just got your allowance!"

"Mine's bareback riding," announced Bumps, "and I'll give my Navajo horse blanket." The others stared. It was a new idea.

"I'll take bobbing for apples," said Jock calmly. There couldn't be much preparation for that that he could see. "I will give my rattlesnake hatband." Everyone was impressed.

"Mine'll be the sliding-down-hill-on-trays one," said Ricky.

"What'll you give?" asked Jock.

"Golly, I don't know," said Ricky slowly. "All my Indian junk's at school. I haven't got a thing. I'll have to figure something out. Say, have you seen Herb on a tray? He's the nuts!"

It was Christmas eve. Everything was still far from done. But Father and Tom had crashed through and helped with some of the heavy work. Phil and Tom's wife were giving Twig some help in the kitchen, but she was nobly struggling to do her share.

The party had grown, too. Tony, the Indian who came around selling sweet-grass baskets, had promised to send his son.

And then came the snow. The children glued their faces to the windows and prayed that it would stop in time, so their guests could get through Christmas afternoon.

"Thank heaven, we haven't got those lights up yet on the living Christmas tree!" said Ricky. "They'd be ruined!"

But just before supper the snow stopped and Father said the snowplough would take care of the road.

Everyone was so relieved that he sat down cheerily to that evening's task—filling gay red cheesecloth bags with the hard candy Phil had bought in ten-pound cans.

They sat down on the floor in the barn and soon their hands were all sticky from the bits of hard candy, and they felt mildly ill from all they had eaten.

"I've got to get some air!" said Ricky, and went out. The night was clear and cold, so that Ricky's breath made white clouds. He was filled with peace and Christmas spirit. How beautiful the dark shadow of a tree before him would be to-morrow, sparkling with lights! Great patches of snow clung to it like bought tinsel, weighting down its branches. But he still had to think of a prize he could give. Surely Herb would win it. He wished he had something really nice to give!

There was a faint crash in the woods at his left. It must be just the wind! Another faint crackle. Then silence. Quickly Ricky felt for the flashlight he always carried and advanced bravely into the deep snow. The light fell on unbroken white. And then suddenly the light picked up—could those be the tiny footprints of some animal? He whistled softly and his heart pounded with adventure as he picked his way on. A dark shadow was on the snow and he shifted his flash to it. Then stopped.

A small head, with big soft ears, was sticking out of the snow! It stared at the light out of liquid brown eyes. It give a frantic struggle, but couldn't free itself from the deep snow.

"A deer!" Ricky breathed it softly so as not to frighten the poor thing. He went softly up to it. He patted its head gently.

The deer gave a funny sound, something between a whistle and a snort.

He felt down with his hand and could feel the terrified beating of its heart. He tried to lift it but it was too heavy. It was a soft-colored tan, with no horns and no spots. Though small, it must have been almost a yearling.

Turning quickly, Ricky ploughed back to the barn and threw open the door.

"Dr. Wetherill!" he panted. "There's a deer—caught in a drift—out there—and I think something's wrong with it—come quick!"

"Boy!" said Jock enviously. And then he remembered he'd once had a coyote.

Everyone went out quickly. Father and Dr. Wetherill and the boys dug the animal out. It hung limp as Dr. Wetherill lifted it in his strong arms. Ricky walked close so people would surely realize it was his deer. Bumps struggled along in the deep snow.

"A reindeer!" she breathed. "On Christmas eve!"

"It's not a reindeer. Besides, if it were, it'd be a rein*doe!*" said Ricky, who felt he knew all about deer.

Back in the house Dr. Wetherill laid the doe in the blankets from Ricky's bed and poured some brandy down its throat.

"I'm really not a vet," he laughed, "but I think your doe will be all right. We'll give it warm milk, and if we're gentle with it in a few days it won't be frightened of us. We lose lots of deer this way in the winter. They go out of their yards to forage, and become exhausted, or their little hoofs sink so deep in the snow they can't get out. You mustn't let this one go till the weather's less severe!"

"I'll say we won't!" said Ricky. He fed the deer through cheesecloth dipped in milk, which it sucked. It was too exhausted for anything else and lay limp—in Ricky's blankets, so he had to get others.

But the children knew they had a lot left to do tomorrow, so at last they went to bed.

Ricky awoke when it was still dark. There was something on his mind. Oh, yes, the prize he still had to think of!

The doe stirred softly in her sleep. She was certainly the nicest thing he could think of. But he didn't *want* to give up the doe—his doe that he'd rescued from freezing to death. Would the old wallet do? No, it wouldn't!

Suddenly he buried his head in the pillow to shut out the doe's breathing. He'd give his doe. He felt much better and went to sleep.

Christmas dawned, sparkling. The powdery snow had packed, and after one coast the children realized nothing would have to be done about the hill. Everyone set to and helped with Bumps's race track and before noon it was ready. Ricky kept dashing back to give his doe evergreens and feed it bread with salt, and milk. Twig was frantic in the kitchen. Bumps polished the horses—Dixie and Pam—and Peter Pan, her pony, as high up as she could reach. Herb, who'd been there since before the

170

children were awake, announced the lighting was ready.

Tom had already left to get the guests in the buckboard when the children had a chance to pause, and lunch on milk and sandwiches and Twig's latest failure in cookies.

They'd barely finished when they heard the buckboard! As Tom, driving Pam and Dixie, drove up with the gay load, a cheer went up from the waiting Sherwoods and Dr. Wetherill. And an answering cheer came, sounding above the trotting of the horses.

As dozens of assorted children piled shyly onto the snow, the Sherwoods were in a jitter of excitement. They were bound they were going to be good hosts.

"Won't you take off your coa—no, that's wrong, we'll do the outside things first!" Ricky led the way to Bumps's outside race track. It was really most impressive, the snow having been shoveled away in an oval, and cinders strewn on it. Tom unharnessed Pam and Dixie, and Bumps proudly led up a shining Peter.

Father and Phil and the doctor stood and judged while the children, with screams of laughter, piled onto the horses' backs in turn and tried to trot around the ring. There were a few spills, but nothing serious, and by the time the young son of the livery-stable man had unquestionably won, Ricky decided the ice was broken and everyone was having a good time. And the little boy was delighted with the horse blanket and put it around his shoulders at once.

At that moment a strange Indian boy appeared, coming so softly no one heard him. He had a brown, quiet face and straight black hair.

"How'd you get here?" asked Ricky. "Come on, it's time for my contest."

"I walked," said the boy. Jock stared at him.

"You *walked!*" he said. "How far?"

" 'Bout eight mile," said the boy. "That's nothing." But he didn't seem to like the stir he caused. He seemed quiet and not used to children.

"Come on!" yelled Ricky. He caught up a large black tin

171

tray, already a bit battered, and everyone followed, mystified, to the big hill. "Listen!" he yelled. "We're each going down the hill in turn—sitting on the tray—and Dr. Wetherill'll stand at the bottom with a stop watch and time us—and whoever does it quickest gets the prize—and, boy, it's a wow! Keep in the middle or you'll get stuck in the snow!" There was a good deal of giggling, and no one wanted to go first.

"Come on, Molasses!" called Ricky. But that little boy shook his head.

"No *sir!*" he said. "I ain't a-gonna go down that hill for *no-body!*" Ricky was in despair.

"I tell you—we'll draw lots!" he decided. So they wrote down numbers and pulled them out of a hat. Mary, the postmaster's daughter, went down first, with ear-splitting shrieks, but only got halfway before she capsized in the soft snow over at the side.

Another flying figure leapt down the hill, hair waving, sweater flashing like a red danger signal, arms outstretched.

"Thirty seconds!" shouted Dr. Wetherill, writing it down. The next two failed. One cut his hand. But it was only a scratch, and Dr. Wetherill turned from timekeeper to doctor and fixed it at once.

"Herb!" With expert balance, Herb started down the hill. Ricky held his breath. Herb landed gracefully at the bottom.

"Perfect! Twenty-seven seconds!" Another.

"Twenty-six seconds! No landing! Twenty-five seconds!" Something had happened. Each one that went down—and got there—did it faster!

"I'm last," said Ricky. Suddenly he felt sober.

"Ready, set, *go!*"

He was off in a flash. He hardly knew he was moving, things whizzed by him so fast. The tray bounded over the snow like greased lightning! The cold burned into his face, making tears come to his eyes.

A cheer went up, and above it he could hear Dr. Wetherill's voice calling, "Twenty-four seconds—winner!"

Ricky sat down weakly in the snow.

"Oh, boy!" he giggled weakly. "I keep my doe!" But when

172

he picked up his tray, he saw why it was. The tray was polished till it gleamed, by the many trips down the hill. It was his drawing the last number that had done it.

It was time to go indoors. Already the cold winter sun was setting.

The children and the grownups, too, gave an "Ah" of admiration when they saw the barn lit up with colored lights and hung with corn, tinsel, and bunches of gourds. And they gazed with interest at the long, crepe-paper covered tables against the wall.

The children's faces were so cold that the water in which they bobbed for apples felt postively warm! The gurgles they gave pursuing the apples filled the barn with cheery, underwater sounds. Unexpectedly, it was the dignified Herb that won Jock's rattlesnake hatband. He had a method of following an apple with his nose, then pouncing on it with a sharp click of his jaws, sort of like an alligator. Though Molasses didn't win, he sat happily on the floor, eating an apple.

It was Ricky who saw that the Indian boy was being very silent. He didn't seem to be having a good time.

"Would—would you like to see my doe?" he asked. The boy nodded and followed him silently over to the house. Ricky softly opened the door to his room. The doe scrambled to her feet and stood trembling. Ricky started to close the door but the Indian boy motioned to him not to. Advancing so quietly that you could only see he was moving by the space there was left on the carpet, he inched towards the doe. When he had almost reached her a soft chk-chk came from—was it her throat or the boy's? Ricky stood stock still. There was something thrilling about the lean boy and the wild creature there together.

"They're sort of alike," thought Ricky, a lump coming into his throat. "They understand each other." The doe and this strange boy who had walked eight miles and gotten nothing in the contests.

"You can have her," he breathed softly. "When she gets well."

The Indian boy's breath drew in sharply. He didn't say "Thank you," but his eyes, when he spoke, looked a little like the doe's.

"I'll come for her," he said. Ricky was somehow satisfied.

Back in the barn, Twig was frantic about the dancing contest.

"I forgot about music!" she wailed. "I was thinking so hard about food!" Tom, the coachman, came forward. He was even redder than his usual weatherbeaten face.

"I'll go git my accordion!" he said. He was back in a jiffy. His music was satisfyingly loud and the rhythm perfect.

"Everybody dance!" shouted Dr. Wetherill. Father and Phil started in with an Irish jig. Soon everyone was dancing or hopping, or whatever he could do.

Suddenly there was a whoop and Molasses streaked to the center of the floor. His feet twinkled, his arms shook. The little boy was part of his strange, rhythmic dance.

Gradually everyone stood back and watched and soon they were clapping their hands in time to his dance. Twig walked up to him.

"Here!" she said, and handed him the stiff five-dollar bill.

Molasses stopped still in his tracks, and stood motionless. His round eyes bulged. He grabbed the bill.

174

"Oh, boy! Oh, boy!" he yelled. Suddenly he had burst into his dance again.

It was time for supper. Steaming platters and napkin-covered dishes came in on the arms of Phil, Tom's wife, and Twig. The children could hardly wait to get to the tables, but were too polite to start before they were told. Twig came in again, last —carrying a large platter.

"It's fudge!" she said anxiously. "My pies *wouldn't* turn out, so there are only six—so I made fudge instead."

There was a dead silence in the room while the children ate —the right kind of silence. In what seemed a minute there was nothing left on the table at all.

"Now," said Ricky mysteriously, his mouth still full, "There's something else. Follow me! Where's Herb?" Everyone followed him out to behind the barn.

"Now!" yelled Ricky. At once the snow was flooded with a

blaze of multi-colored lights and the outlines of the great tree flamed gayly down at them.

"Ah!" burst from the crowd of children and grownups. Phil spoke first.

"For us!" she guessed. "Our tree. Oh, children, there's nothing lovelier you could have done!"

Now everyone was grabbing the red candy bags off the tree, and almost at once it was time to go home. The guests all piled into the buckboard, packages in hand, saying they'd never had a better time.

"Where's the Indian boy?" asked Father, looking around. He had vanished—disappeared as silently as he had come. But Ricky wasn't worried.

"He's gone," he said softly, "but he'll be back."

The Sherwoods were left alone, standing under the lighted tree.

"How about it? Was it worth it, children?" asked Phil.

"Yes!" chorused four slightly hoarse but happy voices.

"Shall we tell them?" Phil asked Father. He nodded.

"This was your Christmas, as we agreed," said Phil. "We've nothing for you to unwrap. But this is a good time to tell you some nice things that are going to happen. Twig, you've more housework ahead. Daisy and Bob and Joe get here tomorrow, to spend a week with you!"

Twig gulped speechlessly. What she had most wanted!

"Boys," Father was speaking. "I'm going to take you on a salmon-fishing trip this summer. Just us, no women." He smiled. "Bumps," he finished, "Uncle John wants you back for a visit to England. He's coming over for you this spring."

No one spoke. No one could. All the things they had wanted most! A strange kind of Christmas, all round—nicer than the unwrapping kind.

"It's the best Christmas I ever had," said Ricky, as they stumbled back to the house. "But I've simply got to go to bed!"

Beverly Cleary

ELLEN'S SECRET

ILLUSTRATED BY *Louis Darling*

ELLEN TEBBITS was in a hurry. As she ran down Tillamook Street with her ballet slippers tucked under her arm, she did not even stop to scuff through the autumn leaves on the sidewalk. The reason Ellen was in a hurry was a secret she would never, never tell.

Ellen was a thin little girl, with dark hair and brown eyes. She wore bands on her teeth, and her hair was scraggly on the left side of her face, because she spent so much time reading and twisting a lock of hair around her finger as she read. She had no brothers or sisters and, since Nancy Jane had moved away from next door, there was no one her own age living on Tillamook Street. So she had no really best friend. She did not even have a dog or cat to play with, because her mother said animals tracked in mud and left hair on the furniture.

Of course Ellen had lots of friends at school, but that was not the same as having a best friend who lived in the same neighborhood and could come over to play after school and on Saturdays. Today, however, Ellen was almost glad she did not have a best friend, because best friends do not have secrets from one another. She was sure she would rather be lonely the rest of her life than share the secret of why she had to get to her dancing class before any of the other girls.

The Spofford School of the Dance was upstairs over the Payless Drugstore. When Ellen came to the entrance at the side of the building, she paused to look anxiously up and down the street. Then, relieved that she saw no one she knew, she

177

scampered up the long flight of steps as fast as she could run. There was not a minute to waste.

She pushed open the door and looked quickly around the big, bare room. Maybe her plan was really going to work after all. She was the first pupil to arrive.

Ellen's teacher, Valerie Todd Spofford, was looking at some music with Mrs. Adams, the accompanist, at the piano in the corner of the room. She was really Mrs. John Spofford and had a son named Otis, who was in Ellen's room at school. Because she taught dancing, people did not call her Mrs. John Spofford. They called her by her full name, Valerie Todd Spofford.

"Good afternoon, Ellen," she said. "You're early."

"Good afternoon, Mrs. Spofford," answered Ellen, and hurried past the long mirrors that covered one wall.

When Ellen opened the dressing-room door, she made a terrible discovery. Someone was in the dressing room ahead of her.

Austine Allen was sitting on a bench lacing her ballet slippers. Austine was a new girl, both in the dancing class and in Ellen's room at school. Ellen knew she had just come from California, because she mentioned it so often. She thought the

178

new girl looked good-natured and untidy, but she really had not paid much attention to her.

"Oh," said Ellen. "Hello. I didn't know anyone was here."

"I guess I'm early," said Austine and then added, "but so are you."

The girls looked at each other. Ellen noticed that Austine had already changed into the required costume of the Spofford School of the Dance. This was a short full skirt of tulle gathered onto a sateen top that had straps over the shoulders. Austine looked chubby in her green costume.

Neither girl spoke. Oh, why doesn't she leave, thought Ellen desperately. Maybe if I wait long enough she'll go into the other room. Ellen removed her jacket as slowly as she could. No, I can't wait. The others will be here any minute.

"This is a silly costume we have to wear," said Austine. "When I took ballet lessons in California we always wore shorts and T shirts."

"Well, I think it's pretty," said Ellen, as she took her pink costume from the rack along the wall. Why don't you go away, she thought. She said, "It's almost like real ballerinas wear. When I'm wearing it, I pretend I'm a real dancer."

Austine stood up. "Not even real ballerinas practice in full skirts like these. They wear leotards. In California . . ."

"Well, I think leotards are ugly," interrupted Ellen, who was glad she knew that leotards were long tight-fitting garments. "They look just like long underwear, and I wouldn't wear one for anything. I like our dresses better."

"I don't," said Austine flatly. "I don't even like dancing lessons. At least in California . . ."

"I don't care what anybody does in California," said Ellen crossly. "I'm tired of hearing you talk about California and so is everyone at school. So there! If you think California is so wonderful, why don't you go back there?"

For a second Austine looked hurt. Ellen almost thought she was going to cry. Instead she made a face. "All right for you!" she said, and flounced out of the dressing room, leaving her clothes in an untidy heap on the bench.

Instantly Ellen was sorry. What a terrible thing to say to a new girl! What if she herself were a new girl and someone had said that to her? How would she have felt? She hadn't really meant to be rude, but somehow it had slipped out. She was so anxious to have Austine leave that she had not thought about what she was saying.

But now that Austine was gone and Ellen was alone, there was not a moment to waste, not even in feeling sorry for what she had done. Feverishly she unbuttoned her sweater. She was starting to unfasten her dress when she heard some of the girls coming through the classroom.

Frantically Ellen looked around the dressing room for a place to hide. She darted behind the costume rack. No, that wouldn't do. The girls might see her when they took down their costumes.

Snatching her pink dancing dress from the bench, Ellen dashed across the room and into the janitor's broom closet, just as the girls came into the room.

If only there were some way of locking the closet door from the inside! Ellen stood silent and rigid. When no one came near the door, she relaxed enough to look around by the light of the window high in the closet. She could see brooms, a mop and buckets, and a gunny sack full of sweeping compound.

Careful not to knock over the brooms and buckets, she leaned against the door to listen. She could hear Linda and Janet and Barbara. Then she heard Betsy come in and, after a few minutes, Amelia and Joanne. Ellen counted them off on her fingers. Yes, they were all there.

Trying to move carefully so she wouldn't bump into any-thing, she took off first her starched plaid dress and then her slip. But she was so nervous that she knocked over a broom. She stood terrified and motionless until she realized that the girls were chattering so noisily they did not hear the thud. If one of the girls had opened the door at that moment, they all would have learned her terrible secret.

Ellen was wearing woolen underwear.

She was wearing a high-necked union suit that buttoned

down the front and across the back. It did have short sleeves and short legs, so it could have been worse. Ellen didn't know what she would have done if her mother had made her wear long underwear.

With trembling fingers she slipped her arms out of the despised garment, rolled it as flat as she could down to her waist, and pulled the elastic of her panties over the bulge. Quickly she slipped into her costume.

"I wonder where Ellen is," she heard someone ask.

"I don't know," someone answered. "Maybe she isn't coming today."

Ellen was limp with relief. She was safely in her costume. No one had seen her in her underwear. Nobody could tease her and tell her she was old-fashioned because, besides being the only girl in the third grade who had to wear winter underwear, she was the only girl in the whole school who did.

She took off her shoes and socks, laced her slippers, and waited, shivering, until all the girls left the dressing room. Then she slipped out of the closet and, after piling her clothes neatly on a bench, joined the others in the classroom.

A couple of girls were running and sliding the length of the room, and others were practicing at the exercise bar that was built along the mirror-covered wall. All the girls stopped when Ellen appeared.

"Well, where did you come from?" asked Linda Mulford.

"The dressing room," answered Ellen briefly, as she took hold of the bar and began to practice a circular movement of one leg that Mrs. Spofford called a *rond de jambe*. She felt uncomfortable, because all the girls were looking at her. She hoped the bulge around her middle did not show.

"I didn't see you," said Amelia.

Ellen pretended to be so interested in rotating her leg that she didn't hear. If she kept moving, maybe no one would notice the goose flesh on her bare shoulders.

"I didn't see you either," said Joanne. "Where were you?"

"Oh, I was there," said Ellen vaguely. "You just didn't see me."

She twirled her leg faster. Then she looked in the mirror and saw Austine watching her. Ellen felt sorrier than ever for what she had said, because Austine looked so unhappy. She was practicing alone at the end of the bar and none of the other girls were talking to her.

Valerie Todd Spofford walked to the center of the room. "All right, girls," she said. "Let's get in line in front of the mirror."

The girls stood several feet apart, in a row. Ellen was careful not to stand near Austine, who, she could tell by looking in the mirror, remained at the end of the line.

Valerie Todd Spofford stood in front of the girls with her back to the mirror. "Now, girls, we will go through the five positions of the ballet. Remember, ballet dancing is based on these positions. To be good dancers we must learn them perfectly. First position." She stood with her heels together and her toes turned out, and held her arms slightly out from her sides. The girls imitated her as she looked critically up and down the line.

"Knees together, Joanne," she corrected. "Turn your toes farther out, Amelia. That's right, Linda. Splendid!"

Ellen was careful to do everything exactly right, because she did not want Mrs. Spofford to call attention to her. The five positions of the ballet were easy for her, because she practiced them every night before she went to bed. Now, as she pointed her toes and held out her arms, she thought more and more about what she had said to Austine. What a terrible person she was to make a new girl unhappy! Again she looked in the mirror at Austine and thought how lonely she looked, standing at the end of the line a little apart from the other girls.

Ellen knew what it felt like to be lonely, because she had been lonely herself since Nancy Jane had moved away. Maybe Austine sat on her front steps and wished she had someone to play with. Maybe she hoped someone in the dancing class would ask her to come over after school. The very least Ellen could do was to be friendly. She made up her mind to tell Austine she was sorry the first chance she had.

"Fourth position," said Mrs. Spofford. "No, Janet. We do not raise both arms over our head in the fourth position." She walked over to Janet and arranged her arms so that one was circled over her head and the other was held out from her side.

Here was Ellen's chance! When she saw that Valerie Todd Spofford was not watching the whole class, she slipped out of her place in line, darted behind several of the girls, and stepped into line beside Austine, where she quickly assumed a perfect fourth position.

"Austine," she whispered, "I'm sorry I said what I did. I really didn't mean it. Honestly, I didn't."

"Ellen," said Mrs. Spofford sharply, "have you forgotten that we do not whisper during our dancing lesson?"

"No, Mrs. Spofford," said Ellen.

"All right, girls. Fourth position again!"

Ellen arranged her arms and legs in the correct position once more. Mrs. Spofford was watching, so Ellen could not catch Austine's eye in the mirror. Had Austine forgiven her? She couldn't tell, but she hoped so. The more she thought about the new girl, the more she wanted her for a friend.

It was not until Valerie Todd Spofford asked the girls to assume the fifth position that Ellen felt her underwear slip. Oh my, she thought, what am I going to do now? How can I hold it up when I have to raise my hands over my head? Carefully she arranged her feet and lifted her arms to form a circle. The underwear slid alarmingly.

As she stood in the fifth position, Ellen heard someone running up the long flight of stairs. When the footsteps neared the classroom, she heard a jingling sound. Oh dear, thought Ellen. That sound could mean only one person—Otis Spofford.

Most of the boys and many of the girls at school owned a cowboy hat or neckerchief. Several even had boots, but Otis was the only one who owned a pair of real spurs that jingled when he walked.

Now he burst into the room, the spurs on his tennis shoes clinking against the hardwood floor. "Hey, Mom," he demanded, "can I have a dime?"

184

"Otis dear, you are interrupting the lesson," answered his mother, as the girls lowered their arms and turned to look at him. "All right, girls, let us do the fifth position again."

Ellen carefully arranged her feet so that the heel of one foot touched the toe of the other foot. Then, just before she raised her arms to form a circle over her head, she gave her underwear a quick hitch.

Looking into the mirror to see if the bulge showed, she saw that Otis was standing directly behind her. He too arranged his feet, made a hitching motion, and raised his arms. At the same time he blew a huge bubble with his gum.

Ellen was horrified. What if Otis guessed her trouble! She was even more horrified when she felt her underwear slipping again. Quickly she put her hand on her hip.

Otis put his hand on his hip.

Ellen raised her arm again. The underwear slid still more.

Otis raised his arm again and blew another bubble.

"Now, girls, we will go through the positions once more. First position," said Mrs. Spofford.

Ellen set her heels together and turned her toes out. She gave her sliding underwear a discreet tug before she held her arms out from her sides.

Otis turned his toes out, tugged, and held his arms out from his sides.

Ellen turned and whispered fiercely, "Otis! You go away!"

Otis looked cross-eyed at Ellen and blew another bubble with his gum.

"Ellen Tebbits," said Mrs. Spofford, "I have already spoken to you about whispering in class."

"I'm sorry, Mrs. Spofford," replied Ellen.

"Second position," said Mrs. Spofford.

Ellen had been pressing her knees tightly together to keep her underwear from slipping. Now she grasped it again, at the same time trying to feel through her costume for the elastic of her panties, and yanked it into place. She could tell that her underwear had come unrolled. Then she held her arms out from her sides.

185

Miserable because she could do nothing to stop Otis, Ellen watched him in the mirror. He copied her movements exactly.

By this time all the girls were watching Ellen and Otis in the mirror. Ellen knew they could not help seeing how thick she was around the middle.

"Third position," said Mrs. Spofford.

Ellen was determined not to tug at her underwear again. Surely it could not fall any farther. She moved as carefully as she could, but once more the underwear slid. Ellen had to grab it and pull it into place.

This time the girls giggled when Otis imitated her. Ellen swallowed and blinked her eyes to keep from crying. Why did Otis have to pick on her? Why couldn't he tease someone else?

Then, to her amazement, Austine spoke out loud. "Otis Spofford! You stop bothering us," she said loudly.

Everyone was startled, because no one ever talked out loud during a ballet lesson. The girls stopped looking at Ellen and stared at Austine. Ellen gave her underwear a good hard tug while no one was watching. Was Austine really trying to keep Otis from teasing her? If only Ellen knew for sure.

"I'm sorry, Mrs. Spofford," said Austine. "Otis is bothering me so I can't do the steps right."

"Otis dear," said Mrs. Spofford, "you know Mother doesn't like her boy to come into the studio while she is giving a lesson."

"Can I have a dime?" asked Otis.

"Mother is busy now, Otis," said Valerie Todd Spofford. "All right, girls. Let's do our exercises at the bar."

Otis clinked across the floor to the piano, where he leaned over the keyboard and amused himself by blowing bigger and bigger bubbles with his gum.

After the exercises at the bar, Mrs. Spofford had the girls practice the Dance of the Falling Leaves while Mrs. Adams played *Rhapsody of Autumn* on the piano and glared at Otis.

Every time Ellen leaped, her underwear slipped. After each leap she had to clutch it and pull it into place. In the mirror she could see that she looked more and more bulgy. Leap and

186

clutch, leap and clutch. Ellen thought they would never finish being falling leaves.

When Mrs. Adams came to the end of *Rhapsody of Autumn,* Otis added to the tune by picking out "Shave and a haircut— six bits" on the bass keys of the piano. Mrs. Adams was annoyed, but Otis looked pleased when the girls giggled. Ellen was glad he had found someone else to tease.

Mrs. Spofford did not pay any attention to Otis. "Once more, girls," she said.

Then it was leap and clutch, leap and clutch again. Ellen stayed as far away from Otis as she could and hoped he would continue to bother Mrs. Adams.

Finally Valerie Todd Spofford clapped her hands for attention. "Ellen Tebbits," she said. "I think you have forgotten. Falling leaves do not put their hands on their hips. They flutter their arms slowly and gracefully." She fluttered her arms slowly and gracefully.

"Yes, Mrs. Spofford," said Ellen miserably. Usually her dancing was praised.

"Try to watch the way Linda dances and think of falling leaves. Think what falling leaves feel like."

"Yes, Mrs. Spofford," answered Ellen, telling herself glumly that she was too busy thinking about falling underwear to think about falling leaves. She noticed Barbara glance at her waistline and whisper something to Amelia.

"All right, Mrs. Adams. We will take it from *tum tum te tum.*" Mrs. Spofford hummed a few bars of *Rhapsody of Autumn.*

The girls leaped and fluttered their arms. By making short awkward leaps, Ellen managed not to clutch her underwear. Then to Ellen's horror, Otis suddenly bounded onto the floor with a loud jangle of spurs. Leaping and clutching, he began to dance beside Ellen. But Otis did not come down lightly on his toes like a falling leaf. He landed with a flat-footed thud. His spurs made more noise that way.

The girls began to snicker. Ellen stopped dancing, but Otis went on leaping and clutching. She could see that he knew the Dance of the Falling Leaves as well as she did. I wish he would trip on his spurs, she thought crossly.

Then Ellen noticed Austine lengthen her leaps. She could not help thinking that Austine did not look a bit like a falling leaf. She was out of breath, and she did not flutter gracefully. She flapped.

When Austine caught up with Otis, who was making an extra-long leap, she suddenly sprang sideways. They collided in mid-air and both sat down hard on the slippery floor.

188

"Ouch," said Austine loudly, as everyone stopped dancing. "Mrs. Spofford, Otis bumped into me."

"I did not," said Otis. "You jumped in front of me."

"Well, you weren't supposed to be there," said Austine, as she stood up and rubbed herself. "Was he, Mrs. Spofford?"

"Otis, run along and play like a good boy," said Valerie Todd Spofford.

"Can I have a dime if I go?" asked Otis, untangling his spurs and standing up.

"All right, just this once." Mrs. Spofford took a dime from her purse on the piano and handed it to her son. Otis made a face at the girls and ran out of the room, the jingle of his spurs growing fainter as he ran down the steps. Ellen sighed with relief.

"Once more, girls," said Valerie Todd Spofford.

Austine smiled triumphantly at Ellen, who gratefully returned her smile. Austine had bumped into Otis on purpose! Ellen knew now for sure that Austine had forgiven her and wanted to be friends. She was very glad, but she began to worry about getting into the broom closet without being seen by the other girls. And what about Austine? Now that they were friendly, she would expect Ellen to talk to her in the dressing room. The lesson certainly could not last much longer, so Ellen danced her way nearer the dressing-room door.

Finally Mrs. Spofford clapped her hands. "Girls, before I dismiss the class I have a little announcement to make," she said. "Next week members of all my classes are going to give a program for the soldiers and sailors in the Veterans Hospital. I should like to have some of you girls put on your little Dance of the Falling Leaves. It is such a sweet dance and it is so appropriate for this time of year, I am sure the men will enjoy it. Those of you who think your mothers will let you go, please give me your names before you leave."

Ellen thought it would be wonderful to dance on a real stage with a real live audience just like a grown-up ballerina. She knew she would dance so beautifully that she would be called

189

back for encore after encore. Eagerly she crowded up to Mrs. Spofford with the rest of the girls.

Then she remembered her underwear. She wanted so much to dance at the Veterans Hospital that she was almost willing to risk having the girls find out about her underwear. Almost, but not quite. She wiggled out of the group of girls, ran across the polished floor, and darted into the empty dressing room. Snatching her street clothes from the bench, she flung open the door of the broom closet. Then she stopped, astounded at what she saw.

Austine Allen was already in the broom closet.

Ellen could not believe her eyes. Austine was wearing woolen underwear.

"Shut the door!" ordered Austine.

Ellen stood with her mouth open. Austine's high-necked underwear buttoned down the front and across the back just like hers.

"Didn't you hear me? Shut the door!"

"Do you—do you wear woolen underwear, too?" asked Ellen, still not believing what she saw.

"Shut the door," ordered Austine for the third time, as she yanked her slip over her head. She poked her head through the slip and said crossly, "Yes, I do."

By now Ellen had her wits about her. She joined Austine in the broom closet and closed the door. "And I thought I was the only girl in the whole school who had to wear it," she said, and sat down on the bag of sweeping compound.

"And I thought I was the only one," said Austine, "until I watched you in the mirror. I sort of thought that was why you looked so bumpy around the waist."

"That old Otis Spofford makes me so mad," said Ellen. "Do you suppose he really guessed? I don't know what I'd have done if you hadn't spoken right out loud like you did." As she hastily stood up again and began to change her clothes, Ellen smiled at Austine. "Promise you won't tell anybody," she begged.

"I promise if you promise," said Austine. "My mother makes

me wear the old stuff because she says it's so much colder here than it is in California."

"I promise," agreed Ellen. "Mother says I have to wear it because I'm thin and catch cold easily. I'd just die if anyone at school knew about it."

"Me too," said Austine.

"How did you keep yours from slipping?" asked Ellen.

"I brought a string and tied it around my waist. Sh-h-h. Here they come."

"We'll have to stay here until they go," whispered Ellen. Both girls dressed quickly and silently. Then, as they waited, they listened to the other girls chatter.

"Where are Austine and Ellen?" they heard Joanne say. "I didn't see them leave."

"I didn't either," said Linda, "and I just know Ellen wasn't in here before the lesson. I wonder where she came from."

"She couldn't have come from any place but here," said Barbara. "Say, where does that door go?"

"That's just the janitor's closet."

"I'll bet they're in there," said Linda, and flung open the door. "There you are!" she exclaimed triumphantly. "What are you doing in there?"

Ellen and Austine looked at each other and began to giggle.

"Oh, we were just hiding," said Austine.

"We just wanted to see if you would miss us," added Ellen. "Come on, Austine, let's go home." She wasn't going to give the others a chance to ask any more questions.

When they were out on the sidewalk, Austine asked timidly, "Do I really talk about California too much?"

Ellen was embarrassed. "Well, you do talk about it quite a lot, but I shouldn't have said anything. I guess I was just worried about someone finding out about my underwear."

"I suppose I do talk about California a lot," said Austine slowly, "but I miss it—all the kids I used to play with there and everything. Here it rains all the time, and I have to stay in the house a lot, and anyway there isn't anyone in my block to play with."

191

"There isn't anyone in my block to play with, either. I live on Tillamook Street. Where do you live?"

"On Forty-first next to the house with the little gnomes in the frontyard."

"I know where that is," exclaimed Ellen. "I like to walk past there and look at the gnomes. I like the one with the spade best."

"He's my favorite, too," agreed Austine. "Second best I like the one with the wheelbarrow."

Ellen thought a minute. "You live only two blocks from my house. Just down the street and around the corner."

"Do I?" Austine was delighted. "Maybe you could come over sometime. Why don't you come home with me now? My mother could phone your mother."

"I'd love to. I'm sure Mother would let me if your mother phones."

"And we can bake brownies," said Austine.

Ellen was impressed. "Do you know how to bake brownies?"

"Sure. I bake them all the time. My brother eats so many they don't last long at our house."

"I can make pudding out of a package," said Ellen, "but I can't do anything hard like brownies. There are eggs in brownies, aren't there?"

"Just two."

Ellen was even more impressed. "My mother let me break an egg once. I hit it on the edge of a bowl just like she does, but when I tried to break it in two, I stuck my thumbs into the yolk and messed it all up."

"I know what," said Austine. "You crack the nuts, and I'll break the eggs and do the rest."

"Swell," agreed Ellen. "I'm good at cracking nuts."

The girls smiled at each other. "You know something?" said Ellen. "I don't mind this awful underwear half so much, now that I know I'm not the only one in school who has to wear it."

"Isn't it funny?" said Austine. "That's just the way I feel."

Margery Williams Bianco

DOLLY JOINS THE CIRCUS

ILLUSTRATED BY *Florence and Margaret Hoopes*

MR. MORELLI stood outside his barn, his hands in his pockets, staring up at the poster on the wall. It was a big poster, and it took up nearly the whole side of the barn. It showed elephants and horses and a tiger, and a lady in bright pink tights jumping through a flaming hoop. In huge letters across the top it said:

WHEELER'S CIRCUS

THE BIGGEST SHOW ON EARTH

In a corner of the empty lot where the barn stood, under the shade of the single oak tree that grew there, Dolly stood drowsing. Dolly belonged to Mr. Morelli. Every morning when Mr. Morelli went round with his milk bottles, Dolly pulled the wagon for him. The rest of the time she had very little to do. The milk route was only a part of Mr. Morelli's business. He had also a small shop in town where he sold fruit and vegetables and Italian groceries.

Dolly was old and very gentle, and blind in one eye. No one, not even Mr. Morelli himself, knew just how old she was. Her mane was ragged; her good eye gazed at one sleepily through thick white lashes. Her white coat had yellowish and grayish marks on it where the harness had rubbed and stained it, and just over her shoulders there was quite a bald spot. But Johnny and Emma, who lived next door to Mr. Morelli's barn and spent a great deal of their time playing in the lot, thought she was a very wonderful horse.

For one thing she looked so wise and sensible, as if she understood everything that was said to her. Nothing ever startled her. If they were playing ball, and the ball rolled between Dolly's feet, she would just look down and stand perfectly still while

193

they crawled under her to pick it up. She had a broad and comfortable back, and when she stood close to the fence it was quite easy to climb up and sit there. Dolly never minded. She seemed to like having people on her back.

Mr. Morelli was still staring up at the poster when the children came in this morning. Johnny and Emma looked at the poster too, though they already knew it by heart. There was a smaller one, just like it, in the window of Tony's barber-shop across the way, and they could see it every time they looked across from their front porch, which made matters all the worse. If it hadn't been for that poster they might have been able to forget about the circus altogether, and pretend that today was just like any other day. But not with the tiger and the elephant and the pink lady staring them right in the face, like that!

Mr. Morelli turned around so suddenly that it made them jump. He pointed with his thumb.

"Circus!" he said cheerfully. "You goin' to the circus, huh?

194

Your pa got lots of money; you tell him to take you. Everybody go to the circus. No?"

That was just Mr. Morelli's joke. Mr. Morelli knew just as well as Johnny and Emma that there was no money this year for circus tickets. He was just being funny. Mr. Morelli smiled, and Johnny smiled back, but he thought that Mr. Morelli had queer ideas about what was funny and what wasn't. Having no money for the circus was not funny at all.

"I guess we aren't going," Johnny said.

"No spend money, huh?" returned Mr. Morelli, every bit as cheerfully as before. "Circus cost two, three dollars, what for? If I want to see circus, I look at the picture. Picture don't cost nothing!"

Mr. Morelli laughed, a deep rumbling laugh, and patted Johnny on the back. Johnny wriggled. Mr. Morelli's pat was as hearty as his laugh.

The children stared at the poster. It said "July 23." Today was July 23. Down in the big meadow behind the railway station the tents were up this very minute. There would be all the gilded wagons stretched in line, the peanut stands, and the lemonade and candy stalls. If one shut one's eyes and imagined very hard, one could almost smell the sawdust and the elephants.

"Goodness," said Emma. "I should think you'd go to the circus if you got a chance!"

"Me?" asked Mr. Morelli. He looked surprised. "I gotta work! I gotta haul potatoes. No sooner one thing done, you got another. The day I haul potatoes, Dolly she must loossa the shoe! Now I gotta take Dolly to the blacksmith. Some day I sell Dolly. I buy a car! Car run all the time!"

More than once when Dolly lost a shoe, or caught cold in winter, Mr. Morelli had uttered this awful threat, which always terrified the children. Emma cried now, "Oh, Mr. Morelli, you wouldn't sell Dolly!"

But Johnny had another idea. He began to hop up and down, tugging at Mr. Morelli's arm.

"Mr. Morrelli, let me take Dolly to the blacksmith! I can

195

take her. I did once. I can ride her down! Mr. Morelli, let me ride her down!"

Mr. Morelli pulled his arm away and began to rub his chin. He really was busy, although he didn't look it. Taking Dolly to the blacksmith meant a whole hour of his time. It was no pleasure to him to take Dolly there, but it would be a lot of pleasure to Johnny. Mr. Morelli was a good-natured man, as well as a busy one. He said, "If you ride that horse, you fall off and then everybody blame it on me!"

"They won't! I shan't fall off. Me an' Emma, we've ridden Dolly lots of times. Mr. Morelli, please!"

"I ain't got no saddle," said Mr. Morelli.

But he moved off toward the tree where Dolly was standing. The children followed him. Dolly was not pleased to be interrupted in her quiet daydreaming. But she trailed obediently back to the barn where Mr. Morelli took hold of her halter, switching her tail and stepping slowly with her big hoofs.

Mr. Morelli began to search among the odds and ends in the barn. There was no blanket, but he found an old black woolen quilt that he used in winter to pack over the milk bottles, and he folded this in a square pad across Dolly's broad back and then strapped it on. He took a rope and tied the two ends to Dolly's halter, one on each side, to make reins; she didn't need any bit.

Johnny scrambled up, climbing by the feed-chest. Mr. Morelli lifted Emma up behind, where she could hold on with both arms round Johnny's waist. He led Dolly out through the yard and opened the gate.

"Now you walk that horse slow, and when you get to the blacksmith you leave her there an' you say Mr. Morelli he come to fetch her. And don't you fall off. Giddap, Dolly!"

Dolly giddaped. She moved off at a slow, easy walk. Riding her was rather like riding a table, except that it was farther from the ground.

Mr. Morelli watched them a little way down the road, before he crossed over to take the short cut that led to his store. He felt quite easy in his mind. Dolly was a very steady horse.

196

Nothing—not even a fire engine—could frighten her, and it was most unlikely that she would attempt to trot. Only on very rare occasions could even Mr. Morelli himself persuade Dolly to trot.

Perhaps if Mr. Morelli had known what was going to happen he would not have strolled back to the vegetable store quite so calmly.

There were two ways of going to the blacksmith's. One way was quite short and only took a few minutes. The other way was a great deal longer. It meant going down the road as far as the church and then making a circle back again. Johnny chose the longer way.

Dolly kept to a steady walk, taking the side of the road where the ground was soft. Johnny held tight to the rope halter and Emma held tight to Johnny's belt from behind. They hardly joggled at all.

They reached the church and turned the corner. It was as they were going along this next bit of road that Dolly suddenly stopped.

She had heard something.

It was music, the kind of music that Dolly had not heard for a great many years. The children heard it, too, and knew at once what it was. It was the circus parade just turning into Main Street.

Dolly's ears pricked, and she seemed to stiffen all over. Her head went up, and the next moment she broke into a trot.

Emma cried, "She's running away! She's running away!"

But Dolly was not acting like a runaway horse. She was acting like a horse that knew exactly where she wanted to go and was very anxious to get there just as soon as possible. Her trot quickened, but it was a steady comfortable trot. After the first moment of surprise, Johnny and Emma found that it was not so very much harder than walking, as long as they held on tightly. Her ears pointed straight ahead, and she sniffed as she went. Johnny tugged at the halter, but he might as well have been tugging at a brick wall for all the attention that Dolly paid to him.

The music grew louder. People were staring from their doorways; boys ran along the sidewalk, hurrying to see the parade. Nobody seemed to see anything strange in a big white horse trotting down the road with two children on her back. Perhaps they all thought that Johnny and Emma were just hurrying to get there, too.

Dolly trotted faster and faster. She turned one corner after another, until suddenly the music blared out louder than ever. There was a tramping of feet and a glitter of red and gold wheels, and almost before Johnny and Emma knew just what was happening there they were right in the very middle of the parade itself, between the band wagon and the clown with his two black mules!

And there Dolly settled down to a walk. But what a walk it was! She held her head high in the air; her feet rose and fell in time to the music. Someone shouted from the band wagon. People stared, and children on the sidewalk cheered her. But Dolly paid no heed to anyone. She belonged in that parade, and there she was going to stay. Nothing should stop her!

As for Johnny and Emma, they could only sit there on her back, holding tight and feeling very shy and strange.

Right down Main Street they went, past the post office and the town hall, past the sidewalks lined with people, past the big red-faced policeman at the traffic stop, past the five-and-

Emma clutched Johnny by the arm. "Look," she cried. "There's Dolly!"

ten, the bakery and—last of all—a small shop doorway where, between piles of potatoes and oranges and red tomatoes, Mr. Morelli himself in shirt sleeves and white apron stood open-mouthed, unable to believe his own eyes. But before he could so much as shout, Dolly had swept past in a triumphant blare of trumpets, the parade had closed in behind her, and not even Mr. Morelli could stop the parade and drag her out!

Past the fire station they went, all the way round the block and then back again to the big meadow down by the railway station, where the circus tents stood like huge mushrooms. But not even then would Dolly stop. Right in she trotted with the other circus horses to the long horse-tent, and took her place at the end of the line as though she had always belonged there.

The circus men gathered around. Johnny and Emma, still bewildered, slid down from Dolly's back, but no one paid much attention to them. Everyone was looking at Dolly.

"An old hand, that's what she is! Did you see the way she slipped in there?"

"She's worked in a show, all right!"

And another man said, "When I was with the Heely outfit years ago, I remember there was a ring-horse looked just like her! I wouldn't wonder. She might have been stolen."

Johnny piped up, "Mr. Morelli didn't steal her! He bought Dolly off a truck pedlar; he told me!"

"Who are you?" asked a man in riding clothes who had just come up. And before Johnny or Emma could answer he added, "Someone take these kids and see they get a good seat for the show. Better telephone their folks first. And hunt up this man Morelli. One of you can give the horse a tryout. If she acts like a good ring-horse we might buy her, now Queenie's gone lame. I hate to see an old circus-horse hauling truck!"

There was no need to hunt Mr. Morelli. He was already making his way through the crowd, hatless and out of breath. But Johnny and Emma had no ears for anything he might say. They were going to see the elephants and the tiger and the flying lady in pink tights. Everything was happening like a fairy tale, with Dolly for the fairy godmother.

It was early for the show, but already people were pushing their way into the big tent. Johnny and Emma didn't mind how long they might have to wait. There was so much to be seen, all sorts of things one never had time to look at properly while the circus was going on—the way the huge canvas roof was stretched, so far above their heads that everything up there looked dim and misty; the mysterious ropes and poles and pullies, the trapeze and the tiny platform high up in the air, that made one dizzy even to look at; the circus ring itself, deep in sawdust, and the red curtains that hid the entrance.

Each with a bag of peanuts and paper cup of lemonade, they sat happily and stared about them.

And then all at once the band struck up, the red curtains were drawn aside. The circus was going to begin!

To Johnny and Emma that afternoon passed like a dream. It was just towards the end, when all the performers were riding round the big ring for the last time, that Emma suddenly clutched Johnny by the arm.

"Look," she cried. "Look, there's Dolly!"

It was Dolly herself, but Dolly as they had never seen her before. She looked ten years younger. Her mane had been trimmed and combed, her coat had been scrubbed till it shone

and the yellowish patches scarcely showed at all. Her hoofs
were blackened; she had a gay saddle and bridle, and the rider
on her back was dressed in pink and silver. Very proudly she
trotted around, her head held high, but Emma was quite sure
that she gave them a friendly wink from her one good eye as
she went past.

So it was true. Dolly had joined the circus for good. It was
dreadful to lose her, but both Johnny and Emma knew just
how pleased she must be feeling about it all. There would be
no more hauling of potatoes and milk bottles. Mr. Morelli would
have the car he had wanted. And next summer, when the circus
came to town once more, Dolly would be there too.

They would begin to save up their pennies, Johnny and Emma
decided, from that very next week!

THE CIRCUS DRUMS
Adelaide Love

I saw the circus parade today;
I heard the great big bass drums play,
And I understand what they tried to say.

"Come—come to the circus," they said,
"And watch the elephant stand on his head
And the little white poodle pretend he's dead.

"See the bareback riders that jump through a hoop
And the man in the auto that loops the loop
And the monkey that eats a bowl of soup.

"There will be ladies in sparkly gowns
And men on trapezes and tumbling clowns
And a lion-tamer that scolds and frowns."

That's what the big drums said, although
It only sounded like "boom," I know.
But I understood and I'm going to go!

201

THE four Clover children, Quintin, fifteen, Marcia Lucinda, almost fourteen, Dorothy, nine, and Peter Jenks Clover, nearly four, having been left orphans, have come to the small town of Woodlea, to live in the comfortable old house left to young Peter by old Peter Jenks, their granduncle. They are not welcomed by the town as a whole, many people thinking they may become a public charge, as the income left to young Peter is very small, and the children seem to be all of them too young to work or assume the responsibility of a house and family. With the help of a few good friends they are struggling to prove that they can take care of themselves. They do, too. Here is one of their adventures.

Mary Dickerson Donahey

MR. DOOLEY
DISGRACES HIS FAMILY

ILLUSTRATED BY *Ruth van Tellingen*

THE next day was Sunday—their first Sunday in their new home. Marty Lu considered it a very important day indeed. They must all of them go to church, and they must all of them look their best and show their best manners.

Peter was of course very young, but he could be trusted. He had been to church many times before and had always been a good baby, listening with delight to the hymns, and going quietly to sleep during the talking parts of the service. He was to go with the rest of the family. His costume caused no worry either. For two years he had been inheriting the clothes of the younger brother of one of their mother's music pupils, and he had the best outfit of any of them. But the other three, though

202

possessed of a sufficient number of everyday clothes, had had
no Sunday best provided for them for many months.

"You'll just have to polish up again, Quint," said Marty Lu,
the worried little manager of the family. "And I do hope you
won't have to brush your clothes to bits, before you get new
ones. Dorry, I think that last white dress of mine will do for
you. I can't squeeze into it any more, and yours, of course, is
too short for anything but a petticoat for you now! I do wish
we didn't have to grow. Whatever am I going to wear, I wonder? Do you really think Mother's things will be all right?"

Quintin and Dorothy said "Yes" to that question, as they had
said it a dozen times in the last few days. They meant it, too.
And yet, when Quintin, polished till he shone, emerged to meet
his family, he realized that something was very wrong. Not
with Peter. His short blond rings of hair shone out against a
dark blue sailor hat, and his sturdy little body was clothed in a
becoming blue sailor suit. Not with Dorothy. Her mop of bronzy
curls looked lovely under a white hat, old but still graceful, and
Marty Lu's dress fitted her very well, while her own blue coat
did not look outgrown if it was left unbuttoned. But Marcia
Lucinda! Quint blinked and stared. She was very wrong indeed,
and Quintin knew it, though how and why he couldn't have said.
If he had only known, there was a lot of pathos behind Marty
Lu's queer looks that day. The poor child had realized fully
why Woodlea people did not want them to stay in town. It was
because they were all so very young. So Marty Lu had decided
that on this day, when they made their first public appearance,
she must look just as old and responsible as she possibly could.
The scantiness of her own wardrobe had helped the idea along.
She would dress in her mother's clothes! Grown-up clothes
would make anybody look grown-up who wore them! To be
sure, she, Marty Lu, was very short. But Mother had been short
too—hardly a shade of an inch taller than her daughter was
now. Lots of grown women were short—shorter than she!

And so, her thoughts of her beloved family and not of herself,
Marty Lu had dressed that day as much like her mother as she
could. She knew well enough the result was not becoming. But

203

she didn't care about that. It made no difference whether people thought she was pretty—in fact, they might think she was a more responsible person if they thought she wasn't! And neither she nor Dorothy, who was still young enough to consider "dressing up" in older people's clothes great fun, realized that she was ridiculous.

She had been gladder than ever that day that she had never cut off her long braid. Mother had hated "bobs" and had cried when Dorry had recklessly butchered her own hair, so that Marty Lu had sighed and refrained from doing likewise—especially after finding out what it cost to maintain a shingled head.

Now she was really glad she had done it, for short hair made old grown-up women, as much as thirty years old, look young. What it would do to her, Marty Lu hated to think!

Today she fondly imagined she had added at least ten years to her appearance by bundling up the mass of yellow hair into a tight hard knot, pinned on the back of her head, not quite in the middle. Marty Lu was not expert at "doing up" hair just yet! Over it was perched a small black hat with purple pansies on it—a hat which young Mrs. Clover had in her turn worn because it made her look more settled and responsible. It may have accomplished its purpose on her. On Marty Lu it was simply funny. Then there was a black taffeta dress, which fitted only in length, but was too tight or too loose everywhere, black gloves, and as a crowning touch of grown-upness, Marty Lu wore on her feet Mother's one pair of high-heeled slippers. Never had she worn high heels before. They were uncomfortable and gave her a queer pitching sort of walk, but she felt she must stick to them. Anything must be borne for her family!

"Geewhillikens!" said Quint, as he studied the absurd little figure his pretty sensible sister had become. But Marty Lu herself was satisfied. She felt she looked grown-up. She took his remark as one of admiration, and not knowing what to say or do to change her, Quintin let it go at that.

"I guess we're all ready," she said, anxiously. "Did you put Dooley in the barn?"

"Yes, and tied him up too," answered Quint. "Dooley's mad

and insulted and hurt. That dog thinks he can go anywhere we do. Just hear him!" Mr. Dooley was indeed voicing his indignation at the top of his lungs. But it did him no good. They all called "good-bye" to him, and then his sharp ears heard them move off down the street.

"Hurry," Dorothy was saying, "Miss Budd said we mustn't be late, you know. Oh isn't it lucky we were born Methodists, when it's her church, and the Smith's church?"

"It was kind of her to ask us to sit in her pew," said Marty Lu primly. She was rehearsing grown-up manners, to match her grown-up clothes.

They were expected at the church. All the Sunday School seemed to be waiting about outside, while a great many grown people were there too—people who generally went in and sat down as good church members should. But everybody in Woodlea was frankly curious about this new and most unusual family.

Their good friend and neighbor, Miss Budd, was nervous. She did so want these pathetic children to make a good impression! That affair between Mr. Dooley and Abijah, the big cat belonging to Miss Anthea Frost, another neighbor of theirs and distinctly not a friend, had been unfortunate. Dooley had bitten off the end of Abijah's tail, and though even Miss Frost had had to admit that Abijah had started the fight, she had not forgiven "that rowdy big mongrel Airedale." Most folks had laughed about it, but others besides Miss Frost were saying it was what the town might expect right along if Dooley and his owners were allowed to remain. Miss Budd felt that all must go well today!

Then her anxious ears heard smothered titters, and she stepped outside the church door. She gave a gasp of horror. Why hadn't she asked what they planned to wear? Why hadn't she realized that they would need help? They came toward her as decorously as children could. Quintin, tall, thin, and awkward, but as clean and neat as a boy could be, his fine pleasant face looking more scholarly than usual because his nervousness made him so pale. Dorothy, beside him, was as pretty as a picture and as dainty as a rose. Behind walked Peter—a perfect love of a baby, well dressed and well mannered. But Marty Lu,

205

who led him—Marty Lu, who could be so sweet and so pretty, —why Marty Lu was a little black scarecrow!

At first gentle Miss Budd was just plain angry. Why hadn't the child had better sense? She must have known the clothes didn't fit her or become her, and that they were too old for her anyhow! And then came a flash of understanding. She knew why Marty Lu had done it! She wanted to look old. She wanted to prove that she was not too young to be the head of a family!

Sudden tears in her eyes, Miss Budd hurried forward to meet the four, of whom Peter was the only one not stricken by sudden terror. As much as possible, Miss Budd hid Marty Lu's queerness between herself and Dorothy, and she managed to get them all into her pew without a very noticeable outbreak of smiles. In fact, so well did she manage that few already inside the church saw any but the satisfactory members of the Clover family very distinctly.

The service began. Quintin and Dorothy had good voices, which had been well trained by their music-loving mother. They sang exceptionally well. Marty Lu, being tone deaf, had been as well trained at keeping absolutely still. Peter hummed through the hymns in a pleasant inoffensive baby monotone. Miss Budd began to beam. Approving looks were being cast in their direction from all over the church. Finally the sermon began. Peter had gone to sleep. The church was very still. Mr. Smith had a rather drony voice, and it seemed to drone more than ever today. The weather was warm. Many heads began to nod here and there. And then suddenly, across the pious Sabbath stillness, came a clicking sound—a sound not usually heard in church, followed by a violent snuffling.

People began to sit up and wonder. Inquisitive heads began to turn. Decorous heads twitched on their well-intentioned shoulders. The clatter ceased but the snuffling grew louder. The best-trained necks in town swung round to observe the cause.

And—the cause was that "rowdy mongrel Airedale dog" of the Clovers'—Mr. Dooley! Mr. Dooley, a grin of doggish delight on his face as his nose told him he was nearing his adored owners. Mr. Dooley, a length of frayed rope dangling from his

collar, his shaggy coat very disreputable from the caked mud
he had accumulated while digging his way out from the old
barn. His sharp claws ceased to clatter on bare boards, just
before he decided he had almost reached his goal. Head up,
eyes shining, he trotted down the carpeted aisle. Miss Budd's
pew being well to the front, the Clovers were last to know what
the commotion was about. It was Dooley who informed them.
Always a silent person, he made no outcry now.

But, pausing beside their pew, he gave a final sniff, smiled
a   knowing   you-see-what-happens-when-you-try-to-leave-me
smile, cocked one ear at them, and then, with a really whispered
"Whoof" of pleased satisfaction, he flung himself down in the
aisle beside their seat, ready to be silent, ready to be good, ready
to be anything at all, if only he could stay beside these people
whom he loved.

But that was exactly what could not be allowed. Dooley might
be silent—the congregation wasn't! It seethed! It giggled! Mr.
Smith, staring down into Dooley's upturned, interested, happy
face tried manfully to go on with his sermon, and then found
his mouth twitching, his eyes twinkling.

"Put that dog out, somebody," came Mr. Stowe's sepulchral
tones, and poor Quintin dragged himself up to do it. In an agony
of embarrassment he rose and stepped into the aisle. "Come
Dooley!" he commanded in a fierce whisper, and started out,
expecting Dooley to follow. But Mr. Dooley did no such thing.
Quint had deceived him and locked him up and tied him once
that day. He wasn't going to let Quint fool him again! Mr.
Dooley wagged a beseeching tail and smiled at the rest of his

family. Surely they weren't against him too? He could trust them to want him!

But "Go home, Dooley—home!" whispered Marty Lu. "Home, Dooley," echoed Dorothy, who generally thought anything he did was right, while even his best-loved Peter, waking up, decided against his friend for once and piped "Go home, bad dog," in any but churchy tones.

Poor Mr. Dooley could not believe his ears. Peter go back on him? Well, he knew how to win his Peter! He'd done it hundreds of times. So, up on his haunches rose Mr. Dooley. He faced Peter, one ragged ear cocked saucily up, the other hanging ridiculously down. Then, instead of merely dangling his paws in the silly way affected by most begging dogs, Dooley began his own method of pleading. His forepaws went out like the arms of some tragic actress. They beat the air—they waved—they pleaded—they besought! No dog had ever appeared so human and so funny as Dooley always did when performing this trick, and he could keep it up a long time, striking new poses, doing utterly ridiculous things with his ears and head and paws every second. He threw his whole soul into his performance now, finally rising to his hind feet and doing a side-splittingly funny little dance, while his forepaws still pleaded for mercy. Smothered giggles were smothered no longer. Mr. Smith was openly laughing in the pulpit. People at a distance stood up to get a better view.

"Down, Dooley! Down—DOWN!" commanded Marty Lu. Dooley took her literally. He rolled over on his side and was unmistakably a "dead dog." If going through all his tricks would keep him in this strange place where his dear family unaccountably wished to remain, go through with them he would, most willingly! The church now rocked with laughter. Quintin, who had reached the church door before he realized that Dooley was not with him, was back by now. He made a furious, frantic grab at Dooley's collar, but the dog eluded him. And then, seeming to realize suddenly that somehow he was all wrong, and evidently in for punishment, Dooley, the wise, the dignified and clever, completely lost his head. He tore away, dashed

208

here and there about the aisles, pursued by other boys, all willing enough to help put him out, and finally made off towards the door, ky-yi-ing as the well-mannered Mr. Dooley had never done before. And his going unfortunately did not end the show, either. For Peter, suddenly realizing that his best friend was unhappy and persecuted, began to cry loudly. "My lants my Mr. Dooley!" he shrieked in his shrill baby voice, losing all his *w*'s even more thoroughly than usual. "My lants to go home too!" And the eyes of the entire congregation, with no funny dog to watch, turned to the ridiculous little woman in black, now forced to lead a wailing baby boy all the long, long way down that church aisle, to the blessed, peaceful out-doors!

Mercifully, Marty Lu did not realize that most of the laughter then was caused by her own clothes. She thought they were still remembering Dooley's antics, and that was bad enough. She met Quintin outside. Dooley had shown his good sense by vanishing. They stopped Peter's yells by methods more forceful than that pampered youngster was accustomed to and started glumly for home. They did not speak till they reached the two giant lilac bushes that guarded the gate of Peter Jenks's house. Then they stopped with one accord and gazed up at the low, comfortable old brick house which now belonged to their Peter, and which had already grown to seem so homelike to their lonely young hearts.

"Well," said Quintin glumly, "I suppose it's all off now! They surely will send us packing after this. And where will we go—what will we do?"

"I just don't know," said Marty Lu, her eyes full of tears. "And we were so happy here—it's such a lovely place—and there *are* folks who like us."

Then suddenly her proud little head went up with a jerk—the fighting blood of all the Clovers who had been soldiers shone in her eyes.

"We won't go, Quint!" she declared hotly. "We can't—and we won't! We'll stay right here and fight it out! I'm ashamed of you, Quintin Lloyd Clover! Didn't Dad and Mother, too, always say we must be good soldiers and never give up no matter how tough things seemed? I tell you we'll stay! Now then—forward —MARCH!"

And all went bravely up the path and began impatiently to await the coming of Miss Budd and Dorothy, with the latest news from the scene of their recent anguish.

When at last they came, their report was not so bad as might have been expected. Of course, Mr. Dooley himself had lost all reputation as a respectable dog, but the broken cord dangling from his neck had exonerated the Clovers in the minds of most people. Mr. Smith, the pastor, and a friend of theirs, was very forgiving. Only a few of the old church members had joined the Stowes, the Powells, and Miss Frost in making a fuss.

"But," said Miss Budd, as she bent to give the head of a crushed and repentant Dooley, who had crawled back among them, a forgiving pat, "it would have been so very much better if it had not had to happen!"

And with that mild comment, everybody concerned was forced to agree.

THE Melendy children have formed a Saturday club. Each child in turn has a Saturday trip around the city—all by himself. Here is Randy's adventure.

Elizabeth Enright

RANDY
AT THE ART GALLERY

ILLUSTRATED BY *Janet Smalley*

OF COURSE Father said yes. But he had certain conditions which they already knew by heart. They were the same ones he had imposed when they started going to school by themselves.

"Don't get run over," he said. "That's the first and most important rule. Look where you're going and watch the lights when you cross the street. This applies to Randy in particular who believes too often that she's walking in another world: a safer, better one. It's the people who make the safety on this

211

earth as well as the trouble, unfortunately." Father glared at the newspaper that lay on the floor beside him. "Sometimes I think the Golden Age must have been the Age of Reptiles. Well, anyway, let me see what was I saying—? Oh, yes. Randy and the lights. And another thing. If you get lost or in trouble of any kind *always* look for a policeman. Sooner or later you'll find one, and he'll know what to do; and don't hesitate to ask him even if he's the traffic cop at Forty-second and Fifth with busses breathing fire on every side. Let's see, what else?"

"Don't talk to strangers," Randy prompted him.

"Yes, that's right, don't talk to strangers. Unless you know by looking at them that they're kind people, and even then think twice. Be home no later than quarter to six, and Randy had better make it five." He picked up his newspaper and flapped it open. "That's about all. Oh, one last thing— See that you do something you really *want;* something you'll always remember. Don't waste your Saturdays on unimportant things."

"Yes, that's one of the rules," Mona told him.

"Is it? Good. Then go with my blessings."

Then they went to Cuffy who naturally said yes, too, but not as if she cared for the idea.

"Well, I hope it's all right, I'm sure. Seems to me like you're pretty young to be kiting all over a big city by yourselves. And one at a time, too, not even together. Don't you get run over now!" They couldn't help laughing at that: all grownups had learned the same set of precautions apparently.

"And it's nothing to giggle about, neither," said Cuffy severely. "I don't want nobody run over, nor nobody lost so's we have to get the police out after 'em. I suppose I can't keep you from getting a little lost once in a while. It'd be against nature. But not so lost that we have to get the police out after you."

Good old Cuffy. It was that sort of thing that made them love her so much.

"If you *do* get lost," she continued, "you can always go up and ask—"

"A *policeman!*" shouted Mona and Randy and Rush in unison.

"Do you think it's polite to take the words right out of

212

people's mouths?" inquired Cuffy, pretending to be offended. "And another thing—"

"DON'T TALK TO STRANGERS!" they cried.

"Well," said Cuffy, giving up. "I can't say much for your manners but I'm glad to see you've got the right ideas at least."

"What about strange policemen?" said Rush, looking innocent.

"Oh, go on with you! Out of my kitchen, the whole tribe of you!" Cuffy made sweeping gestures with the broom. "My patience is worn about's thin as the sole of my shoe."

But that wasn't true, and they knew it. Cuffy's patience was as deep as the earth itself.

After a brief discussion it was decided that Randy as founder of the Club should have the privilege of the first Saturday. For the next five days she worked feverishly in her schoolcraft shop whenever she got a chance, and by Friday evening she was able to distribute four small pins cut out of copper, and each bearing the mysterious name Isaac.

"Swear on your sacred word of honor *never* to tell anyone what this pin means," Randy said to the Club members. And they all swore, even Oliver. It was a solemn moment.

Saturday dawned much the same as any other day, maybe even a little grayer than most, but when Randy woke up she had the same feeling in her stomach that she always had on Christmas Day. A wonderful morning smell of coffee and bacon drifted up the stair well from the kitchen, and she could hear a familiar clattering spasm deep in the house: Willy Sloper shaking down the furnace. Mona was still asleep, a mound entirely covered up except for one long trailing pigtail that looked as if it were awake all by itself.

Randy lay staring absently at the wall beside her bed where pictures hung at haphazard intervals. She had painted all the pictures herself, and there was a reason for their strange arrangement: the wallpaper was old and the pictures served to cover up peeled and faded places. They were all drawings of enigmatic-faced princesses and sorceresses. Each had mysterious, slanted eyes, a complicated headdress and elaborate jewels; each was posed against a background of palaces, rocks, and

213

dashing waves, or forests with unicorns. "Don't you ever get tired of drawing Lucrezia Borgia all the time?" Rush had once asked her.

For a while Randy lay still just being happy; then she stretched. S-t-r-e-t-ch-ed way up and way down. During it she probably grew half an inch. After that she got out of bed, stepping over her bedroom slippers as usual.

"Ow! Is it cold!" Randy complained happily and closed the window with a crash that drew protesting grumbles from the little mountain range that was Mona.

The morning finally went by with Randy pushing it every second. It was awful to sit at the lunch table while Cuffy calmly insisted that she must eat everything on her plate. Everything.

"Oh, Cuffy, even my *beets?*"

"*All* your beets," replied Cuffy inexorably. "And *all* your squash."

Randy looked witheringly at the food on her plate.

214

"Beets are so boring," she said. "The most boring vegetable in the whole world next to squash."

"Not so boring as spinach," said Rush. "Spinach is like eating a wet mop."

"That will be enough of that!" commanded Cuffy in the voice that meant no nonsense.

At last it was over, even the tapioca, and Randy just stopped herself in time from remarking that she considered tapioca the most boring dessert in the world next to stewed rhubarb.

Mona came into their room while Randy was changing her dress.

"How'd you like to borrow my ambers?" she asked.

"Oh, Mona!" Randy was overcome. "Do you mean you'd let me? Honestly? Oh, I'd be so careful of them, I promise I would."

She felt like a princess in her brown velveteen dress with the amber necklace that had belonged to Mother. "It's like big lumps of honey," she said, staring into the mirror.

"Well, don't you lose it now," admonished Mona, not quite regretting her generosity. "Have a good time, Ran, and don't forget you have to be back by five."

"I won't," promised Randy, giving her sister a hug. "Good-bye, you're swell to let me wear the ambers."

She said good-bye to everyone just as though she were going away for a long voyage. Cuffy gazed at her thoughtfully.

"You look awful little to be going off by yourself like this," she said. "Now remember, don't you get run over and don't—"

"I won't, I won't!" cried Randy, quickly running down the steps and waving her blue leather pocketbook in which the dollar and sixty cents rattled wealthily.

My, it's a nice day, she thought. Nobody else would have thought so. The sky was full of low clouds, and the air had a damp, deep feeling in it that meant rain after a while. But being by yourself, all by yourself, in a big city for the first time is like the first time you find you can ride a bicycle or do the dog paddle. The sense of independence is intoxicating. Randy skipped halfway up the block, a leisurely lighthearted skip, and then she walked the rest of the way, stepping over each

215

crack in the pavement. It was very dangerous, she had to be careful, because if she did step on a crack she would be turned into stone forevermore.

In Fifth Avenue the big green busses rattled by like dinosaurs. I'm going to walk though, Randy decided. I'm going to walk all the way and look in all the windows. So that's what she did. The shop windows were wonderful: Woolworth's dime store was just as wonderful as Tiffany's jewelry store, and she reached Fifty-seventh Street in either a very long or a very short time, she wasn't sure which, because the walk had been so interesting.

It was just beginning to rain when she came to the art gallery where the French pictures were being shown for the benefit of war relief. It cost seventy-five cents to go in, so Randy planned to stay a long time and gave her coat to the doorman.

The gallery was hushed and dim after the bright, sharp street. The soft rugs on the floor, the soft neutral color of the walls, with each picture glowing beneath its own special light, made her feel as if she had walked into a jewel case.

"Catalogue, miss?" said a man at a little desk. His eyeglasses flashed in the dimness.

"Thank you," Randy said, and took one of the little folders he offered; then, almost on tiptoe, she stepped into the main room of the gallery. There were a lot of people looking at the pictures and talking to each other as if they were in church, low-voiced and serious. One of the people she knew, and at sight of her Randy's heart sank. It was old Mrs. Oliphant ("the Elephant," Rush called her behind her back) who really was old because she had known Father's father way back in the last century. She was a big, tall old lady with a lot of furs that smelled of camphor, and a great many chains around her neck that got caught on each other. Now and then she came to the Melendys', and once they had all been taken to Sunday dinner at her house when it was raining and everybody ate too much and Oliver got sick on the bus going home. She was nice, Randy supposed, but so far away in her oldness and dignity. She hoped Mrs. Oliphant wouldn't notice her.

Pretty soon she forgot about everything but the pictures. There was a nice one of a girl in an old-fashioned dress playing the piano. She had a snub nose and a long yellow braid sort of like Mona (only of course it was probably a French girl). If she looked at a picture long enough, without being interrupted, Randy could make it come alive sometimes; and now she could almost hear the music the girl in the picture was playing: quite hard music, probably, but played very stiffly, with a lot of mistakes, the way Mona played.

"Marvelous substance," murmured a hushed voice behind her, and another hushed voice replied, "Unbelievable resilience in the flesh tones!"

Gee whiz, thought Randy, are they talking about the picture? And she moved on to the next one; a field all burning yellow in the sunshine. You could tell it was twelve o'clock noon on a summer day; probably July. Randy could nearly smell the heat and hear the locusts in the trees sounding exactly like Father's electric razor in the mornings. She was having a good time. She looked at all the pictures: fat ladies bathing in a brook, a girl with opera glasses, apples and pears on a blue plate, a man in a boat, two dead rabbits, and then all of a sudden she came to the picture that was hers, her very own one.

Randy was always finding things that belonged to her in a special way, though ownership had nothing to do with it. Now she had found the picture. The catalogue told her that the picture was called The Princess, that it had been painted by someone named Jules Clairon in the year 1881. In the picture a girl about Randy's age was sitting on a garden wall and looking out over an enormous city. She had a solemn little face: her long hair hung to the sash of her old-fashioned dress, and her high-heeled boots were buttoned almost to the knee. Among the potted chrysanthemums at her feet sat a black poodle with a red bow on top of his head. On either side the clipped plane trees were almost bare, and in the distance the huge city was spread in a dusky web of blue and gray.

It was easy to make this picture alive. Randy stared at it fixedly, hardly breathing, hardly thinking, and pretty soon she

217

thought she could smell the mixture of damp earth and burn-ing leaves and smoke from distant chimney pots; she thought she could hear the hum of the city and the clear voices of chil-dren somewhere out of sight. A day had come and gone, years ago, and still it was alive. I wish I'd known that girl, Randy thought.

She felt a touch on her shoulder that brought her back to her own world with a start. On her shoulder she saw a knuckly black glove, and against her cheek she felt the prickling of camphory fur. The Elephant, darn it, thought Randy crossly. Just when I was getting right *into* that picture, too.

"Well, well! Why, Mona dear! What are *you* doing here?" inquired Mrs. Oliphant in her deep cavernous voice with its faint foreign accent. "Or is it little Miranda?"

"Miranda," replied Randy politely, with a smile that was nothing but stretching the corners of her mouth.

"Of course, of course. Mona is the one with the hair," said Mrs. Oliphant, whacking Randy's shoulder absent-mindedly. "You seem very interested in this picture, Miranda."

"I think it's beautiful," Randy said, sloping her shoulder out from under Mrs. Oliphant's hand as tactfully as she could.

"It isn't so beautiful as I remembered it," observed Mrs. Oliphant, regarding it with a frown. "But then I haven't seen it for sixty years. Not since I was eleven years old."

"Eleven years old!" repeated Randy. It was impossible that Mrs. Oliphant had ever been eleven. "Not since the day it was finished," the old lady explained. "You see, I was the girl in the picture."

"You!" cried Randy, amazed. Her mouth dropped open.

"That's I at the age of eleven," said Mrs. Oliphant, very pleased at Randy's surprise. "Not much to look at, was I?"

"I think you looked nice," Randy considered the girl in the picture. "Interesting and, well, *nice*. I was just wishing I'd known that girl."

"And how she would have loved knowing you. Sometimes she was very lonely," said Mrs. Oliphant. "Unfortunately she disappeared long, long ago."

218

Randy looked up at her companion's face. What she said was true. The face was so old, crossed with a thousand lines, and the dark, fiery eyes were overhung by such severe black brows that every trace of the little girl she had once been had vanished with the past.

"What was that big city in the distance?"

"It was Paris," said the old lady, with a sigh.

"Who was the dog?"

"Tartuffe, we called him. He was a selfish old beast, and very dull company." Mrs. Oliphant shook her head and laughed, remembering. Then she looked about her questioningly. "Who is with you, Miranda? I don't see any of your family."

"I'm all alone," Randy told her.

"*Alone?* How old are you, child?"

"Ten," said Randy.

Mrs. Oliphant shook her head again. "When I was your age such a thing was unheard of. My aunts would have fainted dead away at the suggestion. What a lucky girl you are!"

Randy agreed. Really, I am lucky, she thought.

"Well, since we are both alone," suggested the old lady, "why don't you come with me and have a cup of tea, or an ice-cream soda, or a chocolate marshmallow walnut sundae, or whatever you prefer?"

Randy was beginning to like Mrs. Oliphant very much. "I'd love to," she said.

Surrounded by an aura of camphor and eau de Cologne, and with all her chains jingling, the old lady swept splendidly from the gallery. Randy followed in her wake, like a dinghy behind a large launch.

Outside the moist air had become moister. A fine mist was driving down. Mrs. Oliphant disentangled an umbrella from her handbag and the tail of one of her furs. When it was opened the umbrella proved to be extremely large and deep. They walked under it, close together, as under a small pavilion. "I've had it for twenty-five years," Mrs. Oliphant told Randy. "It's been lost once on a bus, twice on railway trains, and once at the London Zoo. But I always get it back. I call it the Albatross."

After they had walked a block or two, they came to a large hotel which they entered, and the old lady, having checked the Albatross, led Randy to a large room full of little tables, gilt chairs, mirrors, and palms in fancy pots. At one end of the room on a raised platform there was a three-piece orchestra: piano, violin, and cello. All the musicians looked about fifty years old.

220

A waiter who looked old enough to be the father of any one of the musicians led Mrs. Oliphant and Randy to a table by a long window. After a period of deliberation, it was decided that the old lady would have tea and toast, and Randy would have vanilla ice cream with chocolate sauce.

"And, François, bring some *petits fours*, also."

"*Parfaitement, madame*," said François, creaking agedly away in the direction of the kitchen. Randy did not know what *petits fours* meant, but she did not like to ask.

"Ah, yes," said Mrs. Oliphant when she had uncoiled from her layers of furs, taken off her gloves, untied her scarf, and arranged her necklaces. "My childhood was a very different thing from yours."

"Tell me about it," said Randy. Then "please," as an afterthought.

"Would you like to hear the whole story?"

"Yes, yes, please, the whole story," begged Randy, giving an involuntary bounce on the hard chair. She loved to be told stories.

"Well, it's a long time ago," said the old lady. "Before you were born, even before your father was born, imagine it! The garden in the picture was the garden of my father's house in Saint-Germain near Paris. It was an old house even then, tall and narrow and gray, with patches of ivy. The inside of it was stuffy and dark and full of furniture. When house cleaning was going on, all the windows were opened; never any other time, and I can remember the smell of it to this day: the mixed odors of cloth and cough medicine and age. I was the only young thing in the house, even Tartuffe, the dog, was older than I. My mother had died when I was born, and my father's business kept him in Paris all day, so I was brought up by my aunts and an English governess. They gave me my lessons too, I was never allowed to go to school. The aunts were all maiden ladies years older than my father. They always wore black, took pills with their meals, worried about drafts, and spoke in quiet polite voices except when shouting at *Tante* Amélie, the deaf aunt, who carried a great curved ear trumpet like the

221

tusk of an elephant. Ah, here is the tea."

François arranged the feast before them. *Petits fours* turned out to be the most wonderful little cakes in frilled paper collars: pink, and pale yellow, and chocolate, with silver peppermint buttons on top. Randy's eyes glittered with such enthusiasm that the old lady was delighted. "You shall have some to take home to the other children. François, please bring us a boxful of *petits fours* to take home."

"That will be wonderful," Randy said, not quite with her mouth full, but almost. "Please tell me some more."

"Very well," said her friend. "The English governess was also a spinster, also elderly. Her name was Miss Buff-Towers and she was related in some way to an earl, a fact she was very proud of and never forgot. She had long front teeth, the color of old piano keys, and a huge coiled arrangement of braided hair on top of her head like an orderly eagle's nest. She was a kindhearted creature but she knew as much about raising children as I know about raising coati-mundis. (I'm not even sure what they are.)

"You can see that my life was far from exciting. I knew no children, rarely left my own home at all. If it hadn't been for the garden I might have gone mad from boredom.

"This garden was very large, enclosed by a high wall, and shaded by old chestnut trees that bloomed every spring in great cornucopias of popcorn. There was a tiny bamboo jungle, and a summerhouse with a wasp's nest, and a little lead fountain, and two enormous mossy statues: one of Diana, and one of Apollo. At the end of the garden the wall was low enough to permit seeing the magnificent view of the city. In the distance the whole of Paris lay spread out like a map: golden in the morning, blue in the dusk, shining like a thousand fires at night.

"I spent all the time I could in the garden. I had a swing there, and many hiding places for myself, my dolls, and Tartuffe. I used to take my lessons to the wall at the end, looking up from my dull books every other minute to see the city far beyond. I never tired of looking at it and wondering about it.

"One September evening when I was eleven years old I had

gone into the garden, and was sitting in my usual place on the wall looking at the city and hoping dinner would be ready soon. I heard steps on the little gravel path behind me and, turning, saw my father and another gentleman, a friend whom he had brought home for dinner. I stood up respectfully and was introduced to Monsieur Clairon. He was a tall man with a brown beard and pleasant eyes. I had a feeling, looking at him, that he was more alive than most people.

"'Your daughter makes me think of the princess in a fairy tale who looks out of her tower at the world,' he told my father. 'Someday I would like to paint her just as she was: sitting on that wall.'

"I was flattered and self-conscious, but only for a moment.

"'We mustn't make her vain, Jules,' said my father in a stately voice. 'That plain little face was never meant for Art.' Dinner, for once, was fun. Monsieur Clairon told jokes and stories, everybody laughed, and each story was repeated in loud brays for *Tante* Amélie with the greatest good will.

223

" 'I've been making sketches at the carnival down the street,'
he told me. 'I can never resist carnivals. This one has a camel
and a dancing bear as well as the usual carrousel and fortune-
tellers. It makes good pictures. You've seen it, I suppose,
mademoiselle?' He turned to me.

" 'No, monsieur,' I said sadly. I knew there was a carnival
somewhere in the town. Bursts of music had been drifting over
the wall all day.

" 'But you must see it!' Monsieur Clairon insisted. 'It leaves
at midnight. I should be happy to take you this evening—'

" 'Heaven forbid, Jules,' said my father, with a distressed
smile. 'Gabrielle would come home with smallpox or whooping cough or measles or all three.'

" 'And so *dreadfully dirty!*' added Miss Buff-Towers.

" 'Someone might even kidnap her!' said my *Tante* Marthe,
who always expected the worst.

" 'It's out of the question,' stated my father firmly.

"For the first time since I was a tiny child I dared to defy
the collective opinion of my aunts, father, and governess.

" 'But I want to go!' said I, laying down my fork. 'I want to
go *terribly!* Why can't I? I'll wear gloves and not touch anything, I promise. When I come home I'll gargle. Please let me
go, please please please!'

"My father stared at me. Even his eyebrows and mustache
looked annoyed.

" 'That will be enough, Gabrielle,' he said.

" 'You never let me go anywhere!' I persisted. 'I've never
seen a carnival. Or a real live camel. Or a dancing bear. I'd like
to see *something* besides just this old house all the time!'

"My father's face was dark as the wine in his glass.

" 'Go!' he roared. 'Upstairs, immediately! Without dessert!'

"And up I went, crying into my sleeve and hearing above
my sobs the turmoil in the dining room: Monsieur Clairon in-
terceding for me, my father expostulating, and above that the
loud, toneless voice of *Tante* Amélie saying, 'What's the matter?
Why is Gabrielle crying? Why doesn't someone tell me something?' And *Tante* Marthe bellowing into the ear trumpet:

'GABRIELLE HAS BEEN A VERY NAUGHTY GIRL!'

"After I had gone to bed, and Miss Buff-Towers had heard my prayers and wept a few embarrassing tears over my disobedience, I lay in bed very still and straight and angry. Through the closed window I could hear rowdy strains of music.

"At last I got out of bed and opened the window which looked out over the garden and the distant lighted city spread like a jeweled fabric. For the first time I was sorry that my room was not at the front of the house since then I might have glimpsed the carnival. The music sounded gayer than ever, and I could hear bursts of laughter above the noise. Slowly my anger turned to curiosity and active rebellion. An adventurous flame sprang to life within me. Quickly in the dark I dressed in my oldest dress. Quickly I stuffed the bolster under the blankets just in case someone should look in. But money! I wanted to ride on the carrousel and to see the dancing bear. There were only twenty centimes in my pocketbook, and then I remembered the gold piece! My father had given it to me on my last birthday; at the time I had been disappointed, but now I was glad. I took it out of its box, put it in my pocket with the twenty centimes, and cautiously opened the door to the hall.

"The fat bronze goddess on the upstairs landing was brandishing the gas lamp like a hand grenade. Downstairs I heard my father shout, 'Why don't you move your queen?' and knew that he was playing chess with *Tante* Amélie. I turned back to my room and closed the door behind me. Nothing was going to stop me now. I went over to the window and opened it again. Aged ivy covered the walls at either side, and, scared to death, in my clumsy old-fashioned clothes, I reached out among the leaves till I felt a strong stem like a cable, stepped over the iron grille in front of the window, and with a breathless prayer, began my descent. Very awkward it was, too. I made a lot of noise, and all the sparrows in the ivy woke up and flew chattering away. About six feet above the ground the ivy ripped away from the wall, and down I went with a crash into a fuchsia bush. I sat there listening to my heart and

225

waiting for the entire household to come out with lanterns.

"But nothing happened! After an eternity I got up and stole out of the garden. Both the knees had been torn out of my stockings, I was dirty, and my hair was full of ivy twigs, but it didn't matter.

"In less than five minutes I had arrived at the carnival! It was even better than I had hoped: full of crowds and bright lights and noise. The carrousel with its whirling painted horses and its music was like nothing I had ever seen before. I rode on it twice and when I screamed with excitement nobody paid any attention because they were all doing the same thing. After that I bought a ride on a camel. That took some courage, as I had never seen a camel before and did not know that they possessed such sarcastic faces. Have you ever ridden on one?"

"Never," said Randy.

"You must try it sometime. It made me a little seasick but I enjoyed it. Then I went and watched the dancing bear softly rocking to and fro on his hind paws like a tipsy old man in bedroom slippers. There was too much to see; I was dazzled, and just walked about staring blissfully.

"I was fascinated by the fortuneteller's booth. It was really a large wagon with a hooped roof which you entered by a pair of wooden steps. On one side there was a large placard bearing the words: 'Zenaïda, world-renowned seeress and soothsayer! Advice and prophecy on affairs of business or the heart. Palmistry, cards, or crystal as preferred.' On the other side there was a life-sized picture of a dark, beautiful woman gazing into a crystal globe. I hesitated only a moment, then I mounted the steps, parted the flaps of the tent, and entered. Inside the tent was draped with shabby shawls of many colors; overhead a red glass lantern cast a murky light, and at a small table sat a gypsy woman glittering and jingling with earrings, clattering bracelets and necklaces. She looked almost nothing like the picture outside. She was older, and her fingernails were dirty. I was dreadfully disappointed.

"'What do you want, kid?' she said. Her voice was hoarse and rough as though she had spent her whole life shouting.

" 'To-to-have my fortune told,' I stammered.

" 'Got any money?' asked the woman doubtfully, looking at my torn stockings and dirty dress.

" 'Yes,' I said.

" 'Let me see it,' she demanded.

"I brought the gold piece out of my pocket. The gypsy examined it craftily; then she smiled a wide, delighted smile. One of her teeth was black.

" 'You must have found that in a well-lined pocket,' said she.

"At first I did not understand what she meant. Then I was angry.

" 'I never stole anything in my life!' I told her. 'My father gave it to me for a present.'

" 'Your father? He is a rich man?'

" 'I suppose he is,' I said. 'I don't know. I never thought about it. Anyway I don't think I want you to tell my fortune after all.'

"Quick as a cat the gypsy sprang from her chair and barred the entrance.

" 'Forgive me, mademoiselle,' she wheedled. 'I didn't real-ize— Your clothes are torn, and you have such a dirty face. Come and sit down; I'll tell you a fortune you'll never forget: splendid, wonderful things are going to happen to you. I see luck shining all around you!'

"Well, who could resist that? In spite of myself, I was soon seated opposite Zenaïda, my dirty hand in her dirtier one. Before she began to read my palm she called out in her harsh gypsy voice, 'Bastien!'

"A young man's face appeared at the entrance, and Zenaïda said something to him in a strange language. The young man nodded, looked at me, and burst out laughing. Then he disappeared.

"The gypsy lived up to her word. Never was such a fortune told to a human being! Jewels, lovers, fame, travels into far countries, all were promised to me, and I sat there like a half-wit believing every word.

" 'I must go,' I said at last. 'Please take what I owe you out of this.' I gave her the gold piece trustingly. And that, of course, was the last I ever saw of it.

" 'We will drive you home in the wagon,' said Zenaïda, smiling. I could hear Bastien hitching up the horses outside.

" 'No, thank you,' said I. 'It's not far, only a little way. If you will give me what you owe me I will go.' I realized that the music had stopped, and a sound of hammering and clattering had taken its place. The carnival was being dismantled. I had been in the wagon for a long time.

" 'We will take you home,' Zenaïda insisted. 'It's almost midnight, and we must be on our way anyhow. Where do you live, and what is your father's name?'

"Like a fool I told her.

"Bastien called to the horses, and the wagon began to move; the red lantern swinging in a slow circle overhead.

"I was so busy thinking of my glittering future that it was some time before I realized that we must have left my house far behind. When I began asking frightened questions the gypsy came close to me and grabbed my arm. She told me that I was not going home, but far away, till my father was ready to pay a price to get me back. When I cried and struggled she called Bastien and they bound my wrists and ankles and tied a rag over my mouth. All night I lay on the floor in the dark feeling the wagon lurch and sway, and hearing Zenaïda's snores and Bastien's voice swearing at the horses. I was sick with terror.

"I remained with the gypsies for three weeks. The first day Zenaïda unbraided my hair, took away my shoes and stockings, and dressed me in gaudy rags. She pierced my ears for brass earrings, and, stooping down, picked up a handful of earth and rubbed it across my face. 'There!' she said. 'Now even a gypsy would think you were a gypsy!'

"In spite of her, and in spite of the letter I was forced to write my father during the second week, telling him where to leave the ransom money if he wished to see me again, I enjoyed many things about those three weeks. The wagon and the travel and the going barefoot! The sound of rain on canvas

229

overhead; the noise and smell of the carnival: a noise of bells and talk and music; a smell of garlic and tobacco and people and that camel! But the bad things more than overshadowed the good. Zenaïda was cruel, and so was Bastien when he got drunk, which was often.

"One fine day we came to a small town in the Loire district. There was a big cathedral on the square, I remember, that looked huge and disapproving beyond the carnival's tawdry, jingling whirl of light and music.

"When Zenaïda was telling fortunes in the wagon Bastien was supposed to keep an eye on me. I had to stay near the wagon or run the risk of a bad whipping. But on this particular evening, Bastien, a little tipsier than usual, went to sleep under the wagon with his head on his hat. I saw my chance and wandered away. I had no thought of escape. I was too dirty and dispirited, and I had no money; my sheltered life had taught me nothing of fending for myself or what to do in an emergency. However, for the moment I enjoyed myself watching the familiar sights of the carnival and the many unfamiliar faces.

"Suddenly I saw something that made me gasp!

"Standing under a gas lamp at the outskirts of the crowd was a tall man with a beard. In his hands were a small sketch-book and a pencil. It was Monsieur Jules Clairon who never could resist a carnival!

"I ran to him bleating like a lost sheep. 'Oh, Monsieur Clairon, save me, save me, and take me away from here!'

"Poor man, he looked horrified, and who can blame him? I had accumulated the dirt of three weeks.

"'I don't know any gypsies!' said he. 'How do you know my name?'

"'But I'm the *princess*, don't you remember?' I cried idiotically. And then I explained.

"'Good Lord!' he said, horrified. 'I knew nothing about your disappearance. I left Saint-Germain early the next morning on a walking tour.'

"He took me back to the house where he was staying, and

230

the landlady scrubbed me and gave me clean clothes, while he got the police and went back to the carnival. But Zenaïda must have found out what had happened, for the gypsy wagon had disappeared. Nobody ever saw it again.

"As for me, I was rushed home by train the next day. I was embraced by my haggard father, who was relieved on two accounts: first because of my safe return, and second because the ransom money had never been collected. All my aunts wept over me wetly, and I had to have my hair washed every day for two weeks, but in spite of everything I was glad to be home.

"When my father begged Monsieur Clairon to tell him how he could reward him, Monsieur Clairon replied, 'Allow me to paint the portrait of your daughter.' So that is how it came about. Later on it was he who persuaded my family to send me to school in England. I went to a convent there for seven years which, though it would have seemed dreadfully strict to you, was heaven itself as far as I was concerned."

Mrs. Oliphant opened a pocketbook like a giant clam, extracted some money to pay the bill, and clapped it shut again. "That's all," she said.

Randy rose slowly to the surface and emerged from the story dreamily.

"It was wonderful," she said. "Things like that never happen to us. We lead a humdrum life when I think about it. It's funny how it doesn't seem humdrum."

"That's because you have 'eyes the better to see with, my dear' and 'ears the better to hear with.' Nobody who has them and uses them is likely to find life humdrum very often. Even when they have to use bifocal lenses, like me."

It was dark when they came out. The rain had stopped but the streets were still wet; crisscrossed with reflected light. The shop windows were lighted too. In one bright rectangle floated a mannequin in a dress of green spangles, exactly like a captured mermaid in an aquarium.

"I go up and you go downtown," said Mrs. Oliphant when they came to Fifth Avenue. She held out her hand. "Thank you for coming to tea."

"Oh, thank you *very* much for inviting me," said Randy. "Could I—would you let me come to see you someday?"

The old lady looked pleased. "Do come, child. Come by all means, and I'll show you the brass earrings Zenaïda made me wear. I kept them for luck. I have a lot of interesting things: Javanese puppets, and a poison ring, and a beetle carved out of an emerald, and the tooth of a czarina—"

"The tooth of a czarina!" cried Randy, stopping dead.

"That's another story, my dear," said the old lady exasperatingly. A big Brontosaurus of a bus clattered to a pause. "This is mine," said Mrs. Oliphant, climbing on it and waving her hand. "Good-bye, Miranda!"

Randy crossed the street and boarded a big Stegosaurus going the other way.

At home she went straight to Rush's room. He was having a peaceful half hour before dinner reading, with his feet on the radiator and the radio going full blast. A voice that made all the furniture tremble was describing the excellence of a certain kind of hair tonic.

"Are you worried by the possibility of premature baldness?" inquired the voice in intimately confidential tones that could be heard a block away. "Does it trouble you to see your once luxuriant hair thinning out—"

Randy snapped off the radio. "You don't have to worry about that yet awhile," she said.

Rush looked up from his book. "Huh? Oh, hello. Have a good time?"

"Wonderful. Guess who I met?"

"Mickey Rooney," said Rush.

"No, silly. The Elephant. Only I'm never going to call her that again."

"Oh, just the Elephant." Rush was disappointed.

"Not just the Elephant. She's swell, she's a friend of mine now, and I'm going to see her. She was kidnaped by gypsies and lived with them for weeks."

"Recently?" inquired Rush, startled.

"No, no. Years ago when she was a little girl in France. I'll

232

tell you about it after dinner. And look, she sent you these. All of you I mean."

"What are they?" said Rush, taking a bite.

"Pitty foors," said Randy. "I think it's French. For cakes, probably."

"Pitty foors," repeated Rush mellowly, through chocolate custard. "Not bad, not bad at all. So she was kidnaped by gypsies, was she? Do you think the El— Mrs. Oliphant would care to have me come along with you when you go calling on her?"

"I know she would," said Randy. "And, Rush, let's go soon and often."

Helen Train Hilles

HANDSOME IS

ILLUSTRATED BY *Keith Ward*

TONY hated to leave Handsome at home
every morning. But his teacher (not like the one in "Mary Had
a Little Lamb") wouldn't let him bring a dog to school, and
Handsome was far too timid to be tied outside to wait.

Still, it could have been worse. For Tony's little sister Jane
was at home, and she and her lame chicken, Omelet, took care
of Handsome while Tony was away. Luckily Handsome seemed
to be fond of both of them.

So Tony made up for being away so much by taking the dog
for an early morning walk, before it was time for school. He was
doing that today.

Tony sighed as he stopped to let Handsome chew a thin
blade of grass. His freckled hand loosened on the dog's shiny
red leash. Handsome loved to eat grass and he looked so funny
when he got a long straw of it stuck between his widely spaced
bulldog front teeth that the tight places in Tony eased up a little
bit. And the steady worry he felt about Handsome left him for
a moment.

Handsome, who had always been so frightened of everything,

had improved a little, Tony thought. After he had won the prize in the Pet Show for having the most kinds of dog in him Tony had felt almost happy for a few days. Surely Handsome's winning a prize would shut up Tommy Green, who'd always teased him so about his dog. And when Tony was teased about his dog it hurt more than anything he could think of—except the one time he thought the Family had forgotten his birthday.

Look at Handsome now! His tail was straight out behind him—not stuck between his legs—and he was trotting along contentedly, close by the heels of Tony's galoshes. Tony started to whistle.

And then he saw Tommy Green. He stopped whistling and his throat grew tight. He felt he just about couldn't stand being teased any more. It *hurt* so to be a good sport. It was almost time to turn around and go home. Should he pretend he didn't see Tommy?

No! That would be—that would be somehow too much like the way he *didn't* want Handsome to be! Tony firmly squared his shoulders and thrust out his jaw, though inside he felt all queer and trembly like the time he'd had the measles.

"Hi!" he said. His voice sounded way down deep like Father's, not like his own at all. Maybe—maybe this time Handsome would wag his tail.

"Hi!" said Tommy. His green eyes looked mockingly at Handsome. "What a dog!" he added airily. His scrawny arm waved in the direction of Tony's dog. Handsome cringed as though struck and slunk off as far as his leash would let him, his front paws scraping the ground. The jerk almost yanked Tony off his feet, but he tightened his grip on the leash till his hand hurt. That was the trouble with Handsome. You *thought* he'd improved, but you couldn't *count* on him not to get scared. This time it was all Tommy's fault. Tommy had hurt his feelings—and Tony's, too.

"Your own father gave him a prize in the Pet Show!" Tony's voice was hollow and sort of strangled sounding. That wasn't quite fair, he knew. You couldn't bring fathers into it. But he was desperate.

"Ya! He only got a prize for being so funny looking!" jeered Tommy. Tony was sunk. That was perfectly true. His anger faded, but he stayed hurt.

"He lets Omelet do anything he wants to him," he said in a low voice. Tommy paused, trying to think of something to say. Tony didn't realize that it had always rankled with Tommy that Handsome had gotten a prize. And every kid in the neighborhood envied Janey's lame chicken Omelet, who had hopped into her life the day after the Pet Show.

"He only lets Omelet because he's scared of him—her!" Tommy's voice was high with pleasure at his bright idea. "Omelet's got twice the guts Handsome has."

An awful weight descended on Tony. Was that true? It mattered awfully, because one of the reasons he was almost sure Handsome had improved was the way he let Omelet play with him. Something stung back of Tony's eyeballs, and he turned his back hastily. Handsome was pulling frantically now, his quivering body a streak along the ground. Tony wasn't at all sure he could hold the terrified dog, so the wisest thing was to follow. Maybe Tommy wouldn't know he had to. Tommy's maddening voice followed Tony's back as he rushed along behind Handsome.

"Who's leading who?" it yelled.

"I'll show him—I'll show him—somehow!" thought Tony miserably as he flew unwillingly toward home.

Handsome slowed up and stopped trembling as they drew near the wide opening in the hedge in front of Tony's house. Tony was breathing hard. His right hand felt cold and numb. He was almost mad at Handsome. Had all these weeks of patience and training and—and hope, and standing being teased, been no use? Why couldn't Handsome keep on behaving properly when Tommy was there? He looked almost like any other dog now!

" 'Lo," said a calm small voice. "C'mere and help with Omelet's splinter, will you?" Janey was sitting on the porch, toes turned in, Omelet contentedly in her arms. Her thundercloud face under the thick black bangs looked very tender as she examined Omelet's stiff leg.

236

"Splint, not splinter, you dodo," said Tony. "Sure I will." He couldn't look the way he felt or Janey would notice.

Omelet clucked and stuck her pointed black beak against Tony's sweater. Her round shiny black eyes looked pleasantly mocking. She ruffled her rusty brown feathers and gave an extra cluck in Handsome's direction. Handsome's tail gave what for it was a wag. Tony took a deep breath. He *was* right. Handsome *did* like Omelet. Everything seemed nicer.

"It's just the bandages come a little loose around her—around her knee," explained Janey. Tony was skillful with hurt animals, and it didn't take him a minute to lay the tongue depressor that was the splint comfortably against Omelet's scaly leg and tighten the gauze bandage.

"Daddy says Omelet's almost well and we can take the splint off soon," said Janey.

"Oh, I think she needs it for a little while longer," said Tony hastily. Of course he and Janey wanted Omelet to get well and all that, but still a lame chicken was somehow more exciting than a perfectly whole one. And it was soothing to have one pet that the other children envied. "Golly, I'm going to be late for school!" yelled Tony suddenly after looking at his nickel-plated watch.

He turned and ran down the steps. He didn't really want to leave the quiet of the lawn to go back to Tommy Green's eyes. But he had to. He couldn't resist an anxious backward glance at Handsome as he ran. The dog was lying placidly in the sun and as Tony looked, Omelet, who had escaped from Janey's arms with a funny, one-sided flutter, landed on Handsome's back. There she stood, stiffly upright, flapping her wings as though to take off. Handsome didn't move.

All during school that day Tony felt a new courage. Maybe he was getting somewhere. He even made himself stare at Tommy Green without lowering his eyes. Tommy'd been wrong about the Omelet part anyway!

When school was over he hurried home. He'd thought of a new way to make Handsome less timid. Whenever he found anything the dog was scared of, he'd lead him gently up to it,

237

and then give him an extra puppy biscuit or a nice bone. Maybe that would help. He was quite encouraged by his new idea. He walked a little faster and practiced toeing out, for fun.

While he was still quite far off, through the side part of the hedge that had been winter-killed, Tony could see the little patch of green lawn in front of his house. He could hardly wait to reach it, it looked so peaceful. Janey had fallen asleep on the grass, arm outstretched over her head. Handsome was lying by her. Tony couldn't see whether he was asleep or not (you could tell with Janey, because if she was ever quiet she was bound to be asleep) but he could see one paw lying over Janey's green-and-white checked gingham dress. Omelet was giving a one-sided, slow strut near by, pausing to give an occasional peck at Handsome.

Tony hurried on. But suddenly he stopped short in his tracks. Something so awful was happening that he couldn't move!

A slinky, wolfish-looking thing had sneaked up to the hole in the hedge and was peeking through, blocking the opening. It gathered itself together as if about to spring. At that moment Tony noticed the jingling end of broken chain dangling from its collar. In a flash he recognized the enemy. The Jones' police dog! The watch dog they kept chained up because he killed chickens! He must have broken away!

Power came back into Tony's legs, and he started to run. Panting as he ran he yelled, "Look out! Oh, Janey, look out!" He stumbled and picked himself up again. He was almost there, and suddenly shrieks and cacklings and unknown sounds split the quiet of the street. The sounds roared in Tony's ears. He vaulted the hedge and saw in one relieved moment that Janey was standing on the porch screaming and holding a struggling but live squawking Omelet. Rooster-like sounds were coming from the chicken. Then he saw the whirling lawn. Two big animals were rolling around so swiftly and fiercely that you couldn't tell one from the other. A dogfight! For a moment it didn't dawn on Tony *who* was fighting. Mother had burst out on the porch and was holding Janey, all mixed up with Omelet and a frying pan, tight in her arms. Suddenly Tony knew.

238

"Handsome!" Tony's shriek was full of pain as he ran towards the struggling mass. What could he do? He could never separate them, and that brute would kill his dog!

"Tony!" Mother's voice was tight. She meant it. "Don't go near those dogs! They might hurt you!" She hugged Janey tighter.

Tony stopped stock-still. His eyes strained, trying to follow the motions of the dogs. And inside of him was a feeling of terror. He didn't care what Handsome was like, he didn't want him hurt! He shut his eyes. The sounds grew less—so soft that Tony couldn't stand it and opened his eyes again. Now Tony could see that Handsome had the police dog by the throat!

The noise had roused the street, and the edges of the lawn were packed with people—people you knew every day but who now had the blurred face of a crowd. They were all shouting but nobody was doing anything.

"Stand back!" "How'd he get loose?" "Get some pepper, somebody!" "Keep away!" Tony, standing tense, saw Mr. Jones, white-faced and hair sticking up in wisps, vault the fence with a big whip in his hand.

"I'll separate them!" he said. "Back, everybody!" Tony covered his eyes as he heard the whip whizz through the air. His whole body felt stiff. But they had to do it to save Handsome.

Then it was all over. Mr. Jones had his cowering police dog on a piece of laundry rope and was talking to Mother.

Tony ran blindly to the place where Handsome was and picked him up, all bloody and streaked, in his arms. The dog's heart was beating fast, close against his sweater, as he hugged him, almost sobbing. Handsome *couldn't* be badly hurt. He was licking Tony's ear!

Mr. Jones's voice talking to Mother sounded far away.

"I'm terribly sorry. He must have broken his chain. I don't think he would have attacked Janey, but that chicken! If it hadn't been for your boy's dog! Of course I'll send him away after this. I came as soon as I heard."

Tony's eyes were wet as he looked up from Handsome. A shock of joy plunged through him as he realized what Mr. Jones had said. *Handsome had saved Omelet!* He *was* brave, as dogs should be! Braver—because he must have been terribly scared of the police dog. Tony hugged him tighter.

Mother was down on her knees by Handsome, too, now. In her hand she still held the frying pan she had been carrying.

"Good dog!" She patted him, not minding the blood that was coming from the gash in his flank. "You risked your life to protect us. Tony, I saw it from the dining room. That big brute was going right for Omelet—with Janey between, when Handsome stiffened and growled and sprang! Just think what might have happened!"

But something had happened to Tony. He raised his head high. The admiring eyes of the crowd were on his dog. Suddenly he saw Tommy Green by the fence.

"You shouldn't have worried, Mother," he said loudly and a little disagreeably. "Handsome was there!"

Tommy's mouth dropped open, making him look dumber than ever. And now Tony knew that no matter what happened, he would never mind Tommy Green again.

"Listen," he went on. "I need a basin of warm water—and those—those sterile bandages of yours, Mother! And the iodine and— No, Janey, don't pat him, it might hurt his wounds—"

Many hands offered to help bandage Handsome. But Tony did it all by himself. By the time they were through (though he really hadn't been badly hurt at all) his whole body was done up in sterile gauze with his tail emerging dirty white from the bandages. The dog lay there with what Tony was sure was a new pride in his eyes and listened calmly while everyone praised him. Tony felt thawed out inside and happier than he'd ever been since way back before he got Handsome.

"Well, mercy! I must go in and get lunch! Everything's probably burnt!" said Mother.

At that moment a cart jingled outside and a ragged looking man came in at the gate. With difficulty Handsome rose stiffly to his feet, standing erect and bristly, and looking like a strange thick ghost. From his throat came a low guttural growl.

"Why, Handsome!" Mother laughed. "It's only the scissors grinder. Yes, I've some for you to do."

Tony was staring at his dog.

"Why!" he said. "He's acting so—different!"

"I don't believe he's going to be frightened any more," said Mother. "He was much better anyway, after all your training—and now that he's overcome his fear enough to fight to protect us, I think he'll be cured."

Handsome lay down once more and closed his eyes. Tony kept staring at this bold new dog. This dog looked like Handsome but was just like other boys' dogs.

"I'm saving the roast beef bone for Handsome," went on Mother as she turned to go into the house. And Tony laughed as he heard her voice through the screen door.

"Handsome is as Handsome does!"

241

Chesley Kahmann

THE CREAM–COLORED PONY

ILLUSTRATED BY *Matilda Breuer*

THE new gypsy camp was a world of its own. All the men had disappeared for the day, but women in long, bright skirts dragged feather mattresses into the newly erected tents and stirred the food in the kettles over the smudgy, blazing fires. Already the smell of onions and sage and burning wood had come into the air. And everywhere there was shouting and laughter as children fed the horses and gathered twigs for the fires.

Linji, however, stood a little apart from everyone, staring at old Eldorai, who was hobbling away from her.

"I just can't believe it!" she gasped.

But there it was on her arm, the bracelet that old Eldorai had given her. And Eldorai's words still were in her ears: "It's your own, dearie, for all the good turns you've done an old woman!"

"Even Nareli has nothing so precious!" Linji thought. It sparkled in the sun and the white stones seemed to flash a hundred colors. It made all the other beads and bracelets Linji wore look shabby.

The next moment Linji started toward her sister, Nareli, her

242

wide, ankle-length orange skirts swishing grandly and her jewelry jangling. Nareli was going to tell fortunes at the next fair, but even Nareli had nothing as valuable as this new bracelet.

"Oh!" cried Nareli, who had been stirring a stew in one of the kettles. "Let me see it! Whose is it? Let me have it in my own hands for a small, wee moment!"

"It's mine!" said Linji. "Eldorai gave it to me!"

"Why'd she give it to *you*?" asked Nareli, her face darkening. "You aren't going to tell fortunes at the fair! Here, give it to me!" She grabbed at the bracelet, but Linji jumped back.

The next moment Nareli said, "I'll give you my purple scarf for just one moment's wearing of it."

"No," said Linji, fearful that her sister would not return it.

"I'll give you my red skirt," offered Nareli, impatiently. "And my green earrings." Quickly she took off her earrings and held them out. "See, they're yours!"

But still Linji shook her head.

At that, Nareli reached forward and gave Linji's arm a deep pinch. Linji screamed.

"Hush! hush!" said Nareli. Then, in a low voice: "I won't forget, and that's God's truth! May the dazzling stones in the ugly bracelet bring you the worst of luck!"

"You've no right!" shouted Linji, angrily. "You—you——"

But the next moment she was stalking out of camp, past the three green wagons with yellow wheels, past the tethered horses. Then she was alone in the wood, but still thinking, "She's no right!"

It was a new neighborhood to explore, and Linji began to take deep breaths. To rest her legs she ran forward, stopping only when she had splashed into a hidden spring. She took off her sandals and waded in the water. From that moment, Nareli was forgotten.

Soon she caught sight of a squirrel above her in a tree. At once she began to make strange little sounds in her throat. The squirrel sat listening, his head cocked to one side. Then he, too, made sounds, as if he understood all that Linji said.

243

For an hour or more he followed Linji, chattering and scolding. Occasionally there was a trill from a bird or the sound of a woodpecker drilling. Linji made birdcalls, too, waiting after each one to see if there would be an answer.

But suddenly, above the chattering of the squirrel, came other sounds. Linji stood still and listened. Voices and laughter —but not gypsy laughter—and hoofs upon the ground. She stole toward them. Finally she stood very, very still, peering through a clump of bushes. Beyond were two Gorgios, a girl and a boy. The boy was riding the most beautiful pony she had ever seen —cream-colored with a black mane and tail. He was slightly larger than an Indian pony, and he raised his feet nicely, proudly, and held his head high. The girl rode a lively pony.

Linji, behind bushes where she could see and not be seen, moved closer, hearing talk of school which would open soon, and a dance. She could tell that the boy liked the girl and wanted her to think him superior to other boys. At least he seemed to, with all that talk about football and what he was going to do. He called her Helen and she called him Bob.

Linji followed, thinking: "If I could just ride the cream-colored pony! If I just could!" Cautiously she crawled from

bush to bush. "Oh, I've just *got* to ride him!" Perhaps the boy would let her!

She circled away from the Gorgios and, when far enough so they could not hear her, ran ahead as fast as she could, then back to the path they were following. She climbed a small tree. And there, sitting on a limb which jutted out over the path, she waited for Helen and Bob.

Before long she heard their voices and the feet of the ponies. She sat very still until they were under the tree. Then she moved her legs.

As she had expected, the ponies swerved to one side. With a laugh, Linji sprang out of the tree and grabbed both bridles. The girl, frightened, screamed. The boy pulled on the reins and tried to turn his pony around.

"Oh, don't be scared!" said Linji, repentant of the trick. "I did it only for fun." She wondered what would have happened had the girl fallen and got that clean gray riding costume dirty. Her hair was tucked in under a clean black hat, too, with light curls sticking out.

"Go away!" said the boy.

But Helen stared at Linji's uncombed hair that had never known a hat, at the dirty blouse and wrinkled sash, and the orange skirt that fell to Linji's ankles.

"Who—who are you?" she finally asked. "And where do you live?"

"I live everywhere," Linji said. Then, to Bob: "Come, give me a ride! Give a poor gypsy a ride on the cream-colored pony, and bring yourself a little luck for the kindness!"

At the word "gypsy," Helen seemed to shrink back and at the same time to be interested.

"You—you've just come here?" Helen asked.

"Don't talk to her," advised Bob. To Linji, "Move aside, and hurry up about you!" Again he tried to turn his pony.

"You wouldn't go without giving me a ride, would you?" Linji asked quickly. She still kept her hands on the bridles.

"I'd be smart, now, doing that!" said Bob. "It'd be good-bye, pony!"

245

At that, Linji's black eyes flashed angrily.

"Do you think I'd steal him and be caught for it, and get my people into trouble?" she cried. "I'd be smart, doing that, I would!"

"Move!" commanded the boy.

"I can ride the fastest ponies in the world and not fall off," said Linji in a softer voice. Then, seeing that that kind of talk did not help either, she said, "Here, let me tell your fortunes."

"Do you really know how?" Helen asked.

"Of course," said Linji. She wished with all her heart that she did know how, that she had paid more attention to the older gypsies when they had talked of fortunes. "Here, give me your hand." She looked into Helen's eyes, trying to find a sign which would tell her what to say.

Helen reached her hand toward Linji, but Bob said, "Come on, we haven't time to waste on that!"

Linji ignored the remark, taking Helen's hand into her own, saying quickly, "Your name is Helen."

"Did you hear that?" Helen gasped.

"All the boys like to dance with you," continued Linji, remembering Helen's conversation.

Bob cleared his throat. Oh, surely this fortune would win a ride on the pony!

"Can you tell me what his name is?" asked Helen, pointing to Bob.

"I'll have to look at his hand," Linji said, pretending that she could not know the answer otherwise.

"Give her your hand," said Helen.

"Aw, she couldn't tell!" said Bob. But, obviously because Helen had asked the favor, he condescendingly stretched out his hand. "She hit yours accidentally. Helen's a common name."

Linji turned Bob's hand this way and that. She puckered up her face as if puzzled, finally saying, "Your name begins with a B. It might be Bob."

"Listen to that, now, would you!" said Helen disdainfully.

"Oh, I've got to have a ride, I've got to!" Linji kept thinking. Aloud, she said, "You're going to school sometime." Sooner or

later all rich boys went to school. And Bob looked rich.

"That's right," said Helen. "Maybe next year."

"Sure, she can tell a fortune!" said Bob. "You tell her every-thing, yourself!"

"If you don't believe in fortunes," said Linji, "then you shouldn't listen to them! But from those lines in your hand— several little lines right there"—grabbing his hand and brushing over a number of lines—"it says you are interested!"

"Show me the lines!" said Helen.

"You couldn't see them," said Linji. "You're only Gorgios!"

"Go on, tell him some more!" said Helen.

"You've met a dark-haired friend," said Linji, quickly. "All you have to do is give her a ride on the pony."

At that, Bob jerked his hand back, saying: "Oh, so that's it! All this, so you'd get a ride! Nothing doing!" He said trium-phantly to Helen, "What'd I tell you!"

"Oh, I'm foolish, trying to go so fast!" thought Linji, miserable at the thought of failure. Eldorai often spent a whole week getting something she wanted. But aloud, she said desperately: "You're a good dancer, too. No wonder your friend likes to dance with you."

"Who said she did?" shouted Bob.

Then Linji realized that she had said too much. She must be more careful or the Gorgios would discover that her informa-tion came from their own conversation. But she covered her mistake by adding, "Well, her dancing line is the same shape as yours, that's all." She should not have mentioned dancing at all. Why hadn't she said something about football? That would have appealed to Bob more. But it was too late now.

"Come, give me a wee ride!" Linji begged. When Bob refused, she continued, "You'd let me go to all this trouble, and then not give me a tiny, short ride?"

"Go on, let her!" said Helen. "She won't be long."

"Oh, and that's the truth!" agreed Linji. She stripped herself of all her jewelry except the new bracelet and thrust it into Helen's hands. "Keep it, to prove I'll come back." She patted the cream-colored pony's neck, and the pony rubbed his nose against her hand.

In the end Bob dismounted, but it was plain that he would not have done so had it not been for Helen.

"What's his name?" Linji asked.

"Gregory," said Bob. "Now don't go far away from us."

Linji unfastened the girths of the saddle. "I could never get along on such a thing!" she said. "You keep it." She put the saddle upon the ground, then took hold of Gregory's mane, and in a moment was on his back, her legs squeezed close to his warm sides.

Off she rode, patting Gregory's neck, telling him that she was his friend. If Nareli could just see her riding this cream-colored pony with the black mane and tail! How grand she must look! And how the bracelet sparkled! It was not far to the gypsy encampment. She would show them.

She rode to the tents. Children shouted as she drew near and begged for a ride. Women crowded about.

"What a grai!"

"Let me on his back!"

"Keep away!" warned Linji. "Where's Nareli?"

Learning that Nareli had gone to a farmhouse for food, Linji brushed the children aside and rode to the main road. Sure enough, there was Nareli, trudging along in the dust, dragging a sack behind her. Linji rode to her and stopped.

"*This* is the bad luck the bracelet brought me!" boasted Linji.

248

But Nareli only said, "The potatoes are heavy, fine sister." She rested the sack on the ground, looking at the pony. "And the day is hot, so let's just put the sack behind you on the grai. I'll walk along and steady it." She looked, too, at the bracelet.

"What!" said Linji. "Use him for carrying potatoes! He'd be black instead of cream-colored, after that!"

Then, as Nareli's face darkened, she touched Gregory's sides with her heels. The pony started down the road at a gallop, leaving Nareli in a cloud of dust.

With Bob and Helen again, Linji said, "Oh, he's a good one, and he can go like the wind, just the way I like to ride!"

Helen returned the jewelry. Linji dismounted and gave Gregory back to his master, who promptly swung the saddle over his back. Bob seemed less suspicious of her now.

"A circus wanted to buy him, once," he said.

"But Bob wouldn't sell him," said Helen. Then, "My pony's named Morovan, and I call him Moro."

Linji, feeling guilty that she had not paid Moro any attention before, patted his nose. But she stole glances at Gregory. In all the world there was not another pony like him.

A squirrel darted across the path.

"Let's catch him," said Linji. If she could interest Bob enough, she might get another ride.

"Could you?" asked Helen.

"We'll see," said Linji. "Here, tie your ponies to a tree." She imitated the squirrel's chuckles and chatter and saw the squirrel, who had moved on a short distance, turn to look back at her.

"I'll bet she does have a way!" whispered Helen. She dismounted from Moro. "Come on, Bob, let's see if we can catch him! Wouldn't it be slick if we could learn a trick like that?"

Bob and Helen tied their ponies to a tree. Then they followed Linji as Linji crept almost up to the squirrel. The squirrel darted farther away. Linji coaxed him back a little. The squirrel scolded, chattered, darted away again.

After perhaps half an hour, Bob said: "You're no nearer catching him than you were in the first place! I don't believe you *can* catch him!"

250

"I guess he's not used to you," said Linji. "I guess maybe he's afraid of you."

"We got pretty close, anyhow," said Helen.

"I guess maybe we could have had him in a little while," said Linji. But perhaps it was just as well that they gave up the chase. Bob did seem impatient.

They walked back toward the ponies—over twigs and matted leaves and brushing against prickly bushes. At last they came to the tree where they had tied the ponies. But only Moro was there.

The cream-colored pony was gone!

Seated cross-legged on the ground around kettles of stew, the gypsies ate with special gaiety. For Linji's father, Taimi, had announced that the county fair would open the day after to-morrow and the gypsies had been given permission to tell fortunes there. With the tribe so sadly in need of money, that had been joyous news.

But Linji paid little attention. Instead, she watched the flames rise into the blackness of night, watched burned wood turn white and curl into thin, paper-like pieces.

"Oh, he was such a fine grai!" she kept thinking. "And he had such straight legs, and his mane was so black against his body!" She had searched the wood with Bob and Helen until dark, finally confident that Gregory had gotten loose and gone home by himself, the way a horse would do if he had the chance. Bob had been very angry about everything, but he would see! He would find his pony in his own stable!

Her own people had scolded her for ever having spoken to the Gorgios—and then everyone had forgotten the pony at Taimi's news of the fair.

The meal finished, someone tuned a violin. Two girls moved into the center of the ring and began to dance. Nareli clapped her hands and jumped to her feet, too, swaying this way, that way, to the rhythm.

But suddenly the music stopped and the dancers moved back.

"That's the girl, right there!" someone cried.

251

Bob, accompanied by four men, rushed toward Linji.

"Maybe you know where the pony is!" one of the men said. "I'm the sheriff."

Linji tried hard not to show the anger she felt. So Bob had come with a bodyguard, had he?

Taimi stood before the sheriff, saying: "We wouldn't steal a pony. Not us. But we'd be glad if you'd look around."

Bob kept shouting out the whole story of Linji's riding his pony as the men searched the camp. The more Bob talked, the more silent Linji became. She calmly denied knowing any more about Gregory than Bob did.

"Well, he's not here, that's true," admitted the sheriff, finally. "But tomorrow morning, early, you're to move on—the whole bunch of you. And don't come back, unless you want to camp in jail! Understand?"

It made no difference to the sheriff that the gypsies needed to earn money at the fair. Nothing made any difference. The Gorgios departed, repeating the warning to move on.

"If there's trouble, it's us that're blamed!" wailed old Eldorai.

"There's the one we have to thank for it!" shouted someone else, pointing to Linji.

"Yes, why'd you so much as look at the Gorgios? Don't you know what they are by this time?"

"Yes, it's your fault if we starve!"

Voices rose in indignation and anger, and Linji heard her name on almost every tongue. Miserably she sat before the fire, feeling very much alone. Suddenly Nareli slid over toward her and sat down at her side.

"How fine a ride you could be having in the moonlight while the Gorgios sleep!" Nareli whispered. "It was a fine grai, and he did travel like the wind."

"I wouldn't touch him again!" said Linji, disturbed that Nareli had come so close to her thoughts. "I've forgotten him."

"Oh, no, you don't forget," said Nareli, softly. "Such a pony was made for us who'd understand his ways, not for Gorgios.

"I said to myself," Nareli continued, " 'Linji should have him to ride.' Ha, I saw clear into your very heart."

Linji turned over a log. The wood crackled and gave off a smudgy, sweet odor. The voices of the old women grew louder, grumbling against Linji.

"Come, let's take a walk," said Nareli.

Linji, glad to escape, was soon walking into the black wood with her sister.

"It wasn't my fault the pony ran away," Linji said.

Nareli turned her flashlight from the path to Linji's face, saying, "I thought you understood!"

"Understood what?" asked Linji.

"I said to myself: 'I, and I, alone, can do my dear sister a favor. She won't do it for herself. Only I can borrow the pony and let her have a ride, when the night's quieted down and the Gorgios have given up the search until morning,' " said Nareli.

"You took him?" cried Linji. "And ran the risk of jail, and——"

"It was only borrowing," whispered Nareli. "There's no crime in doing that. After you have had a little ride on him, you can turn him loose, and he'll find his own stable fast enough by himself."

"Where is he?" demanded Linji.

But Nareli was in no hurry to tell. She simply said, "He's

safe enough." And added that she herself had fed him.

"Oh, I will turn him loose!" Linji thought, "after one little ride!" Already she could feel her legs against Gregory's sides, the breeze in her hair.

"And what'll you do for me—for the favor?" Nareli asked.

"Oh!" said Linji, angrily. "You did it for yourself, then, not me!" But the next moment, she was saying: "Show me the pony! And what do you want?"

"Ah, pretty, loving sister, what about the bracelet, for instance?" asked Nareli.

"Show me where he is first!" insisted Linji. "Then I'll give it to you."

The two hurried through brush and over sticks, Nareli saying, "Oh, and I was afraid, after the sheriff came!"

"But not afraid to let them think I stole the pony!" said Linji, angrily.

"I didn't mean any harm!" said Nareli.

But when they came upon Gregory in a place sheltered by three huge rocks, Linji began to forgive the trick. She untied the pony, felt his nose upon her shoulder.

"Here's the old bracelet!" said Linji.

With Nareli lighting the way, Linji rode through the darkness to a road, not the main road but one she knew would surely lead to the town.

"If you'd like to have me watch for you, I will," said Nareli.

"No," said Linji. "Go away."

She galloped down the road, the breeze blowing her hair, night air upon her face. The stars were above, and a long road lay ahead with fields and woods at the side.

"You're as good as my own for the hour!" she whispered.

Three times she let him reach the edge of town, then turned him back into the country, saying: "Oh, not quite yet! One more ride, Gregory!"

The moon slipped under a cloud, and the wind blew a little more strongly. It looked as if it might rain. Before long, Linji found herself not only at the edge of town, but on paved streets. The streets were dark except at the corners where there were street lights. Gregory's hoofs clattered in the stillness.

"I ought to turn him loose right now," Linji thought. But as she saw no one upon the streets, she thought she would wait until the next corner. Before she had gone that far, however, a group of boys appeared. Linji never could be sure where they had come from, but one called out, "Hey, that's Bob Baxter's pony!" and the boys rushed forward.

Linji found herself surrounded by them. Her first thought was to jump and run, but she realized that would be foolish, for the sheriff would know who she was.

"Give him to us!" one of the boys demanded.

"How smart you are!" said Linji. "Why'd I give him to you after all the trouble I've had to get him this far? Didn't I find him in the woods, caught so he couldn't get away? You should have seen him! Twenty men couldn't have found him!" Then, seeing their wide eyes, she continued, "So you've come just in time to show me the way to the Baxter house."

"Gee!" said one of the boys. "Where was he?"

"Caught, I said!" Linji repeated. "And he could have stayed there for weeks, with no food and no water, and all you would have stumbled on had you ever come upon him would have been his bones!"

The boys were glad enough to lead the way to Bob's house. Linji, towering above them, rode through the streets proudly, feeling more like a hero than she had imagined one could feel. More boys joined the procession and to them, also, Linji told the story.

At the Baxter house, Bob and his father and mother rushed out.

"She knew all the time!" Bob said. "She got afraid when the sheriff went out, so she brought Greg back!"

"Bob!" said Mr. Baxter, sternly.

"That's the way it looks!" insisted Bob.

Linji dismounted and handed Gregory over to his master, explaining once more how she had found him when she least expected to; how she had taken the trouble to return him.

Not for worlds would she tell about Nareli's part in the

255

finding. She and Nareli might quarrel within the tribe, but neither would be false to the other outside.

"Come into the house," said Mr. Baxter. "I'd like to talk to you, but it's too noisy out here."

As Bob took Gregory around the house to the barn, Linji followed Mr. and Mrs. Baxter up to the porch. Mr. Baxter opened the front screen door and Linji, head high, walked through proudly. She had never been inside a house like this before. Several times she had gone into the kitchen of a farmhouse, but never into a brick house like this one, through the front door!

Inside, Linji found another world. The living room was large, with polished furniture everywhere—furniture without a speck of dust. And the rug was so thick it made her want to take off her sandals and wade in it.

"Sit down," said Mrs. Baxter.

Linji sat down carefully on the edge of the red silk sofa. She looked about her at the several lamps, the pictures on the wall, the magazines and books on a table. She wished she could touch the keys of the piano across the room. And the long curtains were silk. And the chairs were so soft-looking and clean! How could people keep them so clean? She must remember it all so she could tell her people.

"What is your name?" asked Mr. Baxter.

Linji told him. Then, she told once more of that black wood where she had found the pony caught by his reins. She told about the dense thicket in such detail that it seemed more and more true.

"And my own sister fed him his supper," she added.

"Ugh!" Mrs. Baxter shuddered. "I'm glad Bob didn't prowl around in that awful place tonight!"

Linji wondered if all Gorgio mothers were like that. What was there to be afraid of? She wanted to laugh.

"Well," said Mr. Baxter, digging a hand into a pocket, "I should like to thank you for bringing Gregory back."

"Oh, that's all right," said Linji, rising to go.

"Any money in the house?" Mr. Baxter asked his wife. "I

256

haven't—what I want." Mrs. Baxter shook her head.

"Oh, I don't want any money," said Linji, "if that's what you're talking about."

She heard rain outside. It pattered against the window glass. She was glad it had begun, for she liked to walk along the road in it. But as she started for the door, Mrs. Baxter said: "I can't let you go all that way alone. Your mother wouldn't want you to!"

Linji stared at her. Her mother not want her to! How strange!

"You'd better stay all night," Mrs. Baxter said.

"All night in a house?" thought Linji. "Never. I shouldn't sleep a wink!" But aloud, she said, "The rain doesn't bother me any."

Just then Bob came into the house. His hair was quite wet.

"Yes, stay all night!" said Mr. Baxter.

Bob frowned. He shook his head at his father, as if warning him not to let a gypsy stay all night.

Linji's eyes flashed. There was no reason for Bob to continue this hostility. Not once had he even thanked her for returning his pony. And now he didn't want her in the house!

"I'll stay!" she said, so suddenly that even Mrs. Baxter looked surprised. To herself, she was thinking: "I'll show him! I'll stay in his old house! Oh, I will, even if it kills me!"

"Here's a nightgown for you," said Mrs. Baxter when she had taken Linji to her room. Then she showed Linji the bathroom, giving her two towels and a washcloth.

It was very, very funny, Linji thought. As soon as Mrs. Baxter had gone downstairs, she very carefully hung the towels and cloth on the glass rods with the other towels. They were far too clean ever to use. Then she examined the tub and looked into the mirror over the washbowl where she saw her own dark gypsy face.

She turned on the water. Some was hot; some was cold. The hot water burned her hands. So the Gorgios didn't have to heat it! The tub had both kinds of water, too, she found. Also, she found that the water stayed in the tub when she turned a certain knob. Off came her sandals in a great hurry and in splashed her feet.

"If Nareli could only see this!" she thought.

Before long, she dried her feet on the rug and went to her bedroom. She had seen Mrs. Baxter turn on the lights by pressing a certain button. She pressed it now, herself. The room became dark. Another push, and it became light. For a while she played with the mysterious button, laughing to think how easy it all was.

Then she looked at the bed. Mrs. Baxter had turned down the spread, and the white, unwrinkled sheets showed. The nightgown lay at the foot.

"Ha, did she really think I'd wear it!" thought Linji.

As she walked across the room, she caught sight of herself in a full-length mirror. For a moment she stood looking at her wide orange skirt. She had not known it was so dirty. She retied the sash to make herself look a little better.

On the dresser lay a piece of silver which, overturned, became a hand mirror.

"The Gorgios certainly like to look at themselves!" she thought. "Wouldn't Nareli like to have this, though!" Already she had forgiven her sister for taking the pony.

She could hear the rain now, but not well enough, so she opened a window, letting the rain come into the room and spatter her face. She felt better. How stuffy a Gorgio house could be! As she stood there, she discovered a roof outside. She stepped out onto it. There she could smell and feel the rain

258

better. But the roof was slanting and slippery. She finally returned to the room.

She felt the bed. It was soft and springy.

"But it's just too clean for sleeping!" she thought. It was for a Gorgio, not for her.

She lay down on the floor, but she did not stay there long, for she kept wondering what was behind the door by the dresser. She got up and cautiously opened the door, finding, to her surprise, a room full of dresses.

Her eyes fell upon one dress in particular—a bright red one. She took it out of the closet and stood before the mirror, holding it up in front of herself.

"Gorgeous!" she thought.

She slipped it over her own dress. It was too big, but it looked well. It was by far the gayest red and the most beautiful dress she had ever seen. For several minutes she paraded back and forth.

"I'd look better if my hair was combed, maybe," she thought.

But there were so many snarls that the comb she found in the top drawer would not go through. She tried to brush it next. The brush wouldn't work well, either, and she finally gave up and pulled her hair back as far as she could and stuffed it down the back of her dress.

Then she took a yellow dress from the closet. It had a blue flower on the shoulder and lace around the neck. She put it on over the gay one. She tried several others, too, one on top of the other. But she liked the gay one best of all.

"I'll take it to Nareli," she thought.

One by one she took off the dresses and returned all except her favorite to the closet. That one she folded carefully and stuffed under her blouse. But in the mirror she could see that it bulged too much around the waist. Anyone would be suspicious. So she pulled it out and took off her own dress. Then she folded Mrs. Baxter's lengthwise and wound it around her waist. Over that she put on her gypsy dress and tied her sash as tightly as she could.

"You'd never know it was there!" she thought, proudly. How surprised Nareli would be!

But the next moment, she was shaking her head sadly, thinking, "No, it won't do!" Nareli might wear it and the gypsies find themselves in jail. To protect her people she must not take it.

Slowly she untied her sash, took off her dress, and unwound her new possession. It was badly wrinkled.

"Mrs. Baxter'll know I tried it on!" she thought. She smoothed it out on the bed the best she could and sat on it to press it, but that did not help much. She finally hung it back of all the other dresses, next to the wall where Mrs. Baxter would not see it when she opened the closet door.

"But what a shame to leave it here when it looks so well on me!" she thought.

Her own clothes on again, she dropped to the floor, tired. The rain had stopped. She lay looking up at the ceiling. The ceiling began to worry her, and the four walls seemed to move in on her every time she closed her eyes.

"If only I could let the outdoors into this room!" she thought.

She rose from the floor and sat in the rocking-chair. As she rocked back and forth, she wondered what her people would say if they knew she was in a Gorgio's house, under a ceiling! Why was she here, anyhow? Because Bob had not wanted her to stay!

"Making myself uncomfortable, just to spite a Gorgio!" she thought. "Oh, it's not worth it! I won't do it!"

She jumped up from her chair and crawled out through the window to the slanting roof. It was still wet, but she moved slowly toward the edge on her hands and knees, feeling sure that she could find a way to the ground. Rid of the stuffy Gorgio's room, and under her own sky again, she took a deep breath, filling herself with that damp, fresh smell of things after a rain. But there was something else in the air, too. She sniffed again. Was it smoke?

She looked back toward the window through which she had come. Was the house afire? For it was smoke, all right! Then she looked over toward the barn. It was dark there, but as she looked, she saw a burst of flame in an upper window.

"Gregory!" was her first thought.

Linji scrambled back into the house and ran into the hall, screaming: "Get up! Get up! Your barn's on fire!" She kicked loudly at every door she saw. Then, the family aroused, she dashed downstairs, unbolted the front door, and ran out to the barn. By now the smoke came faster and faster from the upper window.

"Oh, the poor grai!" she cried, pulling at the barn door. But the door would not budge. She kicked it, pulled again.

Then she ran around to the back, hoping that there might be another door. But there was not. There were, however, two open windows. She crawled through one. From somewhere she heard Gregory stomping and whinnying, but grope as she would in the blackness, she could not find his stall.

Then she heard a fumbling of keys at the door. A moment later the door slid open, and someone switched on lights.

"Get Gregory!" said Mr. Baxter to his son. "I'll get the car out or the place'll blow up! Hurry, Bob!"

"Listen," said Bob, turning to Linji, "you don't need to feel so important around here! It's funny how the barn caught fire *tonight*——"

"Get the saddle!" cried Linji. "Something he's used to! So he'll leave the barn!" Smoke was coming into the stable from

261

the hay chute. "Or get a gunnysack! Or something to cover his eyes!"

"Go on out!" said Bob, shoving her. "I can get him myself. Whose pony is he, anyhow? Come on, Greg!"

But Gregory showed no signs of moving. Rather, his legs seemed glued to the floor. He stiffened them, and no matter how hard Bob pulled on the halter rope, they would not budge.

"Get the saddle!" Linji cried. "Don't you know *anything*?"

"Are you crazy?" shouted Bob. "The important thing's to get him out!"

"But he—won't move"—coughed Linji—"without—a saddle— or a gunnysack——" No horse would leave a burning stable unless his eyes were covered or unless one could make him think he was going to be ridden. Oh, the stupid Gorgio! Did he know nothing about his own pony?

A spark from the haymow above fell into the manger. Linji struck the flame with her hands and threw what water was in Gregory's pail onto it.

"Oh, the poor, poor grai!" she wailed. She ran out into the main part of the barn, but she could not find the saddle, or a sack, or anything. Back in the stable again, she found Bob still jerking the halter rope.

Linji's eyes smarted from the smoke that still was coming out of the chute. Suddenly she clutched Bob's arm with her strong fingers. With a quick twist she sent him flying away from the pony.

"That's only a little of what I can do!" she cried. "Now, be quick! Get the saddle! Or you'll have a dead pony and maybe be dead yourself!"

Bob, obviously surprised at Linji's strength, dashed out of the stable, returning a moment later with the saddle. Suddenly the lights went out.

"Oh, and maybe the ceiling will cave in!" Linji kept thinking. She jerked the saddle from Bob, threw it over Gregory's back, and tightened the girths. Then, quickly, she ripped off her long, wide skirt. That she threw over the pony's head and eyes. Then she took hold of a certain place low down on his

Flames leaped against the dark sky. Columns of smoke puffed upward.

nose with her other hand, ignoring the halter rope, and led Gregory out of his stable into the blackness of the main part of the barn. Gregory kept shaking his head up and down, trying to free himself of the skirt.

"It's all right," Linji kept saying. "Don't be afraid."

Outdoors, she pulled her skirt from Gregory's head and eyes and led the pony to a tree a safe distance from the barn, telling Bob he need not bother any more if he didn't want to.

But Bob had already dashed off.

A screeching siren seemed to have awakened the whole town, for neighbors, half-dressed, were rushing into the yard, and a fire engine clanged up the driveway. Soon men in rubber coats and hats were erecting ladders and splashing water over the unburned part of the barn as well as into the haymow.

"But it was me that saved you!" boasted Linji to Gregory. "Me, and not your own master!" She started to pull on her skirt when suddenly she cried: "Oh! Just look, would you! Look what's happened!"

Her skirt was torn from hem to waistband.

Gregory rubbed his nose against her shoulder.

"Oh, I'm not blaming you," Linji said. "No, you're worth a lot more than a torn skirt. But look at him, now!"—she pointed to Bob—"Running around like a wild man, trying to get someone to find his bicycle! Not thanking me, even!"

Firemen spread big rubber sheets over the roof of the garage so the garage would not catch fire. Everywhere there was noise. A hundred helpers, it seemed. Shouting, running about, yet only a few actually doing anything. Linji watched, contemptuously. She put on the skirt with a jerk. It tore in still another place.

Someone was now throwing sacks of grain out of the haymow door. Linji watched. Did the stupid Gorgios think Gregory would eat grain that had been smoked?

Flames were red against the dark sky. Columns of smoke puffed upward. But Linji stood by Gregory, stroking his smooth back, rubbing his nose.

Everybody was giving directions. Bob dashed about as if his

263

excitement would help put out the fire. Everywhere was the smell of burned wood, and pieces of charred wood flew through the air when the hose was turned upon the roof.

Under the chemicals and water the flames gradually turned into smoldering smoke, and Linji could see that the fire was under control. And then she caught sight of a tall man she had not noticed before.

"The sheriff!" she gasped, uneasiness instinctively overtaking her. To Gregory she said: "Oh, I've got to go now! The next thing the sheriff'll say is that I started the fire! Well, good-bye——"

She gave Gregory's neck a squeeze and hastily rubbed his nose once more. Then she started to steal away.

She had gone only a few steps, however, when someone behind her cried: "There she is! Here, Dad!"

Turning, Linji caught sight of Bob.

"Oh, they've thought of it!" Linji said to herself. "Thought of blaming me for the fire!" The picture of jail loomed up before her. "Oh, and what'll my people say?" Already her people were angry at her for having associated at all with the Gorgios.

They would be angrier than ever, now, when they found she had been blamed for the fire, too.

In defense, she turned to Bob, saying: "You needn't speak a word! Look at me! Torn from head to foot, I am, for helping you get your pony out!" She showed him the long rip in the skirt, showed him that anybody could now see the whole length of her green petticoat.

"Gee!" said Bob. "Gee, I'm sorry. That's too bad! Look, Dad, look how she's torn——"

Linji could only stare at Bob. Had she heard right? Or *had* there been a tone of pleasantness in his voice?

But Mr. Baxter was there, too, saying: "Linji, we want to thank you. You ought to give my son a few lessons on horses in general. You saved Greg, all right. Bob never could have. And we'd like you to know we appreciate it. What can we do for you?"

"I——" Linji began. "Oh, I——" For the life of her, she couldn't think of anything. If only she had been a little more prepared for this sudden change in the Gorgios!

Then she realized that Mrs. Baxter was there, too, adding a thank-you.

"We ought to get her a new skirt," Bob was saying. "Look how hers is torn."

Suddenly Linji began to seem a little more herself. In a flash she remembered the bright orange dress in Mrs. Baxter's closet.

"Oh!" she said. "If you're—going to all the bother of getting me a new skirt, maybe—maybe you'd get it the color of the dress upstairs—the orange one——"

Then she stopped abruptly, realizing that she never should have examined those dresses. But Mrs. Baxter was saying kindly, "Which one, Linji?" quite as if everything was all right.

"It's—well, it's orange——" said Linji. "And it's a little wrinkled and——" As well as she could she described it, adding, "It's the one clear in the back of the closet—behind the other dresses."

Mrs. Baxter was nodding her head, saying, "I know the one you mean." Then suddenly, "Linji, how would you like to have *that* dress?"

"Oh!" said Linji. A strange feeling came into her throat. "Oh, it was gorgeous!" She remembered exactly how she had looked in it. "Oh, it was!"

The next minute Mrs. Baxter had gone into the house, asking Linji to wait.

"Sam! Come over here a minute!" called Mr. Baxter.

And then the sheriff was standing beside Linji, clearing his throat loudly.

"He's got something to say to you," said Mr. Baxter.

"I guess," said the sheriff, looking straight at Linji, "you can stay awhile in the neighborhood if you want to. I guess it'd be a good idea to stay for the fair! I guess maybe we need a few good fortune tellers at our fair!"

At the same time Bob was saying: "Listen! Could you come over this afternoon and show the gang how you can ride without a saddle?"

"Oh, I don't hear right!" Linji thought. Inside, she felt very fluttery. But aloud, she found herself answering: "Yes, I could. Oh, I could, without any trouble at all!"

Then Mrs. Baxter was back with the gay dress. In a second, the dress was over Linji's arm—her own. And finally Linji was starting out for her camp, calling back a promise to meet Bob that afternoon to show his friends how well she could ride.

Then, out of sight of everyone, she sighed deeply.

"I'd never have believed it if I hadn't heard him with my own ears!" she thought. "A Gorgio sheriff inviting us to stay for the fair! Saying it as if he really meant it. Oh, what's come over the Gorgios!"

Her feet kept going faster and faster. For above everything that had happened, something else awaited her at camp—her own people's praise. Nobody would be angry now.

As for Nareli . . .

She sighed again. She had done something that even her older sister, Nareli, could not have done.

B. J. Chute

ARCHIE AND THE APRIL FOOLS

ILLUSTRATED BY *Frances Eckart*

"TED," said Jimmy Brewster, coming into the living room rather suddenly, "I hate to mention it, but there's a giraffe in the backyard."

His brother roused himself from the study of a photograph, gave Jimmy a puzzled look, then glanced at the calendar. A peaceful smile dawned upon his face. The calendar unquestionably proclaimed the fact that it was April first.

"Run away, my good man," said Ted. "I'm busy. You know, Jimmy, there's definitely a light leak in our camera. We've certainly got to get a new one, as soon as we have enough money."

"We're going to get a projector," Jimmy reminded him, "and, while I hate to mention it again, there is a giraffe in our backyard."

"I know, I know. And there's a baby hippopotamus in the kitchen sink, too, but don't bother me with that now. Just put April Fool's Day out of your mind." Ted sighed. "What kind of camera do you think we should get?"

"Projector," said Jimmy, gazing thoughtfully out of the window. "I take it all back. There *isn't* a giraffe in the backyard."

Ted said: "That's better. You can't catch me on those old April Fool gags."

"He isn't in the backyard," said Jimmy, "because now he's in the sideyard."

Ted fixed his brother with a glittering eye. "Now look here, you poor cluck, enough's enough. Once is funny, but—" He broke off, his gaze drawn to the window by Jimmy's intent stare, and made a noise like a drowning suction pump.

"You see?" said Jimmy reproachfully.

Ted saw. He rushed to the window and peered out wildly. Jimmy nodded in sympathy. He knew how Ted felt. But there was no getting away from it—the large spotted object in the Brewster peony bed was a giraffe.

"I hope," said Jimmy, with dignity, "that this will be a lesson to you to trust me. I was deeply hurt—"

"Stop babbling," Ted requested, recovering slightly. "What are we going to do about this—this monster?"

Jimmy gazed out at the giraffe, which had left the peony bed and was munching a convenient tree, its head out of sight and its long thin neck looking like a large spotted serpent.

"I read a book once," said Jimmy.

"This is no time to discuss your literary exploits," his brother told him fiercely. "Great howling buttercups! We've got to *do* something."

"This book," said Jimmy, undiscouraged, "said that giraffes can run faster than most horses."

"Yoicks! We've got to catch him. He probably belongs to the zoo."

"Maybe it would be better just to leave him alone," said Jimmy. "The book also said they kick with their hind legs, and, while naturally gentle, are capable of making a stout resistance."

Ted, who had been about to leave the house and organize a giraffe hunt, stopped in his tracks. "Stout resistance, huh? Perhaps we'd better call the zoo first."

"You watch the giraffe, and I'll call 'em." Jimmy grabbed for

268

the phone book. "Circle 2-1023. Hurry, operator . . . Hello, hello. Look, this is Jimmy Brewster, out on the Pine Road. We've got a giraffe here . . . A GIRAFFE. One of those things from Africa with long necks . . . I want your what? Your accounting department? I do *not* want your accounting department. I want—" He broke off suddenly. "Look, what number is this? . . . Oh. Oh, I see. I'm sorry." He hung up, rather sadly. "That was the bank. They said I wanted their accounting department."

"Get going," Ted advised. "He's eating the lilac bush now."

"Circle 2-1023," Jimmy said again into the phone. "Ted, if you were a bank, would you refer a giraffe to your accounting department? . . . Hello. Is this the zoo? . . . Well, have you lost a giraffe? Yes. Yes? You have? . . . Well, it's here in our peony bed."

"Lilac," said Ted.

"Lilac bed," Jimmy corrected himself. "What do you want us to do?" There followed a brief, rather one-sided conversation, then Jimmy said, "Thank you. Yes, sure, we will."

He hung up.

"What'd they say?"

"It belongs to the zoo all right. They're sending men out with a truck, and we're to keep the giraffe here until they come." He paused. "Ted, there's a $25 reward for the thing. He said we'd get it, if we caught the giraffe."

"Zowie!" Ted shouted. "We can get that camera."

"Projector," said Jimmy automatically.

"Camera," said Ted. "All we have to do—" He stopped short. "Faster than a horse, huh? Suppose it runs away when it sees us? Maybe it's scared of people."

"Frankly," said Jimmy, "that would make it unanimous. I'm scared of it."

Ted waved his hand airily. "Don't be difficult. Look, you go and get the encyclopedia and see what it says about giraffes, while I watch the beast out the window."

Jimmy dashed off and returned with the required volume. Ted, who had been watching the giraffe anxiously, said: "One of the advantages of living in the country is there's plenty of

269

giraffe food around. He's eating the ivy now. Mother and Dad won't be pleased."

"Well, if they were home," said Jimmy reasonably, "they could tell Archie so."

"Archie?"

"That's his name. The zoo man told me." He began to read. "The giraffe or camelopard—good night, is that what he is? A camelopard!"

"Go *on*," said Ted.

Jimmy went on. "Native of Africa—occurs generally in herds of from five to forty. Whoops! Not here, I hope. Feeds on leaves and small branches of trees. Yes, we'd guessed that. Seven vertebrae in neck. Hey! That's all *I've* got. It hardly seems fair. Look at the length of his neck compared to mine."

"If you don't get a move on," Ted warned him dangerously, "there won't be any Archie here to have a neck."

Jimmy read on hastily. "No vocal chords—well, anyway, he can't answer back then. . . . Generally seeks safety in flight. That's not so good. . . . Large, clear eyes. Nice for Archie, but no use to us. Ah, here we are!"

"About time," said Ted bitterly.

"What I said about their kicking with their hind legs," said Jimmy, "is true. But it seems they only kick lions."

"What do you mean, they only kick lions?"

"Well, the lion is their natural enemy, so, when attacked by a lion, they kick it—naturally."

"Very sensible point of view," Ted approved heartily. "Well, you and I aren't lions, therefore Archie won't kick us. Elementary, my dear Watson. Let's go."

Jimmy looked unhappy.

"Twenty-five dollars reward," Ted reminded him, "means we can get that camera."

"Projector," said Jimmy.

"Camera," said Ted. "Come on."

His brother came.

They let themselves cautiously out the back door and, by creeping, managed to get within ten feet of their giraffe, before it noticed them. At that point, however, Jimmy fell over the garden hose and into an empty pail, and, the clatter being considerable, Archie withdrew his narrow head from the treetop.

"Shush!" said Ted, fiercely.

Jimmy removed himself from the pail with as much dignity as possible. "I couldn't help it. Some silly idiot left that hose across the path."

"You did," said Ted. "Last night."

The giraffe was regarding them in a benign and lofty manner. "The man said to be awfully careful with him," Jimmy said. "He cost $3500."

"That thing?" Ted regarded Archie with profound respect. "Well, I'll be hornswoggled! What's he got that I haven't got?"

"More neck," said Jimmy, "and spots with white edgings."

Ted treated this remark with the contempt it deserved. "This is going to be quite simple," he announced suddenly, in a competent manner. "He's perfectly friendly." He stretched out one hand placatingly and began to advance, a step at a time. "Here, Archie, Archie. Nice Archie. . . . Oops!"

Archie gave him one look, shied violently, wheeled, and departed around the corner of the house, his sloping body rolling in a ridiculous amble. "Now, look what you've done," said Jimmy. "There goes our projector."

"Camera," said Ted. "Come on. We've got to catch him."

They rushed around the house and stopped short.

"There he is!" Jimmy panted, pointing. "He's stopped. Hey! Ought he to do that?"

The giraffe had sighted a yellow crocus in the grass, and it had evidently roused in him a desire for dessert. Accordingly, he had spread his thin forelegs out at an impossible angle and was lowering his head earthwards, in a way that looked extremely perilous.

"He doesn't look safe to me," said Ted. "Besides, for all we know, crocuses aren't good for giraffes. Do they have crocuses in Africa?"

"I don't know," said Jimmy, "but I'll go and get the encyclopedia, while you figure out a way to—"

271

"Oh, no, you don't," Ted said firmly, grabbing his brother and hauling him back. "I've already figured out a way. How soon do they expect to get here from the zoo?"

"Dunno," Jimmy admitted regretfully. "It's quite a ways, and they may not find our place right off, although I gave 'em directions. Why?"

"If that giraffe leaves," said Ted, "our new camera leaves."

"Projector," said Jimmy.

Ted ignored him. "And the chances are that Archie isn't going to hang around just to oblige us. So *my* idea is to get him into our barn. It's got a good high roof, and—"

"May I ask just one simple little question?" said Jimmy. "*How* are you going to get him into the barn? You can't lead him, you know. He's all neck and legs. There's nothing to hang onto."

Ted said dramatically, "Look at his tail!"

Jimmy looked. It was a goodish tail, not beautiful, perhaps, but certainly utilitarian, with a tuft on the end. It would be a most satisfactory tail to hang onto.

"Well?" said Ted.

"I can think of two objections," Jimmy said. "One is, do you think you can pull a giraffe around backwards? Because, if so, I'm going to leave the whole thing to you, and you can have the projector all to yourself. I have my life to live."

"It's going to be a camera," Ted said firmly, "and we don't pull him, you goof. We urge him forward gently. The tail is just for emergencies, in case he starts to run."

"Oh," said Jimmy. "Well, the other objection is the location of his tail."

"It's in the usual place, I believe," Ted said stiffly.

"Well, naturally, but the usual place is so awfully near his heels." Jimmy looked mournful and quoted, " 'They kick with their hind legs and are capable of making a stout resistance.' "

"So what?" said Ted. "Archie won't attack anything but a lion. You read that yourself from the encyclopedia. We aren't lions, are we?" There was a short pause.

"I see what you mean," said Jimmy. "Are we men or are we lions?" There was another short pause. "Personally, I'm a mouse. You do it, Ted. You're more the executive type. I'll watch."

"You will not," Ted told him. "It's perfectly simple. I'll go in front and urge him on with some grass, and you go behind and hang onto his tail."

"Me?" Jimmy croaked. "Hang onto his tail?"

"Certainly. You just said I was the executive type, didn't you? Well, the executive type always leads. Come on, Jimmy."

Ted gave him a shove from behind, and Jimmy staggered mournfully toward Archie's tail, stared at it for a moment, took a deep breath, and grabbed.

Things after that happened very quickly. Archie's left hind leg kicked out at a fantastic angle and landed a powerful and accurate wallop. Jimmy described a parabola in the air, rolled over twice on the grass, got to his feet, and started running.

Ted joined him. Archie galloped in enthusiastic pursuit. His two would-be captors shot up into the branches of the nearest apple tree, and Archie came to a disappointed halt. Jimmy and Ted climbed upward as far as they could and came to rest near an abandoned bird's nest. They looked at each other.

"Kicks only lions," said Jimmy bitterly. "The executive type. Bah!"

"You read the book yourself," Ted accused and looked down thoughtfully at Archie's head, weaving around among the

273

branches. The tree was not tall, and Archie was. After a moment, Ted broke off some juicy-looking leaves and handed them down to Archie, who accepted them courteously. Ted broke off some more.

Jimmy got the idea and began to help. "If we can only keep him here until the zoo men come—"

"I hope the tree lasts out," said Ted. "Sit down, Jimmy. You're rocking the boat."

"Thank you," said his brother with dignity. "I'm more comfortable standing up."

Ted said, "Oh," with polite sympathy, and Jimmy added: "In case you want to know, being kicked by an even-toed ungulate is the same as being kicked by anything else, only rougher."

"By a what?"

"An even-toed ungulate. That's what that thing down there is. And, personally, I wish he'd go off and ungulate somewhere else."

"Think of the camera," Ted urged.

"I am thinking," said Jimmy, "of the projector." He added broodingly: "So he wouldn't kick me, huh? He wouldn't kick me because I didn't have a mane. Phooey!" He then said, "Whoops!" and nearly fell out of the tree.

A large, purposeful-looking truck had just turned into the driveway.

"The zoo men!" Ted shouted. "The marines have landed. Jimmy, we're saved." He hesitated, and added: "I wish we weren't up here, though. It doesn't look so good. They might almost think Archie caught *us*."

"If they give that giraffe the reward," said Jimmy, "I shall blow a fuse."

"Hey!" said a voice. A stout man in blue overalls was peering up at them, one arm wound affectionately around Archie's neck. "What you doing up there?"

Jimmy said, "We've caught the giraffe for you," and there was a hearty burst of laughter in response.

"Look who's caught who, will you?" said the stout man. "A nice, tame, little fellow like Archie, too!"

"Tame!" said Ted under his breath, and then addressed the stout man quite coolly. "We couldn't find much for him to eat, and we thought feeding him was the best way to keep him here." He paused impressively. "We're up in this tree, where we can get more leaves."

The stout man was silenced in his turn, and Jimmy and Ted descended with admirable dignity. "Well," the man admitted finally, "that was pretty smart. Yessir, that was real bright. We're much obliged. I'll see you get that reward all right."

Indoors, Jimmy glared at the encyclopedia. "Only lions," he muttered.

"We can get our camera," Ted offered consolingly.

"PROJECTOR!" Jimmy howled.

"M'mmmm," said Ted, "I'll tell you what. We'll compromise. Next time we'll buy a projector. This time we'll buy a camera. Now run along and get some cookies, there's a pal. All that brain work has made me hungry."

Jimmy gazed upon his brother in mingled awe and fury, said "Compromise!" in a strangled voice, then departed suddenly. He came back, a moment later, both hands full of cookies and a strange glitter in his eyes.

"Ted," he said, "I hate to mention it. But there's a rhinoceros in the backyard."

Ted let out a wild scream and dashed into the kitchen. A moment later, Jimmy heard the back door slam. A gentle smile dawned on his face.

"Ah, well," he murmured, "we can't all be the executive type."

He looked affectionately at the calendar, which still proclaimed unmistakably that it was April Fool's Day, smiled again, and began to eat his cookies. He felt much better.

THE BEST RIDE OF ALL

Adelaide Love

Riding in buses and trains is a very
Nice way to travel. A trip on the ferry
Is fun, but there is only a short way to go,
Not even as far as my daddy could row.
I like to ride ponies, and once at the zoo
I rode on the back of an elephant, too . . .
But a ride through the air in a plane with a whizz
And a roar is the jolliest ride that there is.

WHEN MRS. DOUGLAS heard from her husband that his expedition to Labrador had been caught fast in the northern ice and he would not be able to get home until the following spring, she called her four children together. Jim, the eldest, at sixteen, Elspeth and Alan, twins, and little Posy, the youngest, helped her decide to save money by staying all winter in their old summer home on Great Porcupine Island. Cousin Ronnie Douglas, who had been traveling all over the world with his step-father, arrived at the island just as winter was starting. The twins, who were searching for some long-lost treasure, made him a member of their secret society, the Red Rovers, and the three conspired to keep Jim from finding out about the treasure hunt. Thad Crawford, an island native, was also secretly looking for the treasure, so there was keen competition. The search was slowed down when Ronnie became sick, but he soon was better and ready to join the others in the Christmas party.

Louise Andrews Kent

AN ISLAND CHRISTMAS

ILLUSTRATED BY *Jill Elgin*

THE three days before Christmas passed in a pleasant bustle of preparations. In the kitchen Mrs. Douglas and Elspeth consulted the precious receipt book written in Grandmother Douglas's firm, unfaltering hand, and the house was full of delicious smells. The brick oven in the living-room chimney proved to be as good for baking as it had ever been. Into it went mince turn-overs, pumpkin pies, a certain dark rich fruitcake—familiarly known as huckleberry gingerbread—loaves of golden pound cake and great pots of baked beans. Jim was busy with the cider press and made several gallons of the delicious amber-colored juice. A big turkey from the Crawfords' was hanging up ready to be stuffed and go into the brick oven.

277

In the living room was a pile of what had originally been marshmallow cans. Elspeth had lacquered them in various gay colors, and the boys were busy filling them with fudge and peanut brittle while Posy scraped saucepans and ate enough crumbs to have endangered a weaker constitution. Fortunately a cast-iron digestion was part of the Douglas standard equipment, so Posy throve on scraps of unfamiliar food, snapped up while no one was looking.

An old trunk in the attic had yielded a supply of Christmas tree ornaments, and the big tree was beginning to shine with gold and silver bells, balls of different sizes and colors, flocks of birds with rainbow wings, fish like no fish ever pulled out of Frenchman's Bay, flowers that would make the orchids of the Amazon jungle look pale and dull. Jim spent most of one afternoon on a stepladder among the upper branches of the tree, fastening on candles and ornaments, while his assistants operated lower down, not without argument and the consequent breaking of some of the fragile treasures. At last nothing was left to do but fasten the star at the top. The stepladder was too short, so that Jim finally climbed out on a beam and reached down from above.

"I feel like Michelangelo painting the Sistine Chapel," he remarked as he slid to the floor and surveyed his work with approval.

"Except that he lay on his back and worked looking up while

278

you lay on your stomach and worked down," suggested Alan.

"Well, anyway, I don't believe it looked any better," said Jim modestly.

"It doesn't," said Ronnie. "I have seen it. This beats it all empty."

"Hollow," corrected Alan, who was giving Ronnie what he described as a course of easy lessons in American.

Even allowing for family pride, the barn on Christmas Eve looked very beautiful. To Posy, looking up beyond the shining tree to the dim obscurity of the roof, it seemed as vast as a cathedral. The great beams hewn from the primeval trees of the island two centuries ago, the rafters, the walls and the floor, all softened by time to a mellow gray brown, made a pleasant background for the rows of small spruces that stood along the walls. Elspeth had fastened above them a row of gleaming tin sconces with orange candles ready to light. Under each sconce she had hung a hemlock wreath studded with tiny cones and the scarlet berries of the black alder. Ronnie and Alan, somewhat hampered by Posy's assistance, had piled orange pumpkins, purple cabbages, and green squashes at the base of the

smaller trees where they made bright splashes of color. Around the foot of the big spruce was a steadily increasing pile of mysterious-looking packages, tantalizing to everyone, but especially to Posy, who walked around the tree prodding any bundle which bore the magic letters P-O-S-Y, surveying her own somewhat battered-looking contributions with great satisfaction.

Toward evening it stopped snowing. The wind shifted to the south and almost died down. Occasionally a puff would blow some of the light snow from the top of a drift into the air, but for the most part there was stillness. It grew warmer than it had been for weeks, there were no Northern Lights, and the stars shone less brilliantly than they had on the freezing nights before the storm.

"It looks as if the Cap'n were right this time," said Jim, as they watched from the living room for the arrival of their guests. "If it keeps as warm as this, we'll have a real thaw."

Soon troops of dark figures began to come from both directions, plodding through the soft snow and leaving a dark wave of footprints behind them. Jim and Elspeth hurried to light the candles in the sconces and on the tree, so that by the time the Crawfords and Whittakers had stamped the snow off their feet, the barn was fragrant with the smell of warm spruce, while the tree was a dazzle of light and color in the scented dimness.

"Make yourselves at home and don't take off your things," said Jim as the Whittaker family filed in. "Cap'n, I wish you'd sent us the warm weather a bit earlier. There's enough cold left in this barn right now to freeze Eskimos. We'll go in where it's warmer pretty soon."

No one seemed to mind the cold. The small Whittakers and Crawfords stared open-mouthed and silent at the glistening tree, accepting the gifts that Jim took from the pile at the foot with shy thanks and beaming faces. Even Thad seemed somewhat more gracious than usual, while the older members of the party uttered choruses of "Well, if that don't beat all!" "Say, Zeke, wish we could catch some fish like that!" "Now, that certainly is real pretty!" Mrs. Douglas moved about in her friendly way making everyone feel welcome, and Posy skipped

in and out bumping enough people so that soon there was very little formality left.

No one—from Captain Whittaker to little Marion Crawford—had been forgotten. Besides the boxes of candy, Elspeth had made cards with appropriate snapshots and verses underneath. These had been composed by Alan and Ronnie and were full of local allusions that seemed to please the recipients. Zeke's purported to come from Paul Bunyan, and he chuckled delightedly as he read the doggerel lines. Finding something for Thad had been a problem. Alan had insisted that a picture of the Den with the fish hawk's nest above it would be the most suitable thing. It was with great difficulty that he had been persuaded to destroy the verses, dark with mysterious hints, that he had composed to go with it. He was at last convinced that if the treasure were actually in the cave, he was running a real risk of giving the secret away, and consented to the substitution of a picture of Thad holding up a halibut almost as big as himself. The remarks about Thad's talents as a fisherman that accompanied the picture brought such a smile to his usually sulky face that even Alan was obliged to admit that it was possible for Thad to look pleasant.

Both families were glad to get bags of the much-needed flour. Mrs. Whittaker was made perfectly happy by a cut-glass water pitcher which she had often gazed at with yearning eyes as she helped Mrs. Douglas clean the china closet. Her daughter-in-law, Ed's wife, the mother of the three tow-headed, stolid children, received a preserve dish equally heavy and shiny. Zeke's wife was suffering from a cold and had not been able to come, but bundles containing similar treasures had been sent to her. Zeke's son Ashur, his pretty young wife, and two small black-eyed girls, who somehow suggested their cousin Thad more than they did their good-natured-looking father, were all remembered. Mrs. Douglas had the satisfaction of feeling that what she called her home-grown presents had found their way to the right owners.

The last candle had burned down by the time the visitors had received their presents. The family except for Posy, had left theirs for later distribution. It was too much to expect her to wait while all the other children tore open papers and yanked off ribbons. Her eyes were now impossible to keep propped open any longer, and when she went into the warmth of the schoolroom she promptly curled up on the sofa and went to sleep. Mrs. Douglas covered her and her armful of treasures with a soft-green-centered Paisley shawl and left her there.

"Oughtn't she to go to bed?" asked Elspeth, who had stern ideas about the upbringing of her young sister.

"I suppose she ought," replied her mother, "but it won't hurt her for once, and her nerves must be good or she wouldn't sleep through the noise."

The little Whittakers and Crawfords had entirely lost their shyness by this time. They chased each other under tables and over chairs blowing trumpets and whistles in each other's ears, rolled over on the floor, pulled hair with consequent squeals, and generally made themselves at home. Zeke was tuning his fiddle to the piano with a scraping whine. The other men were having a heated discussion as to the chances of the ice breaking up. The women chattered happily about children, clothes, and cooking.

Suddenly Zeke called out in his high voice, "Take partners for the Portland Fancy." The furniture, from under which the youthful islanders now had to be hauled forth and shaken apart,

282

had been moved back against the wall so that there was plenty of room for two sets of dancers.

They were an odd sight as they paired off: Jim with the youngest tow-headed Whittaker girl; Caleb's lean figure towering above a small monkey-like Crawford; Mrs. Douglas with Bob Whittaker's tousled head and hot pink face coming almost to her elbow; Ed Whittaker with the other lively little Crawford; Ashur returning the compliment by leading out Rebecca Whittaker. Ronnie, after some hesitation, made a shy bow to Cap'n Caleb's vast white-haired wife. Mrs. Ed Whittaker and Mrs. Ashur Crawford declared with giggles that they didn't need beaux and would dance together. This left only Elspeth and Thad, who had been peering about the warm candlelit room with his sidewise look.

"Bet he's hoping for another look at the map," thought Alan, who sat turned around on the piano stool waiting for the dancers to take their places. If Thad had any such intention, he was disappointed, for the map had been put away when the room was cleared for dancing. Prodded by his Uncle Ashur,

283

Thad came across to where Elspeth was standing and ducked his head with a gruff "Will y'please be m'partner." Elspeth curtsied politely, and the sets were ready.

There was a chord from the piano, a scrape from the fiddle.

"Eight hands around," squeaked Zeke in his nasal treble, and the dance began.

Alan, looking over his shoulder occasionally as he played, caught glimpses of a picture that he would always remember. Candles flickered and smoked in the seven-branch candlesticks that Grandfather Douglas had brought from Russia, and a great fire of blazing birch logs threw its light on the whirling figures: Captain Whittaker bending his gently twinkling face over his small partner; his mother, with the light shining on her bronze hair, smiling as she and Bob got mixed up on the right and left; Ronnie looking hot and anxious as he swung the light-footed but enormous Mrs. Whittaker into place. Jim, Alan thought, looked more like their father than ever, strong, kind, courteous, moving with unexpected ease and grace. Occasionally came a glimpse of Thad's sulky face and awkward movements, or of Elspeth's slim figure with her short red curls bobbing above her flushed cheeks and shining eyes. Through it all Posy slept, comfortable under her scarlet shawl.

Zeke and Alan went through their repertoire—"Hull's Victor," "Morning Star," "Money Musk," and last of all the "Virginia

Reel." When the clapping and reeling were over, they struck into "Auld Lang Syne" which was sung by the whole company. Ed Whittaker's roaring bass voice, the treble squeaks from the smaller children, Zeke's nasal tenor, Elspeth's clear soprano, all the other voices whether off the key or on it somehow blended into harmony—perhaps because everyone felt happy and friendly. As the last notes ceased, Mrs. Douglas led the way into the living room, where the little Whittaker's eyes were bluer and rounder than ever as they saw the loaded table. In the center was a great silver bowl of apples and oranges and around it glass pitchers of sparkling cider, big platters of dough-nuts and mince turn-overs, dishes of nuts and raisins, plates of little frosted cakes decorated with red-and-green candies to look like holly. The children stuffed themselves quietly and systematically. Mrs. Douglas felt thankful that Posy was still asleep. At last, when no one could eat any more, the visitors put on their mittens and comforters and with a chorus of thanks and good wishes went out again into the starlit night.

"That was a nice party," said Mrs. Douglas as they cleared away the remains of the feast and straightened the disordered room.

"It isn't over yet," remarked Jim, looking at his watch. "It's just time for the best part of it. Come into the schoolroom."

The fire had burned down to a great bed of glowing coals, the candles were burning low in the gleaming candelabra, Posy still slept peacefully on the sofa. Jim went to the corner, turned the switch of the radio with a click, and twisted the dials. There was a low hum, a whisper of a voice which quickly grew louder. Ronnie caught the words "Polar Broadcast" and gasped "Oh, Jim!" in an ecstatic whisper. The voice, very clear and business-like went on:

"Our first message is to Robert Ellicot, Hudson Bay Trading Post. Davis Inlet, Labrador. It says:

" 'We spent Thanksgiving at Mother's. Everyone well. Bobby has had the measles, but is back in school. He played tackle on the team. We were glad to get your message through the Douglas Station. Send when you can. Merry Christmas. Mary.' "

285

"The Douglas Station!" said Elspeth excitedly.

"Hush!" whispered Alan. "Here comes another."

" 'To David Blenkinsop. Canadian Mounted Police. Father died November thirtieth. Come home as soon as you can. I am well, but you are needed for business reasons. Mother.' "

"Poor woman!" murmured Mrs. Douglas.

The voice went on.

" 'To Dr. Samuel Allerton. Medical Mission, Labrador. We miss you, but everything goes well here. Keep smiling, Sam. Cheerio. Bill and Barbara.' "

Mrs. Douglas choked a little and wiped her eyes, hoping that she was unobserved. The messages brought more clearly than ever the sense of the loneliness, the cold and darkness, in which these men were living. The announcer's voice went on steadily, bringing cheer to some, grief to others, impersonal, and yet somehow friendly. Most of the messages were simply Christmas greetings, but here and there was something at which the listeners chuckled. A dashing Canadian Mounted Policeman received messages from four different girls, all of whom were doubtless listening in. One of the missionaries was reproached by his wife for taking all the keys to the house with him when he left. As they were laughing about the predicament of these gentlemen—Alan prophesying that neither of them would ever come home—they heard the words:

" 'To Commander James Douglas, Radio Station near Cape Chidley, Ungava Bay, Labrador.

" 'We are spending the winter on Great Porcupine and having great fun. Uncle Ronald's son is with us. Mother is coaching me for my exams. By next spring we all hope to be healthy, wealthy, and wise. We got one message from you through the A.R.L. I have had no luck picking up your station, but shall keep trying. Good luck, Dad. Jim.' "

"Oh, Jim, do you think he'll get it? Won't he be pleased?" exclaimed Elspeth, her eyes shining, while Alan pounded him on the shoulder and Ronnie looked at him with admiration.

"I think there's a good chance," Jim answered. "You see how clearly it's coming through tonight. Mother, do you mind if we all sit up till one o'clock and listen for his answer? That's when he said he'd send, you know. Between one and two on the nights of the Polar Broadcast."

"Of course we'll stay up! I wouldn't go to bed for anything," said his mother.

"Let's open our presents while we wait," suggested Elspeth. "That will keep us awake."

Ronnie and Alan ran into the chilly darkness of the barn and brought back the piles of treasures.

"Let's open them one at a time to make it last longer," said Alan. "Mother, you begin."

"Then I'll open Posy's first. How simply too precious for anything! Did you help her, Elspeth?"

"Not much. There wouldn't have been such gobs of paste on it if I had. I told her how to spell the words, but she thought of them."

"I feel sure of it. 'Alan and the Pigs. Alan has on his slicker.'"

"Handy way to tell them apart!" Elspeth dodged out of her twin's reach. "Jim's is characteristic too."

Jim chuckled good-naturedly as he looked over his mother's shoulder and saw the announcement in rather straggling letters, "This is Jim looking Cross at a Cow."

Elspeth's picture was labeled, "Elspeth trying to kick Alan," although as Alan was nowhere to be found in the picture this act of sisterly devotion seemed to have missed fire. No photograph of Ronnie was to be had, so Posy had drawn his portrait.

"It's a wonderful likeness," said his aunt, "especially about the hair, and how cozy having the elephant and the tiger beside you—I'd know it anywhere. Did you tell her how to fix her own, Elspeth?"

Elspeth admitted that she had. It was called "Posy in the Fish Hawk's Nest," and had been made by pasting a small picture of Posy on top of one of the big trees, with its bristling crown of sticks.

"The poor hawks!" exclaimed Alan. "If she kicked them the way she did me when she got into my bed this morning, there'd be no hawks on Great Porcupine."

Mrs. Douglas put down Posy's work of art and picked up a small package marked "From R.D."

"I always think the small ones are very exciting," she said as she opened it. "Why, Ronnie, how beautiful! It can't be for me."

"It was my mother's," said Ronnie shyly. "My father gave it to her when I was born. I think they would like you to have it if they knew——" he paused, leaving the sentence unfinished.

Mrs. Douglas spread the beautiful rope of tiny pearls on the table. The strands were caught together here and there with bosses of fragile exquisite goldwork, and at the ends above the heavy pearl tassels were emerald-studded circlets.

"I thought, perhaps," said Ronnie, "that you would wear it and keep it some day for Posy, because you were my first friends. See, it will look pretty on your black velvet." He put it gently around his aunt's neck and knotted the fringed ends together.

"I'll keep it for you and wear it sometimes," said Mrs. Douglas, "but I'll save it for your wife, Ronnie. Thank you for trusting me with it. I've never seen anything so beautiful."

"He'll be getting snapped up by some designing female for it," complained Elspeth.

"Nonsense," contradicted Alan. "Ronnie and I will both be married for our beauty. Our faces are our fortune, ladies."

"Until you find the treasure," suggested Jim. "How are your prospects, Alan? I have an idea you've got a competitor in Thad. He's asked me three times about where Elspeth got the idea for the map."

"Much good may that do him," said Alan more calmly than he felt. "I suppose you told him all you knew, didn't you?"

"No, I only said she used an old map she found in the house," said Jim, and went on without hearing Alan's grumble of "You might as well have"—"I'm going to open your present next, Ronnie. I hope it's the Kohinoor. It looks about the right size."

"You'll like this better," said Ronnie. "I bought it in Bar Harbor the day of our pleasant trip. It's quite suitable, I think."

"It's a peach!" Jim turned the handsome pocket compass around admiringly. "I'll get lots of use out of it, I know. Thanks a lot, old scout."

Before long the schoolroom was littered with papers and ribbons. New treasures kept making their appearance: the trim model yachts that Jim had made for the boys; tiny carved ivory elephants and boxes from Ronnie's bottomless bag—as Alan called it; knitted ties and belts of colored cord patiently knotted by Elspeth's quick fingers. It was midnight when the last bundle was opened and even interest in the presents could not keep Alan from yawning.

"We've got an hour to wait," he announced, picking up a steamer rug from the end of the sofa. "Come on, Ronnie. That's the third yawn I've seen you swallow. Your manners are perfect as usual, but you'd better lie down with me in front of the fire and take a nap."

They both curled up on the polar bear skin that Commander Douglas had brought home and went on to sleep like puppies. Elspeth picked up a mass of crumpled papers and threw them into the fireplace. The candles had burned out, and the room was dark except for the blue flames flickering around the big log. They burst with a bright blaze as they ate into the papers, and in the light Jim saw that his mother, too, was asleep in her chair.

"Lie down on the other end of the sofa, Elspeth," said Jim in a low voice. "You and Mother must be about done up with all you've put through today."

"How about you?" asked Elspeth. "Of course you haven't done a thing. Just sat with your feet up comfortably, I suppose, while the women did the work."

"Never mind about me. I'm not a bit tired, and anyway, we can all sleep late in the morning."

"I'll lie down a few minutes. I shan't go to sleep, though."

Elspeth curled up at one end of the big davenport taking care not to disturb Posy. For a few minutes she watched Jim. He had put on the earphones and was listening intently and apparently with satisfaction to some distant music. Elspeth could hear the faint buzz of it even without the loud-speaker. It was a drowsy sound like the hum of insects on some warm July afternoon, and the room was warm—as warm as it would be picking raspberries near the old cellar hole. Elspeth's eyelids closed, but she dragged them open again with a determined effort. The firelight still flickered softly on Jim's intent profile and black hair. How funny he looked with that headpiece and a tuft of hair sticking up above the band! The sap in the wood hissed and sang, and there was that faint monotonous buzzing from the radio. Elspeth's eyelids shut again, this time to stay closed. Jim was left alone waiting, listening.

He turned the dials through their whole range. Station after station came in with wonderful clearness. The air seemed saturated with Christmas carols. Trumpeters outside the cathedral at Boston sent out the glad tidings of Christ's birth. In Davenport, Iowa, men's voices were singing, *Oh, little town of Bethlehem*. Montreal resounded with *God rest ye merry, gentlemen*, and *Good King Wenceslas*. From Pittsburgh came the echoes of an Irish Christmas tree—"Little Mickey has just received a handsome piccolo. Sure an' if you listen you can hear the little chap tryin' to pick a low note on it. . . ."

A carillon in New York rang out *Adeste Fideles.*

The fire had settled down to a steady glow now. Jim stepped across the sleeping boys and put on a fresh stick of wood. Everyone looked very comfortable in the warm half-light. He went back to his corner, put on the earphones again, took a notebook from his pocket, and turned his flashlight on the page where he had jotted down the wave length that his father had said he would use. He had remembered it correctly, but there was still half an hour to wait. He turned the dials slowly again. After the final burst of carols, the stations seemed to be quieting down. Jim could hear one after another signing off. He turned the dials to the point at which he hoped to hear from Labrador. There was a sharp crackling sound, then a low buzz. He yawned and stretched his arms. He had not realized how tired he was. The earphones felt heavy on his head, and the singing buzz of the radio made him dizzy. Somehow he couldn't seem to hold his head quite straight. Perhaps if he rested it a minute on the edge of the table, it would feel better. Sometimes a few minutes' rest made all the difference . . .

It was not, he decided, so cold in Labrador as he had expected, and it was surprising to find the Eskimos using Chesapeake Bay dogs instead of Huskies for their sledges. It was queer to see Bruce and Wallace hauling a sledge in this place—not that it looked very different from Frenchman's Bay. In fact the dogs, with Posy in her fur suit driving them, seemed to be

291

starting out across the Halibut Hole. But they mustn't go—it wasn't frozen all the way. He must run and stop them. What was that crackling sound? The ice, the ice giving way under his heavy feet that wouldn't run. It was cracking more and more every way he turned and above the noise came his father's voice calling to him. "Jim, Jim Douglas," it said. He could hear it plainly.

Jim sat up with a jerk. The room was quiet. No one had stirred and he could hear nothing from the radio—not even the crackling of static. Suddenly he noticed that the plug was pulled out. Good gravy! He'd jerked it out when he woke up from that dream. Poor boob, asleep at the switch. He glanced at his watch—it was after one—then thrust the plug in savagely.

". . . families will be glad to hear that everyone connected with the expedition . . ." This was no dream, this faint whisper of a voice that he could hear even through the waves of static. Jim turned one of the dials a fraction of a millimeter. The voice went on more clearly ". . . wish you could see how warm and comfortable we are. Our ship is frozen into the ice and we are living on it in our own cabins and bunks . . ." then another great wave of static stifled it. Jim clenched his fists—he *must* hear it. He moved his dials again—now he had lost it completely, there was nothing on the air at all. Ah, that was better! By some trick of the ether, the static had cleared away. Some thunderstorm in Africa had cleared up, perhaps, or possibly the Northern Lights had changed their direction. The reason didn't matter. Jim pulled out the plug and pushed in the one belonging to the loud-speaker. The room filled suddenly with that deep friendly voice that seemed to have a smile hidden in it somewhere.

". . . tell you, first of all, that we shall start home as early as we can get out through the ice. In June sometime, we hope . . ."

Jim turned and looked at the sleepers. He must wake them— they mustn't miss another word, he thought, when there was a stir from the sofa, and Posy's voice called out. "It's Daddy. I hear my nice fat Daddy talking. Wake up, Mother. It's Daddy."

Mrs. Douglas woke and held out her arms for Posy, both

their faces flushed and shining with excitement. Jim shook the
boys and Elspeth awake. No one spoke—they were all too
anxious not to miss a word—but all listened intently as Commander Douglas's voice went on.

"Jim," he was saying, "if you're listening—and somehow I
know you are—get a pencil and take down these messages. Any
of you other amateurs do the same, and right here I want to
thank every one of you boys who have sent me messages and
have passed mine on for me. Now if you're ready, we'll begin.
Our boatswain, Bill Todd, wants to say to his wife: that he
never felt better and that he'll bring her his Christmas present
next June. Better late than never. I may add myself that she's
missing something not seeing Bill sitting here smoking in his
red flannels. He's a pretty picture, Bill is. Weighs about 210
right now in his present costume. That's to Mrs. William Todd,
Orange Street, Malden, Massachusetts. Did you get that, Jim?
Well, here's another. Dave Lewiston to his mother, Mrs. Robert
Lewiston, Spring Street, Barre, Vermont. He just wants to say
that he's well and to wish her a Merry Christmas. Now I'm
going to let some of these boys deliver their own messages. Bill
and Dave are Mike-shy. I couldn't get either of them to stand
up in front of this little round gadget and talk. They're all right
wrestling with polar bears and tickling walruses in the ribs, but

when it comes to this business, they're scared pink. Here's a chap, though, who's got his nerve with him. He's our cook, Rastus Johnson, and he's not scared of a thing—except cockroaches. Here, Rastus, speak your piece!"

A voice, unmistakably belonging to one of the darker-skinned members of his party went on:

" 'Deed I ain't afraid of no cockroaches this trip, 'cause there ain't none of them visitors on this boat. No, sir—ain't going to be neither if I have anything to say about it. Well, now I'd like to speak to Miss Pomona Wendella Phillipa Washington, on Myrtle Street, Boston. I disremember the number, but I'd just like to remind her that June's the time for orange blossoms . . ."

Rastus's radio courtship faded away at this point. Jim put on the earphones again. He could hear very faintly that different voices were speaking from time to time, but could catch only an occasional word. At last the sounds became stronger and he switched back to the loud-speaker. A drawling, nasal voice was saying:

" . . . want to thank our friends particularly for the twenty-one different brands of cigarettes there are on board this ship. In case any one needs a signed testimonial from me, I am willing to go on record as saying there's not a sneeze in a hay-bale. Commander Douglas and I don't smoke, but we feel sure that it's due to being fumigated with such fine grades of tobacco that's kept us from having colds in our heads and feet. Now I guess I shrink from publicity about as much as any of the well-known explorers, but for the good of civilization I'll say right here that the first offer to me of two hundred dollars for my photograph and the above statement, neatly written and signed, will receive due consideration. This is Ebenezer Bunker speaking. Stand by for the Commander."

"That's Cap'n Whittaker's nephew," whispered Alan to Ronnie. "I knew his voice right away."

There was a moment of silence. Everyone in the room listened more intently than ever. Ronnie and Alan had edged gradually over to the radio and were sitting as close as they could get to the loud-speaker. Their faces were flushed with

Suddenly Zeke called out, "Take partners for the Portland Fancy."

excitement as well as from their sleep by the fire and the re-
semblance between them was particularly striking. Mrs. Douglas had moved her chair with its back toward the fire so that
no one could see the tears that somehow persisted in coming
into her eyes. Posy, entirely rested by her long nap, squirmed
around happily on her mother's lap, but kept her usually active
tongue remarkably quiet. Elspeth sat on a low stool, leaning her
head against her mother's knee and occasionally squeezing her
hand in moments of enthusiasm.

In a moment they heard Commander Douglas's voice again.

"Now we've heard from every one of our party and I'm going
to spend the few minutes left to talk to my own family. Thank
you all for your message. We could hear the Polar Broadcast
perfectly this evening, and you can guess whether I was glad
to hear from you. I was surprised, of course, to hear that you
were on the island, but I think I understand your reasons and
I thoroughly approve. I want you to know that we have plenty
of food here, as we were provided for the winter in case we
had to stay. Jim, you will be glad to know that the station is
doing even more than we hoped in getting messages through

295

to people in this part of the country. I hope you're having good luck with your own set. Alan, I know you're helping Jim all you can. I don't expect he gives you much time for treasure-hunting, but perhaps you get a day off once in a while. If you do, I bet I know how you spend it! I know how fast the wood-box gets empty, too. Elspeth, I can see your red curls bobbing about while you dash around doing things for your mother. Posy, I suppose you're fast asleep . . ."

"I am not," said Posy indignantly.

". . . but I want you to know that I've seen reindeer up here, but no sign of Santa Claus. I've looked hard, but I guess he must be farther north. I want Ronald to know that I welcome him just as much as if I were there and that the island belongs to him just as much as to the others. I wish I knew how he got there, but I'm delighted that he is. Mary, you know everything I want to say to you and I'm not going to broadcast it. I know you're listening. I feel perfectly sure of it. I shall stop at the island on the way home and expect to find you there, so look out for the *Osprey* coming up the channel some day in July. Now my time is up, and you ought to be in bed. Good night. Merry Christmas. Station at Cape Chidley, Labrador, Jim Douglas signing off . . ."

"Jim," Mrs. Douglas said in a rather shaky voice, "it's the best present I ever had. I don't know how to thank you. It makes Christmas perfect. I feel as if he'd been here."

Posy threw her arms around Jim's neck and hugged him. The twins and Ronnie slapped him on the back, all talking at once.

Jim at last disentangled himself from their embraces.

"I knew I'd get it," he said, his usually grave face beaming with pleasure over his achievement. "Didn't it sound as if he were in the room? Who turns up their nose at radio now?"

"No one except Ronnie," said Alan maliciously, and soon found himself in a frenzied scuffle with Jim's staunchest supporter.

"I'll put you both in the snowdrift," threatened Jim. "Didn't you hear Dad tell you to go to bed? Snap out of it."

HERE is another adventure of the Melendy family—Mona, Rush, Randy, Oliver, and their dog Isaac. Their man-of-all-work, Willy Sloper, and Cuffy, the housekeeper, and Father have all moved with them to a funny old house they call "The Four-story Mistake."

Elizabeth Enright

CLARINDA, 1869

ILLUSTRATED BY *Janet Smalley*

"IT'S snowing!" cried Randy one Saturday morning from her roost in the cupola. She had gone up there with a book of Father's called *Jean-Cristophe* which she didn't understand. "Real snow!" she shouted exultantly, forgetting all about the strange boy in the book and tumbling down the steps to the Office. "First I thought it was just ashes from the chimney but I watched and it melted right on the window sill!"

Rush stopped playing the piano. Mona stopped writing her play. Oliver stopped trying to draw a battle between fourteen airplanes and thirteen submarines, all on the same sheet of paper. With one accord they went downstairs, put on their coats, and, as an afterthought, their galoshes, and went outdoors. None of them had ever seen snow in the country. At first it wasn't very exciting, really. The sparse, papery flakes flew down, alighted, and vanished without making any difference on the landscape.

But Oliver made a discovery.

"Look," he said, examining the snowflakes on his sleeve. "They're shaped like little sort of fuzzy stars."

Oh, everybody knew *that!*

"Didn't you really ever notice it before, Oliver?" Randy sounded astonished. Nevertheless, she ran into the house and

297

borrowed one of the lenses from Rush's microscope and she and Oliver took turns peering through it at the snow crystals. How wonderful they were! So tiny, so perfect, down to the last point, the last feathering of frost. There were little stars, and miniature geometrical ferns and flowers, and patterns for fairy crowns, and tiny hexagons of lace. And each was different from all the others.

"How can they ever think of so many patterns?" wondered Randy, relinquishing the lens to Oliver.

"How can *who* ever think of them?" said Oliver, breathing so hard on the flake he was examining that it turned into a drop of water.

"God, I suppose," Randy answered, catching some snow on the tip of her tongue and eating it.

"Does He draw them first, or does He just go ahead and cut them out and drop them?" Oliver wanted to know.

But that was too much for Randy. Snowflakes were a mystery altogether.

"Come on," she said. "Let's go up through the woods to the top of the hill and see how it looks from up there."

By lunchtime the valley was lightly coated, like a cake with confectioner's sugar; and by half-past three the snow was of a respectable depth: halfway to the tops of their galoshes. There was white fur on the antlers of the iron deer and on the melancholy boughs of the Norway spruce.

They cleared the front drive with Willy, built a snowman for Oliver and a fort for all of them. "But, gee, if we only had a sled!" Rush said finally. Oliver stopped digging, leaned thoughtfully on his spade, and in a moment or two drifted inconspicuously toward the house.

Scrape, scr-a-a-pe, went Willy's industrious shovel. The millions of little white stars twinkled down, and down, and down; an endless supply. Mona bent over and wrote her name, big, on the snow with the point of her mitten.

MONA MELENDY.

Then she stood off and looked at it. It was the kind of name

298

that would look well in lights when she was famous. Oh, yes, of course, Mona Melendy. Isn't she wonderful? The most perfect Juliet I ever—

"Ow! Rush, you devil!" yelped Mona furiously as a wet, generous handful of snow down her back brought the glorious daydream to a close. The fight was on. Half in earnest, half in fun, they pelted each other, rolled on the ground, got soaking wet. Rush was strong, but Mona was bigger. She got him down, finally, and was sitting firmly on his chest combing her disheveled hair when she saw Oliver returning.

"Why, look what he's got!" she exclaimed, rising suddenly and liberating her victim.

"Sleds, gee whiz," murmured Rush, in awe. They were sort of funny, shabby old things with high, rusted runners, and names painted on them in fancy letters. "Snow Demon," one was called. "Little Kriss Kringle" was the other. Yes, they were strange, but never mind, they were sleds!

"Where'd you ever get them, Fatso?" inquired Rush.

"Me? Oh, I just found them," replied Oliver vaguely.

"But *where?*"

"Oh, just around."

"What do you mean *around?* I never saw any sleds lying around the Four-story Mistake. Come on, Oliver, give us the dope, like a good guy."

"I can't," said Oliver firmly. "It's a secret."

Randy couldn't resist boasting a little. "I know where he got them," she crowed. "But I promised not to tell." And she and Oliver exchanged a wink of the greatest satisfaction and good will.

The sleds turned out to be all right, though not greased lightning by any means. Rush had an inspiration, too, and went and got two large dishpans from the house; so each of them had a suitable vehicle for traveling down a snowy hill. The dishpans were particularly exciting, because they not only descended rapidly, but spun round and round while doing so. At the bottom of the slope you rose with difficulty, staggered, and discovered that you were the exact center of a world that re-

volved about you like a mammoth merry-go-round. Oliver was
the only one who didn't care for this. His stomach resented
the spinning of the dishpan, though for some reason it did not
resent being slammed down belly-whopper on a sled over and
over again.

Even Willy Sloper came and joined them for a while, and
the picture of him going down the slide in a dishpan, arms
and legs waving like an old-fashioned windmill was one that
none of them would ever forget.

"I know what let's do," Mona said, when they were all

exhausted and hot and red-cheeked. "I read about it in a book. They made snow ice cream in this book. Why don't we make some?"

"How do you do it?"

"Well, first we have to beg a bottle of milk and some sugar from Cuffy. You do it, Rush. You're best at it."

"Okay," said Rush, who was hungry, trotting obediently toward the house.

"And some cups," called Mona, "and some *spoons!*"

Then she and Randy and Oliver went looking for the cleanest, purest patch of snow they could find, which was in the middle of the front lawn: untouched, unmarked, it looked as though it had been created to be eaten.

It tasted very good, too, though rather flat, later on when Rush had brought sugar and milk to mix with it. Oliver ate so much that his alert and responsive little stomach felt strange again, and he retired to the house.

Mona and Randy gathered up cups and spoons and went back to the house, too. But Rush left them and took a walk up into the woods. It was dusk, but the snow lent a strange radiance to the world. Flakes still fell, melting cold on his cheek, whispering with a feathery sound. There was no sound but their whisper, and his boots crunching softly. Isaac bounded at his heels with a white beard and ear-fringes.

"Just think," Rush said, "almost a year ago I found you. And in a snowstorm like this." He leaned down and patted Isaac, who looked up at him lovingly with one cold paw raised out of the snow.

"Let's go back," Rush said. The woods were beautiful and mysterious; but suddenly he was cold; he longed for noise, and warmth, and light. Isaac understood; he turned with a little yelp of joy and galloped beside his master down the hill toward the bright windows of the kitchen.

The next day, Sunday, was a great disappointment to them all. During the night, by some strange alchemy, the snow had turned to rain. The spruce trees looked dreary and uncomfortable, like monstrous, wet crows. Only Oliver took any

301

pleasure in the morning, slopping about and digging in the dissolving snow. The rest of them did their chores, their homework, and snapped at each other. After dinner when they started a noisy game of dumb-crambo in the living room Father came out of the study and asked them to go up to the Office. "I can't even hear my typewriter," he complained, "let alone my own thoughts!"

Silent and out of sorts they retired to the Office. By now it was pouring. What is worse than a rainy Sunday afternoon when you've eaten a heavy dinner?

Randy sat down at the piano. She played the piece that Rush had taught her. It was a simple air by Bach, and the oftener she played it the better she liked it. First she played it as if she were very happy, and then as if she were very sad. (It sounded wonderful when played sadly, so she did it several times.) She also made it into a dance; into a thunderstorm, a picnic on the first day of spring, a funeral march, and a witch's lament. It sounded beautiful to her in all its transformations, she never got tired of it, but after half an hour Mona looked up from her book and said, "If you play that tune one more time, Ran, I'm going to start screaming and I don't think I'll be able to stop!"

"Oh, all right, if you feel like that." Randy folded her hands in her lap and sat very stiff on the piano bench. She hoped she looked deeply hurt, and stared coldly at the cutout pictures on the wall above the piano.

"Well, that's funny," she exclaimed a moment later, standing up and peering closer at the wall.

"H-mmm?" Mona's voice came vaguely from the distant regions of Castle Blair.

"I said, well, that's very funny," repeated Randy remembering to sound offended.

"What is?" Rush looked up languidly.

"Why, goodness! Come here, Rush! Look!"

"I don't see anything," said Rush, standing beside her. "Just those same old pictures pasted up. I practically know them by heart."

302

"No, no," Randy was excited. "See how the paper's sort of broken along here?"

"It's just a crack between the boards," Rush said.

"No, I don't think so," Randy persisted. "Look how it goes: up to here, and then across to there, and then down again. And look, there's kind of a bulge on that side. Like a hinge!"

"Like a hinge," repeated Rush, light dawning. "Creepers, Ran! Do you suppose it could be a door?"

"That's what I think," agreed Randy, as solemn as an archaeologist who has discovered the relics of a lost primitive race.

"Come on, kids, help move the piano out so we can see." But they didn't need to be asked; already they were pushing and tugging and the piano moved slowly outward, squealing on its casters.

"Where's your knife, Rush? Why don't you slit the paper along those cracks?" suggested Mona.

"No, let Randy," said Rush honorably, unsheathing the wicked-looking blade of his scout knife. "After all, she discovered it."

Rush was wonderful, Randy thought. Almost trembling with excitement she slit the ancient paper along the crack upward from the floor. But she wasn't tall enough to reach along the top.

"It's a door all right," whispered Rush, as though an enemy lurked beyond the partition. "But it's nailed shut: I can feel the nailheads under the paper. Here, hand over the knife, Randy. I'm taller. I'll do the top."

"Think how long it's been shut," Mona said, awed. "The pictures on this part of the wall are the oldest in the Office; I've noticed that before. There's a date down here above this newspaper engraving that says 1875!"

"What do you think's behind the door, Mona?" said Oliver, looking a little worried.

"Ah, that's a question, Fatso," Rush told him. "Maybe gold, maybe jewels, maybe a rattrap, maybe nothing."

"Not—not anything alive?" Oliver looked relieved.

"After almost seventy years? Not likely."

"Maybe a ghost," said Randy ghoulishly. "Maybe a skeleton hanging from the rafters."

"Mona?" Oliver's fat hand crept into hers.

"They're just joking, darling. Of course, there's nothing like that." But she didn't sound too sure herself.

"Funny there doesn't seem to be a trace of a latch or a handle of any kind," said Rush, feeling along the right side of the door with his long, sensitive fingers. "But I *think*—hmmm—I think *maybe* if I dig a hole just here with the point of my knife I might—just possibly—yes! It is! Look there's a keyhole!"

A keyhole!

"You look first, Randy," Rush said nobly.

"I'm almost scared to," Randy confessed. But then she knelt down and glued her eye to the keyhole while the others held their breaths.

"For heaven's sake!" she exclaimed.

"What do you see?" They all asked it at the same time.

"Are we ever dumb!" said Randy.

"Why, what do you see?" Oliver was dancing up and down with impatience.

"I see a window," Randy replied slowly. "I can see the spruce branches beyond it."

"What else?"

"Just floor and some wall: it's got green-flowered wallpaper on it. But are we ever dumb!"

"I don't see why," said Rush, gently but firmly pushing her out of the way so that he could get a good look himself.

"Well, because we *know* there are dormer windows all around the roof," Randy explained. "Twelve of them there are: three on each side. You can walk around the house outdoors and count them if you want to. Now just look at the Office. How many windows do you see?"

"Seven," said Mona. "I catch on. Three windows on the west wall; two apiece on the north and south. None at all on the east; just plain wall and pasted-up pictures." She knocked on the wall. "And listen how hollow it sounds. Why don't we ever notice!"

"Unobservant," Rush told her. "And dumb, just like Randy says. Very, very dumb."

"But not even Father noticed," Mona said. "Not even Cuffy."

"And you can't call *them* dumb!" Oliver was shocked at the mere idea.

"No, you certainly can't," Rush agreed. Suddenly he stood up. "Listen, kids. I'm going to get a hammer and a pair of pliers: we've got to get this door open. Oliver, you go find the library paste. Mona and Randy, you'll have to patch the places I tear in the paper. This must be kept secret, do you understand?"

They all understood perfectly. There had never been any doubt in their minds about that.

"Because who knows what we'll find when we open it," Rush continued darkly. "We *might* find a skeleton at that, or —or a torture chamber, or—"

"Or a ghost," repeated Randy, as a chill ran over her scalp. Oliver looked dubious.

305

"Ghosts!" scoffed Mona. "Honestly, Randy! And at your age." Nevertheless, her cheeks were pink, her eyes shining with excitement.

"I move we take a vow of secrecy. A blood vow," Rush said. "What do you think?"

"Oh, yes, a blood vow!" cried Randy, with a rapturous leap. "The only other blood vow we ever took was when we swore not to tell Cuffy or Father that we'd been exposed to whooping cough that time."

"Well, they just would have worried, and anyway we never got it," said Rush, as if that had justified the act. "Now, who has a pin?"

Mona had a safety pin in the ripped hem of her skirt. Providentially she hadn't mended it days ago when she was supposed to.

"But first it has to be sterilized," she insisted from the depth of her first-aid wisdom. So they sterilized the pin in a match flame. Of course Mona knew that the whole performance was nonsense but there *was* something rather solemn about the way they pricked their thumbs and made a scarlet X on a piece of paper opposite their names.

Mona and Randy, and Rush, that is. Oliver was firm in declining to yield his blood to the enterprise, so finally they had to let him use red water color instead.

"Though it's not really legal and binding," Rush warned him.

"I don't see why it matters," Oliver maintained stoutly. "Just two different kinds of juice, that's all. You can't tell the difference on the paper."

"But it's the principle of the thing," Rush argued weakly. "Oh, well, nuts. I'm going down to get the pliers and hammer now, and we'll get to work."

What an afternoon they had! It took ages to get the nails out; they were old and rusty, and had been in the wood so long they had almost become a part of it. Each one squeaked protestingly as Rush yanked it out.

In the middle of all this they heard Cuffy coming up the stairs and had to shove the piano back into place at once. There was a scuffle as Rush and Mona returned to their books, Oliver to his drawing, and Randy sat down on the floor and covered the nails and hammer with her skirt. Four scarlet faces confronted Cuffy as she heaved into view.

"What mischief are *you* up to?" she inquired suspiciously, looking at them.

"Us? Nothing," replied Randy. And a loud, nervous giggle escaped from her.

"We-e-e-l-l—" Cuffy was skeptical. Still the place looked no more upset than usual, and nobody seemed to be crying, so maybe it was all right. "I just came up to see if any of you would like to lick the bowl. I've just made a chocolate cake for supper, and there's lots of frosting left over."

What was the matter with them? They followed her so politely down the stairs, almost as if they were reluctant to come, instead of racing and bumping into one another, each in an attempt to get there first, as they had always done on similar occasions. And when they did get there they lapped up the chocolate fast as if they wanted to get it over with. Even Oliver failed to follow his customary procedure of licking his spoon so slowly that he could hold it up when everyone else had finished and say, "Look at all I've got left!" Yes, something was up, no doubt, but Cuffy was too busy to bother about it now. The children thanked her politely, if hastily, and lunged for the stairs, racing and bumping, each in an attempt to get there first. Cuffy sighed. That was more natural.

By four o'clock it was almost dark, but Rush wouldn't let anyone turn on the lights. Instead he went down to his room and got his flashlight and worked by the light of that. "This is much safer," he told them. "Less revealing." Randy secretly thought he just liked it better that way: it made the whole enterprise more dramatic. She didn't blame him; she liked it better that way herself.

"The Egyptians used to blow anthrax dust into the cracks of the royal tombs when they sealed them," Rush recounted with relish. "Whoever broke them open was supposed to get the disease and die in agony a few days later."

"What's anthrax?" said Randy. "It sounds like something Cuffy might use in the kitchen."

"I trust not," replied Rush, with the dignity demanded by the setting. "It's a very bad disease. Cows get it, I think. Well, anyway, *inside* the tombs they put a spell on all the gold and jewels and stuff, so that any robber or explorer, or anybody who fooled around with them would meet a dire and dreadful fate. Even if it was thousands of years later."

They were silent, thinking of the old tombs: each with its sarcophagus staring into the dark.

The sleety rain brushed the windows, the spruce branches sighed funereally in the wind, and the last nail came out of the door.

"There!" said Rush. He stood up, put the tip of the pliers into the keyhole, and pulled gently. At first the door refused to budge, but after a moment or two it yielded gingerly. Rush

308

only opened it a crack; then he handed the flashlight to Randy.

"Madam," he said, "the honor is yours. You go in alone first."

What? After all that talk about skeletons, and ghosts, and anthrax dust, and ancient Egyptian curses? Oh, no, Randy wasn't going through that doorway by herself.

"You come in with me, Rush," she insisted. "Right beside me. And Mona and Oliver you stay close behind."

"Okay, ready?" Rush opened the door and slowly, half fearfully they stepped into the secret chamber. The windows admitted only the frail, pearly glow of a wet twilight, and Rush flashed his light into the room. It was a long, narrow room, they saw: merely the sliced-off end of an attic, but it had five windows of its own and the walls and even the ceiling were covered with the pretty old-fashioned green-flowered paper. Rush flashed the lamp more thoroughly about the room.

Who was that!

Randy screamed. Even Rush made a startled sound, and Mona and Oliver leaped back into the Office as though they had been shot. Randy was right on their heels.

"A ghost, I saw a ghost!" she was gasping. "I knew there'd be a ghost, and there was!"

Oliver began to cry.

"No, no, kids. Come back!" called Rush. "It's only a picture! That's all it is. Honest. Just a big picture. Come on back and see."

Reluctantly they went back into the room. As for Oliver, he just peeked around the edge of the door until he was sure.

It was a picture, all right. Life-size, too, and set in the heaviest, fanciest, dustiest gold frame any of them had ever seen. It was a portrait of a young girl, almost a child; she might have been anywhere from twelve to sixteen, though her clothes were grown-up, old-fashioned clothes. She wore a silvery dress with a tiny waist and a long full skirt, and lots of buttons, and loops, and fringes all over it. The artist hadn't missed a single one. Her head was bent slightly to one side, cheek resting on one finger in a sentimental attitude. Her great mane of dark ringlets fell sideways, too, like heavy tassels on a curtain, and in her half-opened, curly little mouth each tooth was painted carefully, white and gleaming as a pearl. In her right hand she held a rose about the size of a head of Boston lettuce, with a big tear of dew clinging to its petals. Below her left hand (the one that supported her cheek), her elbow was poised upon a marble balustrade. She was painted against a classic background, with what appeared to be a mighty thunderstorm sweeping across the sky.

"Who is she?" whispered Randy, in awe.

"Why's she standing in the middle of a cemetery?" said Oliver.

"That's not a cemetery, Fatso," Rush explained. "That's just a lot of ruined Greek columns in the background."

"Why're they ruined? Did a bomb drop?"

"No, they're just old; they fell to pieces."

"Oh. Well, why's she standing in the middle of all those busted columns?"

"Search me. In those days people were always painting people beside temples and ruins and stuff."

"Look," said Mona. She leaned down. Attached to the frame at the bottom of the picture was a small gold plate with something engraved on it. Mona dusted it off with the tip of her finger.

"'Clarinda,'" she read aloud. "That's her name, I suppose. Just 'Clarinda,' and then a number, or a date I guess it is: 1869."

"Clarinda, 1869," said Rush thoughtfully. "Who was she, do you think? I bet she was a Cassidy! Clarinda Cassidy; very euphonious. It goes with all those curls. She looks kind of nice, though, doesn't she? I wonder how she could ever bend over without snapping right in half. Her waist looks about as big around as a doughnut."

"Why do you suppose she was ever nailed up in this room all by herself," said Randy, "all these years and years?"

That was a mystery no one could explain. They stood there in a little silent cluster staring at that tilted head, that narrow waist, that pearly smile. It had been a pretty exciting day altogether. First a hidden door; and then a secret room which

310

had been closed for seventy years, and now an imprisoned maiden in a golden frame. Clarinda, 1869. What more could you ask on a wet Sunday?

A piercing blast from the kitchen shattered the stillness. Cuffy's police whistle. That meant it was time for Oliver's supper; time for Randy to set the table, and for Mona to clean the Office, since it was her week. Hurriedly, they left the secret room, closed the door, and shoved the piano back in place. Like conspirators, they separated in the directions of their various tasks. Rush's pockets were full of rusty nails that had to be disposed of; Mona remained in the Office with the lights on, hurriedly pasting back torn strips of paper so old that they kept crumbling like ashes in her fingers.

"My," said Cuffy at suppertime. "What in the world was you doing all afternoon? I thought I heard furniture being pushed around, and then everything quiet for hours, and then a lot of squeals and a kind of stampede. Some new kind of game?"

"Sort of, Cuffy," Randy said uncomfortably, with her fingers crossed under the table. It was true in a way, wasn't it?

Rush seemed to have developed a sudden consuming interest in the Cassidy family.

"Fourteen children you said, didn't you, Father? I wonder what happened to them all!"

"Somebody or other told me about one of them who's still alive. A rich old gentleman out west someplace: hasn't been back in forty years," said Father. "There may be others scattered about, and doubtless many descendants."

"Why didn't they hang onto this swell place, I wonder?" Rush said. "I should think they'd have wanted to keep it in the family."

Father shrugged his shoulders; that was a question. "Perhaps they thought it was a funny old place; aesthetically it's sort of a freak, you know. I bought it through the agents of the estate of the two daughters who owned the property: two old spinsters they were; lived here till they died a few years back."

"What were their names, Father?" Rush put down his fork. So did Mona. So did Randy.

"The old ladies'? Well, let's see. One was named Minnie, or Lizzie. Lizzie, I believe, and the other—"

"Not Clarinda, by any chance?" Rush demanded.

"Clarinda? No, it was Christabelle. I remember because the contrast of the two names seemed so marked. Why on earth should it have been Clarinda?" Father wanted to know.

"Oh, I—I just read the name someplace," Rush said lamely. "It's an old-fashioned name and I just thought—" But he didn't have to cross his fingers under the table, for it was the simple truth.

That night the children dreamed all night about Clarinda and the secret room. Mona and Randy and Rush, that is. Oliver dreamed that he was driving a Greyhound bus full of policemen across the Brooklyn Bridge.

THE OLD COACH ROAD
Rachel Field

There's hardly a wheel rut left to show
The way the coach road used to go.
Trees straddle it and berries grow
Where coaches rumbled long ago,
And horses' hoofs struck sparks of light,
Many a frosty winter night.
Here gypsy faces, lean and tan,
Peered from some lumbering caravan,
Or peddlers passed with bulging packs
And sheep with sun aslant their backs.
Now, only berry pickers push
Their way through thorn and elder bush—
But sometimes of a night, they say,
Wheels have been heard to pass that way.

313

HAVING lived on Bright Island with only her family for company, Thankful Curtis was both frightened and angry when her parents decided that she should attend high school on the mainland. Up until this point she had never studied with a group of young people.

The first days of school were very difficult for her. But she found two friends, her Latin teacher, Mr. Orin Fletcher, and old Mr. Dinkle, who owned a boat and had accepted Thankful as a Saturday sailing companion.

Among the students shy Thankful had a hard time. Her own shyness as well as their lack of understanding of her home life made them spurn her company. The first dance at the school was a costume ball, and Thankful dressed as a Scottish lass. She danced with Robert, who had befriended her, and did miserably. Both he and her roommate, Selina, were amazed when later on at the dance Thankful was introduced by Mr. Fletcher, asked to dance the Highland Fling, and did it beautifully, receiving much applause. She was a success at the dance and with all the students except Robert and Selina, who thought that she had fooled them with her shyness and was just showing off with the Fling. Thankful has a chance in the following adventure to show them their mistake.

Mabel Robinson

FALSE SUMMER

ILLUSTRATED BY
Armstrong Sperry

THE Indian summer sun lay soft on Thankful's eyelids. She stretched into comfort on the pebbly beach and waited for old man Dinkle to come. He was going to haul up next week so that she would have no more Saturdays on the water. She knew it was time. This pale sea and soft light were false summer. Already they had twice fought their way around the course on Saturdays when the fall wind had whipped the bay feather white. She knew, but she could not face the

314

procession of weeks ahead when no shining day barred off each end.

Still there was today. The sun poured over and soaked into her, but without much heat. Winter was coming. She heard fewer crickets now in the harsh grass, and the bayberry twigs were stiff with dull blue clusters. The berries had been jade green when she left Bright Island.

It was curious, she thought, how Bright Island never left her. Always the feeling of it was in her senses, apple green of the sky, the taste of its fog on her lips, its lovely quiet. She knew now that she would never be tuned to the noise of many people. That she would always be troubled by their strange ways.

She sighed deeply as she thought of Robert and Selina. Since that dance they had dropped her entirely. When Selina had said, "Well, you had a swell time showing off, didn't you?" Thankful had slashed back against her hurt. And then there had been quiet between them, but not the peace of this quiet in the sun. An ugly stillness. The kind that brooded before a storm broke. Thankful had never known it between humans before.

Robert she understood better. Boys were easier to understand. He was so gay, so irresponsible. He valued people who gave him a good time. She had failed him at that dreadful dance, had touched his vanity. Probably he thought that she showed off, too. Queer what Robbie's plaid had done for her that night. She now could hear Robert's voice, "Gal, where've you kept all those good looks!" and she saw Selina's staring woman's eyes. Anyway, she rolled over and felt the freedom of her overalls, anyway she was part of the rest of the school now. Though even they looked at her puzzled sometimes as if trying to reconcile two different people. It was those dreadful clothes that the girls had bought her. She wished that the tide would carry away the dress which she had tucked behind a rock when she put on her overalls.

Those overalls! She had had them on last week when Mr. Fletcher suddenly appeared on the beach. The gloom left her as she thought of last week, and she felt light and comfortable again. She and old Dinkle had been busily loading the dinghy

315

when there he was, leaning against a rock.

"Hullo," he said, and "Hullo," they both said.

"So you do have some fun, don't you?" he came up to the boat and handed Dinkle the oars. Thankful had introduced them as well as she could with old Dinkle shoving the boat. Mr. Fletcher took hold, too, and they got it to the water's edge in no time.

"Have a good haul," he said and he managed to look wistful.

Old Dinkle held the dinghy back with an oar. "Want to come, young feller?" Just as if he had been one of the boys. Robert, if Robert could be imagined there! And without waiting to answer, he had given the bow a push and leaped aboard. He had on old clothes, too, though they didn't look like Dinkle's.

Dinkle asked him what his name was, though Thankful had already told him. Orin Fletcher. And if the old man didn't call him Orin! Just as if he had been one of the boys. So easily that Thankful did it herself once. She turned scarlet now as she thought of it. He had started to cast off too soon and she had shouted from the wheel, "Hold her, Orin, hold her!" She was glad he hadn't noticed it and was very careful after that. But curiously enough she found herself thinking of him as the old man called him, Orin with the first letter drawled a little. Perhaps it was because on an island you called people quite simply by their own names. She sighed. There she was back to the island again.

But it had been easy to talk about Bright Island that day. Not while they were hauling, though that was fun too. He had been so quick in his motions that Dinkle said he was through before he had begun. And Thankful had to show him how to do so many things that she entirely forgot that he was usually the teacher. He seemed to forget it too, and they laughed a great deal over his mistakes.

It was while they had their snack that they talked so much about Bright Island. Thankful was surprised when she remembered how much she had told him. Luckily he had a sandwich of his own, and a whole pocket full of chocolate bars. Old Dinkle had relished those! Thankful hardly got one for herself, and she didn't see Orin—Mr. Fletcher—eat a single one.

As Thankful lay there on the beach and recalled the fun they had had, it seemed surprisingly the best trip yet. If she had considered beforehand including someone who was so Latin wise, she would have been sure of a spoiled day. But he really had added something which she couldn't quite define. The day seemed saltier, with more flavor. Fuller of laughter and quick gay talk. Not once his sardonic tongue.

Thankful sprang to her feet and ran to help old man Dinkle slithering over the beach grass with his mended spray hood. "May need it before we get 'em hauled today," he grunted, and Thankful nodded, wise to the November sea.

Before he shoved off, the old man squinted up and down the shore. "Orin comin'?" he asked.

Thankful had looked, too. "I guess not," she said. "He might think he was pushing himself in."

"Good comp'ny," Dinkle pulled short hard strokes to his power boat. "Good choc'let."

Thankful reached in the pocket of her jeans. "I brought you some."

317

Dinkle's eyes gleamed under bushy brows. "Might try a chaw when we get her off," he said.

The power-boat chugged smoothly out of the cove with Thankful at the wheel. She knew the location of each lobster pot now. But today instead of rebaiting the slatted cage and dropping it back again, Dinkle piled the pots neatly in the bow. As they putted briskly around the next point he cocked a withered eye toward the shore.

"That fool sloop goin' out today? Should 'a' been hauled up two weeks ago."

Thankful didn't want her happiness spoiled. This last day. They had passed her in a car, Robert and Selina. No bus when his boat had been ordered up the first of the month. Selina had hired the car because Robert was always broke, and it was one way to make him take her sailing. Thankful had heard all this gossip from the girls, but she didn't want to think about it now. Her thoughts must leave them alone, and the clean white sloop, and their lunch together on an island. If she could but set foot on an island again, a wild sweet-smelling island! She swung the wheel and slid up to a bobbing buoy. It was enough to be out with the gulls this morning. They swirled and shrieked after the discarded bait. She thought of Limpy, strong and free. And Dave! She missed Dave suddenly, and then forgot him. Robert's brown hair smooth and close to his head, Robert's quick grace, oh, she wished that Robert would keep out of her thoughts! She wanted all of them for this last day on the water. Where was her pride to let them wander away to those young people who had no thought of her? The sloop fell behind the wooded point and she whistled urgently to her sad heart.

She and Dinkle had a companionable snack none the less appetizing from the smell of dead herring which hung over the boat. Not even a crust for the screaming gulls who followed to the last haul. Some pots must be left for another trip but now there was work enough to stow these into the shed above the tide line. Back and forth they trudged, the old man strong and gnarled, the girl young and straight in her faded jeans. One on each side until the last pot was piled away for the winter.

318

Out at the mooring old Dinkle fastened down the spray hood. "Blow before night," he said, and they jogged their heads together at the piled ranks of wind clouds in the north. "Spell o' weather on the way. Hope that fool boy'll haul up his sloop now."

Robert back again in her thoughts when she just cleared him away. He must have come in long ago. It was late. Stacking the pots had taken so long. She must run. It was good-bye then. And "Come a good day in March, we'll get her off again." March. Months away. So long to wait! And then she remembered that when March came she would be only two months from Bright Island and she ran with swift glad steps as if toward that time. The old man plodded through the pasture without looking ahead or behind.

At the turn of the road where the coastline stretched to either side, Thankful paused and looked. Looked again, and then again to be sure. Robert's boat was not at its mooring. Then she remembered with a quick lift of her breath that he might have sailed it down to the yard where it was to be hauled up for the winter. "Of course," she thought. "Of course he did. He wouldn't want them to know up at school that his boat was still out." Though she knew how little he cared in his gay insubordination, and how gentle with him the authorities were. "Spoiled, he is," she said, and then she saw the car still braked in the beach grass. Robert and Selina becalmed out there somewhere were waiting for those black rolling clouds to bring them wind. And they little knew how much, she thought grimly.

It was curious how much she knew of their plans in spite of the indifference she had worked so hard to achieve. A sail to Hogback, a swim, a driftwood fire, steak, marshmallows—a stolen picnic which no one would permit; and stolen, all the better. But what if this escapade ended other than they planned? Thankful could already see the whitecaps edging the outer bars. A November nor'wester was too strong medicine for that little boat. She was built for summer seas.

A slap of wind, chilled as if from the bottom of the sea, struck her sharply. She shivered down into her sweater though not from cold. Best wait around a few minutes, she thought. They'll be right in now the breeze has come up. She hated to get back to school late. Miss Haynes let her have these Saturdays knowing her need, and that she would be back on time. Thankful could not bear to worry her. But, she thought swallowing her pride, I'll ride up in their car and save time. I must be sure about them.

The windclouds swept low now and helped to darken the brief November day. Thankful watched the water ruffle and break into gray fragments under them. Not too squally, she thought, they could weather this. Hope they've plenty of warm clothes. But she had seen Selina dress in her smart linen slacks and shirt, and the coat she wore to cover them was slung across the car seat.

Why didn't they hurry? Didn't they *know*—know what, that the day was darkening, that the wind from those overhanging clouds could break them, that she was waiting, oh, what could she do if that small boat did not sail around the point soon!

Across the road the ground rose in a brief knoll which might overlook the wooded point. Thankful pulled herself up through wild rose brambles which tore at her, into alder brush, and out on the flat granite top. There it was! Flitting over the dark water

toward her like a small pale moth. The relief was so sharp that
it hurt. She was consumed with anger toward that pair for the
anguish they had caused her. Let them make their mooring as
they could! She would run for it now and reach the campus as
soon as they did.

The sloop went about, tacking close into the wind. Thankful
stopped short at the edge of the rocky summit. "The fool! The
fool!" she cried. "Why don't you reef your sail!" her voice blew
back into her throat. All sail on to make time, and no thought
about consequences. She knew, she knew what Robert would
do. She could see his dark figure bent over the wheel, and a
crouched huddle of white which spelled Selina. Were they
frightened? Reckless, reckless lad to pay no heed to that wild
wind! It blew her hair into her eyes, and she pushed the pale
mop back and peered distractedly under her hands.

The sail from her knoll looked almost flat on the water. Selina,
backed against the rail, was braced erect now. The sloop shoved
itself nose deep through choppy waves rushing crazily at each
other. Its keel was bare. "The good little boat! The good little
boat!" Thankful cried to it watching it wallow. "You can make

321

it!" Oh, if he'd only reefed her! "Robert! Robert!" she screamed, "Robert! Head her up! Head her up!" and then she was running, running blindly, purposefully, through brush and brambles. The sloop had capsized.

Her feet took no caution that she knew, but they bore her sure and swift as wings. Down to the road, up the shore, to the dinghy pulled high from the tide. Dragging, tugging at the heavy stern, until waves crashed over its edge. Her breath stopped in her throat now, and she panted like a dog. Into the water beside the boat until it cleared the chop, and then over the side, and pull, pull, pull. Almost as much water inside as out. But nothing could sink that dory. Oh, could those two hold on until she got there! Could she hurry any faster! If she could only breathe!

She leaped aboard the power-boat, and flung the dory's loop over the mooring pole. Here, here in the diddy box he kept the key. Dave had always rolled up the wheel. She thought of Dave now. She knew how, but she had no breath. And if it would not catch! Oh, she couldn't think of that—she reached down and gave it a mighty roll.

It caught! And she flung herself against the tiller. Broadside she must run, no easing her off. Robert and Selina struggling in that icy water, clutching at a slippery keel—oh, hold on! Hold on! I'm coming. If she could ever get beyond the point where she could see if—where she could see if—she pushed back what she might have to see. Her breath was easier now, and she felt every elastic muscle stretch and pull at the boat's speed. It was so slow! When the motor coughed once she felt sick and faint.

She took a chance at rocks and cut close to the point. Around it, leaning out to prick into the space ahead. In the gloom, nothing. Nothing but crazy fighting waves. Thankful moaned, pushing hopelessly on. Then her terror found voice and she heard herself above the wind screaming their names. "Where are you? Where are you? I'm coming!" If the wind would be quiet to let her hear.

She was almost on them when she saw them, Selina lurched over the flattened rudder, Robert hanging to the bowsprit.

322

Water dashing over them and the flat white sail. Instantly Thankful felt her wild pulses quiet. They were here, and she could get them. Calm and sure, she slid at low speed as near as she dared.

"Catch!" she hurled one of the ropes old Dinkle had used to tie his lobster pots together. It curled over the half sunk bowsprit and into Robert's numb fingers. He made a clumsy hitch and cried hoarsely, "Hurry!"

Her arms, her heart, pulled her toward him first. Robert. He could so easily slip now! His poor stiff hands—but Selina *was* slipping. A limp, huddled heap. Thankful dragged at her rope, drifted closer, grabbed at the white slacks, and Selina had tumbled into the bottom of the power-boat. Thankful could hear her gasping, "Oh, I'm so thankful, thankful, thankful," and thought she was calling her. But she had no more heed for Selina.

Robert tried valiantly to help her, but she thought that she had lost him twice. Somehow he caught the rope each time he fell, but the waves dashed over his white drowned face and Thankful thought he must let go. She talked, talked, talked to him. Not that he could hear her words. But her steadying voice, her set determined face swaying above him, her strong young arms, finally they got him aboard. He rolled down beside the engine and was very sick. She thought, perhaps he will mind this most of all, and looked sharp for a chance to free their mooring to the wreck.

She was still enough of a sailor to feel that she cut away something alive. But there was no more that she could do for the sloop. It would wash ashore, and with luck it would make the sheltered cove. They would come down tomorrow and retrieve it. Thankful swung out in an arc until, the wind behind her, she leaped with the waves toward the mooring where the dinghy bumped.

Bitten to the skin by the icy spray, the cold wind pouring over her wet body, Thankful still was conscious only of a warm core that could not be reached. Down there, cowering close to the engine box in the lee of the gale, were two live people.

Wretched, half frozen, water streaming from them, Selina sobbing and Robert ghastly with shut eyes, yet there! Alive and—she held the dinghy with one hand and pushed them into it with the other—almost ashore.

No one could help her pull the dory back above high water except the tide which was at the full. I'll give it an extra hist tomorrow, she promised herself. She measured the task ahead of her. How to get this numb stumbling pair as far as the car. They waited for her to decide, motionless where she had dragged them from the dinghy. She could not manage both of them at once.

"Robert, you come with me and we'll drive back for Selina." Oh, if she only could drive that car! Would Robert? It would take so long for her to run back to the school for help. They would freeze down here waiting. "Robert!" she spoke more sharply. "Come along with me. Exercise will warm you best."

He stood dripping and looked at her vaguely. Her heart was wrung. "Come on," she seized his arm and propelled him toward the road. Selina moaned, "Don't leave me," but no one noticed her. His feet slipped back over the loose pebbles, and she could see his knees begin to fold. She thrust a strong, tired arm around him and hoisted him over the bank to the road. How slight and fine he felt!

"Now faster, just a little jog trot, see like this," she urged and prodded until she could feel his muscles under her arm come to life. She thought there had never been a piece of road so long. Then she could see the car settled down into the gloom of the dark beach grass.

"Can't drive it," Robert muttered. The car smelled stuffy and warm. Robert folded his arms over the wheel and rested his wet dark head on them. Thankful could have cried.

"That's perfect blethers!" her mother always broke into Scotch when she scolded. "I cannot abide such softness. Pick up your head off that wheel."

Robert raised startled eyes, and she met them with her dark-browed frown. "Now get on with you," she was relentless in her need. "We'll not leave Selina to chill on the beach. You

can go that far, and if need be I'll run it the rest." She watched
his shaking hands start the car, and kept a hand on the wheel
as it swerved down the road. "It's not unlike enough to a boat
to bother," she said. "You can leave the steering to me. Though
I don't know as I can bring her around."

The turn was a problem, and the car sheered crazily about
the road before it faced home. But Selina was aboard and
Robert was still at the wheel. At the gate he pushed Thankful's
hand from the wheel. "I'll take it in," he said shortly. She
thought, he is remembering now the hard words I said to him.
Oh, Robert! But because his hand was steady she let him go.

There could be nothing secret about this return. Through the
lighted windows of the dining room their empty places proclaimed them. Thankful saw the great roast, and hunger brought
her first weakness. She trembled as she watched the maid bear
it away for the dessert. Suddenly she felt the sorrows of the
world bear down upon her, and she wept. This last straw had
broken her.

Robert was ready to dominate again. She heard his voice
running on to Miss Haynes. But she did not care what he said.
The lost roast stood for a spar which would have saved her from

drowning. She crept up to her room and dropped her wet clothes on the floor while Edie helped Selina into bed.

Edie left them and went out. Thankful crawled shivering under the blankets. The wind and the fear and her hunger had beaten her down. She seemed hollowed into the bed, flat and lifeless. Her hair dried in wisps on the pillow, her lashes were feather dark. She felt that nothing could rouse her again.

Edie held the door back with her foot and pushed her way in. The curling smell of hot roast beef woke Thankful's tired senses. Edie set the tray down between the beds. "Want I should feed you?" she asked. Selina moaned assent. Thankful sat up briskly. She took the loaded plate from Edie and silently set to work through the roast and vegetables while Selina fussed over a glass of hot milk. But before the last spoonful of ice cream was reached, she slid back on the pillows with the soft breathing of untroubled sleep.

SNOWFALL

Janet Norris Bangs

Delicate as frosted dew
   That remembers starry flowers,
Snowflakes, caught in cloud, sift through,
   Light as feather-showers.

Over valley, hill, and town,
   Snow foams softly in the night,
Shovel tons of thistle-down
   Carve a world of white!

Summon fay or pixy, call
   Gnomes or brownies—I'll believe
Any myth while snowflakes fall
   Cool upon my sleeve.

He made a clumsy hitch and cried hoarsely, "Hurry!"

When Mr. Ellis was called at the last minute to join an expedition, the four Ellis children and their mother, whom they affectionately called Penny, moved to an old farmhouse in Connecticut to save money. They knew that there would be many hardships, but when Penny was called away to care for a sick relative, the going became extremely difficult. As Caroline and Martin were too young to be of much help, the responsibilities fell to Kay, the artist, and Garry, the tomboy. With the help of Neal and Mary Rowe, the neighbors across the road, and Edna, the town "good neighbor," they get along very nicely until the storm Neal predicts comes upon them. Then things really begin to happen.

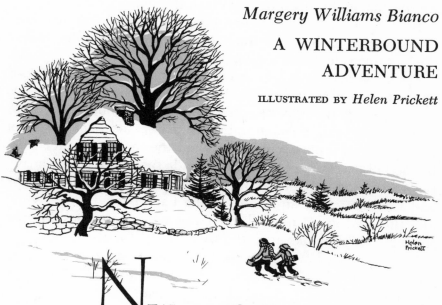

Margery Williams Bianco

A WINTERBOUND ADVENTURE

ILLUSTRATED BY *Helen Prickett*

NEAL was right. Next morning there was an ominous grayness in the air. By midday the snow began to fall, first in big whirling flakes, then closer and denser, shutting out the landscape like a white curtain, packing against the door sill, and drifting high in the hollows. The children came home from school shouting and red-cheeked, snow clinging thickly to their clothing and sifted down their necks, shaking themselves like dogs as they ran in through the door that Garry held ajar against the rising wind.

327

"There's four inches now. If it keeps up Jimmy says we won't get down to the state road tomorrow, not unless they get the snowplows out."

It did keep up. Garry and Martin worked hard bringing in armloads of wood before the big outdoor woodpile should get snowed under, till their fingers were frozen through their wet gloves.

"Gosh, there's enough here to last us through a blizzard!" Martin exclaimed, dropping his last heavy load on the shed floor.

"So you think," said Garry darkly. It was her job to tend Big Bertha, and she knew how much that monster ate.

By suppertime the snow had piled halfway up the window-panes on the north side of the house, and when Caroline pulled the curtain aside it was to peer out on a white and buried world.

There was no going to school next day. The kitchen door opened onto a snowbank, and Martin stepped out above his knees. Jimmy brought the milk over a good hour later than usual, floundering through unbroken drifts, and between them they shoveled a narrow path as far as the mailbox. Later Neal hitched his two horses to the homemade snowplow, three heavy timbers spiked together to make a rough triangle, and the boys and Caroline clung squealing to the back bar while it swung and slithered down the hill, breaking a track and pushing the snow into high banks against either side of the road.

Down on the lower road the town plow was busily forging its way, an impressive noisy monster that threw the loose snow up in showers as it chugged along. Neal, about to turn his horses at the foot of the hill, drew up and waited with the children to see it pass.

"Hey, what you tryin' to do—spoil the sledding?" he shouted as the engine drew abreast.

The driver grinned back.

"Better take them horses off of the road before we scrape 'em up!"

Road and hedgerow shimmered through the hot air from the exhaust. The horses' breath came in white clouds as they stood

waiting. Neal's sturdy figure planted with feet braced well apart on the snowplow, the children in their knitted caps and mufflers, old Sam, the Walker hound, sitting down beside them with his tongue lolling out—the whole made a cheerful picture, sharp cut against the heaped, sparkling snow.

"Me an' my horses, we're making a decent job of it," Neal drawled. "By the time you're finished muckin' up the roadbed with that old pushcart we'll have to get to work an' pay for havin' it all put back again."

"Oh yeah? Didn't see you at the Grange dance Friday night."

"You didn't. My best an' me was all fixed up to go, but she turned it down at the last minute. Seems she heard you was goin' to be there. Bad news always gets around, some way. Giddap, Dolly!"

The horses swung round into the cleared road, making a wide circle. The snowplow driver leaned out and waved. Then they were breasting the hill again, the heavy wooden frame lurching like a ship at sea while the children clung to one another to keep their balance.

"Good as toboggan ridin'," said Neal. "Hang on tight. When we get back I'll take a turn round the barn and then we're through. I'll clear you a nice track there for sleddin' on."

The horses pawed and floundered through the drifts on the pasture slope, where the plow left a wide curving track, smooth and close packed for the sleds to run on, with a soft snowbank on either side.

The bright, clear cold was growing steadily colder by afternoon, and a steely haze crept over the hills. Neither of the boys wanted to give up coasting, but Caroline left them early and came back to warm her pink chilled hands at the stove.

Kay was deep in her rug, sorting colors by the window.

"Had enough sledding, Caroline?"

"I guess so."

"Then take your things off quickly. The snow's just dripping off you!"

Caroline began to tug in a half-hearted way. She was so long about it that Garry had to come and help.

330

"Anything happened out there?"

"No. . . . I just got tired."

"You're all chilled through," said Garry briskly. "You should have had sense enough to come in before."

Caroline flounced aside.

"I'm not. I'm burning hot, if you want to know. And I guess my head aches, too."

Kay and Garry exchanged glances.

"I'll tuck you up on the sofa, and you can take a nap till suppertime."

In spite of Big Bertha the windowpanes were already beginning to freeze over, earlier than they had ever done before. Garry scratched a fingernail across the transparent ice. "Look at that already! It's going to be pretty cold tonight."

"Five degrees now," cried Martin excitedly when he came in, cheeks burned red with the frost. "And it's going down all the time. Neal says it'll drop way below zero tonight."

Caroline felt no better by suppertime. She was cross and irritable, drank a glass of hot milk under protest and was tucked up in her bed, which had long ago been shifted into the room where her sisters slept, warmed by the floor register just above Bertha's towering head. That register made an isle of comfort on which to dress or undress in chilly weather, and the girls were doubly glad of it tonight.

"I'll make up a good big fire that'll keep till morning," Garry said.

She wedged chunk after chunk into Bertha's cavernous mouth before closing the drafts. But the wind changed during the night; instead of smoldering as they should the logs burned themselves out and when Garry came down in the early morning there was only a handful of graying ashes left. A chill light filtered through the ice-covered windows. In the kitchen everything was frozen solid.

Garry gave one grim look around her, pulled on a windbreaker, and went out in the shed to split fresh kindling, for Martin had forgotten his job in the excitement of sledding yesterday and the woodbox was nearly empty. The pump handle only gave a dismal croak when she took hold of it, but luckily there was still water—or rather ice—in the kettle. She got the kitchen fire started, set the frozen coffeepot over it, and returned to struggle with Bertha.

Martin heard her stirring and stumbled drowsily out in bathrobe and slippers, his teeth chattering.

"What's happening? Did the fire go out?"

"Oh, no! I'm just trying to keep the heat down!"

Ashes were flying in the room. Garry, poker in hand, turned a smudgy and exasperated face on him.

"Wrap a blanket around you and go sit by the kitchen stove till I come—and keep it *going*. And watch that coffeepot. I'll be right out."

She laid fresh kindling over the still warm ashes, with a fresh log on top, and opened the drafts. Bertha could be depended upon to do her best.

Martin was peering into the percolator. "Do you suppose frozen coffee's bad for one?"

"No, of course it isn't; I've drunk it dozens of times." Garry knew her Martin; he had a horrible memory for scraps of information read in newspapers, especially relating to what he called "chemical reactions." The slightest hesitation on her part, and that precious coffee would have gone straight into the slop pail. She snatched the pot from him barely in time and set it back on the stove. "There's enough for us two there and I'll make some fresh as soon as the water's thawed out. You get some cups out and for heaven's sake don't make any racket; I want Kay to go on sleeping till the house has warmed up."

The kitchen stove was burning cheerfully by now; they sat with their feet on the oven ledge and drank the left-over coffee, while little by little the room grew warmer and tiny misted spots appeared on the windowpanes.

"Thirty-six," said Garry presently, going to look at the thermometer which hung by the doorway between the two rooms. "Lord knows what it's like outside."

They were to look at that thermometer many times before the day was out. Neal's cold snap had come with a vengeance. Martin was all set to go to school in spite of the temperature, but learning when Neal came over with the milk that Jimmy was staying home, he thought better of it, and spent the morning across the way instead. Even that short dash across the road made him feel like an arctic explorer.

"Eighteen below last night," Neal told them. "Mary and I sat up all night to keep the fires going. It's all of ten below now, or I miss my guess. No sense letting those kids walk down to the school bus and back this weather."

And yet there was something exhilarating in the cold, Garry thought when she went out into the yard and felt the keen sting of the air against her face, a sort of excitement in knowing what real winter weather could be like.

Kay was worried about Caroline, who huddled near the stove, listless and shivering. Her cheeks were burning and her hands cold and clammy.

"It's a straight old-fashioned cold," said Garry. "If Penny were here she'd give her a good dose of something and put her back to bed. I'll light the drum stove upstairs and we'll get the room good and warm before she goes up."

For once Caroline made no objection to anything. All she wanted was to curl up in bed and lie there, and it was this

333

unwonted submissiveness more than anything else that frightened her sisters.

"If only I knew what she felt like, I'd know more what to do," Kay said helplessly. But Caroline wouldn't even tell them what she felt like. She lay and snuffled into her handkerchief, refusing all comfort and only wanting Penny—Penny who had always been on hand every time before when she felt sick.

And Penny was in New Mexico.

Garry went over to the Rowes, sure strength in all emergencies, and returned with Mary and the clinical thermometer.

"Hundred and a half," said Mary. "I don't believe it's anything more than a cold. You could call the doctor up, but he'd have eight miles to drive and the roads are awful. Neal says there'll be hardly a car out today. I tell you what. If her temperature goes up, or if she isn't any better by tomorrow, why don't you call Miss Hussey? She's the district nurse."

"Would she come?"

"Of course she'll come. And she hasn't so far to drive, either. I'd as soon have her as anyone. She was grand when Shirley was sick last spring. And if you need a doctor she'll tell you right away. I'll write her number down for you, and I'll leave the thermometer here."

She went, and the little wave of reassurance she had brought somehow vanished with her.

"Do you suppose it *is* anything?" Kay worried.

"Anything" meant pneumonia, Garry knew. That unspoken word hung in the air between them.

"She'd have a worse temperature than that, if it was."

Miss Hussey, over the telephone, sounded cheerful and unperturbed. There were a lot of bad colds going about just now. Keep the little girl in bed, and she would come over and have a look at her tomorrow.

"Well, I suppose that's all we can do," said Kay.

She went upstairs to sit with Caroline. She found *Alice in Wonderland* on the bookshelves and began to read to her, but in the middle of the Hatter's tea party the print began to dance up and down before her eyes; her teeth chattered, and she was

334

conscious of a steadily growing ache through all her limbs. When Garry came up with a cup of hot tea it was to find two patients instead of one.

"I g-guess it's flu all right," Kay said. "I've had it before. Anyway we know what it is, now."

"Everything *would* happen at once," Garry thought, as she tucked Kay, too, into bed and marched down to fetch the thermometer and fill fresh hot-water bottles. The kitchen ure had gone down by the time she had Kay fairly settled; the pump was frozen up again, and when she did get water boiling at last the kettle tipped over the open stove hole and scalded her wrist as she made a hasty grab to catch it.

Martin ran for the olive oil in the pantry, but that too was a solid lump in the bottle, so all she could do was to smear butter on, biting her lip as Martin wound a bandage round with shaking fingers.

"That'll be all right; I don't give a hoot if it *is* septic—it takes the pain out anyway. Now pull my sleeve down—ouch! Thank goodness it's my left hand, or we'd be in a worse fix yet."

It was colder than ever that night. With Kay and Caroline in bed there seemed a gloom over the house. Garry and Martin ate their supper by the stove, and as she glanced at the windows Garry remembered those early winter days when they had asked one another: "Do you suppose it ever gets much colder than this?" This cold was like a living enemy. It seemed to prowl round the house, pushing at the doorsills, snatching at every possible cranny to get in, and if it weren't for the snow which had sealed many of the cracks it would have been worse yet.

No taking chances on the stoves tonight, Garry decided. With Martin's help she dragged the sofa across the floor, cautiously so as not to wake Kay and Caroline upstairs; Martin brought a mattress and blankets from his own room, and together they camped in the circle of Big Bertha's comforting glow, like sentries round a campfire.

"Aren't you going to undress?" Martin asked.

"Not tonight." She lit the stable lantern, set it on the floor by the stairway with the wick turned low, and lay down on the sofa with her clothes on and the old warm comforter from the spare room wrapped about her.

"Then I won't sleep either."

"Don't be silly," said Garry.

The shadows stretched high on the walls, making queer pictures among the cracks and bulges of the old plaster. Now and again a log shifted in Big Bertha's interior, sending a little tongue of flame leaping up the stovepipe. Out in the pantry a rat, undismayed by the cold, was gnawing busily. Garry's wrist began to bother her. At the time she had been too busy to notice it much, but now the warmth was bringing out the pain.

Martin, for all his determination to keep her company, soon fell asleep, the blankets hugged tightly around him, but Garry lay long awake, watchful for a movement in the room above her, listening, as night drew on and the cold grew more intense, to the strange snapping and creaking of the frost outside—sudden sharp cracks and muffled thuds, as though the house itself were fighting desperately in the grip of the enemy, its old

336

timbers about to fly apart at any moment. Frightening sounds to one who had never heard them before. They seemed to come from underfoot, from all around. One, louder than the rest, cracked like a pistol shot on the stillness, and in the dim light from the lantern she saw Martin's face, startled and wide-eyed, raised from his mattress.

"What was that?"

"Only the frost cracking, I guess. Go to sleep again."

He snuggled under the blankets.

"I don't like it. Say . . . Garry?"

"What?"

"Suppose the whole house was to crack up?"

"It won't. I guess it's stood worse frosts than this."

She got up to put more wood on the kitchen stove and crept halfway up the stairs to listen if Kay or Caroline was stirring. But there was no sound; only the queer watchful emptiness of the house about her, the crackling of the frost outside. It was just two o'clock. She pulled the covers round her once more and settled back to doze.

When she opened her eyes again it was daylight. Martin was awake before her: he had set the kettle over and made fresh coffee. In his anxiety to have it good and strong he had used double measure and let the percolator bubble frantically; Garry winced at the first bitter mouthful, but it did her good.

Kay's fever had gone down, but she felt weak and miserable. Martin was a tower of strength that morning, helpful as only a boy can be when he suddenly realizes a crisis in the familiar machinery of home life. He brought in wood, swept up the living room, washed the dishes, and kept looking anxiously at Garry as though he expected her, too, at any moment to keel over before his eyes. As a matter of fact she wasn't feeling any too good herself; her head was buzzing, the floor had a tendency to rise and drop unexpectedly under her feet as she moved about, and more than once she paused in what she was doing to clinch her teeth and mutter angrily: "Garry Ellis, just pull yourself together, you blame fool. You *can't* get sick now."

The morning dragged by and at midday, when Garry had

337

almost given up hope of her, Miss Hussey arrived. The mere sight of her brought comfort. She was stout and motherly and deliberate in her movements. She took off her numerous outer wrappings, unpacked her little black bag on the table, tied a fresh apron over her uniform, and went out into the kitchen to peer into the kettle and poke the fire up, chatting to Garry about the weather and asking after the Rowes (particularly Shirley and Tommy, both of whom, it seemed, she had helped to bring into the world)—as though driving six miles over icebound roads in zero weather to look after a family of strangers were quite an everyday matter, as it doubtless was to her.

"Good thing Neal Rowe got that road plowed out before it froze up on him," she remarked cheerfully, "or I'd have had a hard job getting up here, chains or no chains. It wouldn't be the first time they've had to pull me out of the drifts, either. Sure as we get a real hard cold spell or a big snowfall, someone up the back roads gets sick. I never knew it to fail. And this road's nothing to where I have to go, sometimes."

Upstairs she took temperatures, straightened beds, and shook pillows with a masterly hand. She gave Caroline a hospital bath from head to foot, which filled that young person with a sense of great importance and did much to raise her spirits, and she rubbed Kay's aching limbs with alcohol.

"Now I guess you're all set for a while," she said when she rejoined Garry downstairs. "I'll look in again day after tomorrow if you need me, but I guess you won't. Keep that child indoors till after the cold spell's over, and don't let your sister there get up till she has to. Two or three days in bed ought to put her straight again. How do you feel yourself?"

"All right," said Garry.

The shrewd eyes rested on her approvingly.

"Don't overdo it, and if you get any temperature go right to bed and call me up. We don't want you sick, too, if we can help it. What did you do to your wrist, burn it?"

"The kettle spilled over."

"I'll fix it for you." She unbuckled her bag once more to take out salve and a roll of bandage. "There's nothing like cold

338

weather for things happening. A day like this it seems like all your fingers are thumbs and everything you take hold of either spills on you or cuts you or you drop it on your toe. That feel any better?"

"It certainly does. Thanks a lot." Garry pulled her sleeve down gratefully over the cool soft dressing. "I . . . we . . . Mary didn't say what we owed you for coming."

"Fifty cents," said Miss Hussey briskly, buttoning up her coat.

She picked up her little bag again and was gone, driving off down the hill to visit other households in affliction, leaving comfort and cheer behind her.

For five more days the frost held. Kay and Caroline were up and about again but there was no going out except for Martin, who spent long hours skating with Jimmie on the little pond at the foot of the hill. Life was a monotonous round of watching the thermometer and tending stoves.

On the sixth night Garry woke up towards dawn with a

sudden queer sensation of something having happened, an un-familiar feeling in the air. Sitting up in the darkness, it took her a full minute to realize what it was. The cold spell had finally broken.

Freezing still, but the bitterness had gone from the air. It was good to stand outdoors again, to be able to draw breath freely.

Edna drove over to see them. She had telephoned twice during the combined cold-and-flu siege to ask how they were getting along, but had not been able to visit.

"Just a lame shoulder," she explained, "but I wouldn't have dared try and hold the wheel straight over these roads. But I was bound to get up and see you all today, even if I had to drive with my teeth!"

Edna was resplendent in a new hat, a new scarf and sweater, and a pair of smart fur-lined driving gloves, a Christmas gift from one of her devoted "old ladies."

"I put everything on to show you," she laughed. "I got a pair of red bedroom slippers, too, and if it wasn't for driving I'd have worn them. And that reminds me: back in the car there's a Christmas present we got and couldn't keep, because we've two like it already, so I brought it along for Caroline."

"Couldn't you get it exchanged?" Kay asked.

"Not this one you can't. It comes in all sizes, but only one make." She went back to the car and returned carrying a square grocer's carton tied securely with twine. "Open it and see."

Garry cut the string. There was a stirring and rustling inside, and a black suspicious nose poked out from a nest of tissue paper.

"A coon kitten from the state of Maine," said Edna. "My aunt and uncle up there have more cats than you can shake a stick at. Every so often they send us one down. He runs a dairy farm there, and the barns are simply running with cats. Sum-mer visitors always like them, so they get rid of a few that way. Uncle is always talking about getting his gun and clearing some of those cats out, but when it comes right down to it he wouldn't touch a hair of 'em, and there's plenty of milk and scraps going, so I guess they don't bother anyone much. This 'un looked real smart to me, but we've two cats already and that's too many for anyone living in town. I wish clothes lasted as long as cats do! Our old Susie will be thirteen next month."

The coon kitten had hoisted himself out of the carton and was beginning a wary tour of the room. His long thick hair was jet black all over, his eyes a deep glowing amber. While Garry ran for a saucer of milk Kay exclaimed:

"Caroline will love him. He's just like a Persian, only prettier. Are they always that color?"

"Black or yellow, mostly. Though there was a grand black and white with white paws I remember as a child; he used to run wild in the woods back of the house, and no one could ever get near him. You'd just get a glimpse of him sometimes, along towards fall when the hunting began to grow scarce. Aunt has a family of yellow ones, too, but the yellow kittens mostly get picked up by the summer folk. Either black or yellow's a good

color for cats in the country; if you have one of these grays or tabbies they're like to get taken for a rabbit or a squirrel some fine day, and you lose 'em. Neal Rowe's more careful with his gun than most, but there's lots of hunters don't bother to look twice when they see something moving."

Caroline had gone back to school that day for the first time. Edna had brought sliced ham and a home-baked pie, so the three of them ate lunch together in the living room while the coon kitten prowled and explored.

"I thought I'd kill two birds with one stone today," Edna said as she drank her third cup of coffee. "There was a job up this way I'd heard about, but I guess I can't take it. It's a woman down here on the state road, right opposite the milk station where the school bus stops. They've got a little nursery business called Roadside—raise flowers and seedlings. We always get our tomato and pepper plants from them in spring. The husband's lame. She had her first baby a few days ago— right in the middle of that cold spell it was—and her sister was staying there, but now she's had to go home and they wanted someone to look after things round the house till Mrs. Collins gets about again. But it would mean going there every day, and I can't manage it."

"I didn't know you took jobs," Kay said.

"Anything I can get, when the taxi business is slack. I clean folks' summer cottages and close up for them, and I do spring cleaning once in a while. When you live in the country you learn to turn your hand to most anything. I felt sorry about these folks—she's a real nice woman—but the most I can do is to try and find someone else for them."

There was the latest Santa Fé news to be told, scraps from Penny's letters to be read aloud; all the exchange of local and family gossip that always took place on Edna's visits. When at last she rose to go Garry said,—

"Guess I'll ride down the road with you a little way, and walk back."

She pulled on rubber boots and a windbreaker. When they were halfway down the hill she said,—

"I'm going after that job myself, if I can get it."

Edna smiled as her foot pressed down on the brake.

"Good for you. I can drop you right there. She'll be pretty glad."

"What does it mean?"

"Housework, getting the dinner—maybe a little washing. Miss Hussey comes in every day, so you won't have much to do with the baby."

"I guess I can do all that. I don't know an awful lot about cooking, but she can tell me how she wants things done."

"I always said you'd fit in anywhere, all right," Edna said. "You see, there isn't much of regular hired help around here, but when folks are in a fix anyone will do what he can. I guess they haven't got an awful lot of money, but she's willing to pay ten dollars a week."

"That's ten dollars more than I ever earned before," Garry returned. "Just the other day I was saying that there wasn't any way to earn money in the country, and here it is. Only I didn't want to say anything in front of Kay—not till I know whether I've got the job or not."

There was another reason too perhaps, which Edna perfectly understood.

"I remember as well as yesterday," she said as they turned

the corner into the lower road, "the time I was fourteen and I wanted to get a new dress for the church picnic where we lived, and I didn't have more'n a few cents saved up for it. So I marched off and hired me out, to a woman that took in boarders, to wash dishes and clean the kitchen up twice a day. My aunt was staying on a visit with us, and the way she carried on when she heard about it you'd have thought there was something disgraceful in washing other folks' dishes instead of one's own. But my mother was the sensible kind. She said, 'If Edna wants money let her set to and earn it, and then it'll mean something to her. As long as there's dishes to wash I never heard that it mattered what house you wash 'em in, so long as you wash 'em clean.' So I got my dress, and a nice dress it was, too. I spent all of eight dollars on it, and that was a lot in those days."

When Garry reached home a couple of hours later, having trudged the long steep hill road with more buoyancy and self-confidence than she had felt in some time, she found Martin and Caroline already back from school. She entered whistling, tossed her cap on the table and announced:

"Well, I've got a job!"

Caroline was too absorbed in the coon kitten to pay any attention, but Martin lifted his head.

"What job?" And Kay exclaimed: "Garry, not that job Edna was talking about? I might have known you were up to something when you sneaked off that way. You can't do that sort of thing!"

Garry's chin went up.

"I don't see why. It wouldn't be the first time an Ellis turned her lily-white hands to something useful. And I want to tell you that I feel right like a million dollars this minute. I never knew anything could give one such a lift. The only thing is I hate to take their money for doing just everyday things, because I don't believe by the look of the place they've got a cent more than they can manage with, and the woman is a dear. She's young and pretty—she looks a little bit like you, Kay—and

344

the baby's a darling; I never saw anything so tiny! If you'd been there yourself, Kay, you wouldn't have thought twice about it. She was sitting up in bed with a flowered jacket on, with the baby tucked up in a clothesbasket beside her, and she was peeling potatoes and hushing the baby at the same time. When I said what I'd come for she acted kind of scared of me at first because she'd heard we were city people, till I told her all about the family and how we were fixed, and I took the potatoes right out of her hands and started doing them myself, for I thought I'd show her I could do that much, anyway."

Garry smiled, remembering the expression on Mrs. Collins's face when the potato bowl was whisked away so promptly. Edna had sensibly refused to come in, feeling that Garry would make her way better alone, as she certainly had. But it was the baby who had really settled the question, for Garry adored all small things, and the sight of her eager face bent over the clothesbasket had outweighed any last doubts Mrs. Collins might have had about "city people."

"Ten dollars a week, and I start tomorrow. I wish it would last all winter, but it won't. Still, it's given me a good idea. If I

345

suit all right I shall get Mrs. Collins to give me a reference. In the country people are always having babies and if I keep in touch with Miss Hussey I might get a lot more jobs when this one's over."

Kay had to laugh, for Garry's ideas always spread in widening circles like a stone thrown into water.

"Wait till you see how you like this one. Are you really sure you want it?"

But Garry was quite serious, even though it meant getting up early every morning to walk the mile and a half to the state road. There was a thrill in having a job of any kind for the first time, and she was still young enough to feel work in another person's house more of an adventure than a task. She washed dishes, scrubbed pantry shelves, swept floors, and cooked dinner in a businesslike way; she did the baby's laundry without wincing; and she even learned to sterilize feeding bottles and to prepare formulas as though she had been used to it all her life. Miss Hussey, coming in on her visit to bathe the baby, gave her a friendly approving smile.

"Well, well, so you've got a new job these days! Not enough to do up home, huh? How's the family?"

"All fine. Caroline's back at school again."

"Good."

Garry enjoyed these daily visits. She liked Miss Hussey's brisk cheery ways and amusing gossip and hurried to get her work forward so that she could watch the bathing and dressing rites. It was all good experience, for she had never had anything to do with a baby as tiny as this, and she learned a lot that she had not known before. Anything small and young Garry loved; baby animals, baby plants, she was used to tending and handling, but this human specimen was something new and every detail of its care absorbed her.

Mrs. Collins, her first shyness worn off, was friendly and talkative, glad of Garry's company as well as her help. Both she and her husband were newcomers in the neighborhood; before their marriage Mr. Collins had worked for a firm of nursery gardeners and had only started in business for himself three years ago. He was a kindly, rather silent man, lame from a shell wound in the War; Garry rarely saw him except at mealtimes, or when he tiptoed in once or twice during the morning to look at the baby and perhaps stroke its small hand gently with the tip of one finger as though it were some rare and delicate seedling that he was almost afraid to touch. Most of the time he was busy in the greenhouse or potting shed.

Garry longed to talk to him about his work but never quite found the courage. The greenhouse where he raised his plants and cuttings had been built onto the house and opened directly from the small living room; as Garry stood at the kitchen sink rinsing clothes or washing dishes she could see the rows of flowerpots behind the glass panes and whenever the door was opened a warm breath of earth and moisture filled the house. Many a time she was sorely tempted to cross the floor and open that door herself, just to take a sniff and look inside, but she reminded herself sternly that she was there to do chores and keep house, not to indulge her own particular hobby. Still the temptation was very strong, and one morning she gave in to it. Her hands happened to be still soapy; the doorhandle slipped unexpectedly in her grasp, and she all but fell down the two steps on to Mr. Collins's broad back as he stooped over a tray on the lower shelf. He looked taken aback at this entry, but relieved to find it was not an urgent summons for help, and grinned as he pulled her to her feet.

"Those steps are a bit tricky when you aren't used to 'em," he said. "Did you hurt yourself any?"

"Not a bit. I'm awfully sorry, but I just had a minute to spare and I've so wanted to have a look at your plants. I love greenhouses and I hardly ever get a chance to poke round in them."

"Look at all you want to," said Mr. Collins.

He stopped his work goodnaturedly to show her round, explained how the house was heated and the moisture controlled, let her linger over the rows of potted seedlings and the cuttings set to root in trays of wet sand. Following him as he limped down the aisle between the growing plants Garry found that here was a man who loved his work and could forget all his

347

awkwardness in talking about it. She was full of eager questions and real understanding, and the time flew till she suddenly remembered the potatoes on the stove and the unset dinner table.

After that she was free of the greenhouse whenever there were odd moments to spare, and as Mrs. Collins was now sitting up and the district nurse's visits becoming fewer, Garry could generally manage by working at extra speed to gain a little time. When the baby was fed and sleeping, Mrs. Collins settled for her afternoon nap, and the dishes put away, she would slip out and help Mr. Collins. There were plants to spray and water, sometimes seedlings to be repotted or rooted cuttings set out, empty pots to be scrubbed and stacked away, or potting mold mixed in the big trough at the end of the greenhouse—jobs she enjoyed far more than scraping saucepans and mopping floors.

"Well, I'll give you a regular job any time you want it," he said one day jokingly, and Garry took him up at once.

"Would you let me work here, if you want extra help later on?"

"Well, there's always plenty to do, come spring. But I don't know as you'd call it a young lady's work, exactly, except once in a while like now, when you feel in the mood." He seemed to overlook entirely the kind of work Garry had been doing, this last week. "Handlin' earth and pots an' that isn't any too good on your hands."

"I've handled plenty," Garry told him. "I'm only a beginner, Mr. Collins, and I wouldn't want you to pay me. But there's a whole lot I could learn working with you, and I'd be glad to do it. I could take care of some of the easier jobs and leave you more time for the rest."

Mr. Collins considered.

"There's rock-garden plants," he said. "Folks are crazy about them, right now. If I had money it would pay me to go in for the real Alpines, but there's plenty others that I'm beginning to have a steady sale for, for there's one thing they can't always raise from a packet of seeds. Divisions they increase from, mostly. I've got a lot of young plants on hand in the cold-frames, and I thought I might do a good bit in that line this year. That'll

348

call for a lot of dividing and settin' out, and I don't know but you might try your hand at that, if you'd care to. But we'll see later on. Come spring you'll have plenty doing in your own garden."

"I couldn't get a promise out of him," she told Kay that evening, "but I mean to try again in the spring. It's just the chance I need, and I don't mean to let it slip."

There was little doing in the way of business at Roadside Nurseries just now. So far not a single customer had stopped by during the week that Garry had spent there, but towards the end of her stay one car actually did draw up, a smart sedan with two well-dressed women in it. Mr. Collins had gone to town that afternoon; Mrs. Collins was giving the baby her two-o'clock bottle, and Garry had just finished her third batch of diapers and was hanging them on the line behind the kitchen stove.

"Good afternoon. I got such nice cyclamens here last year, and my friend was wondering if you had any more."

Mrs. Collins looked flustered.

"Mr. Collins would know, but he's out just now. That's too bad. I suppose you couldn't . . ."

Garry turned promptly.

"There are some nice ones just coming into bloom. Would you like to see them?"

She left the washtub, gave a businesslike hitch to her overalls, and led the way into the greenhouse. Roadside Nurseries wasn't going to miss its one sale of the week if she could help it.

"They're down at the end here. Mr. Collins had to go into town to see about a new consignment of plants, but I expect I can help you just as well."

Mr. Collins's trip had been to arrange for a renewal of his bank loan, as Garry very well knew, being by now practically a member of the family, but that explanation wouldn't sound quite so impressive. The cyclamens (Garry thanked heaven it was an everyday plant she did know, not something unusual with a long Latin name) were on a warm shelf at the far end of the house, and she led her visitors purposely by the aisle

349

where the best-looking plants and seedlings were ranged. The elder of the two women happened to be a genuine gardener; she had taken a fancy to Garry's voice and appearance and was inclined to linger more than once on the way to chat about this or that.

"They're all very nice," said the younger woman presently, as Garry reached down pot after pot to set before her. "I don't like dark red so much, do you, Mary? There's a white one up there . . . is that the only one you have? It looks rather . . ."

Garry patiently took the last pot down from its shelf.

"The only one; I'm sorry. But this pale pink is lovely, and it's full of buds. It ought to be perfect in just a few days." (What, oh what did Mr. Collins charge for cyclamens?)

The young woman still hemmed and hawed, turning the pots about.

"I saw some just like this in town. They were asking forty-five cents. Isn't that what you paid last year, Mary?"

Garry looked at the elder woman's smooth ringed hands, at her companion's costly fur coat, and thought of the Collins baby, asleep at this moment in a clothesbasket under two cheap cotton blankets.

"These are seventy-five cents each," she said firmly. "They ought to be more, really, but they're the last we have."

"That seems very dear, doesn't it?"

"Detestable female!" thought Garry, and added aloud: "These are particularly well-grown plants, Mr. Collins won't stock anything that isn't good."

"Hm. . . ." Her eyes rested on Garry inquisitively. "Do you work here all the time?"

"Only when Mr. Collins is short-handed."

In the end she chose three after much deliberation, while the elder woman, left to wander by herself, had discovered other things that she wanted. Garry swathed the pots carefully, carried them out to the back of the car, and returned proudly to lay six dollars and a fifty-cent piece on the baby's blanket.

"That'll help to buy her something useful, I guess!"

"How much did you dare charge them?"

"Seventy-five for the cyclamens and two dollars each for the little evergreens. There are plenty more of the same kind, but those two happened to be standing all by themselves and she took a shine to them. She was so pleased I was scared after that I'd undercharged her, but I'm pretty sure I didn't," said Garry. "And I let her have a strawberry begonia for a quarter, just to make up."

"The first sale in ages." Mrs. Collins smiled gratefully. "Wait till George hears about it. I guess you brought us luck!"

"The older woman will be back again; she said so, and she likes the place. She's interested in rock plants, too. I wouldn't care if we never saw the other one again. Wearing a three-hundred-dollar coat and wants to save thirty cents on flowers!"

"Lots of 'em are that way," said Mrs. Collins, who had had experience. And she added: "I wish you could stay here always."

So did Garry. In these ten days she had come to feel so much a part of the little household that when she pulled her rubber boots on for the last time, hung up her apron, and stooped to kiss the small curled fist lying outside the covers it seemed as if she was leaving a part of herself behind. It was with an empty almost homesick feeling that she climbed the hill that evening with ten dollars in her pocket (she had stubbornly

351

refused to take more for the extra days), a promise to stand godmother to small Julia when the time came, and a store of new experience and self-confidence that was worth far more to her than any wages.

Much of the snow had melted, but a new light fall had come to cover the unsightly patches of bare earth. It was a soft misty night; there was no wind and though the mercury stood at just about freezing the air felt mild. Just the night for fox hunting, Neal announced. He had long promised the two boys a moonlight fox hunt, and the moon would rise about nine.

When Garry reached home she found Martin all excited. He fairly bolted his supper and was ready long before Neal and Jimmie knocked at the door.

"You wrap up well," Kay admonished.

"Walkin'll keep 'em warm," drawled Neal. "We ain't settin' out for the North Pole. That leather jacket's all you need, son, with a good sweater under it, and I bet you find that too much. I'll look out for him all right." He winked at the two girls. "Sorry you ain't coming, Garry. I reckon if we git one fox apiece that's all we'll want to carry, but maybe if we meet up with a fourth one and he's extra good, we might bring him back for you."

"I'll bet you don't get one!" Garry scoffed.

"Is that kind? Didn't I pick this night special? Moon just right, everything just right, and old Sam fairly bustin' hisself to get out on the job. Wait till you hear him singin', once he hits a good scent. We're goin' out over Crooked Hill and work round towards Bear Hollow and the big ledges. I ain't hunted over there yet this winter and I bet you we pick up something before we're through."

His deep leather pockets bulged with a package of sandwiches on one side and a thermos flask on the other. "See you later," he nodded as he picked up his gun from the corner by the door.

"Why didn't you go along?" Kay asked when the door had closed behind them.

352

"It's Martin's party," Garry said. "Besides, I don't like seeing things shot, even if Neal does the shooting. . . . Well, it seems funny to be home for keeps again." She opened the stove door and pushed a fresh log into Big Bertha. "Remember how we hated this stove when Penny first brought it home? I bet if there are any auctions in Santa Fé she's having the time of her life. Think of all the things she'll want to bring back with her!—Kay, I want to make something for that baby down the road, and I've got to think what."

"There was that pink sweater wool," Kay debated. "Only I gave it to Caroline to learn knitting with when she was sick and I guess it's pretty mussy by now—what's left of it."

"Uh-uh. I hate knitting anyway. I'll go and take a look round."

She went upstairs, where Kay could hear her dragging trunks out in the room overhead.

"Just the thing," she exclaimed when she came down again. "That peach robe I got Christmas before last. The front's worn but the back is all right, and I had it cleaned just before we came up here. It'll make a grand cot cover."

"Are you going to cut that up?" Kay looked ruefully at the shimmering quilted silk.

"Can you see me trailing a peach silk negligee around this place—or anywhere else for that matter! It's lamb's wool inside, so it will be beautifully warm." She took the scissors and began to slash. "If I piece a bit more in these two top corners and just turn the edges in all round it makes quite a good-size spread. I can use that pink sewing silk out of your workbox. Kay, now that Penny has to stay longer than she thought, don't you think it would be fun to get the house fixed up a bit by the time she gets home?"

"I'd love to. Only . . ."

"There's this ten dollars; part of it anyway. I might get another job of some kind, and if we ever hear anything from our advertisement woman there'd be some of that money, too."

"She'd have written long ago if she was coming," Kay said. "We'll never hear from her."

"The old buzzard," Garry commented. "People just make me sick anyway. I think she might answer even if she isn't coming." She spread the silk out, viewing it critically as it lay across her knee. "What's your trouble *now*?"

A faint wail had drifted down through the register from the room where Caroline was supposed to be asleep.

"All right. I'll get him for you." Garry laid aside her work to hunt round the room for the coon kitten, who, with the ingratitude of all cats towards those who seek to do them undesired kindness, had fled the warmth of Caroline's bed and was sitting with tucked-in paws as far under the sofa as he could squeeze. "That's the third time I've hauled that wretched kitten upstairs. Nothing will persuade Caroline that coon cats don't like being cuddled. I hope the next time someone gives her a pet it'll be a tortoise; at least they can't run so fast.

"Do you know, Kay," she went on when they were settled once more, "I had an idea the other day. I don't know that it's brilliant, but it might work. Remember those funny pictures you used to make up for the kids when they were little—the Pilliwig family?"

"*Those* things?" Kay looked puzzled. "Martin used to like them. I haven't thought of them in years. I don't even remember how they went."

"I do. I'd remember Mrs. Pilliwig's hat and the way the little Pilliwigs looked if I lived to be a hundred. You used to make up the story and draw the pictures as you went along. Kay, I believe if you were to do a series of those any children's magazine in the world would want them."

"But they were just nonsense."

"Some of the best stuff in the world is nonsense," said Garry stoutly. "It's what everyone likes, anyway, and there's precious little of it that's any good. Those were fine just because they were nonsense and you weren't worrying about how they came out, but just went ahead and drew them."

"Wait a minute. I remember now I once made some on the back of another drawing."

Kay rummaged through a portfolio of old sketches.

354

"It was when that little Cary girl came to tea. I wanted . . . Yes, here it is. It's about the zoo."

She smiled as she held out the paper for Garry to see. Garry was right. There was life and humor in the ridiculous little figures. There was more, too: a freedom of expression and a sure use of line that Kay didn't always get in her more studied drawings.

"See what I mean?"

"I don't know. I might be able to make something out of them if they were better drawn."

"There you go!" said Garry. "They don't want to be better drawn. They want to be just like you have them there."

"Eleven o'clock." Neal looked at his wrist watch. "What do you say we push on towards the ledges there and find a place to eat our sandwiches?"

They were halfway up the last rise of hillside. Below them there stretched a bare sparkling slope broken only by the track of their own footsteps and by a few gray bowlders thrusting here and there above the snow. Overhead the moon sailed in a sky dotted by tiny scudding clouds.

They had walked for miles, but Martin didn't even feel tired. There was something in the pure keen air, the dazzle of moonlight on the snow, just the excitement of being out at night in an unfamiliar place, that went to his head like wine and made

355

him feel wider awake, more alert to every sight and sound about him, than ever he had felt in the daytime. Everything looked strange and different. The patches of black shadow cast by bush or pasture wall stood out sharp and distinct; an old twisted wild-apple tree took fantastic shape in the moonlight, and the occasional faint lights of houses snuggled far down in the valley seemed to belong to another world.

So far they had seen one fox only. They were following an old wood road when he crossed their path unexpectedly in a clearing just ahead, a silent furtive shape that stood for a moment, head turned, and vanished. Jimmy had fired, but his hands shook with excitement, and when the smoke cleared only some scattered pellet holes in the snow showed where the fox had stood.

"Passed clean through his fur and never touched him," Neal said, pointing to the marks. "Too bad!"

Across the shoulder of the hill now they could hear old Sam baying on another scent, two high-pitched notes, clear and mournful, like the sound of a bell at intervals on the frosty air. Neal listened.

"He's working round towards this way. We'll sit up there by the ledges and wait for him."

They climbed the slope to a little plateau between flat outcropping ledges of granite. Neal found a sheltered hollow where they could sit, their backs to the rock and facing the open.

"See that big flat rock ledge straight in front of us?" he said. "When a fox is bein' hunted and he gets far enough ahead he'll always make for the highest place he can, so's he can take a good look round. Once you know that, and you know the country pretty well, you don't need to waste time followin' the hounds. You can get a good idea of which way they are workin' by listenin' to 'em, and then you go ahead and wait right where you know the fox is bound to come out. He'll be comin' up the other side of the hill now, and right there on that flat ledge is where he'll be likely to show himself, square against the skyline. He ain't in any hurry, no mor'n we are. We'll hear from old Sam when he's getting nearer."

He laid the gun down beside him and pulled the sandwiches out of his pocket.

"Guess some hot coffee'll taste good. You ain't cold, Martin?"

"Not a bit."

They ate their sandwiches and drank their coffee in turn from the little cup on the flask, talking in whispers. At intervals old Sam's voice reached them on the still air, sometimes nearer, sometimes further off.

"Workin' in a circle," Neal said. "He'll be another half hour, maybe."

Yesterday's wind had blown the loose snow from the ledges; in this sheltered angle it was warm and still. Martin finished his sandwich and leaned back against the flat slope of rock, his hands behind his head. Watching the moon as it fled in and out between the small fleecy clouds, rainbow hued in its halo, he felt as if the whole hillside were turning under him, and he sat up suddenly to find everything about him dizzy and strange. Neal laughed.

"That's the way folks get moon-struck. When I was a kid mother was always telling me if I lay in the moonlight I'd go looney. That was one of her ideas, and the other was about night air being bad for you. Well, I managed to grow up in spite of both of 'em!"

The sandwiches were gone, the coffee finished. Neal racked his brain for hunting stories to while away the time as the minutes slowly passed. Jimmy was getting chilled and restless; he hated to keep still for long at a stretch and his missed shot earlier in the evening still rankled. He shifted his position several times to peer about, fidgeted here and there, and finally settled down again facing the other two, the .22 always ready in his hands. For a long time old Sam had been silent.

Suddenly, in the middle of a sentence, Neal's voice paused. He made a movement towards his gun, then drew his hand noiselessly back, and instead his fingers tightened on Martin's arm beside him. Martin looked up.

There on the flat rock just above and behind Jimmy's head stood the fox. Unseen he had crept round behind them and now

357

he was so near that Jimmy, had he known it, could have put out a hand and touched him. Martin could see the drawn-back silent snarl of his lips, the fixed eyes staring. Every hair of his coat stood out sharp and electric like spun glass in the moonlight. For what seemed a full minute he stood there motionless, one paw lifted, while Martin scarcely dared draw breath. Then Jimmy turned his head; the spell was broken. There was a blur and a flurry on the snow, something whipped past them like a flash of color and was gone. Neal rose to his feet, but it was too late.

"What a shot! Oh boy, what a shot!"

"Where—where?" Jimmy clutched at his rifle, staring wildly round.

"Right back of your head! I could have got him easy, but I wouldn't have risked it. Just sneaked up on us from round those boulders, and us sittin' here all the time. Well, he got the laugh on us this time, I reckon."

A moment later old Sam loped up to them, puzzled and disappointed, to stare from one to the other and then thrust his black muzzle reproachfully into Neal's hand.

"No more hunting tonight," said Neal cheerfully, shouldering his gun. "That's settled it, hey, Sam? Don't know about you boys, but I'm just about chilled through all of a sudden. Guess we'll make tracks for home, and better luck next time."

It was as Neal said. For the first time Martin felt suddenly chilled and stiff. The excitement of the evening had dropped from him; drowsiness was creeping through his limbs. There was still a long walk before them, and by the time they had crossed the last stone wall into the pasture and saw the lighted kitchen window shining through the dusk he was ready to drop with sleep.

As he closed his eyes that night he seemed to see again, like a picture flashed on darkness, that swift moonlit vision of the fox in the snow.

Garry trudged the long steep hill road with buoyancy and self-confidence . . .

Elizabeth Rhodes Jackson

CHRISTMAS EVE AT REGINALD'S

ILLUSTRATED BY *Marguerite Davis*

PERHAPS it's because Reginald was a real Christmas puppy, born on Christmas Eve, that he has so much love in his heart for everyone and has so many dear friends.

When he goes walking with us, perfect strangers that we meet are not strangers to him at all. Boys in the street that we have never seen before say, "Hello, Reggie, old boy," and very proper old ladies in old-fashioned hats, taking a morning walk around Louisburg Square, pat him very gently and say, "Good morning, Doggie. How nice to see you again!"

Once he ran right up to a lovely young lady who was sitting talking at the Esplanade and put his paws on her white dress. She wasn't even annoyed. She shook hands with him, and the young man with her said, "Is that your dog? We've known him a long time and we wondered where he belonged." And the young lady said, "He's one of our very best friends."

After that, almost every time we went to the Esplanade, we

359

used to see them, and no matter how earnestly they were talking together, they would stop to pat Reginald. But one day the young man was sitting there all alone, looking very gloomy. Beany, who sometimes says the wrong thing, asked him, "Where's the young lady?" and he said shortly, "She hasn't come." After that we never saw the young lady, but we often saw the young man alone, and he always rubbed Reginald's ears very kindly.

One day—it was Election Day—Reginald was walking with Jack and me and we passed a voting place, and Reginald recognized the policeman outside and poked his nose into the policeman's hand to be petted, and the policeman said to him,—

"You ought to be after running for office yourself today. As popular as you are, you'd carry the ticket."

We were very much surprised because we had thought that that policeman didn't like Reginald. He had been very cross one day because Reginald followed and came running after us into the Public Garden when we were going to the swan boats. The policeman had stopped us and said, "Don't you know you can't bring that dog in here? There's a sign at the gate, 'No dogs allowed except on leash.'"

"Yes, we saw it," said Beany politely, "but Reginald didn't. At least, he couldn't read it."

"Don't tell me that dog can't read," said the policeman. "As smart a beast as he is!" So we really had thought the policeman didn't like Reginald.

But Reginald loves everyone, and he goes all over town by himself to make new friends. He crosses the street with the traffic lights to get to Boston Common. He likes to watch the children swimming in the Frog Pond and bark at the squirrels that chatter at him from tall elms. We never go to the West End because once when Jack went there to look at a beautiful ship model in the window of an antique shop, a big boy knocked him down and took ten cents away from him. But our ash-barrel man told Beany he often meets Reginald in the West End, and the children playing in the street pat him and love him.

360

Once, just before Christmas, he was gone all night, and in the morning we went up and down Beacon Hill, asking at every door, "Have you seen a dog named Reginald? White with black spots?"

Most of the people said, "Why, I know Reginald. I do hope you'll find him."

One very stately lady with white hair and a Paisley shawl was just getting into her car when we asked her, and she said, "Dear, dear! How sorry I am! He is such a good dog."

Then we came to a house where there is a beautiful white door with a fan light and a shiny brass knocker. It is our favorite house on the Hill. On Christmas Eve it is always brightly lighted, and the curtains are drawn back to show a great painting of the Christ Child in his mother's arms.

We lifted the knocker, and after a moment the door was opened by a very straight butler. I asked, "Have you seen a dog named Reginald? White with black spots?"

He cleared his throat and looked embarrassed. "Why, the

fact is, Miss," he said, "there was a dog answering to that description on the front steps yesterday, and I was given orders to take it away, and—" he stopped and coughed as an old gentleman came into the paneled hall behind him.

"What's this? What's this?" said the old gentleman. "Don't hold the door open, Bates. What's this all about?"

"This young lady is asking about her dog, sir," said the butler very respectfully.

"Dog?" said the old gentleman. "You took it to the Animal Rescue League, I hope, Bates, as I ordered you to?"

"Yes, sir, quite so, sir," said the butler.

"Quite right," said the old gentleman. "I've contributed to

the Animal Rescue League for years. About time I made some use of it. Proper place for a lost dog."

"But Reginald isn't a lost dog," said Beany. "He knows his way home."

The old gentleman looked at Beany very hard. "Well, well!" he said. "If he knows his way home, why does he spend his time sitting on *my* doorstep?"

"Probably he sat down to rest," said Beany. "Probably he likes your house. Probably he admires your fan light."

Beany choked a little, and Jack and I knew he was thinking of Reginald shut up in a cage and hoping we would come for him. Jack said comfortingly, "Anyway, now we know he's safe and we know where to go for him."

"And we do thank you," I said to the old gentleman. "We know you meant to be helpful."

The old gentleman looked at Beany and from him to Jack and then at me. It reminded me of the surprised way Beany looked the first time he saw a giraffe at the circus.

"Most extraordinary!" said the old gentleman. "Bates, you may order the car."

"Yes, sir," said Bates.

In just a minute or two the car was in front of the house, and we all went out and got in. Jack sat in front with the chauffeur, and Beany and I sat in back with the old gentleman. We drove through Park Square to the Animal Rescue League on Carver Street, and sure enough, there was Reginald. When they brought him in to see us, he rippled from his nose to the tip of his tail and jumped all over us and even tried to jump up to kiss the old gentleman. Then we all rode home together, and when we got out of the car and said good-bye, the old gentleman took his hat off as if I were a grown-up lady.

The next day the lady in the Paisley shawl came to our house to see if we had found Reginald. She was so glad when he got up from the fireplace rug and stretched himself to welcome her. She stayed and talked a while with Mother, and they had tea, and when she went she said, "They say the fashion of making calls is out of date, but Reginald has re-

363

vived it. I hope you and your children and Reginald will soon return my call."

After she had gone, Beany said, "I wish all Reginald's friends would call on us, don't you, Mother?"

"Mercy!" said Mother. "You don't realize how many friends he has. We'd have a constant procession of callers."

"Well," I said, "why can't we give a party and have them all at once?"

"Oh, let's have a party," said Beany. Beany loves parties and thinks we all ought to have birthdays twice a year.

"Couldn't we, Mother?" I said. "Reginald has gone to dinner with so many people—it really is his turn to invite them."

"I know what," said Jack. "Christmas Eve is Reginald's birthday. Let's have 'open house' for him with candles in the windows and all his friends invited."

Mother looked doubtful. "How could you invite them?" she said. "You don't know who his friends are."

"But *he* knows," said Beany. "Let's tie the invitation to his collar, and everywhere he makes his calls, they'll read it and come."

We got out our box of Christmas cards and wrote the invitation that very day. We chose a card with three camels across the top, and Jack printed on it. "Reginald invites all his friends to Open House on Christmas Eve from seven to eight-thirty," and the address. Then we tied it to Reginald's collar with a green and red Christmas ribbon. Reginald thought it was very decorative, and he went off proudly with his head in the air.

I don't know how many people read the invitation, but after a few days it was very much soiled and a little bit torn, and we wrote a fresh one. This time the card had a Christmas tree on it. When that card got worn out, we gave him one with Santa Claus in a sleigh with reindeer.

Sometimes he would come home with a note tied on, "Thanks. I'll be there," or "We accept with pleasure." And, one said, "Sorry, I can't come. I've got the measles."

Reginald and Beany met the gloomy young man one after-

noon on Beacon Street. Reginald, of course, stopped to greet him, and the young man saw the card. It was the Christmas tree one.

"What's all this?" he said. "Whose Christmas package are you?"

Then he read the invitation, and his gloom all vanished.

"I say," he said. "Is this true about Reginald's Christmas Eve?"

"Oh, yes," said Beany. "He's inviting all his friends."

"I say. That gives me an idea," said the young man. "I'd like to borrow Reginald for a while. Don't be worried about him. I'll see that he's safe." Reginald trotted happily along with him and didn't turn up till evening.

The week before Christmas is a very busy one. There are always last things to do to get our presents finished and write the labels and mail Christmas cards and unpack the tree ornaments. And this time we were especially busy the day before Christmas, getting ready for Reginald's "open house." I helped Mother make sandwiches and cut them star-shaped, and Jack put the candles into their holders and set them in rows on the window sills and sashes, and Beany polished the silver. We were all working hard when the knocker sounded at our apartment door, and Beany went to open it.

We heard a voice say, "I cain't come to the party, Honey, 'cose my folks is having open house theirselves. But I sure did appreciate getting invited. Reginald walked into my kitchen with the butcher's boy, and he turned his haid for me to read the invite as much as to say, 'You is personally invited.' So I done made a birthday cake for the party."

It was a beautiful cake, all frosted, with Reginald's name in red icing on top. We put the cake in the middle of the mahogany table on Mother's best lace tablecloth. There was a bowl of holly at each end and the silver candlesticks with tall red candles. Mother was to serve the coffee, and I was to pour the cocoa. Jack would pass the cups, because Beany sometimes spills, and Beany could hand the sandwiches, and Daddy said he would take care of the doughnuts.

When we heard the church bells chiming, "Noel, Noel," and saw houses up and down the street shining out in a blaze of light, we knew that Christmas Eve was beginning, and soon the streets would be crowded with people who had come into town to hear the carolers singing on candle-lighted Beacon Hill and visit their friends who were keeping "open house." While we were lighting the candles in our windows, a band of carolers went by, singing, "Oh, little town of Bethlehem," and Beany whispered to me, "Can you believe that it really is Christmas Eve at last?" and I knew just how he felt. Then someone lifted our knocker, and we all ran to open the door to Reginald's first guest.

It was the cross policeman. He was carrying a little boy in his arms, and behind him was an anxious-looking woman.

"This is my boy, Jimmy," said the policeman. "And nothing would do but he must come to the dog's party. So I said to the Missus I'd bring him myself, and I'll be after coming for him a little later. Where can I put him down, Ma'am?"

Then we saw the boy couldn't walk. He had iron braces on his legs. Mother moved the cushions and made a place for him on the sofa, and Reginald jumped up and lay beside him.

Jimmy's mother said, "That's what he always does—cuddles down on the bed next to Jimmy. It soothes him something wonderful when he's fretful after one of his bad nights, awake with the pain and too sick to listen to the radio."

The next visitor was the pretty young lady. "I had to come,"

366

she said, "because Reginald came all the way to my house to invite me. I heard him barking at the door. He must have shut himself into the vestibule in some way, and he was so glad when I opened the door to him." Reginald heard his name and wagged his tail as he lay on the sofa.

Then the lady came who wears the Paisley shawl, and brought Reginald a Christmas box of barley sugar dogs. She was just drinking her coffee when the old gentleman came in who had sent Reginald to the Animal Rescue League. The Paisley lady said to him, "So, James Saltonstall, you're another of Reginald's friends!" And the old gentleman said, "By all means. Consider it an honor." And then he said to Mother, "Most extraordinary dog. Comes and sits on my doorstep regularly. Admires my fan light, your surprising son said. Unusual architectural appreciation."

All the evening people kept coming until the room was all one hum of pleasant sound, and Cherio, my canary, began to sing so loud we couldn't hear the carolers outside. The butcher's boy came. He couldn't stay because he was so busy delivering turkeys, but he brought a big bone for Reginald tied with a red paper bow. The boy from the West End who had taken Jack's ten cents came, and was very much surprised and embarrassed to see Jack. But Reginald greeted him for an old friend, and the boy accepted a big piece of the birthday cake and asked for another.

The Admiral came, too. He lives on Brimmer Street, and, of course, everyone in the neighborhood knows who he is. We were very proud that our Reginald had gained the friendship of such a brave and distinguished man.

When Jimmy saw him, he almost stood up. "Gee, Admiral," he said. "Can I shake hands with you?"

Reginald heard "shake hands" and he lifted his paw, too, and the Admiral shook hands with both of them and then pulled a chair up close to the sofa.

"Say, Admiral," said Jimmy, "that was great stuff, that broadcast. I didn't miss one of them. I could hear the ship a-creaking and the waves swashing in the wind, and I felt just like I was

at the Antarctic myself. When I grow up—and get well, you know—do you think I could go along? I could be a cabin boy or something, couldn't I?"

I didn't hear what the Admiral answered, because our knocker sounded just then, and I opened the door to the young man who had borrowed Reginald. "Merry Christmas!" he said, and then he saw the young lady near the door.

"You came," he said.

"Of course, I came," she said. "Reginald asked me specially."

"I know," said the young man. "I shut him into your vestibule. I had to see you. I had to explain. I say, you must let me explain. Where can we go to talk?" he said to me rather wildly.

I showed him the bay window with the wide seat. "Really," said the young lady coldly, "I don't see that there's anything to explain." But she sat down with him in the window seat, apart from the others. Reginald followed them and nuzzled into their hands, trying to get them to pet him, but they didn't seem to know he was there.

When it was nearly half-past eight, Mother went to the piano and played some carols, and we all stood around her and sang. The boy from the West End had quite a good voice, and the policeman, who had come again to carry Jimmy home, came in strong on the bass. Then people began to leave. Just as the old gentleman was going, he put a package into my hands. "Merry Christmas to Reginald!" he said. "Most remarkable dog!"

It was a fine leather collar, and on the plate was engraved Reginald's name and address, and underneath, "He is not a lost dog. He knows his way home."

The policeman carried Jimmy out very carefully with his mother trailing behind calling back, "God bless you and a merry Christmas," and we heard Jimmy telling his father, "Gee, Dad, you can bet I won't forget this Christmas Eve."

"Now everybody's gone," said Jack as we closed the door, "let's hang up our stockings."

And then we saw that not everyone was gone. The young lady and the young man were still in the window seat.

"Oh, we thought you had gone," said Beany.

"Oh, are we the last?" said the young lady, very much surprised, and they got up quickly.

Beany realized that he hadn't sounded very polite.

"Oh, don't hurry," he said. "Do stay. Because as soon as you go, we shall have to go to bed."

But they did go at last. And the young man shook hands with Reginald and said, "Thanks a lot for the Christmas present."

And the young lady's face got pink, and she took Reginald's head in both her hands and kissed him on the black spot between the ears.

Then Reginald, in his shining new collar, lay down on the hearth rug with his nose between his paws and went to sleep. We blew out the candles in the window and on the tree, and we hung our stockings at the fireplace. We could hear the carolers in the distance singing, "God rest you, merry gentlemen," and when it ended we heard the chime of church bells on the frosty air. But nothing disturbed Reginald. Only his tail moved very gently in his sleep; so probably he was having happy dreams about his loving friends.

Reginald always wears his new collar now, to tell everyone he knows his way home; so no one will ever take him for a lost dog again.

Index